BROTHERHOOD PROTECTORS BOXED SET 5

BOOKS 13-15

New York Times & USA Today
Bestselling Author

ELLE JAMES

SEAL Justice Copyright © 2019 by Elle James

Ranger Creed Copyright © 2020 by Elle James

Delta Force Rescue Copyright © 2020 by Elle James

All rights reserved.

No part of this book may be reproduced in any form or by any electronic or mechanical means, including information storage and retrieval systems, without written permission from the author, except for the use of brief quotations in a book review.

AUTHOR'S NOTE

Brotherhood Protectors Series
Montana SEAL (#1)
Bride Protector SEAL (#2)
Montana D-Force (#3)
Cowboy D-Force (#4)
Montana Ranger (#5)
Montana Dog Soldier (#6)
Montana SEAL Daddy (#7)
Montana Ranger's Wedding Vow (#8)
Montana SEAL Undercover Daddy (#9)
Cape Cod SEAL Rescue (#10)
Montana SEAL Friendly Fire (#11)
Montana SEAL's Mail-Order Bride (#12)
SEAL Justice (#13)
Ranger Creed (#14)
Delta Force Rescue (#15)
Dog Days of Christmas (#16)
Montana Rescue (#17)
Montana Ranger Returns (#18)

Visit ellejames.com for more titles and release dates
and join Elle James's Newsletter at
https://ellejames.com/contact/

SEAL JUSTICE

BROTHERHOOD PROTECTORS BOOK #13

New York Times & USA Today
Bestselling Author

ELLE JAMES

SEAL JUSTICE

BROTHERHOOD PROTECTORS

NEW YORK TIMES BESTSELLING AUTHOR
ELLE JAMES

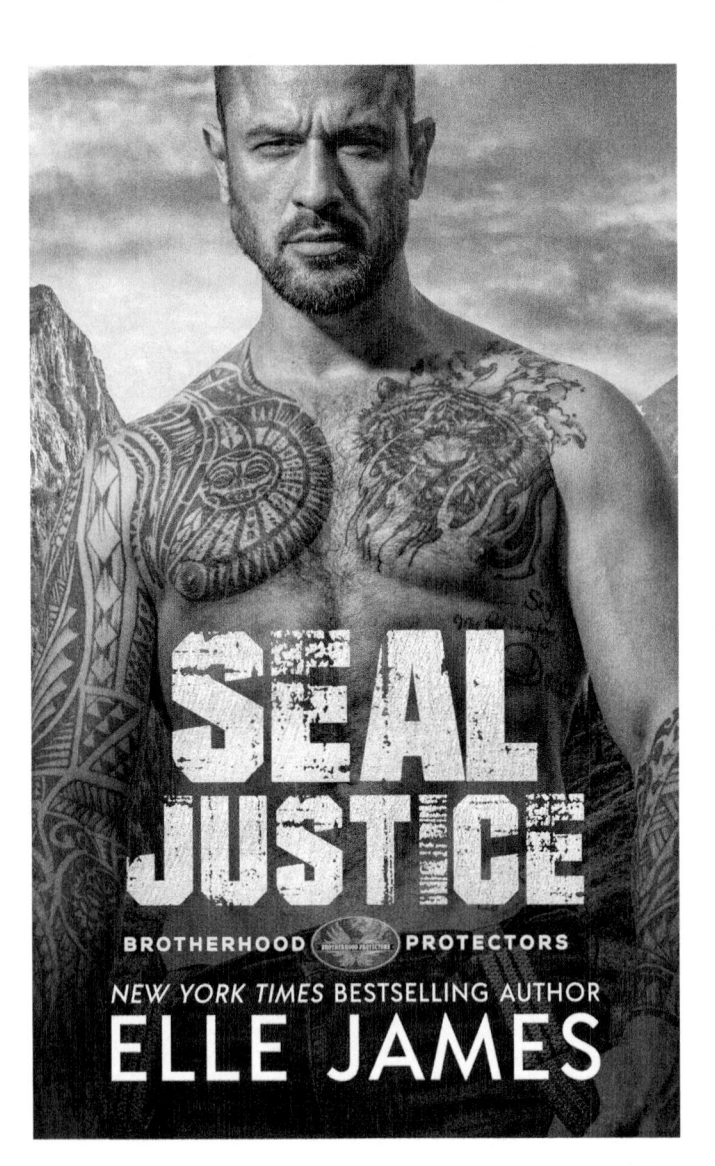

CHAPTER 1

Reggie McDonald held her breath and listened for him. She shivered, her naked body chilled by the cool damp air of her prison. Though her brain was murky, her thoughts unclear, and her strength diminished, she knew what she had to do. When she could hear no sounds of boots on the wooden steps leading down into the earthen cellar, she continued digging. Inch by inch, she scraped away at the soil of her cell, praying she was correct in assuming hers was on the edge of the group of cells. If she dug long enough, she might see daylight and find a way to escape the hell she'd been trapped in for what felt like a lifetime.

Using the tin cup she'd been given to drink from, she scooped dirt from the corner behind the door. That small space was hidden from her captor when he came to feed her or shackle her to take her up to the big house where he tortured her and the other young women he'd kidnapped and held in the horrible dungeon beneath his house.

If she got out, she'd find help to get the other women out and save them from the sociopath who forced them to bow to his bidding. If they didn't do what he said, he whipped them with a riding crop or shocked them with a cattle prod. Sometimes, he burned them with the lit end of the cigars he smoked.

To keep them pliant to his will, he drugged their food and water, making them weak and groggy, unable to form clear thoughts or fight back.

Reggie had caught on to what he'd been doing. She couldn't quit eating or drinking completely, but she'd skip a day and use that time of semi-clear thinking to work through the problem to come up with a solution. On those clear days, she'd acted just as drugged when she'd been shackled and taken up the wooden stairs to the Master's house. When she could see out a window, she'd determined the house sat on the side of a hill, the slope dipping downward from the back of the structure. Though the women were trapped in the cellar, the earthen walls of their prison couldn't be that thick, especially on the far end where she was being kept. The hill sloped sharply on that end, giving her hope that, with steady digging, she'd eventually break free of captivity and escape.

Reggie prayed she was correct and scooped faster, pushing the soil she'd dislodged into the sides of the walls and floor, packing it down so that her captor couldn't tell it was fresh dirt.

She paused again as a sound penetrated the wooden door of her cell.

Footsteps.

"He's coming," a voice whispered. Reggie recognized Terri's voice. She was in the first cell, closest to the stairs. She'd been there the longest. A single mother of a little girl, she'd held out all those days, suffering through the torture in hope of seeing her little girl again. Lately, she'd fallen into despair of ever escaping.

Quiet sobs sounded from other cells along the row.

Reggie emptied her cup, quickly patted the dirt she'd removed into the ground, dragged her tattered blanket over her naked body and moved to the opposite corner where she curled up and pretended to be asleep.

Boots clunked down the steps to the bottom.

Silence reigned, even the few sobs ceased as the women held their breath, praying the Master wouldn't choose them for the trip up the stairs.

Reggie waited, listening. When a door hinge creaked, she braced herself.

"Please, no. Please," a woman's voice pleaded with the Master. It was Beth, a young college student who'd been captured on her way home from a night class. "Don't hurt me," she cried.

"Shut up and move," the Master's harsh voice echoed in the darkness.

"No, please. I can't." The sharp crackle of electricity sparking was followed by a scream.

Reggie winced and bit down hard on her tongue to keep from yelling at the man for hurting Beth. She couldn't draw attention to herself. Not now. Not when the hole she'd been digging was already two feet wide and as deep. If he took Beth up to the house, he'd be distracted long enough Reggie might finally break through.

Beth cried as she stumbled up the stairs, the Master's footsteps sounding as he climbed up behind her.

As soon as the door clicked closed at the top of the stairs, Reggie grabbed her cup and went back to work, digging furiously, scraping the dirt away with the cup and her fingernails. The Master usually kept a woman up in the big house for at least an hour before he brought her back to her cell. She didn't have much time.

She abandoned quiet for speed and dug as fast as she could.

"What are you doing?" Terri whispered, her voice barely carrying above the scraping sound of the cup on dirt and rocks.

Reggie ignored her, determined to get as far as she could before the Master returned.

Her cup struck a large rock. Undeterred, she scraped around the edges, her heart beating faster, her breath coming in ragged gasps. The drugs in her body slowed her down, making her want to crawl into her blanket and sleep. But she couldn't.

"Stop whatever you're doing," Terri said.

Reggie halted and listened. When she didn't hear footsteps or the quiet sobs of Beth being returned to her cell, she went back to work on digging around the rock.

Soon, she found the edge of one end of the stone and worked her way around it.

After scraping and digging for what felt like an hour, she poked through the dirt and felt cool, fresh air streaming through a tiny hole onto her fingertips.

Not trusting her hands, she pushed her head through the tunnel and sniffed fresh air, the scent of decaying foliage a welcome scent from the earthen cell. She inhaled deeply, her breath catching on a sob. She'd been right. Her cell was on the edge of the hill. If she dug a little more, she might be able to push through. The large rock was in the way. If only…

She pulled her head out of the tunnel and shoved her bare feet in and pushed as hard as she could.

The rock didn't move.

Lying on her back, the cool dirt floor making her shiver, she scooted closer, bunched her legs and kicked hard with her heels, over and over until the rock moved. Hope blossomed in her chest and gave her the strength to keep pushing and kicking.

"You have to stop," Terri said. "When one of us crosses him, he punishes us all."

Another one of the women sobbed. "Please don't make him mad."

Reggie didn't want any of them to be hurt by her actions, but the Master was hurting them every time he took one of them up into the house. She had to get out and get help for all of them. Using every last bit of her strength to kick and shove at the boulder until it rocked and gave, she finally pushed it free of the soil, and it rolled down the hill. Loose dirt fell into the tunnel, blocking the sweet scent of fresh air.

Using her feet again, Reggie pushed at the dirt. More fell into the gap. She scrambled around and shoved her arms through the tight tunnel and patted the loose dirt against the walls of the tunnel, shoving the excess out and down the hill.

"Shh!" Someone said from one of the other cells. "He's coming."

A door opened above them. Sobs sounded as Beth descended into her prison, followed by the clumping sound of the Master's boots.

Reggie hadn't taken the time to pat the dirt into the walls this time. If the Master came into her cell, he'd catch her at digging her way out. She looked through the hole. Gray beckoned her. She shoved her shoulders through the tunnel. It was tight. Really tight. But if she could get her shoulders through, she could get the rest of her body through. Desperately inching and wiggling her way inside, she prayed she could breach the exit before the Master jerked open her door, grabbed her by the ankles and yanked her back inside. He'd beat her and chain her. And he'd throw her into the wooden box beneath the stairs where he kept the "naughty" girls.

No way. She couldn't let that happen. Not when she could taste freedom.

With her body blocking the tunnel, sounds of weeping and cries were muffled. Reggie couldn't tell if the women were informing the Master of her scratching and digging. She wasn't sticking around to find out. Once her shoulders were free, she braced her hands on the edges of the hole and pushed as hard as she could. Her body scraped through until her hips were free of the tunnel. Grabbing onto nearby branches, she pulled her legs out of the hole. Once all of her was free, gravity took hold, and she tumbled down the hill, her skin torn and gouged by sticks, rocks and bramble.

The jabs and tears made her cry out with joy. The pain wasn't inflicted by the Master but delivered by nature as a testament she was out of that hell.

She came to a stop when her head hit the big rock she'd pushed free of her tunnel. For a long moment, she lay still, her vision blurring, pain raking through the base of her skull.

Then she heard the sounds of dogs barking, and her heart froze. The Master had two vicious looking Rottweilers he'd kept tethered when he'd brought her up into the big house.

Reggie staggered to her bare feet and shivered. The cool night air wrapped around her naked body. Swallowing the sobs rising up her throat, she ran, following the hill downward. She didn't know where she was or which way to go, only that she had to get as far away from the house and the dogs as possible. She hadn't come this far to be ripped apart by his maniacal dogs or dragged back to house and beaten until she couldn't remember who she was or why she cared.

Sticks and rocks dug into the soft pads of her feet, drawing blood. She kept running until her feet were as numb as her skin and mind. The dogs were getting closer. She had to do something to lose them.

The hill continued downward. A cloud crossed over the sky, blocking what little starlight penetrated the tree branches. Her lungs burning and her heart beating so fast she thought it might explode out of her chest,

Reggie was forced to stop long enough for the cloud to shift, allowing the starlight to illuminate her way.

When it did, she stared out at a dark canyon. She stood on the edge of a precipice. Easing to the edge, she could see the glint of starlight off what appeared to be a river forty feet below where she stood.

The barking dogs were close now.

Reggie turned right then left. No matter which way she went, the cliffs were still as high as the one in front of her. She couldn't backtrack. The dogs were so close enough, they'd find her.

She refused to give up. But what else could she do? Die from the vicious rendering of sharp Rottweiler teeth, go back willingly to the Master's house to be beaten, or jump off a cliff into water of which she had no idea of the depth?

When the barking sounded right behind her, Reggie spun to face the two Rottweilers, emerging from the tree line…stalking her.

A shout from behind them made her heart leap into her throat. The Master.

Without further thought or mental debate, Reggie turned and threw herself over the cliff.

As she plunged downward, she steeled herself for the impact against rocks or whatever lay beneath the water's surface.

Crossing her arms over her chest, pointed her toes and hit the river feet-first, sinking deep. The chill shocked her body, but she kept her mouth shut tight, and struggled, kicking hard to rise. Just when she thought she would never breathe again, she bobbed to the surface and gasped. Above her, she heard the wild barking of the Rottweilers.

The cold water helped clear her foggy brain. She had to make the Master think she was dead. Taking a deep breath, she lay over, face-first in the water and floated as far as she could before turning her head to the side to take another breath. She did this for as long as she could hear the dogs barking above. The Master had to think she'd died in the fall from the cliff. It was the only way to get away and make him think she couldn't tell the authorities about what he had hidden in his basement.

After a while, the sound of the dogs barking faded. Knowing the dogs couldn't follow her scent in the water, she let the river's current carry her along as she treaded water to keep her head above the surface.

The cold sapped what little energy she had left. She rolled onto her back and floated into the shallows where she dragged herself up onto the shore.

Darkness surrounded her, embraced her and sucked her under. As she faded into unconsciousness, her last thought was...*I'm free*.

CHAPTER 2

"Well, Talon, welcome to the Brotherhood Protectors." Hank Patterson held out his hand with a grin. "Glad to have you aboard."

Sam "Talon" Franklin held out his hand to his new boss. "Thanks, Hank, for having faith in my abilities. I hope I live up to your expectations."

"If I didn't think you could do the job, I wouldn't have hired you," Hank said. "You being a Navy SEAL, I know you have the key ingredients necessary to take on any assignment that might come your way with the Brotherhood Protectors. We can always use a weapons expert who's also good at hand-to-hand combat. I think you'll fit right into the team. Flexibility and being able to take charge in difficult situations will come in handy in this job, as it did in your SEAL days. No matter the mission, you're up for the challenge." He shook his head. "We get all kinds of assignments. Some more exciting than others."

"I look forward to my first mission," Sam said. "I

guess I should go by Sam, now that I'm no longer a part of the Navy SEALs."

"Noted." Hank nodded. "I'm looking through our most recent requests. I'll have something for you by the time you come back from your fishing trip." He glanced around the little cabin. "Will this old hunting cabin be enough for you and your dog until you can find more suitable accommodations?"

"It's perfect. Small enough it won't take me much time to clean. It has a bed, which always beats the cold hard ground, electricity, a refrigerator and heat. Most importantly…it's off the beaten path, so I'll have all the privacy and quiet Grunt and I can stand." Sam grinned. "Tell your wife we appreciate her finding it for us. It'll work out fine."

"Sadie likes to help out when she's on hiatus from her work. She's in the middle of a two-month break and getting a little stir-crazy."

"I've seen some of her movies. She's really talented," Sam said. "Don't you get jealous when she kisses other actors?"

Hank nodded. "Like mad. But she always comes home to me and Emma. I know how much she loves me, and I love her more than life itself."

Sam's chest tightened. He'd pretty much given up hope of ever finding that kind of love. It just wasn't in the cards for him.

"Enough about me and my family. You have a vacation to start." He pulled a device out of the bag he'd carried into the cabin. "We finally got satellite phones. Cellphone coverage can be non-existent out here.

Swede, our computer guy, will man the satellite phone while in the office. If you need to get hold of me, he'll pass on the message. But you won't need this until you start work. Now, go." Hank waved toward the door. "Sadie filled the small pantry with some canned foods, stocked the refrigerator and freezer with meats, vegetables, milk, juice and beer. And she put clean sheets on the bed for you when you get back from your fishing trip."

Sam shook his head. "Remind me to thank her. She went way above and beyond anything I could have expected."

"We wanted you to have a smooth transition to your new job and life. If you need anything, all you have to do is ask."

"Thanks," Sam said. "I appreciate all you've done for me."

Hank clapped his hands together. "Did you get with the outfitter I told you to try?"

With a nod, Sam stepped out of the cabin onto the porch. "I did. He fitted me out with all the paraphernalia associated with fly fishing. Now, I just have to remember how to do it."

"There's no science to it. Just do what feels natural." Hank chuckled. "The fish don't always follow the rules anyway."

"Are you sure you don't need me for the next week?" Sam asked, half-hoping Hank would put him right to work.

"Nope. Go. Enjoy your leave. We'll have you working before you know it." Hank clapped a hand onto

Sam's back. "See ya in a week." He climbed into his truck and left Sam standing on the porch.

Sam wasn't sure how to relax. Being on his own for an entire week without anyone shouting, shooting or harassing him, even if good-naturedly, would be a new experience. One he wasn't certain he was equipped to handle. Already, he missed his brothers in arms, the only family he'd known for the past eleven years, and he wondered if he'd made the right decision to leave the Navy and join the civilian world.

He left the cabin Sadie had found for him and drove up into the Crazy Mountains, following the directions the outfitter had given him to the river he'd recommended for fly fishing.

Once there, he unloaded his gear from his truck and looked around. The light green of the grassy glen contrasted sharply with the dark green branches of Lodgepole pines climbing up the hillside. The river in front of him was shallow and meandering through an idyllic valley. Instead of making him relax, the quiet and emptiness of the landscape made his shoulders tense. What if he got bored? What if he found he couldn't stand to be alone? What if he wasn't any good at civilian life? Would the Navy take him back?

Sam slipped into his waders and pulled them up to his waist like the man in the outfitter store had shown him. He gathered his fly fishing pole, the lures he'd purchased, and then let Grunt out of the back seat of his pickup.

The sable-colored German Shepherd leaped to the

ground and ran a circle around the truck before he tore off into the brush.

"Grunt!" Sam called out. He wasn't quite sure the dog knew to stick around. They'd only been together for three days since he'd arranged to adopt the retired military war dog. He'd picked him up from San Antonio, Texas before he'd begun the long trek to Eagle Rock, Montana, where he'd met his new boss, Hank Patterson, former Navy SEAL and entrepreneur.

The two men had known each other from having served in Afghanistan several years ago. Sam had heard about Hank's new venture in protective services. In a corps as small and close-knit as the Navy SEALs, word got around.

When Sam had decided it was time to leave the Navy, he'd contacted Hank, hoping he had room for one more highly trained combatant. He promised he could be retrained to provide protection to those who needed it and could even live with the cold temperatures found in the Crazy Mountains of Montana.

Hank assured him that he had room for more good men in his agency, the Brotherhood Protectors. All Sam had to do was get to Eagle Rock, Montana.

He had arrived that day, met with Hank and gotten the low down on what was expected. Because he was still on terminal leave, he wanted to postpone his actual start date until he'd had a chance to unwind from his last mission.

His fingers tightened on the fishing pole as the events of that final mission came back to him in waves of anger, regret and grief. Pushing thoughts of the men who hadn't been lucky enough to return home on their own two feet and the civilians who'd been caught in the crossfire, Sam baited his hook with a fancy lure, walked out into the middle of the shallow river and cast his line out the way the outfitter had taught him.

He flicked the line, dragging the lure across the water and willed the tension out of his shoulders. He was supposed to be relaxing and unwinding from active duty. The new job wouldn't start for another week, giving him the time he needed to adjust to civilian life. No uniforms, no rank, no one shooting at him. Life would be very different. No surprises. How hard could being a bodyguard be?

A loud splash in the water behind him made Sam jump. He spun and crouched in a combative position, ready to take on the enemy.

Grunt bounded through the water, came to a stop beside Sam and promptly shook the water from his fur, spraying Sam where he'd planned on staying dry. "Hey, shake somewhere away from me."

As if he understood Sam, Grunt took off for the riverbank and sniffed through the reeds until he disappeared into the brush. Sam shook his head. Grunt had seemed so happy to be rescued from his kennel. The dog had jumped up into Sam's arms and slathered him with sloppy kisses. He remembered him from when they'd been together in Afghanistan, before the last mission. Sergeant Tyler Bledsoe, his handler, had been killed when a Taliban rebel had tossed a grenade down the narrow alley they'd been sent into. The dog and the handler had been hit by shrapnel. Sgt. Bledsoe's protective vest hadn't saved him. He'd taken a hit to his neck, severing his carotid artery. He'd bled out before anyone could do anything to slow the bleeding.

Grunt had lost an eye and was laid up with shrapnel wounds. Thankfully, he hadn't been put down on the spot. He'd been evacuated back to the States with other human casualties aboard a C-17 equipped with a critical care team to Germany. A veterinarian cleaned out the shrapnel and arranged for the dog to be transported back to Lackland Air Force Base, where he'd been officially retired and put up for adoption.

That mission had been Sam's last before he'd separated from the Navy a month later. He'd followed Grunt's progress and expressed his desire to adopt the animal once he'd been released from active duty. He'd felt he owed it to Grunt's handler to give the dog a home.

The least he could do for Sgt. Bledsoe was take care of the dog that had meant as much to him as any other member of his family and give him a forever home in his retirement. Grunt had served well, saving the lives of so many soldiers, SEALs and Delta Force. He deserved a good life.

Sam cast the line out again, trying to get the hang of fly fishing, scooting the lure across the water again.

Grunt barked...not something he did often. The sound drew Sam's attention away from his fishing.

About that time, something hit the lure and dragged the line down.

Grunt's barking became more insistent, almost desperate.

With a fish on his line, Sam hesitated. The outfitter in Bozeman had warned him that the mountains and streams in the area were inhabited by bears. He should be looking out for them while he fished.

Grunt continued barking, the sound getting louder.

Sam waded back to shore, tossed aside his expensive fly-fishing pole and tromped along the river bank toward the sound.

He saw Grunt before he saw the source of his distress.

Sam pulled his handgun from the holster beneath his jacket and wondered if a bullet from a 9 millimeter pistol would slow a bear long enough for him to get Grunt to safety. Or would it just piss him off?

Though he searched the brush beyond Grunt, Sam couldn't see a bear. And the dog wasn't barking upward at a bear but into the brush bordering the river.

His gun drawn and ready, Sam approached, wondering if Grunt had cornered another animal.

Flicking the safety off, he edged toward Grunt. As he neared the dog, he noticed the bank sloped sharply down to a grass-covered sandy beach between him and Grunt. Something pale and smooth lay among the grass and reeds.

As Sam got closer, he realized it was a body. A naked body. Beyond the body, Grunt stood, the ruff on the back of his neck standing at attention. In front of Grunt, was a wolf, standing in the shadows of the brush, crouching low, ready to spring.

Sam pointed his gun into the air and fired one shot.

The wolf bolted, ducking into the woods.

Once the wolf was gone, Grunt backed toward the body and sniffed.

Sam scrambled down the slope and hurried to the inert form, lying naked in the sand. As he closed the distance, he could tell by the shape of the hips, it was a woman, lying face down in the sand.

At first, he couldn't tell if she was breathing.

He knelt beside her and felt for a pulse at the base of her throat. He couldn't quite tell if he had his fingers in the right place since she was lying face down. He was hesitant to move her in case she'd suffered spinal injuries. But if she wasn't dead, she'd die soon enough from exposure. Gently, he rolled her over and touched his fingers to the base of her throat. His breath lodged in his throat, and he prayed for a sign of life.

Just as he felt a faint pulse, the woman moaned, and her eyelids slowly lifted.

She stared up at him, her eyes widening. Then she slapped at his hands and kicked her feet in a pathetic attempt to fight him off. She was too weak to escape his hold.

"Hey, I'm not going to hurt you." He let go of her long enough to strip off his jacket and lay it over her naked body, trying not to notice her breasts, the tuft of hair at the juncture of her thighs and how perfectly formed she was, even though her skin was bruised and scratched, and her feet looked like hamburger meat. She had to have been running through the woods to get that beat up.

"We need to get you to a hospital." He scooped her up and straightened to stand.

She tried again to fight free of him, but he only held her tighter. "It's okay. You've been injured. I'm going to get you to a doctor."

"No," she whispered.

He frowned down at her. "No, you weren't injured?"

"No doctor," she said.

"At least let me contact the police. You had to have been running from someone to get all these injuries."

"No doctor. No police." She shook her head. As if that little bit of effort was too much for her, she passed out in his arms.

"Well, damn." Sam trudged along the river and headed back to his truck. He opened the back door and laid the woman on the bench seat. Then he stripped out of his waders, threw them into the back of the truck. He didn't want to waste time retrieving his fishing pole. If it was there when he got back, good. If not…oh well. He held open the driver's door. "Grunt. Up."

The dog flew into the seat, over the console and onto the passenger side.

Sam climbed into the truck and turned in his seat to stare at the woman lying unmoving. Every instinct told him to get her to a hospital as quickly as possible. And to have them run a rape kit on her. Someone had probably kidnapped, raped her and dumped her body. Whoever had done that needed to be caught and prosecuted. Hell, he needed to be shot.

Anyone who could abuse a woman and leave her naked and exposed to wild animals and the elements deserved a bullet through his black heart.

But the woman had specifically said no doctor and no police.

Why?

And what was he supposed to do with her if he couldn't take her to the hospital or to the police?

"I'm taking you to my boss," he said out loud.

"No," she croaked.

He turned in his seat to see she was looking at him, pulling his jacket over her nakedness.

She opened startlingly green eyes as if it took all her strength to do so. "I can't be seen."

Sam shook his head. "I have to get you some help."

She moaned and reached out her hand. "No. Please."

"I don't understand." He stared into her gaze. "You need help."

"No one can know I'm alive," she said. "I have to stay…dead." Her eyes closed and her voice faded off on the last word as if she'd truly died.

Sam fought the urge to climb into the back seat and start CPR. For a long moment, he stared at the jacket resting over her breasts, willing it to move.

When it did with the rise of her chest, Sam let go of the air arrested in his own lungs.

Hell, if she wouldn't let him take her to a hospital, the police or his boss, he had to do something to make sure she didn't die on him. He shifted into drive and pulled back onto the dirt road he'd come in on. Minutes later, he was on the highway heading to the cabin Sadie and Hank had rented for him. It was the only place he could think of where he could take her without her protesting.

He turned up the heat in the cab of the pickup. How long the woman had been exposed to the elements, he didn't know, but she had to be kept warm until he could get her somewhere safe and dry.

Thirty minutes later, he pulled up to the little cabin in the woods. He dropped down from the driver's seat.

Grunt leaped to the ground beside him.

Sam yanked open the back door and stared at the woman, wishing he'd gone with his first instinct. She needed to go to the hospital.

She lay with her eyes closed, the jacket having slipped down, exposing the rounded curve of a breast with a rosy nipple, puckered against the cold.

He slipped his arms beneath her, lifted her out of the back of the truck and carried her into the small cabin, against his better judgment.

Thank God, Hank's wife had stocked the cabin with sheets, towels and pantry goods. Sam hadn't thought that far ahead, preferring to get straight to his vacation and the alone-time he'd needed to decompress.

He hadn't had more than a couple hours by himself before he'd found the woman. So much for decompressing in peace and quiet.

Sam laid her on top of the hand-sewn quilt Sadie had draped across the bed. His jacket slipped off her body, exposing how scratched and bruised she was. He couldn't lay her between the sheets like that, but he didn't feel right cleaning her up. Hell, he didn't know her, and he didn't have her permission.

But she was unconscious. The wounds would get infected if he didn't clean and dress them. His training in the Navy had taught him self-aid and buddy care. He just had to think of her as one of his teammates and get the job done.

He located his duffel bag and pulled out his handy first-aid kit. After locating a washcloth, a large bowl and filling it with warm soapy water, he went to work on cleaning up the woman and dressing her wounds with antiseptic ointment and bandages. She lay almost comatose while he worked, gently wiping away the dirt, mud and blood. When he was finished, he dressed her in one of his clean T-shirts and slipped her between the sheets.

Grunt sat beside the bed and laid his chin on the quilt, his gaze shifting from the woman to Sam. The dog whined softly.

"I know. We should have taken her to the hospital," he whispered, patting Grunt's head. "She could have internal injuries from a fall."

As he stood there, he fought the urge to shake her awake. If she didn't have brain damage or internal injuries, sleep would be the best elixir on the path to getting her back on her feet.

As he waited for her to wake, he shoved a hand through his hair and shook his head, the enormity of what had happened hitting him square in the gut. Holy hell, how had he ended up with a naked, unconscious woman on his vacation? He was supposed to be relaxing and finding his footing in the civilian world. The way things were going thus far, civilian life might be every bit as dangerous as his military world.

CHAPTER 3

The scent of something cooking tugged at Reggie's empty belly. Warmth wrapped around her and made her want to keep her eyes closed to continue sleeping. However, her stomach rumbled and ached, finally forcing her to open her eyes and seek the source of the enticing smell.

For a moment, she couldn't focus. Something dark and damp was in front of her, but she couldn't make it out in the dim light.

She pulled her blanket up around her, only it wasn't her blanket, and she wasn't naked beneath it. The dark damp thing in front of her moved and breathed hot breath on her face.

Reggie jerked backward with a muffled cry. Tangled in fresh, clean sheets, she couldn't roll to her feet. Instead, she fell hard onto a wooden floor, jolting her insides and shooting pain through the hip on which she landed.

The animal leaped up onto the mattress above her

and stared down at her, his tongue lolling and his tail wagging. She realized it wasn't a wolf, but it was another kind of canine that could inflict a lot of damage if he was trained to do so.

"Grunt, *platz*," a firm, deep, male voice sounded from somewhere on the other side of the bed.

Reggie fought to free her legs from the sheet and scooted into the corner of the room, as far as she could get away from the animal and his master.

The Master.

A terrified shiver rippled across every inch of Reggie's skin. Where was she? Had the Master gotten a new dog? Had all her efforts to escape landed her back in the hands of the man who'd kidnapped her and other women? She searched the immediate area around her for a potential weapon but found none. Her fingernails were broken and stubby from digging. She was weak with hunger and the lingering effects of the drugs the Master had fed her. But she'd rather die than go back to the torture and abuse at that madman's hands. If she had to, she'd kill the bastard to get away.

"Hey," the voice said from the end of the bed. A man appeared, dressed in jeans, a black T-shirt and bare feet. "Are you okay?"

She stared at him. Was he the Master? Had the Master removed his mask and taken on a different tactic to gain her trust and cooperation before he destroyed it and beat her into submission?

"Need help getting back into the bed?" The man had dark hair and brown eyes. He didn't look like a sociopath. But then she hadn't met another sociopath until the Master. And though he wore a mask when he took the women up into the big house, he couldn't hide his steely gray eyes that showed no emotion until they were sparked with anger.

"Take my hand. I'll help you up." The man held out his hand.

Though she was convinced this man wasn't the Master, Reggie wasn't sure it was safe to trust him. He could be working with the Master to kidnap women.

He moved closer. "You need to get back in the bed. It's supposed to get down below freezing tonight. You'll want to conserve your strength."

She shrank back even more, pulling his T-shirt down over her legs, her body shaking. "Are you going to rape me?"

His eyes widened. "Hell, no. And I'm not the one who put those bruises, cuts and scratches on you." He shook his head. "Look, lady, I could have left you in that river to be eaten by a wolf or bear, or you could have died from exposure. If you hadn't protested so adamantly, I would have dropped you at the nearest hospital and been done with my good Samaritan act. Now, are you going to let me help you? Or are you going to die anyway?"

Even through her fuzzy head, she could tell he was impatient with her. Reggie frowned. "Not much of a bedside manner," she mumbled.

"Not much of a patient," he shot back. He held out his hand without moving closer. If she wanted his help, she'd have to meet him halfway.

After what she'd been through at the hands of her captor, she wasn't ready to trust any man.

Then her rescuer's voice softened. "Look, I don't want to hurt you. I've had more than enough opportunity, if I did. I'm on vacation and just want to be left alone. The sooner you're well, the sooner you're out of here, and I can get back to my solitude."

She stared into his eyes and then her gaze shifted to his hand. Finally, she reached out and laid her fingers against his palm.

The man closed his hand around hers and gently pulled her to her feet.

His hand was cool and dry. As soon as she was upright, her head spun, the room dimmed, and she lost all control of her muscles. She sank into a black abyss.

IF SAM HADN'T CAUGHT her, she'd have fallen on the floor. He lifted her in his arms and swore.

Her body was on fire.

He laid her on the bed and hurried to wet a cloth with the cool mountain water from the tap. From what Hank had told him, the water was from a well that tapped into a spring. Cool, refreshing and just what the woman needed to bring down her fever.

He carried the cloth to the bed and placed it on her brow.

The woman moaned but didn't open her eyes.

Grunt stood beside Sam and rested his chin on the bed. His gaze shifted from Sam to the woman. He let out a soft whining sound.

"It's okay," he said. "She's going to be all right."

He pulled one of the kitchen chairs up beside the bed and sat with her for the next hour, rewetting the cloth and applying it to her forehead, her neck and cheeks. The longer her fever lasted, the more concerned he became. She could die if he didn't take her to a doctor.

Grunt held vigil as well, refusing to lie down for the first hour. Finally, he curled up beside the bed and slept fitfully, waking up every few minutes and lifting his head to look at Sam, as if asking how the patient was doing.

After two hours with no break in her fever, she lay completely still and unresponsive.

Worried, Sam picked up the satellite phone Hank had left.

The woman didn't want anyone to know she was alive. No hospitals, no police. Hell, that tied his hands when he didn't know who she was or if she had family who could come to her rescue. The only other person he knew who lived close enough to help was Hank Patterson, his new boss.

He entered the number Hank had given him with the phone and pressed send. If he didn't do something to help the woman, she could die.

Not on his watch.

Hank answered the phone immediately. "Sam, I thought you were out fishing and camping?"

"I was, but I've got a situation." He went on to explain about Grunt finding the woman, and how she'd begged him not to take her to a hospital or the police.

"She's burning up. If I don't do something soon, she'll die. I don't have anything to give her to bring the fever down. Cool compresses aren't touching it. I can't leave her to go to a pharmacy. What I'm telling you is that I need help, but it needs to be discreet."

"On it. I'll have someone there in the next thirty to forty-five minutes." Hank ended the call.

Sam set the phone on the kitchen table and returned to the bed.

The cool compress he'd laid across her head had fallen onto the pillow, leaving a damp spot.

Her head rolled from side to side, her brow puckered. "No," she whispered. "Don't hurt them."

Sam leaned closer, hoping to learn more about this stranger. He didn't even know her name.

"Don't hurt who?" he asked softly.

"Don't hurt…" she said, her voice fading.

"Who are you?" he asked, shifting the cloth back to her forehead.

"Dead," she murmured. "Must be dead…"

"What's your name?" he asked.

"Dead." She tossed her head a couple more times, and then lay as still as death. Her cheeks were flushed a ruddy red and were covered in a sheen of perspiration.

He had to get her cooled off or the fever would fry her brain.

Sam lifted her into his arms and carried her into the small shower. Turning on the water, he stood holding her in his arms as the water sprayed over both of them, drenching their clothing and skin.

She struggled weakly, but not enough that he feared

he'd drop her. She was in no shape to fight back. And he had to get her body temperature down.

After five minutes in the shower, the color in her cheeks had returned to a more normal peachy pink. The T-shirt he'd dressed her in was soaked and lay plastered against her skin, revealing the beaded peaks of her nipples and the rounded swell of her breasts.

When she shivered violently, he switched off the water, hooked a towel with his fingers and stepped out of the shower onto the floor mat. He tried to stand her on her feet so that he could dry her body, but she kept sliding down his front.

Giving up, he scooped her into his arms and carried her back to the bed, laying her on the hastily spread towel.

He grabbed another towel from the small bathroom and dried her as best he could. Digging another of his T-shirts out of his duffel bag, he pulled the damp one over her head and dressed her again in a dry shirt.

He'd just finished tucking her beneath the sheet when a hard knock sounded on his door.

Sam stiffened. He glanced from the woman on the bed to the door and back. The only person who knew she was there was Hank.

He took his gun out of the holster he'd hung on a hook on the wall and crossed to the door. "Who's there?"

"Sam, it's me, Hank."

"Are you alone?" Sam asked.

Hank hesitated. "No. I brought Sadie. She worked as

a medical assistant in a hospital before she made it to the big screen. Let us in. We can help."

Sam unlocked the door and edged it open.

The sky had darkened to a steely gray. The sun had settled behind the Crazy Mountains, leaving the land cloaked in the dusk before dark.

Hank stood before him, his wife, Sadie, beside him, her hands covered in oven mitts, holding a container.

"We brought chicken noodle soup and some medicines that should help to bring down the fever," Sadie said.

Sam stepped aside.

Sadie entered, followed by Hank.

Sam peered into the growing darkness for a moment before he closed the door and twisted the lock.

"Who's watching Emma?" he asked.

Sadie shot a smile over her shoulder as she laid the pot of chicken soup on the small kitchen counter. "Chuck and Kate were visiting when Hank got the call. They stayed to babysit Emma."

Sam frowned. "You told them?"

"Not that you had a woman up here," Hank assured him. "Only that a friend was ill, and we needed to help. Chuck and Kate were happy to stay. Their little girl, Lyla, loves Emma. Now that Emma is walking, the two of them are all over the place." She held out her hand for the bag Hank was carrying.

He handed it to her and glanced at the bed. "How long has she been out?"

"I found her about four hours ago. She's been out most of that time. She came to briefly, got out of the bed and promptly passed out again. Her body is hot. I put her in the shower to cool her off, but that didn't wake her."

Sadie ran a digital thermometer over the woman's forehead and shook her head. She stared at the reading and shook her head. "She's running a 104 degree temperature." Sadie turned to Sam. "She needs to be taken to the hospital."

Sam drew in a deep breath and let it out. "When she was lucid, she was adamant. No hospital and no police. I didn't know where else to take her."

Sadie set the thermometer aside and held out her hands for the satchel Hank had carried in. After she dug through the contents, she pulled out a bottle of pills. "She's not going to die, if I have anything to say about it. Help me sit her up. We have to get these into her to help reduce the fever."

Sam hurried forward and helped brace the woman in an upright, seated position on the bed. He held his arm around her shoulders and spoke to her. "Hey, you need to wake up and take some medicine."

She moaned and shook her head.

"Please," he said. "We need to bring your fever down. Come on, open up." He rubbed his thumb across her cheek.

The woman leaned into him and opened her mouth enough for Sadie to push two pills between her teeth and hold a bottle of water with a straw up to her lips.

"Drink," Sam ordered.

For a moment, she didn't move, but then she sucked

the water up through the straw and swallowed, and then swallowed again and again.

When Sadie tried to take away the bottle, the semi-conscious woman reached out and grasped Sadie's hands, bottle and all, and kept drinking.

Sam's heart constricted. The woman was ravenously thirsty. He took one of her hands and squeezed gently. "Slow down, sweetheart. You can have more in a little bit."

Sadie took the water away.

The woman on the bed moaned, her head rocking back and forth.

"It's okay. We'll take care of you," Sam said. "We won't let anything bad happen to you."

"What do you think happened to her?"

"Based on the scratches and bruises, she's been running from something or someone," Sam said. "Or she was dumped in the river to die. Since she was naked, I'd bet sexual abuse is not out of the question." His teeth ground at the thought. In his opinion, any person who sexually abused another should be shot. Studies had proven those kinds of people were sick and couldn't be rehabilitated.

"Hey, sweetie." Sadie applied a cool compress to the woman's forehead. "Can you tell me your name?"

Again, the woman moaned and tossed her head right and left.

Sadie shook her head. "She needs to be at a hospital. If the fever doesn't come down soon, you should take her, whether she likes it or not."

The woman shot up into a sitting position, her eyes

wide and bloodshot. "No. I have to be dead. He'll kill them."

When she started to slump back, Sam sat on the side of the bed and held her in the upright position. "Who is he?"

She looked at him as if she didn't quite see him and whispered, "The Master." Then her body went limp against him.

Sam looked to Hank. "The Master?"

Hank frowned. "She's running a high fever. She could be hallucinating. Even if she'd named a name, we couldn't be sure it was a correct name. But *The Master*... I have no idea who she's talking about. Could be the guy who left her to die in the river."

Sam eased the woman back until she lay against the mattress. He retrieved the cool compress that had fallen onto the pillow and placed it across her forehead. "It would help if you could tell us your name," he whispered. He didn't like calling her *the woman*.

Sadie stood with her hands on her hips. "She needs to be at the hospital. If she's been raped, they need to run a rape kit on her."

"I know that, but you saw her." Sam nodded toward the unconscious woman. "She's adamant."

"What do you think she meant by she has to be dead or he'll kill them?" Sadie asked.

Hank's frown deepened. "Could be that whoever had her has others. If they think she's alive, she might lead them back to him. He might kill the others and dump the bodies before the police can catch up to him."

Sam's fists clenched. "Is there any way we can search for her face among reported missing persons?"

"I can have Swede tap into facial recognition software and see if we can come up with a match." Hank pulled out his cellphone and snapped a photo of the face of the woman lying in the bed.

"I wish we knew her name," Sadie said. "It would be much easier to find her family and let them know she's alive." She glanced up at Sam. "She wouldn't be, if you hadn't found her in the river."

"I didn't find her," Sam said. He nodded toward Grunt. "He did."

Grunt had moved up beside the bed and laid his chin on the mattress, stretching his neck so he could sniff the lady lying so very still. He whined and looked up to Sam.

Hank smiled. "I think he knows she's not well."

"Yeah. He's been by her side since he found her."

"I've found dogs to be a good judge of character." Hank held out his hand to his wife.

Sam snorted softly. "Even characters who happen to be comatose?"

Sadie took her husband's hand, her gaze going to the dog and the woman. "I'm leaving you some warm soup. When she comes to, she'll be hungry. The soup will be a good start to filling her empty belly. I can come back tomorrow with a casserole, if you like." She met Sam's gaze with a hopeful one of her own.

"You've done a good job of stocking the pantry and refrigerator with food. I've been on my own for years. I can rustle up some grub, when necessary.

"We'll stop by tomorrow, anyway," Hank said. "To check on her progress."

"I'd stay, but—" Sadie started.

"No, really, I can handle it from here," Sam said. "You've got a little one to go home to."

"You know, I have half a mind to ask Mia Chastain to come out. She's a rape survivor. If your lady has been assaulted, she'd be a good resource and a shoulder to lean on during her recovery." Hank turned to Sam. "Bear Parker's one of my recruits from Delta Force. He's a good guy. Mia's an award-winning screenwriter. She's amazing."

Sam held up a hand. "I appreciate that, but until I know what she's afraid of, I don't want too many people knowing about her. You heard her, she insists on playing dead. And maybe that's the best thing we can do for her until she can tell us why."

Hank and Sadie both nodded.

"Let us know what you find out," Hank said. "And congratulations. This can be your official first case as a Brotherhood Protector." He held out his hand to Sam.

Sam gripped Hank's hand and shook on it. "Thanks. I couldn't take on anything else until I know what's going on with her."

Sadie touched her husband's arm. "We'd better get back before Chuck runs out of patience with Emma." She grimaced toward Sam. "Now that she's mobile, she's a handful." Her grimace morphed into a joyful smile. "I never knew how much work and how much fun a baby would be."

Hank laid a hand on the small of his wife's back.

"She's all that and more." He gave a chin lift to Sam. "I expect to hear from you with any changes to her condition. In the meantime," he held up his cellphone, "I'll have Swede run that facial recognition software and see if we get a match on the missing persons databases."

"Thank you." Sam hated to see them go, but at the same time, he was glad when they did. Once their truck left the yard, he returned to sit beside the bed and removed the damp cloth on her forehead. After wetting it and wringing it out with cool clean water, he leaned over her, placing the cloth over her brow and whispered, "Hurry and get better so we can get whoever did this to you."

CHAPTER 4

Reggie blinked open her eyes and stared up at wooden beams rising at a steep angle to the apex of a vaulted ceiling. Those beams weren't the plain two-by-fours that had been the flat ceiling of her earthen-walled cell.

A soft light burned from a lamp on an end table, spreading a golden glow over the corner of a small room. The scent of wood smoke gave her a feeling of warmth and security like she hadn't felt in a while. Her hands moved, her fingers touching smooth sheets and soft jersey covering her body.

Sniffing sounds next to her ear made her turn sharply.

A black snout lay beside her. Before she could scream, a long, wet tongue snaked out and swiped her chin.

Reggie jerked away. A squeal shot up her dry throat, coming out as more of a croak.

A face appeared over her.

Fear ripped through her, paralyzing her.

"Hey," a deep, resonant voice said. His warm, minty breath brushed across her face.

A hand holding a cup with a straw moved into her view.

"Thirsty?" he asked and held the straw to her lips.

She shook her head.

"It's just water," he insisted.

And whatever drug he'd decided to add to it. She shook her head again and stared at him through narrowed eyes. "Who are you?" The words came out as a whisper. Her dry throat disallowed any real sound from making it past her vocal cords.

"My name is Talon. Er…Sam Franklin." He smiled. "What's your name?"

"Reggie McDonald," she answered automatically. Her eyes narrowed even more. Were those the eyes behind the masked man who'd kidnapped her and held her captive for so long? The voice didn't fit, but she wasn't completely clear-headed. "Talon?"

He shrugged. "That's the nickname they gave me in BUD/S training.

She shook her head, trying to clear the lingering fog. "You lost me."

"BUD/S. Basic Underwater Demolition/SEAL training. I'm a Navy SEAL." He cleared his throat. "Or I was. I left active duty a few days ago."

She wasn't sure she believed him, though he looked sincere. "Where am I?" she said, continuing to whisper.

"In my cabin, outside of Eagle Rock."

The black-nosed animal slipped beneath the man's elbow and lay on the bed beside her.

The man smiled and rubbed a hand over the dog's head. "This is Grunt, also recently released from active duty. You can thank him for finding you."

She stared at the dog. He had one bright black eye. A jagged scar sliced over the dog's face and his other eye. That eyelid was forever closed, appearing to be sewn shut. "Does he bite?" she asked, forcing the words past her vocal cords, tired of whispering. The croaking sound was worse.

"Please, drink this. You've had a fever. The liquid will help your body recover from it." He held the cup and straw toward her again.

She shrank back. "How do I know it's not drugged?"

His brow formed a V. "Drugged?" He looked down at the cup. "Why would I drug you?" When he glanced back up, his frown deepened. "Is that what happened to you? Someone drugged you?"

She nodded.

He put his lips to the straw and drank from it. "There. If it's drugged, I'll be drugged too."

She stared at the cup again, her mouth so dry she felt as if Death Valley had taken up residence on her tongue.

"Look, if I'd wanted to hurt you," he said. "I could have done it while you were out for the past twenty-four hours." He shoved the cup in front of her. "If you like, you can have Grunt taste it, too. I promise, it's just water."

She tried to sit up but fell back against the pillow.

Talon set the cup on the nightstand, slipped an arm

around her and helped her into a sitting position, stacking several pillows behind her then laying her back against them.

Once she was positioned, he handed her the cup.

She held it for several seconds. The water inside looked so wet and inviting she couldn't resist another moment. Reggie drank until the cup was empty, and sucking through the straw made a loud, empty sound.

Talon, or Sam, chuckled. "Want more?"

She wiped her hand across her mouth. Her lips were chapped, and her hand shook. She realized she was weaker than she thought. For a moment, she closed her eyes and let the water settle in her empty belly. "What do you want with me?"

He laughed. "To get you well enough to tell me what the heck happened. And now that you're my assignment, I need to see that it doesn't happen again."

"Assignment?" She shook her head and lifted her eyelids. "What do you mean...assignment?"

"I just started working for an organization called the Brotherhood Protectors. My boss, Hank Patterson, and I are former Navy SEALs. He hired me to do personal security work. You know, like bodyguard, private investigation, or whatever is needed." He raised his hands, palms up. "Since I found you in the river, he's taken your case and assigned me to figure it out. That is, if you want me to help."

Her head spun. "Look, Talon—Sam—whoever you are, how do I know you don't work for him?"

"Call me Sam," he said. "By *him*, I assume you're referring to *The Master*?"

Her eyes rounded, and that fear rippled through her again, making her cold all over. "You know him?"

Shaking his head, Sam pulled the sheet and a quilt up over her. "No, but you mentioned him when you were delirious with fever. Is he the one who hurt you?"

She nodded.

"Do you know who he is?" Sam asked.

She shook her head. "No. He wore a mask. I never saw his face."

Sam frowned. "That will make it more difficult to track him down."

"Why would you help me?" She pinched the bridge of her nose. "You don't even know me."

"Well, for one, my boss just made you my assignment." He glanced down at the dog. "And Grunt likes you. I'm told dogs are good judges of character." He scratched behind the German Shepherd's ear. "Right, Grunt?"

"Grunt?" She snorted softly. "That's his name?"

The dog barked, startling her, sending a shiver of terror through her. She shrank away from Grunt. A flash of déjà vu rippled across her memory. Dogs had barked as they'd chased her to the edge of a cliff.

Sam touched the dog's head. "Grunt," he said in a stern voice. To her, he said, "Are you okay? Grunt didn't mean to scare you."

"No," she said, holding up her hand. "He d-didn't s-scare me," she lied. "It's just..." Reggie swallowed hard with her suddenly dry throat. "Could I have more water?"

He hurried to the faucet in the kitchenette on the

other side of the one-room cabin, filled the cup and returned, handing her the cup and straw.

She drank, thinking back over what had happened that had led to him finding her in the river. As she remembered, the terror of her escape washed over her. She trembled all over, and her hand shook so hard, she spilled water on the quilt.

Sam took the cup from her and set it on the nightstand. "Hey, it's okay. You're safe here."

When she continued to shake, he eased over to sit on the bed beside her and pulled her into his arms. "I promise, I won't hurt you. And I won't let anyone else hurt you."

He held her stiff body for a long moment. When she didn't relax, he leaned back and looked into her eyes. "Is my holding you making you uncomfortable? If it is, I'll let go." He shifted his body, loosening his hold around her.

She shook her head and leaned into him. "No. It's just… Oh, sweet Jesus. I'm free. I can't believe I got away." All the horror of captivity threatened to overwhelm her. The trembling increased until she realized she was crying. Sobs wracked her body and left her wrung out and weak.

The arms around her were loose enough she could get away easily, but strong enough to make her feel protected for the first time since she'd been abducted.

Sam smoothed back her hair from her forehead and held her until she ran out of tears. Still, she leaned against him, soaking up his warmth and strength. When she finally pulled away, the cool air made her shiver.

"I'm sorry," she said, wiping her damp cheeks with the back of her hand.

"No need to be." He shifted back to the chair beside the bed and waited for her to pull herself together. "When you're ready, could you tell me what happened and why you want to be dead?"

She nodded, gathering her breath and the courage to share what she'd gone through. She had to. If she wanted to get the others out, she had to accept help. From what Sam had told her, he was there to help her. The women still being held captive needed help if they were to be freed, and soon. Before the Master discovered she hadn't died in the fall over the cliff into the river. That didn't give her much time to find him and the women he held captive below his house.

Only problem was, she didn't know who he was. How could she find the man if she didn't know his name and hadn't seen his face? She'd been taken to his house unconscious, and she wasn't sure how far downstream she'd gone before she'd washed ashore. She wasn't even sure if she'd traversed one river or multiple rivers before she'd been discovered by Grunt and Sam.

All she knew was that she had to find the others and free them before the Master killed them. And he would, if he thought she was alive and looking for him.

She leaned back against the pillow and closed her eyes for a moment, wondering how much she should tell Sam and how much she could leave out. What she'd been subjected to was demoralizing and dehumanizing. For the sake of the others, Reggie couldn't hold back what she had to say. If Sam was to help her, he had to know what kind of monster had held her captive.

Sam waited patiently for Reggie to open up and tell him what had happened that had led her naked, bruised and scratched on the shore of the river where he'd been fishing. Rage burned inside at the thought of anyone subjecting another human to the pain and humiliation of being held captive and without clothing. She had to have been desperate to make a break for it despite her lack of clothing or weapons to defend herself against a wild animal attack. She was lucky to be alive.

Reggie opened her eyes and glanced at him briefly before she began to talk in a clear, soft tone, reciting the facts of what had happened to her over the past couple of weeks.

"I was walking home from work in Bozeman, when I heard footsteps behind me. When I turned, someone flung a bag over my head and jammed a needle into my arm. I don't remember anything from that moment until when I woke up in a cool, damp cell, completely naked with only a thin blanket. I was scared and called out. I was shocked at a number of female voices answering my questions in the pitch darkness."

"You say females?" Sam frowned. "How many more of you were there?"

"Four, that I know of. Beth, Terri, Marly and Kayla." She looked up at him. "I have to get them out. No human should be subjected to what we had to endure. The man used a cattle prod to make us stay in line. Any time we protested or talked loud enough he could hear us, he used that damned cattle prod, turned up to its highest voltage." She rubbed her arm over what appeared to be burn marks, as if she'd been hit there on multiple occasions and didn't want a repeat of the pain.

"He used a cattle prod on you and the other women?" Sam said slowly, anger simmering.

She nodded. "He treated us worse than animals." Her lip curled up on one side. "If I ever get the chance, I'll kill the bastard."

The low, angry tone, filled with determination and anger, showed Reggie's strength despite what had happened.

"What can you tell me about where he held you and the others hostage?" Sam gently encouraged.

"We were kept in tiny earthen cells in what must have been the root cellar of an old house. He took us upstairs into the big house when he wanted to…" she glanced down at her hands clasped together, "hurt us."

Rage roiled in Sam's gut. For Reggie's sake, he refrained from cursing. He had to know everything in order to locate the house, the other women and the man who'd captured and incarcerated them.

"How did you get away?" he asked.

She gave a tremulous smile. "I dug my way out using the tin cup he'd given me to drink out of." Reggie stared down at her dirty fingernails. "The house was built on the side of a hill. My cell was at the end, up against the side of the hill."

"Wow." He lifted her hand and stared down at her dirty fingernails. "You must have been terrified."

She pulled her hand from his and curled her fingers into fists, more to hide the dirt than as a display of her anger at having been forcefully taken and abused. "I have to get the others out. If he thinks someone will come looking for them, he'll kill them all and hide the bodies."

Sam's back stiffened. The thought of other women like Reggie trapped and tortured, made his stomach knot and his fists clench. "We can't let that happen."

Reggie nodded. "I won't let it happen." She tossed aside the quilt and scooted her legs to the edge of the bed.

"What are you doing?" Sam asked.

"Going back."

"You're in no condition to hike up the side of a river. And you don't know how far you drifted before you washed up on shore. The river could have joined another along the way. You could have been in the water for miles."

"I can't sit around waiting for my world to align," she said. "Those women are in danger. The Master will hurt them because of me. He will take out his anger on them for letting me escape without alerting him." She snorted. "Hell, he's probably already done something to every one of them, lashing out in anger over my escape." Her eyes filled with tears. "One of the women is a young mother. She just wants to go home to her little girl." Reggie pushed to her bare feet, shivering in the cold. For a moment, she stood straight. Then her eyes rolled upward, and her face paled.

Sam reached out in time to keep her from falling to

the floor. He lifted her in his arms, amazed at how light she was, even as deadweight. Gently, he laid her on the sheets and pulled the quilt over her body, tucking in the sides to keep her warm in the cool mountain air. "You need rest," he said, quietly, though she didn't hear. She'd passed out and lay as still as death.

Sam stayed at her side until she woke a couple hours later. By then, her fever had broken, and her skin was cool to the touch.

"What happened?" she asked in a gravelly voice.

"You passed out."

"I can't..." she whispered, struggling to lift her head.

"You had a high fever for quite a while. Your body burned a lot of fuel it probably didn't have to burn. You need to eat and regain your strength before you go looking for the others." He hurried to the table where Sadie had left the pot of soup. The side of the pot was still warm. He found a bowl and ladle and dished out some of the fragrant, homemade chicken noodle soup.

A moan sounded from the bed as he carried the bowl to her side. "Up to eating something?"

Reggie's eyes widened, and she inhaled deeply. "Oh, sweet Jesus, yes."

He set the bowl on the nightstand and helped her sit up, packing several pillows behind her. When he had her propped up, he gathered the bowl, dipped the spoon into the soup and raised it to her lips.

"I can feed myself—" Reggie started.

Sam slipped the spoon into her open mouth.

Her chapped lips wrapped around the spoon. Her

eyelids drooped, and another moan rose from her throat.

"Are you okay?"

She nodded. "Better than okay. I don't think I've tasted anything as good." She looked up at him. "More, please?"

One spoonful at a time, he fed her the soup until he'd emptied the bowl.

By then, Reggie's eyes were half-closed, and she leaned further back against the pillows. "I'm so tired."

"You've been ill." Sam rose, place the empty bowl in the sink and returned to the bed.

By then, Reggie had rolled onto her side and slid down a pillow to lay her head on the mattress.

"Rest."

"But the others…" she whispered. "They're in danger."

"You won't be any good to them as weak as you are." Sam tucked the quilt around her and removed some of the pillows to allow her to rest her head on just one. "I'll let Hank know what you told me. He can start the hunt for the house you escaped from."

Reggie shook her head. "You can't. It will alert him that someone is looking for him. He'll kill them."

Sam touched her hand, amazed at how soft her skin was. "Hank's a smart man. He won't jeopardize their safety. He'll conduct a search on the down low."

"*The Master…*" She cupped her cheeks in her palms and stared at the wall. "He's smart. He targeted each of us, studying our habits, waiting until he knew no one would be watching before he made his move."

"He might have gotten away with it in the past," Sam's jaw tightened, "but we will find him and put an end to his brand of terrorism."

"Yes, please," Reggie said, her eyelids slipping downward to cover her bright green eyes.

"Rest, Reggie." Sam brushed his knuckles across her cheek, brushing a strand of her strawberry-blond hair back behind her ear. "Get your strength back. We have work to do."

CHAPTER 5

Light shone through a glass window, edging past the slits of her eyelids, nudging Reggie awake. The bed was so soft, the sheets fresh and clean, and she was warm for the first time since she'd been taken. The scent of wood smoke gave her the feeling of being home, even though she knew she wasn't.

She stretched and shoved her hair out of her face, feeling how dirty it was. She needed a shower, a chance to cleanse the dirt of the past couple of weeks off her skin. Would she ever feel clean again, after what she'd endured at the hands of the Master?

When she turned onto her side, a long pink tongue snaked out and licked her cheek.

The dog Sam had called Grunt sat beside the bed, his chin on the mattress. His tongue shot out again, his entire body wagging along with his long tail. The German Shepherd appeared to be smiling, if dogs really could smile.

Reggie reached out and scratched the dog behind the

ears. When she rolled onto her back, she saw dark hair on the bed beside her.

Sam had fallen asleep with his butt in the chair beside the bed and his head on the mattress beside her hip.

She resisted the urge to touch the dark hair and feel the strands beneath her fingertips. This man had saved her life.

Grunt nudged her other hand, reminding her that he had been the one to find her. In her fevered mind, she'd thought Grunt was a wolf. As large as the German Shepherd was, he could be just as dangerous as a wolf.

Reggie smiled. The animal only wanted to be scratched behind the ear and possibly fed.

She glanced around the room illuminated dimly by the light finding its way through the windows on either side of the wooden door. There wasn't much to the room, but it had everything one would need to live comfortably, from a small kitchenette with a stove, sink and refrigerator, to a rough-hewn table and chairs, a single brown leather sofa, a small closet and a bed. Reggie assumed the door in the corner led to a bathroom. She eased out from beneath the sheets and quilt and let her legs dangle over the opposite side of the bed from Sam. She didn't want a repeat of the last time she'd attempted to get out of the bed. With Sam sleeping, he wouldn't be there to catch her if she fell.

The thought of his large, capable hands catching her made her feel warm all over and in places she hadn't expected to ever feel warm again. The thought of why made her cold all over again. The Master had used her and abused her in the worst possible ways. As he was doing to the other women held in captivity beneath his house. A shiver rippled across her skin. She felt dirty. Yes, she was dirty from running through the woods, falling into the river and lying on the muddy banks. The kind of dirty she knew wouldn't wash off was the kind that would take years to overcome. Still, she wanted a shower, more than she wanted her next meal.

When she was fairly confident she wouldn't pass out, she eased to her feet and stood for a long moment. Her head didn't spin, and she didn't wobble. Though her legs were weak, she could make it across the floor to the bathroom. Once inside, she relieved herself, washed her hands and stared into the small mirror over the sink.

Holy hell, she looked horrible! Her face was scratched and bruised, her hair lay in matted hanks with pieces of leaves and sticks twisted between the strands. She eyed the small shower for a second, checked the lock on the door and patted the fluffy white towel on the counter. The water was easy to turn on but took a few minutes to warm up. Meanwhile, she stood on the wood floor, her bare feet and legs cold from the chill mountain air.

When the water was warmer than room temperature, she stripped out of the T-shirt and hung it on a hook on the back of the door. That's when she realized she had no undergarments. She'd been naked when she'd run from the Master's place, and she hadn't cared. Her goal had been to get as far away as fast as she could.

If she'd been naked when she'd left her prison, she'd been naked when Sam and Grunt had found her.

Her cheeks heated.

She couldn't do anything about the past. So, Sam had seen her naked. She hadn't been in the best condition. He must have dressed her in the T-shirt as well. And her body wasn't all that muddy from having been in the river. Had he cleaned her up before dressing her in one of his T-shirts?

Reggie's cheeks burned. With consciousness and clarity came shame and embarrassment. She lifted her chin. It didn't matter what Sam had seen and done, as long as he hadn't taken advantage of her while she'd been out of it. Her gut instinct told her he'd been a gentleman and had done only what was necessary to keep her alive and comfortable.

Reggie stepped beneath the spray and let the hot water wash away the remaining dirt and smudges she'd acquired during her race against death. She squirted shampoo into her palm and rubbed it into her hair, working up a thick lather. Then she ran the suds across her face, shoulders and breasts. Pouring more shampoo into her palm, she scrubbed lower, rubbing hard in an attempt to wash away the filth of her captor's hands and body parts. She'd never feel clean again. Not after what she'd been through. The man deserved to be shot. She prayed she'd have the pleasure of pulling the trigger. That bastard had to be stopped. Too many had already been hurt by his madness. And those Reggie knew about might not be all he had harmed.

She poured some conditioner into her palm and

worked it through her hair, finger-combing the tangles free. When she'd rinsed most of it out of her hair, she turned off the water, reached for the towel and patted her skin dry. When she was done, she wrapped her hair in the towel, feeling more like the Reggie she'd been before she'd been taken. With nothing else to wear, she pulled the T-shirt back over her body, stepped out of the bathroom and ran into a solid wall of muscles.

"Oh." She stumbled back a step or two and looked up into Sam's eyes. "I thought you were asleep."

Sam gripped her elbow to steady her. "I was worried about you," he said. "You were in there a long time."

Her gaze left his and found its way to the floor and her own bare feet. "I had to scrub all of the dirt away," she murmured.

He nodded. "I was more worried that you might have fallen. It's a good thing you came out when you did. I was about to go in after you."

Warmth filled her chest and rose up her neck into her cheeks. "It's nice to have someone worry about me. Thank you."

"My pleasure." He frowned. "I might have another clean shirt you can use."

"No need. This one will do."

He turned away and dug inside a duffel bag, pulling out a solid black T-shirt. He held it out. When she didn't make a move to take it, he shook it gently. "Seriously, you sweated in the other one when you were burning up with fever."

Her nose twitched. "When you put it that way..." She

took the shirt. "Thank you. And thank you for rescuing me from the river."

Sam grunted a response and walked to the refrigerator. "What do you like for breakfast? Sadie stocked the refrigerator with eggs, bacon and soup. I make mean fried eggs, or you can have some of the soup she brought last night."

"Eggs would be good. Do you want me to make them?"

He shook his head. "I've got this. I might not know how to cook anything else, but I can cook an egg and a steak. Though my preference for the steak is to cook on a grill." He pulled a carton of eggs from the refrigerator and set it on the counter beside the small stove.

Reggie returned to the bathroom, whipped off the shirt she was wearing and replaced it with the clean black one. It smelled of men's cologne or aftershave, like Sam. She liked its woodsy scent. It reminded her of her father when he'd taken her mother out for date night.

The Master had worn a cologne. It hadn't smelled anything like this. His had had a strong, sweet scent that made her stomach churn every time he'd come near her. She'd never seen his face because he'd worn a ski mask every time he'd brought her up to the big house. But she'd recognize him by his scent.

Once she had the clean black T-shirt on, she stepped out of the bathroom. She'd like to have undergarments, but a T-shirt was more than she'd had for weeks. She wouldn't complain.

The aroma of bacon frying made her stomach rumble loudly. Reggie pressed a hand to her sunken belly. She'd lost weight while she'd been held in captivity. The Master only fed them once a day. And then it had been oatmeal or dry cereal. Protein hadn't been part of their diet. Sometimes, when he took one of them upstairs, he let them eat his table scraps, if he was in a good mood. Most of the time, he only brought them up for one thing, and if they didn't cooperate, he shocked them with either the cattle prod or a taser.

The first time he'd brought her up to the big house, he'd zip-tied her hands to keep her from fighting back. She'd waited until she was out of the basement, and then kicked him hard in the shin and ran for the front door. She hadn't gone far when she'd been struck in the back with the prongs of a taser. She'd landed face-first on the floor and lay twitching. Completely incapacitated, she'd suffered through his violation of her body. The next time he'd brought her up, he'd reminded her of what had happened the last time. Brandishing the taser, he'd led her into his bedroom and kicked the door shut behind them.

When he was kicking the door with his foot, Reggie had taken careful aim and kicked him in the balls. Then she'd kicked the taser out of his hand. Unfortunately, he'd fallen to his knees in front of the door. She'd run to the bathroom and locked herself inside. While he'd pounded on the door, she'd searched for something to cut the plastic zip-ties binding her wrists. There had been nothing sharp enough to cut through the plastic. By the time she'd realized it, the door swung open and the Master had stood holding the key up in one hand and his taser in the other.

She'd ducked, but not soon enough. The prongs hit her in the chest, and she dropped like a sack of potatoes onto the cool tiles of the bathroom floor.

Once again, she could do nothing to defend herself. The entire time he'd raped her, she'd prayed that she would die. And if she didn't, she vowed revenge on the bastard. Somehow, she'd break free and come back to make him pay for what he'd done to her and the other women he held in his cellar.

Sam stepped in front of her, holding a plate filled with eggs, bacon and toast. "Hey. Are you all right?"

She shook free of the memories and nodded.

Sam frowned, apparently unconvinced. "Have a seat before you fall."

"I'm not that weak," she protested, but did as he suggested and sat in one of the two chairs at the little table.

He set the plate of food in front of her and went back to the stove for the other. He set it on the table and pulled two tin cups from a shelf on the wall and filled them with milk from the refrigerator.

All the while, Reggie stared at the food in front of her, salivating, waiting until Sam took the seat across from her.

"You didn't have to wait," he said. "Eat."

She grabbed the fork and dug into the eggs, shoveling them into her mouth as if this might be her last meal. After what she'd been through, she didn't take any meal for granted. Nor did she take her freedom for granted. Never again would she let a man do what the Master had done to her. She'd kill her attacker first or die trying. The problem was, she'd been tased before she could do much to defend herself. Then she'd been knocked out using some kind of drug. Even if she'd wanted to, she couldn't have fought back. The best she'd been able to do was stop eating and dig her way out of her hell.

The food she'd just eaten sat like heavy wet socks in the pit of her belly, reminding her there were other women being held just like she'd been, locked up in cold, damp cells, being raped and abused by a monster.

Sam reached across the table and covered her hand with his. "If you want to help the others, you have to be able to help yourself. You need to fuel your body to have the strength to stand up to whoever captured you and held you against your will."

She nodded and pressed a hand to her belly. "I know you're correct. But it doesn't feel right filling my face with food when the others are starving and being abused."

"They would eat, if they had the opportunity. Don't let it turn your stomach. You have to get well enough to help me find them." He gently squeezed her fingers and lifted his fork. "When we're done with breakfast, I'll call Hank and see if he's learned anything."

Her eyes filled with tears. "I wish I knew more. The Master never mentioned his name. He wore a mask, and he didn't allow us to talk or ask questions. When one of the ladies cried, he hit her with the cattle prod. We learned quickly to keep our tears and questions to ourselves." She stared down at her fork full of eggs and took the bite. Sam was right. To help the others, she had to be strong.

Soon, her plate was empty and her belly full. Setting her fork aside, she glanced up at Sam. "I'm ready to start looking."

He finished his last bite and nodded. "First, we have to get you some clothes. You can't go about town dressed like you are."

She shook her head, her brow dipping. "I can't be seen. If the Master catches wind I'm not dead…"

"We'll think of something." He took his plate and hers to the sink and ran water over them.

Reggie pushed to her feet and joined him, taking up a dishtowel. "You wash, and I'll dry."

The simple act of washing the dishes felt so normal, it made her feel guilty. It didn't take long, but this wasn't getting them to the Master's house to free the others.

Sam took the dishtowel from her and dried his hands. "I know you're anxious to get started. I was hoping to hear from Hank before we set out looking."

As if on cue, a knock sounded at the door.

Reggie's eyes widened, and her heart skipped several beats. She stepped to the side of the door and stood close to the wall, out of the way and out of immediate sight of anyone who might come inside.

"Sam?" a male voice called out. "It's me, Hank."

Sam opened the door and let his boss inside.

A blast of cool air swept into the cozy cabin along with Hank.

"Sadie sent me over with things she thought you might need." He carried an armload of clothing. He looked around the room, finally spotting Reggie. "Oh, good, you're up and getting around. Sadie will be glad to hear that."

Reggie nodded. "Please thank her for the soup and medicine."

Hank nodded. "I will. By the way, I'm Hank Patterson. And you are?"

"Reggie McDonald," she said.

"Nice to meet you." He shoved the stack of clothing toward her. "These are for you. Sadie figured you could use some clothes, seeing as you didn't have any when Sam and Grunt found you."

Reggie's cheeks heated as she took the proffered items. A rush of warmth filled her chest. "That was very nice of her to think of me."

"She was horrified to hear about what happened to you. She said to tell you that if you need anything, just ask. She'll be happy to assist." Hank smiled. "She'd have come herself, but she didn't have anyone to watch Emma for now." Hank turned to Sam. "I put Swede on searching land plats from where you discovered Reggie upstream. There's a fork in the river not far from there. He'll search both branches. It would help to know more about the topography of the land around the house where you were held captive."

Reggie shook her head. "I don't remember much. But what I do know is that the house was situated on a hill. I dug my way out of the cellar because it opened up on the side of a hill."

"Do you remember how far you ran until you came to the river?" Hank asked.

She shook her head. "All I know is that I had to get away from *him* and his Rottweilers. He had two of them."

"Did they attack you?" Sam asked.

She shook her head. "No. I got away before they could catch up to me."

Sam's eyebrows shot up. "How did you do that?"

Reggie shrugged, the moment coming back to her, making her knees shake. "The dogs were almost on me. My only two choices were to give up and go back with them or jump off a cliff." Her gaze met Sam's. "I jumped."

CHAPTER 6

Sam shook his head. Reggie had to have been terrified. He couldn't imagine what she'd gone through. No one should ever be that scared that she'd throw herself over a cliff rather than go back to what she'd come from. "You jumped off a cliff. Sweet Jesus."

"I did. Into the river below." She closed her eyes. "I hit the water hard. For a moment, I thought I'd hit rocks, it was that hard."

Hank whistled. "How high up were you?"

She opened her eyes and shook her head. "I don't know. Twenty or thirty feet? I sank all the way to the bottom." Reggie's gaze shifted to the window. "I didn't think I'd ever make it back to the surface. But I did."

"You're amazing," Sam said.

Hank stared at her. "When you hit water from that high up, if you don't do it right, it's like hitting concrete. You're very lucky to be alive."

She nodded, wrapping her arms around herself. "The water was so cold."

"The streams up in these mountains are fed by melting snow," Hank said.

Reggie shivered. "I let the river carry me as far as it could, but my arms and legs were getting numb, and I was having a hard time keeping my head above the water. That's when the river slowed, and I was able to crawl out onto a sandy bank." She shrugged and gave Sam a crooked smile. "That's where you found me."

Sam would never forget the feeling in his gut when he'd realized the figure on the riverbank was a human.

Grunt nudged her hand.

Reggie gave the dog a soft smile. "Sorry. That's where Grunt found me."

"I can't imagine what would have happened had we not been there fishing at that time." Sam drew in a deep breath and let it out. "Grunt was barking, or I never would have gone to look."

Reggie scratched the dog's ears. "Thank you, Grunt."

Sam's jaw tightened. "He was standing between you and a gray wolf. He saved your life."

Reggie's eyes widened. "A wolf?" She lowered her head, rocking it back and forth. "I thought that was part of my nightmare." She looked up at Sam. "You mean, he was real?"

"Very real," Sam said. "I fired a shot over his head, and he ran off."

"It wasn't your day to die," Hank said.

"I was lucky to get away." Reggie hugged herself tighter. "I pray the other ladies can be saved before something worse happens to them."

"We're working on it," Hank said. "I also contacted one of my guys and his woman. She's an FBI agent."

Reggie shot a frightened glance between Sam and Hank. "No one can know I'm alive. It's crucial to let the Master think I died in the fall. I floated face-down in the river for a long time to convince the Master I was dead."

"I have them in my strictest confidence. They're going to kayak upstream from the point where Sam found you. Molly, Kujo's woman, has skills with drones. She's going to record what's on both sides of the river as they go."

"Wouldn't it be easier and faster if we hired a helicopter pilot?" Sam asked.

Hank nodded. "And noisier. Reggie's abductor could spook and decide to get rid of the women he has locked in the basement. We have to sneak up on him. Drones are much quieter."

Reggie nodded. "Makes sense."

"In the meantime, I need the names of the other women, so Swede can be searching the missing persons databases. If we can track where they were taken, we might discover a pattern. He might work near the places where the victims were taken."

Reggie frowned. "He had me locked up for at least two weeks. During that time, he would disappear for days at a time."

Sam's fists bunched. "With no food or water?"

Reggie snorted. "He left us with a bottle of water each."

"For days?" Hank stared at her, his face reflecting his horror.

"When he came back one time, he brought Kayla." Reggie again looked toward the window. "She was sobbing. I could hear the crackle of the cattle prod and her screams."

Hank touched her arm. "I'm sorry this happened to you and the others. We're going to do the best we can to keep you safe and rescue the other women." His eyes widened. "Wait. I forgot something Sadie sent." He hurried through the door.

Grunt followed him outside.

In a moment, Hank was back with a small box. He set it on the little table. "Sadie sent these things as well. She figured you might want to get out and about while still hiding. These are some of her props she uses when she wants to move about incognito." He lifted a dark-haired wig out of the box and held it up. "She used this the last time we were in LA together. Sadie's hot as a brunette." He smiled and dug into the box again, this time pulling out an auburn wig. "Hmm. I haven't seen her in this one. I'll bet she's hot as a redhead, too."

"Sadie is hot no matter what color her hair is." Sam grinned.

Hank grinned. "You're right. She is." He shrugged. "Anyway, there are sunglasses, hooded jackets, lipstick and wigs in this box. If you don't want anyone to recognize you, these items will help you hide in plain sight."

She gave a nod. "Good. Because I can't sit back and wait for everyone else to find the bastard. I vowed that if I was able to escape, I'd be back to help them."

"And we will help in that effort," Hank said. "First, you have to recover."

"I'm recovered," Reggie insisted.

Sam shook his head. "Less than twenty-four hours ago, you almost died."

"But I didn't." Reggie sat up straighter, as if to prove she was ready to start the journey to free the others. "The longer I wait to go back, the worse it is for them. I have to get them out. Now."

Hank nodded. "As I said, we're working on finding the house. After all you've been through, do you think you could find the house? Did you see where you were going when he took you there?"

She shook her head her shoulders drooping. "But I can't give up."

"Did you see the exterior of the house in your flight to get away?"

Her entire body sagged. "No. I was in a hurry to get away. I didn't look back." She buried her face in her hands. "How will we find him, if I won't recognize the house?" Tears leaked through her fingers.

Sam's chest tightened. "We'll find them. It'll just take a little longer."

"What gets me is that he's probably from around here," Hank said.

Reggie's head jerked up, her cheeks damp, her eyes wide. "I was abducted from Bozeman. I'm not sure where the others were taken."

"That's a scary thought to think he might be someone everyone knows." Sam reached out and gathered Reggie's hand in his. "We'll find him."

Hank nodded. "Yes, we will."

"Hopefully, before it's too late," Reggie whispered.

"We'll do our best to get to him before anything happens to the others." Sam couldn't promise more. If the man got spooked by Reggie's escape, there was no telling what he would do.

"I need to get back to the ranch and check on Swede's progress. You two might want to stop by." He tipped his chin toward Sam. "I have an arsenal of weapons and gear for you to choose from, should you need it. And communications equipment, if we do a team extraction."

Sam nodded. He wanted to see Hank's setup. "If Reggie's up to it, we'll stop by later today."

"I'm up to it," Reggie quickly assured them.

Sam's lips twitched. "We'll see. You've been through a lot."

"Those ladies are still going through a lot. If I can help in any way, I want to be there. Besides, I was there. Something might trigger a memory that could be significant in our effort to find this guy."

"She's got a point," Hank said. His eyes narrowed. "But to keep him from learning that you're alive and well, you need a cover story if someone should see you riding around town with Sam."

Sam tilted his head. "I'm new in town. People don't know me. If I show up in Eagle Rock with a woman, they'll assume she's with me."

Hank grinned. "For all they know, she could be your girlfriend, fiancé or wife." He glanced at Reggie's finger. "You might be the same ring size as Sadie. I'll see what she has in her jewelry box she's willing to loan you for an engagement or wedding ring."

"Let's go with a simple gold band. Reggie can be my wife."

Reggie chewed her bottom lip. "Lies have a way of growing and becoming more complicated."

"Then we need to get our stories straight," Sam said. "We were married two years ago in San Diego where I was stationed as a Navy SEAL."

She murmured. "I've never been to San Diego."

"It's sunny on the coast, and beautiful," Sam said.

Hank chuckled. "Don't worry, most folks around here have never been to San Diego, either."

"I can't go by my real name," Reggie said. "He knows me by Reggie. And since he followed me enough to know my habits, he might also know my last name."

"Do you have another name you can remember to respond to?"

She nodded. "My full name is Regina. My mother called me Reggie, but my high school friends called me 'Ginnie.'"

Sam dipped his head. "Ginnie Franklin it is."

"Ginnie Franklin," she said, as if rolling the name on her tongue. "Married two years ago in San Diego." She turned to the pile of clothing and the wigs Hank had brought. "I'll go change, then I'll be ready for whatever we need to do." Gathering the items in her arms, she crossed to the tiny bathroom and disappeared inside, closing the door softly behind her.

Hank faced Sam. "I'm worried. We need to get

moving on finding this guy ASAP. He sounds like a sociopath."

"I'm worried, too. If he does away with the other women and finds out Reggie is still alive and might be able to identify him, he'll come after her."

"Ginnie," Hank corrected. "And you're right. Ginnie is in danger, either way. He could kill her to keep her from coming back for the others, or to keep her from testifying against him." He pushed to his feet. "She'll need twenty-four-seven protection."

Sam nodded. "That's where I come in." Whether Hank assigned him to her or not, Sam had been the one to find her. He felt a sense of obligation to keep her alive. No. More than an obligation. He liked her. She'd been through hell. Instead of running away, she wanted to go back to save the others. That took a lot of courage. He admired a woman who stood up for what was right no matter the danger to herself.

"I'm headed back to see what Swede's found on the other missing women and the folks who own property along the rivers."

"We'll be there as soon as Reg-Ginnie's ready."

Hank grinned. "Congratulations on your wedding, though I'm two years late. Make sure she wears a wig. That reddish-blond hair is a dead giveaway."

Sam nodded. "We'll be sure to make her disguise a good one." He walked with Hank to the door and out onto the front porch. "And Hank, thanks for the opportunity. This might not be the assignment you had in mind for me, but assignment or not, it's the one I'll follow through to a resolution."

Hank shook Sam's hand. "That's why I hired you for the Brotherhood Protectors. We don't leave things undone." He drove away in his pickup, kicking up dust on the dirt road leading toward the highway.

Sam turned back toward the cabin to find Reggie standing in the doorway, dressed in jeans, a bulky gray sweater, black ballet slippers and the brunette wig covering her strawberry-blond hair.

Her green eyes shone brightly out of her pale face. "I'm ready to go."

"Oh, sweetheart, are you sure you can hold up?"

She squared her shoulders. "I feel much better since having something to eat. I'll make it now." Reggie lifted her chin. "Those women need me to be strong. So, I will be." Her green eyes swam in unshed tears she wouldn't let fall down her cheeks.

Sam wanted to pull her into his arms and hold her until all the bad stuff went away. But no amount of hugging would save those women. Only speed, action and determination would bring them out of captivity alive.

Reggie swayed on her feet. She straightened and pushed her shoulders back. Sam would bet she was fighting exhaustion, afraid he'd leave her behind if he thought she was too weak.

"All right then, let me grab my keys, and we'll follow Hank out to his ranch." He brushed past her, his shoulder bumping against her arm. A spark of electricity ignited in his bloodstream.

This woman had been tortured, probably raped and had nearly drowned. Top that with battling a raging fever, and she still insisted on going to the rescue of the others who were still trapped.

Sam grabbed his keys, slipped his shoulder holster over his arms and buckled it in place. Then he slid his 9 mm pistol into the holster, shrugged into his jacket and looked up to see Reggie watching his every move, her hand resting on Grunt's neck.

"You don't happen to have another one of those, do you?" She nodded toward the holster, now hidden beneath his jacket.

"Sorry. I don't. But I have a conceal carry permit. Do you?"

Reggie shook her head. "Never thought I needed to carry a gun." She snorted softly. "I guess I was wrong."

"Having a gun doesn't guarantee you'll be safe. Being fully aware of your surroundings at all times is even more important."

"I thought I was pretty aware of my surroundings." She shrugged. "I guess I wasn't aware enough."

"We can ask Hank for a weapon for you." He held the cabin door open for her. "Have you ever fired a gun?"

She passed him, her shoulder rubbing against his chest. Her eyes widened for a brief moment, and she swallowed. "My father taught me how to fire his rifle. He always wanted to take me deer hunting, but he died before I turned eleven."

"I'm sorry to hear that."

Reggie's lips twisted. "He thought he had a headache and ignored it a little too long. It turned out he had an aneurysm. He went to bed that night and never woke up. It was me and my mother against the world until she remarried after I finished high school."

"And your mother? Is she still alive?"

Reggie nodded. "As far as I know. She moved to Florida a couple years ago with her new husband. I wonder if she even knows I disappeared." Reggie shook her head. "I usually call her once a week. It's been at least two since I last talked to her. She must be beside herself, wondering why I haven't contacted her."

"We can make that call from Hank's place while we're there," Sam suggested.

"No," Reggie said. "The Master knew my name. He might be able to trace my previous calls to my mother. If I place one now, he'll know I'm not dead."

"Good point."

"I hate to leave my mother in a panic, but I can't let any more people know Reggie McDonald is alive."

"But Sam and Ginnie Franklin are alive and well and can move around without trouble." Sam snagged her arm with his hand, holding her with a light touch. "Come on, sweetheart, we'd better make this look real."

"I'd like to go back to the place where you found me."

"Will do." He held the truck door for her and helped her up into the passenger seat. She leaned on his arm as if it took a lot of effort to climb up on the running board.

He might be a fool to allow her out of the cabin so soon, but he was also convinced she'd leave without him, if he didn't let her help in the investigation. He chose to go with the flow. If she passed out, he'd lay the seat back in the truck and let her rest until she regained her strength.

With Hank and his team working on locating the house where Reggie and the other women had been held captive, Sam could concentrate on keeping Reggie alive and well. Though she would soon grow tired of him stalling her efforts.

The drive to White Oak Ranch, where Hank based the Brotherhood Protectors, took only thirty minutes. They had to pass through Eagle Rock along the way.

Reggie had slipped a pair of sunglasses over her eyes that Sadie had provided.

As a mega-movie-star, Sadie knew all the tricks of remaining incognito. Otherwise, she'd never catch a break from the paparazzi. The public was voracious in their appetite for anything to do with Sadie McClain. From what Hank had told Sam, Sadie had escaped to Montana to live a normal life with her husband and baby girl, Emma.

Reggie had an entirely different reason to remain undercover. Her life and the lives of Beth, Kayla, Terri and Marly depended on keeping their tormentor from knowing Reggie had survived her plunge over the edge of the cliff.

At the gate to White Oak Ranch, Sam pressed the button and waited for the someone to answer.

"Sam, I didn't expect you to get here so soon," a voice said over the intercom. A camera pointed down at the cab of the truck. Hank could see the driver of the truck. "Is Ginnie with you?"

Sam nodded. "She is."

"Good. I have something I want to show the two of you."

Already, the black iron gate was sliding open.

Sam pulled through and drove along the paved road to a sprawling cedar and stone ranch house perched on a knoll, with the Crazy Mountains rising up in the background, covered in Douglas fir, Lodgepole and Ponderosa pines. The sky was a deep blue with fluffy white clouds floating over the peaks.

Before he'd left the military, Sam had never been to Montana. He hadn't been sure about the move but working with Hank had drawn him to the cold north. He'd heard the winters were brutal, but he couldn't imagine any place as wild and beautiful.

As Sam pulled up to the house, Hank stepped out onto the porch. Sadie, his wife, emerged to stand beside him, holding a little girl on her hip.

The mega-star was beautiful even without all the Hollywood makeup and costumes. Her baby, with her soft blond curls, showed every sign of being as stunning as her mother. Hank slipped an arm around Sadie's waist and waited for Sam and Reggie to join them on the porch.

Sam hurried around the front of the truck to the passenger side.

Reggie had the door open and was sliding out of the passenger seat when he came to a stop beside her.

He waited to see if she could climb down on her own.

She placed her foot on the running board and slipped out of the seat. Her knees buckled, and she would have fallen, but her hand on the door slowed her descent.

Sam reached out and helped her the rest of the way to the ground. "Well enough, my ass," he muttered.

She shot him a narrowed glance. "I am. I just… missed my step." Reggie squared her shoulders and marched toward the porch.

Sam jerked open the back door and let Grunt out. Then he hurried to catch up with Reggie, one hand ready to grab her if she "missed her step" again.

When they neared the porch, Sam cupped her elbow and helped her up the steps.

Sadie held out her free hand. "You must be Ginnie." She winked. "Sam's told us so much about you, I feel like I know you already."

Reggie shook the proffered hand and smiled. "I can't believe I'm shaking hands with Sadie McClain."

"Sadie Patterson around here." She smiled up at her husband. "My husband made an honest woman of me."

"I don't know about honest, but if you mean I made you my wife…" Hank tightened his hold around her waist and bent to kiss her lips. "I'd say you're all right. Mmm. And you taste like sugar cookies."

Sadie laughed. "Because Emma and I just made some." She smiled at Sam and Reggie. "Come in. I have cookies fresh out of the oven. Would you like milk, lemonade, tea or coffee?"

"Coffee, if it's no trouble," Sam said.

"Milk for me," Reggie said with a crooked smile. "I like to dip my cookies."

"So do I," Sam said. "In my coffee."

Hank held open the door.

Sam turned to Grunt, *"Bleib,"* he said, giving him the German command for "stay".

The dog sat on the porch, his single eye bright and alert.

"Good boy," Sam praised the animal and followed Reggie inside.

"I'll bring the drinks and cookies down to the war room." Sadie handed Emma to Hank and strode across the massive living room to the entry into what appeared to be a kitchen beyond.

Hank tickled his daughter's belly. "Hey, you. Want to take Sam and Ginnie down the stairs to see what we've discovered?" He led the way to a door, pressed his thumb to a bio scanner and waited for the door to slide open. Stairs led down to a cool, white hallway.

Sam stood back and let Reggie follow Hank down into the basement below.

The white hallway opened out into a wide room. One wall was lined with computers, keyboards and an array of monitors.

A big man with white-blond hair sat in front of one of the arrays of monitors, clicking away on a keyboard.

"Swede," Hank said. "Meet the newest member of the Brotherhood Protectors. Sam Franklin, formerly known as Talon."

Swede glanced up and held out a hand. He didn't rise and kept his other hand on the keyboard. "Nice to meet you."

Sam crossed to the man and shook his hand. "Swede your name or nickname?"

"Axel Swenson," Swede said. "But everyone calls me Swede. Do I call you Sam or Talon?"

"I go by Sam now that I'm a civilian." Sam peered over Swede's shoulder at the monitors in front of him. Half of them were filled with images of the Montana countryside. A river ran through the middle of each screen. "Are those images of the river I was fishing on?"

Swede nodded. "Kujo and Molly are working their way upriver by kayak with a drone flying overhead." He clicked on the keyboard and four of the six monitors changed to images of women. Two were driver's license photos, two were snapshots. All were young, pretty women. One of the snapshots was of a woman with a toddler girl.

"I pulled these from missing persons reports," Swede said.

Sam leaned closer and read the names beneath the pictures. "Beth Snow. Marly Miller."

Reggie stepped up beside Sam and continued, her voice shaking, "Kayla Long and Terri Thompson." She pressed a fist to her lips, and tears spilled down her cheeks. "All missing."

"Kayla's family is offering a reward for information leading to her return," Swede said. "She's been gone a week. Marly's been missing for over a month. Beth for three weeks and Terri for about the same time." Swede ran his fingers across the keyboard again and brought up one more photo.

Reggie gasped as her driver's license photo displayed on a monitor.

"Apparently, someone turned you in as missing," Swede said.

Sam slipped an arm around her.

Reggie leaned into him, her body trembling. "Missing for two weeks," she whispered. "It felt like a lifetime."

Swede brought up a map with points illuminated. "The highlighted dots are where each of the women were taken." He touched a finger to the monitor and drew a circle around the dots. "He seems to be consistent about taking women within this area."

"That's a pretty wide area," Sam said. "It covers several counties in Montana."

Swede tapped his finger on the desk, staring at the images. "He's targeted women from Bozeman to Kalispell."

CHAPTER 7

"How does a man who goes to all these towns not get noticed?" Reggie asked. "These aren't big cities where people get lost in them."

"Research shows that predators with this level of experience are usually repeat offenders. Many have been caught before." Swede pulled up another monitor. "I've run a check on the Sexual or Violent Offender Registry and come up with a couple names we can check on." He brought up images of the men in the area who were on the registry for sexual offenses. "It would take less time if we could enlist the help of the Montana Division of Criminal Investigation."

"No." Reggie shook her head. "We can't let the Master know we're coming for him. He has to think I'm dead, and he will have no one looking for me or him."

"Do any of the people on the registry live along the rivers?" Sam asked.

"The house could be off the river a little way," Reggie said. "I ran through the woods a considerable distance before I reached the edge of the cliffs overlooking the river."

Swede nodded. "I came up with three potential suspects." He brought up the first mug shot of a man who appeared to be in his early forties. "Matthew Ogletree was convicted of raping a thirteen year old girl in Bozeman eighteen years ago. Released on parole two and a half years ago, he lives along this highway in a house owned by his parents."

Reggie squinted at the photo. "I wish I could, but I won't be able to recognize a face. He wore a ski mask every time he came to get me. Now, if you had a voice recording...I might be able to pick him out. I think he had dark eyes."

Swede clicked on a satellite image of the address and zoomed in on a small cabin.

Reggie shook her head. "The house seemed much bigger than that, and it stood on the side of a hill."

"He could have been using an abandoned house nearby," Hank suggested. "We've had a lot of wealthy people from California come to Montana to buy land and houses. They rarely come out to live in them, and only vacation in them once a year."

Reggie pinched the bridge of her nose. "I can't remember much about the place. He kept us drugged for the most part. I had to stop eating what little food he gave me to avoid the drugs he laced them with."

Sam's jaw tightened. The bastard had to die. "The sooner we find this guy, the better."

Reggie nodded. "He's pure evil. I just hope the other women are still alive."

Sam held out his hand. When Reggie placed hers in his, he held it firmly. He wouldn't let that man hurt her again. He turned to the monitors. "Who else?"

Swede brought up another image of a man with a scar stretching from the middle of his forehead to his right cheek. His eyes were brown, almost black, and his lip was curled in a snarl. "Ed Knowles spent time in prison for raping a waitress who worked in Whitefish. He lives here." Swede brought up the address on the satellite image and zoomed in. The address was a mobile home with what appeared to be abandoned vehicles strewn around the yard.

"Again, not a house and not on a hill," Reggie said. She raised her hand. "True, they could be using an out-of-state resident's house, but let's see who else you have."

Clicking on his keyboard, Swede brought up a mug shot of a man with gray eyes, bushy brows and salt-and-pepper hair. "Timothy Thomas was convicted of two counts of rape. He spent twenty-five years in prison and has been out for less than a year." Swede brought up the rapist's address on the satellite image. "He lives closest to the river in a house he owns."

Sam pointed at the house. "It's bigger than the others, and it appears to be on a hill."

"I don't know," Reggie said. "His eyes aren't as dark as the Master's."

"It could have been the lighting in the house or the ski mask that made his eyes appear darker," Hank said.

Sam watched the expressions pass over Reggie's face.

Her brow puckered, and she chewed on her bottom lip. Reggie sighed. "I wish I'd seen his face."

Sam touched he arm. "If you had, he might have killed you. He seemed pretty concerned about keeping his identity from all of you."

"I'll have Bear do a covert check on Thomas's residence," Hank said. "We can probably rule out the houses of the other two, though we can't rule out their involvement altogether. Where do these guys work? I can get some of my guys to follow them and see where they go during or after work."

"Two of them work in Eagle Rock. Ogletree works at the feed store. Knowles works at Lucky's Automotive as a mechanic. Thomas works at home as a contractor, doing graphic design work. They all report to the same parole officer in Eagle Rock."

"I don't suppose you can hack into Thomas's computer remotely?" Sam asked.

"I'm working on that," Swede assured him. "I have to get to his internet account, and through that, I can obtain his IP address. It'll take a little while."

"Good. Let us—"

"If I find anything," Swede concluded. "You'll be the first to know…after Hank, since he's been working with me in this effort."

Sam nodded and looked toward Reggie. "In the meantime, Reggie and I want to retrace our steps to the place I found her on the river."

"Just be careful," Hank warned. "If the kidnapper is concerned about finding Reggie's body, he might be out looking for her."

"Ginnie and I have our cover story, and she's rocking the wig Sadie gave her."

"We should be all right," Reggie said.

"But we'll keep a low profile to make sure no one suspects her of being the woman who got away," Sam said.

"How far up the river will you go?" Hank asked.

"As far as we can walk in an hour?" Reggie said, looking at Sam.

He nodded. "I have my pistol. Reg—Ginnie would like one as well. I can show her how to use it while we're out by the river."

Hank tilted his head toward another door. "Follow me." Sam's boss led them into another room and switched on the light. The room lit up, displaying an impressive number of weapons of all shapes and sizes, from AR-15s to .40 caliber pistols.

Reggie gasped. "I don't think I've ever seen so many weapons in one place, other than at a gun show or pawn shop."

"You've been to a gun show?" Sam asked. "And a pawn shop?"

She shook her head. "Not actually. I saw advertisements for one that was to be held at the Expo Park in Great Falls one year. Guns for as far as the eye could see. Or so it seemed. I used to go to pawn shops with my mother, looking for antique jewelry." She shrugged. "My mother liked the old pieces best."

"Is your mother still alive?" Sadie asked as she entered the room, carrying a tray loaded with cookies, milk and coffee.

"She is. She remarried and moved to Florida. They'd had enough shoveling snow to last a lifetime." Reggie chewed her bottom lip, a habit Sam noticed she did when she was worried about something. "I hope she doesn't come looking for me before we find the Master and free those women. My mother can be like a pit bull with a bone. She won't give up until she gets what she wants."

Sam fought a grin. "Much like her daughter."

Reggie nodded. "Damn right. Especially in matters of life and death. My mother won't take my death lightly."

Hank chuckled. "We'll consider ourselves forewarned." His smile faded. "Are you sure you don't want to let her know you're okay?"

She shook her head. "Too many people know I'm alive already. I can't risk it. Besides, if my mother shows up, it's one more reason for the Master to believe I'm dead."

"Fair enough. Could you hold Emma, please?" Hank handed his little girl to Sam and grabbed the tray his wife held, setting it on a counter.

Before Sam could lodge a protest, he found himself holding the child awkwardly, not sure what to do with her.

Emma had no such qualms. She smiled, giggled and planted a wet kiss on his cheek.

"She likes you," Sadie said with a smile.

Sam grinned back at Emma. "You're a little sweetheart, aren't you?" He held her closer and looked up to see Reggie staring at him.

"You look like you belong together," Reggie said. "I never thought to ask you if you were married or have children?"

He lifted one of Emma's hands. "No to both. I was never in a place, mentally or physically, to have a family. Navy SEALs belong to the Navy, twenty-four-seven. It's not a stable life for families." He shrugged. "Although some manage, others end in divorce." His gaze met Reggie's. "It's one of the reasons I left the Navy. I wanted to get on with my life."

Reggie's eyes widened. "As in having a family of your own?"

He shrugged. "Someday." He bounced Emma on his arm. "If all babies were as sweet as this one, the world would be a better place."

"I thought I wanted to have children once," Reggie murmured.

Though he wasn't staring right at Reggie, in Sam's peripheral vision, he could see her face pale and shadows darken her eyes. His heart squeezed hard in his chest. After what Reggie had gone through, he doubted she'd ever want to have sex again. Any woman who'd been raped multiple times would be rightfully wary of men. He was glad she hadn't shied away from him when he'd only wanted to help and protect her. Intuitively, he knew she needed tender care and kid gloves to get her through what was her own hell of Post-traumatic Stress Syndrome or PTSD. Finding and stopping the bastard who had done this to her and the other woman would help in her road to recovery.

He snagged a cookie for Emma and glanced at Sadie. "Can she have one?"

Sadie nodded. "Just one, though, or she won't eat her meal."

After giving Emma a cookie, Sam grabbed a glass of milk and a cookie from the tray and handed them to Reggie. "Sit and eat a cookie." He led her to a chair and urged her to sit.

"But I want a gun," she protested.

"You can choose from here. I'll bring them to you." Sam hurried toward a light, sleek .40 caliber pistol, lifted it in his free hand and felt its weight in his palm. "This one should do." He carried it to Reggie and waited while she laid her cookie and milk to the side and took the gun in her hand.

"Isn't bigger better?" she asked.

Hank chuckled. "Only if you can hold it steady." He brought her a .45 caliber pistol, a little bigger and definitely heavier. "Hold this out in front of you for thirty seconds." He took the .40 caliber from her and waited while she held the other pistol as he'd told her. After the first few seconds, her arms shook, and she nodded. "I see what you mean."

Hank handed her the .40 caliber H&K.

She held it in front of her longer than she had the other before her arms shook. "Yes, this one is better. But will it stop a man or a Rottweiler?"

"Depends on where you hit him," Sam said.

"If you hit him in the heart, it'll drop him where he stands. If you hit him in the side, he could still come at you."

"Right," Reggie said. "I need to practice."

"And we will, once we get out to the river," Sam promised. He looked to Hank. "Do you have a shoulder holster for this gun?"

Hank dug in a cabinet and pulled out what they needed, handing it to Reggie.

She slipped the straps over her shoulder.

Sam balanced Emma on one arm and adjusted the buckles with the other hand so that the straps fit snuggly against Reggie's body. His knuckles accidently brushed against the side of her breast.

Reggie sucked in a sharp breath.

"Sorry," Sam said and jerked back his hand.

"No. Really. It's okay." She gave him a hint of a smile and slid the pistol into the holster.

"Won't do you much good without ammo," Sadie noted. She handed Reggie a box of bullets.

Reggie patted the weapon, her cheeks pink. "Right. I'll take those, but I won't load until I've had a chance to familiarize myself with how to fire the gun."

"And how to use the safety switch," Sam said, his lips thinning. "Finish your milk and cookies. I'd like to get out to the river."

Reggie dipped her cookie in the milk and took a bite. Then she upended the cup and drank down all the milk. When she finished, she wiped her face with the back of her hand. She smiled at Sadie. "Thank you, Sadie. The cookies are great."

"I'm glad you liked them." Sadie wrapped four cookies in a napkin and placed them in Reggie's hands. "Here, take some extras with you. Sometimes, the guys keep working and forget we have to eat to keep up our strength."

Sam grinned at Sadie. "Hank's lucky to have you, Sadie."

"Are you kidding? I'm lucky to have him. I wouldn't be alive today, if it weren't for Hank." She took Emma from Sam. "And Emma wouldn't be here if Hank hadn't come along when he did. We're both lucky to have him in our lives." She blew a raspberry into Emma's belly. "Aren't we, sweetie?"

Emma giggled and grabbed Sadie's face, making an attempt at blowing a raspberry against her cheek. She made a loud grunting sound and slimed Sadie's cheek with spit but came up giggling.

Sadie laughed and wiped her cheek. "I'm teaching her all the wrong things."

"You're teaching her how to have fun and laugh," Hank said. "In my book, that's all the right things." He slipped a hand around her waist and pulled her and Emma into an embrace. "I'm lucky to have you both in my life."

Sam watched the display of love and devotion and envied them for what came so naturally for them. He'd known Hank when they were deployed together many years ago. He'd never seen the man as happy as he was now. It gave Sam hope for his own future.

If Hank could find happiness, so could Sam. He just had to give it time.

He turned to Reggie and studied her while she was busy adjusting the shoulder holster beneath a jacket Sadie had loaned her with the stack of clothing she'd sent earlier that day. He was amazed that she had gone from lying naked and nearly dead on the riverbank to being the cool, calm badass she appeared to be in front of him.

When he got ready to choose a woman to share his life with, he hoped he'd find someone as courageous and determined as Reggie.

Why was he even thinking in that direction? Because that was the reason he'd left active duty. He wasn't getting any younger. He'd move aside for the newer crop of Navy SEALs to take up the gauntlet, so that the life he'd put on hold while he'd served his country could begin. He wanted what Hank and Sadie had. That same level of love and companionship. And now that he'd held Emma in his arms, he had to admit, he wanted children.

Perhaps because he was so ready for this next step in his life, he was eyeing Reggie. Hell, it could be any woman he might be considering for the future Mrs. Franklin. But deep in his heart, he knew that wasn't true. He wanted someone like Reggie. He hadn't known her long, but his gut told him she was the kind of woman he needed in his life. And his gut had never steered him wrong.

Reggie wouldn't be ready or willing to embark on exploring any kind of relationship for a while. She had to work through the physical and emotional trauma of having been sexually abused. Until she'd had the time to do that, she would be strictly off limits. He wouldn't want to start something that was doomed to failure through no fault of his own.

The beauty of being out of the military was that he was on his own clock now. Nothing said he had to rush into a relationship. If someone was worth waiting for, he could wait. Not only would waiting give Reggie time to recuperate and get any help she might feel she needed, it would give him time to decide if she was really the one.

CHAPTER 8

Reggie stuffed the cookies into the pocket of her jacket on the opposite side of the .40 caliber pistol.

Every move she made, she could feel the cool, hard metal of the pistol against her side and the inside of her arm. Knowing she had a weapon didn't make her feel any safer than when she hadn't had one. Perhaps once she learned how to use it, she'd gain some measure of comfort. Until then, she'd just have to get used to it feeling awkward and unwieldy. Heck, maybe that feeling wouldn't get any better. Still, having something to protect herself and others was better than having nothing. She could put up with a little discomfort.

Sam tilted his head toward the stairs. "Ready?"

She nodded.

"Oh, wait," Sadie said. "I have one more item you need to add to your disguise." With her free hand, she fished in her pocket, pulling out a plain gold wedding band. She held it out to Reggie. "It's not fancy, but it's a wedding band. And if you want people to believe you two are married, you really need to wear one. It's all about what people expect to see."

Reggie frowned. "I can't take this."

"It's okay," Sadie said. "It belonged to my mother. She wasn't into wearing expensive jewelry. She was all into cooking and didn't want a big diamond to get in the way of kneading dough or washing pots and pans."

"But it's your mother's." Reggie shook her head. "I can't."

"If you don't wear a ring, people won't believe you're really married. Even if you show them a marriage certificate." Sadie placed the ring in Reggie's palm and curled her fingers around it. "I think it'll fit."

Reggie opened her hand and stared down at the simple gold band.

Sam took the ring from her and grasped her left hand. "Sadie's right. Folks will automatically assume we're married as long as they see you and me together with a wedding band on your ring finger." He slipped the ring on her finger and smiled. "I do so solemnly swear to be the best pretend husband you could ever have and to protect you from harm to the best of my ability."

Her pulse quickened, and her body flushed with heat at Sam's softly spoken words. "And I promise to be your best pretend wife…oh, and not to forget your name."

He grinned and brought her hand up to press a kiss to the backs of her knuckles. "There. Married, and it was pretty painless, if you ask me." He winked.

Reggie smiled, though her smile faded at the thought of what they'd have to overcome to really be married.

Or rather, what she'd have to overcome. Having been raped several times by the Master, she wasn't sure she could ever enjoy sex again. She never wanted to be in the position of being trapped beneath a man, forcing himself on her. A shiver rippled down her spine at the images seared into her memory.

Sam brushed a strand of her hair back behind her ear. "It's okay. I won't let anyone hurt you," he whispered.

How did he know what she'd been thinking? She looked up into Sam's eyes. In her gut, she knew he would never be the kind of man to force himself on a woman. He'd been a gentleman the entire time he'd been taking care of her. He'd handled her with care and concern. Sam was the kind of man who, if they weren't in such dire circumstances, could make her want to date him and eventually let him touch her intimately. "Thank you," she responded, turned and led the way out of the basement and through the massive living room to the front door. Grunt lay on the porch in the sun. When they came out, he sat up, stretched and trotted over to stand beside Sam.

Once outside, Reggie drew in a deep breath and let it out along with some of the tension she hadn't known was tightening her shoulders while they'd been in the Brotherhood Protectors war room basement.

She drew in another deep breath as if she couldn't get enough.

Sam touched a hand to the small of her back. "Are you okay?"

She nodded. "I don't think I'll ever like being in a

basement again, no matter how nice it is, or how well-lit. It's still in the ground."

"And makes you feel trapped." Sam nodded. "I'll try to remember that and avoid taking you down there in the future."

She shook her head. "Don't worry about me. We needed to see what Swede had found. And what he showed us gives us a starting point, which is more than we had before arriving here."

Sam opened the passenger door of his truck and held it for Reggie. "Hopefully, Kujo and Molly will have some luck exploring the river with the drone."

"Meanwhile, I'd like to do some of my own exploring on foot," Reggie said as she climbed into the seat.

"Not too far," Sam said with a frown. "Remember, you fought a fever last night. You don't want to end up having a relapse."

"I'm feeling better every minute." She patted the cookies in her pocket. "And I have extra sugar to fuel me for a while."

Sam rounded the hood of the pickup and held open the back door open for Grunt. The German Shepherd leaped up into the back seat.

After closing the door, Sam settled behind the steering wheel.

As they drove toward town, Reggie viewed the countryside. "I've lived in Bozeman most of my life, and I've been to Yellowstone, the Tetons and Glacier National Park, but I can't recall ever driving out near Eagle Rock."

Sam tilted his head toward the hills basking in the midday sun, the peaks still coated in patches of snow. "Hank tells me those are the Crazy Mountains. He grew up near here."

"But you didn't?" Reggie asked.

"No. I grew up in California close to San Diego."

"How does a San Diego boy come to live in the cold north?" She gave him a crooked grin. "You do realize it gets down well below zero during the winter, don't you?"

"I've heard," he said, a smile quirking at the corner of his lip. He slowed to take a tight curve. "I've been in cold climates before."

Reggie snorted. "Cold, yes. But have you been in minus 45 degrees with a windchill factor of minus 65?"

"Not quite. But I'm sure I can handle it."

"Not many people who've always lived in the warm southern climates last long up here," Reggie warned.

He chuckled. "Don't worry. I'm not easily scared away by a little weather."

She crossed her arms over her chest and stared forward, nodding her head, a smirk pulling at her lip. "Yeah. We'll see."

"I came here because of the job. But more because of the Brotherhood."

Reggie turned to stare at him. "You and Hank mentioned the Brotherhood Protectors. What is that?"

"Hank was medically retired from the Navy SEALs and came back to his home in Montana because his father needed help on his ranch. He reunited with his high-school sweetheart."

"Sadie McClain is his high school sweetheart?" Reggie shook her head. "Wow. That's an interesting fact."

"Hank said Sadie was being stalked and terrorized. Someone was trying to kill her. Hank stuck to her like glue and soon figured out Sadie's sister-in-law was jealous of Sadie and was trying to kill her."

"Wow. I didn't know that. How come I didn't see that in the news?"

"Hank and Sadie wanted to spare her brother. He wasn't involved. The ex-spouse is now in jail." Sam continued, "Anyway, Hank realized Montana had become a mecca escape for rich folks. And rich folks come with their own baggage and the need for protection. He started the Brotherhood Protectors to provide a security service for people who need help and don't know who to turn to."

"Like me."

He nodded. "Like you."

"Where does he get people he can trust to do the job and not be corrupted?" Reggie asked.

"He mans it with men who've been highly trained in weapons and combat skills. Men who are good at thinking on their feet and would do anything to protect those they are responsible for. He hires former special operations men from the Navy SEALs, Delta Force, Marines and Rangers."

"Men with some serious skills in combat and self-defense," Reggie said. "Wow. I'm impressed."

"Not only does he have skilled men, he gives these skilled men a place to work, using the skills they've trained so hard to acquire. Some leave the military like Hank having been medically retired. Others, like me, are looking to start living outside a war zone."

As they neared Eagle Rock, Reggie pulled the visor down and checked her disguise in the mirror. She adjusted the dark wig and settled the sunglasses over her eyes.

"Don't worry," Sam said. "You don't look anything like the woman I found on the riverbank."

"Good." She studied the houses and streets as they passed several buildings. One had a sign hanging in front of it proclaiming it the Blue Moose Tavern. Further along was a building marked Sheriff's Department. As they left town, they passed an elementary school with cars parked out front.

"It's a cute little town," Reggie remarked. "Hard to think a serial rapist lives here or nearby. And none of the women he's holding captive came from here."

"Sounds like he doesn't want to target women too close to where he lives," Sam said.

They headed out on a highway leading west of town and soon turned off onto a narrower paved road. A few miles farther, Sam turned left onto a dirt road that became increasingly bumpy as they went.

"I don't remember anything about you bringing me out of here," Reggie said.

"That's because you were out cold in the backseat." He shot a glance her way. "When I found you, I wasn't sure you were alive. If I'd been a few minutes later and Grunt hadn't been there…" He faced forward, his jaw set in a grim line. "The outcome would have been significantly different."

Reggie nodded. She would have been dead. Beth, Marly, Terri and Kayla would have had no one out here trying to find and free them from that monster.

Sam finally pulled to a halt in a grassy area that sloped downward to the river.

For a moment, Reggie sat staring at the water, mesmerized by how smooth and peaceful it seemed. The last time she'd been in that river, she had been fighting to stay alive, first by escaping a madman, and then his dogs. Then she'd struggled to keep her head above water in the frigid snow melt that came from the mountains.

"We don't have to do this," Sam said quietly beside her.

For a moment, she debated telling him to turn around and go back to the little cabin where he'd taken her to recuperate. But she couldn't hide. Lives depended on her.

Reggie squared her shoulders. "No. I'm okay."

Sam dropped down from the truck and hurried around to open her door and the back door to the pickup. Grunt leaped out and ran off.

Reggie frowned as she accepted Sam's hand and let him help her down onto the uneven ground. "Will he get lost?"

"So far, he's come back every time."

"How long have you had Grunt?"

Sam snorted. "A week. I adopted him after he'd been retired from military service. His handler was killed on our last mission. Grunt was injured, he lost an eye, and he spooks too easily over loud sounds since he was caught in an explosion. Because he'd become too skittish for a war zone, they put him up for adoption. Fortunately, I'd already let them know I wanted him. He deserves a forever home with someone he knows and who knows him."

"Were you and his handler close?" Reggie asked.

"As close as you get when you're deployed together. Sgt. Bledsoe and Grunt saved our asses on more than one occasion, locating explosives before we walked over them. Unfortunately, a Taliban rebel tossed a shrapnel grenade in front of them in a narrow alley. They didn't have a chance to dodge it or get away."

The tightness in Sam's voice made Reggie's chest constrict. She'd been through a hell of one kind, but Sam had been through the hell of war. She reached out and touched his arm. She couldn't think of any words that could take away the pain of losing someone you cared about, so she stood for a moment in silence.

Grunt broke the silence by loping into view and coming to a skidding halt in front of them, his tongue lolling, the damaged eye appearing like more of a wink than a battle scar.

Reggie laughed. "I believe Grunt has the hang of being a civilian already."

"I'd never seen an animal happier to see me than Grunt when I picked him up at Lackland Air Force Base in Texas. He's even a good traveler."

"You drove all the way from Texas to Montana?"

Sam nodded. "We did." He scratched behind Grunt's

ear. "He's relaxed a lot, but he's still a highly trained animal. We just don't have a lot of need for his skills sniffing bombs. But he does come in handy for finding and protecting damsels in distress."

Reggie reached out and patted the dog's head. "He is an amazing animal."

Sam took Reggie's hand. "The bank is a little steep and can be slippery if it's wet."

She didn't pull her hand free, preferring the help when her knees were still a little weak. She'd never admit it to Sam, though.

He led her to the bank where a fishing pole lay in the grass. Sam bent to retrieve the pole, shaking his head. "I'm surprised this is still here."

"I'm sorry I ruined your fishing trip," Reggie said. "That gear has to be expensive."

"You didn't ruin my fishing trip. You made it…" he smiled, "more interesting."

Reggie snorted. "Interesting is the word you use when you don't want to insult the person you're talking about by saying *it sucked*."

"No, really," Sam said. "I've never been fly fishing. A lot of my buddies told me how great it was, and that I should do it since I was going to Montana." He shrugged. "I had a week to kill before I officially started work. So, I bought the gear and did what people do when they come to Montana. I tried my hand at fly fishing." He raised his eyebrows. "I think I like the old cane pole and worm kind of fishing better."

"You had a week to kill before starting to work for the Brotherhood Protectors?" Reggie frowned. "So, you didn't get your week of vacation. I'm so sorry. You were active duty and a Navy SEAL. I'm sure you needed it."

Sam shoved a hand through his hair. "Actually, I wasn't sure what to do with it. I've spent most of the past eleven years surrounded by people. It kind of scared the shit out of me going on a vacation by myself." He smiled. "So, you see, you saved me from a fate worse than death…being alone on my vacation."

Her heart swelled at his kindness. He was a balm to her ravaged soul. Just what she'd needed after what she'd endured. "You had Grunt," she pointed out.

"You might not have noticed," Sam nodded toward the dog, sniffing at a frog, "but he's not much of a conversationalist."

The frog leaped. Grunt jumped back.

Reggie laughed. "He might not talk much, but he's good entertainment. And I'm sure he's happy you saved him from life in a kennel."

Sam's smile faded as he looked at Grunt chasing after the frog. "There were so many more awaiting adoption. I'm thinking Grunt needs a friend."

Reggie watched Sam, glad he was the one to find her and sad at the same time. If only they'd met under different circumstances. She still felt dirty and violated and wasn't sure when that feeling would fade or ever go away.

She squared her shoulders. "Okay, Grunt, time to go to work. Where did you find me?"

Grunt looked up at his name and tilted his head to one side, his bad eye winking at her. He took off downstream.

"Is that the way he found me?"

Sam chuckled. "He's not much of a conversationalist, and he can't understand all human words. No. He's headed downstream. We found you upstream." He cupped her elbow gently.

Reggie didn't even flinch when he did. Because she was still a little on the weak side, she appreciated his assistance moving along the uneven ground, working their way upstream.

When they came to a grassy area and a small sandbar jutting out into the river, Sam stopped.

Reggie gulped, swallowing a lump forming in her throat. "Here?" She looked up to Sam.

He nodded. "You were lying face-down in the sand. I thought you were dead."

Reggie's gaze followed the footsteps to an imprint in the sand where her body must have been. She knelt and touched the cool sand, her eyes filling. "Thank you," she said.

Grunt loped up to stand beside her, his gaze on the brush on the other side of the sandbar.

"What's wrong, Grunt?" Reggie stared in the same direction as the dog but didn't see anything in the shadows of the bushes. "What's he growling about?" She turned toward Sam.

Sam had his hand in his jacket, reaching for his gun. He pulled it out, his mouth set in a grim line. "He had a stand-off with a wolf the last time we were here."

As quickly as he'd started growling, the dog stopped and bumped her playfully with his wet nose. He ran over to the brush and sniffed around before he hiked a leg and peed on the lower branches.

Reggie laughed. "I guess he's marking his territory in case the wolf comes back."

Sam nodded, his shoulders relaxing as Grunt ran back to where they stood. The dog appeared relaxed, as if no danger existed in the immediate vicinity.

Reggie straightened and walked along the river's edge, heading further upstream. The more she walked, the more her gut tightened.

"Kujo and Molly have to be quite a way up the river by now." Sam looked into the distance where the river curved to the north. "We'd be better off going back to Hank's and reviewing the video from the drone."

"I know it's crazy to think we could walk all the way back to the cliff where I jumped. It could be miles away," Reggie said, continuing to walk along the bank, not ready to turn back and admit defeat. "The river was moving much faster there. Not like it is here. I'd call this meandering, barely flowing. Where I jumped in, it was deep, and the water swept me away."

Grunt ran ahead, plowing into the water as if he saw something moving beneath the surface and running back out to shake away the water from his coat.

As Sam kept pace with Reggie, he slipped his hand from her elbow to capture her fingers with his. She liked the way his big hand held hers firmly so that she wouldn't fall. Yet, she knew if she wanted to let go, he wouldn't hold on. He'd release her. Knowing she had the choice made her want to keep holding his hand.

The terrain grew steeper and rockier. Reggie

climbed up a hill that overlooked the river below. The hill sloped back down on the other side and rose again to an even higher hill covered in Lodgepole pines and other evergreens. She didn't see any actual cliffs in the distance, but then the river curved back behind the next hill, and there weren't any houses close to the river. At least, none that she could see.

She sighed. "I don't know what I expected to find, but it's not here where I can see it." She turned to face Sam. "I guess we'd better head back before it starts getting dark."

Gunfire ricocheted off the hills.

"Get down!" Sam jerked Reggie's arm, hauling her down to the ground.

Something crashed through the trees and underbrush, running in their direction.

Grunt shot off in the direction of the noise, his usual barking silent.

"Grunt!" Sam called out.

The dog didn't slow or stop, disappearing into the underbrush.

Another shot rang out, and the crashing ceased.

Reggie froze close to the ground, her heart pounding.

CHAPTER 9

Sam had his gun out, his gaze glued to the direction Grunt had gone. He prayed the last gunshot hadn't been aimed at the retired military war dog. If Grunt was dead, Sam would kill the bastard who'd shot him.

Who would be firing off rounds during this time of year? It wasn't hunting season. Whoever had been shooting couldn't be target practicing with only two shots, unless the gun had jammed. The only other reason Sam could think someone would be shooting was at them. He hated leaving Reggie, but he had to find out who was doing the shooting and at what. If it was someone shooting at them, he'd take him out. And he couldn't do that with Reggie at his side.

He glanced around and found a large boulder near to where they were crouched below the top of the hill. "See that boulder?" he whispered.

Reggie's gaze darted to where he was pointing, and she nodded, her eyes wide, her face pale.

"We're going to crawl to that boulder and get behind it."

Reggie made no move toward the boulder. She remained frozen in place.

"Come on, Reggie. I'll go with you. But you have to move." He took her hand. "On three. One...Two...Three." He started toward the boulder, tugging on her hand.

Eventually, she moved, crawling on her hands and knees until she rounded the boulder and hunkered behind it.

Sam waited for a moment and tipped her chin up to face him. "Are you okay?"

She nodded.

"Let me hear you tell me you're okay."

She swallowed hard and whispered. "I'm okay."

"Good. I want you to stay here. Don't move. Don't make a sound. I'm going after whoever fired those shots."

Reggie's hand shot out, grabbing his arm. "No. Don't leave me."

He patted her hand and disengaged it from his arm. "We can't stay here and hide forever. It'll get dark and make it dangerous for us to walk back along the river."

"What if he was shooting at us? What if he shoots you?" She turned her hand and gripped his. "I don't want you to die."

"Reggie, this is what I do. I'm trained for this kind of mission. I'll be all right." He brushed his lips across her forehead. "Trust me."

"Promise me you won't die," she said, her gaze on his, a frown marring her brow.

He held up his hand as if swearing in court. "I promise. Now, let me go before he finds us or gets away. And I need to check on Grunt."

Her frown deepened. "Do you think he shot Grunt?"

"I won't know until I go look." He uncurled her fingers from his jacket sleeve and gave her a pointed look. "Stay down and keep quiet. I'll be back as quickly as I can."

He left her hunkered low behind the boulder and eased his way through the brush in the direction Grunt had gone. The dog had a good nose for finding more than bombs. If anyone could find the shooter, it was Grunt. Sam prayed the last shot hadn't been at the dog.

Sam moved through the trees and underbrush, keeping to the shadows, his gun drawn.

Rustling in the leaves made him stop and listen.

Grunt's bark made him start moving again. If the dog was barking, he hadn't been injured. Sam reasoned that Grunt would whine if he'd been hit.

He followed the sound of Grunt's barking and came to a small forest glen between tall pines.

Grunt stood near the center, barking at something lying on the ground.

The figure on the ground kicked four long, slender legs.

From what Sam could see, they were the legs of another animal. It was too small to be an elk. It had to be a deer.

Sam sensed more than saw movement at the other

side of the clearing. A teenaged boy stood near the edge of the glade, a rifle raised to his shoulder, aiming at Grunt.

Sam's heart skipped several beats. "Don't shoot!" he shouted and ducked low.

The boy swung his weapon toward the sound of Sam's voice and fired off a round.

The bullet went wide, missing Sam completely.

The boy's eyes widened, and he muttered a curse and took off running away from the glen, the deer and Sam.

Sam holstered his gun and ran after him. Grunt ran ahead.

"Grunt, *bleib!*" Sam yelled, afraid the dog would get caught up in the chase and rip into the boy.

Grunt skidded to a halt and remained where he stood as Sam ran past.

It took him far too long to catch up to the teen. Only by anticipating his moves did Sam finally catch him in a flying tackle.

The boy slammed to the ground, his rifle skittering out of his reach in the dust.

"Let me go!" the teen grunted, pinned to the ground beneath Sam's heavier body.

"Not until you tell me what the hell you were doing?" Sam sat up, yanked one of the boy's hands behind his back and up between his shoulder blades.

"Hey, not so hard," the young man said. "That hurts."

"Yeah. And being shot at can get a man killed." Sam gripped the teen's elbow and yanked him to his feet. "Explain yourself."

The teen dipped his head, refusing to look Sam in the eye. "I don't have to explain anything. I got just as much right to be out in the woods as anyone else. It's a national forest, which makes it public property. Now, let go of me." He jerked his arm but couldn't free it from Sam's grip.

"You might have a right to be in the woods, but it isn't hunting season. Let's go back to that clearing and see what you've been up to."

"I don't know what you're talking about."

"Maybe going back there will remind you." Sam started for the clearing.

"I can't leave my rifle. It's all I have."

Sam reached down and grabbed the rifle in one hand without letting go of the teen. Then he marched the young man back to the clearing where the animal lay on the ground near Grunt.

It was a white-tail deer, shot through the chest, no longer kicking. It lay still. Dead.

"Care to explain where that wound came from?" Sam used the rifle to point at the bullet hole.

"It was an accident," the boy said. "I was doing some target practice when that deer ran out in front of my bullet."

"Yeah, and I'm George Washington."

"You're George, and I'm Abe. So, let go of me." He leaned away from Sam, his feet digging into the ground.

"Why are you hunting out of season?" Sam demanded. "You might as well tell me. I'm not letting you go until I get some answers."

The teen twisted and turned but couldn't break free

of Sam's stronger grip. Finally, he stood still, his shoulders slumped, a scowl on his young face. "Hunting season is dumb."

"Why?"

"A person's gotta eat more than just in the fall during hunting season. What's he supposed to do the rest of the year?" He kicked his worn boot across the ground.

Sam stared closely at the young man. He was painfully thin, and his clothes were torn and threadbare. The oversized jacket he wore hung on bony shoulders with holes in the elbows. His boot laces were only tied halfway up as if the laces had been broken off too many times to go any higher.

"You're hunting for food?" Sam asked, his voice less stern, concern replacing anger.

"What do you think I'm doing? A guy's gotta eat." He tipped his chin toward the deer. "That'll feed us…me for a week." He glared up at Sam. "You got your answers. Now, let go of me."

Sam's eyes narrowed. "If you were hunting for food, why were you aiming at my dog?"

"I shot that deer fair and square." The boy's chin lifted, defiantly. "I wasn't going to let no stray dog eat it before I got the chance."

"What's your name?" Sam demanded.

"I told you," he said. "You're George, and I'm Abe."

"Where do you live?" Sam asked.

"I ain't gotta tell you nothin'," Abe said.

"Okay, then, you're coming with me." Sam led him back the way they'd come, collecting Grunt along the way to the boulder where Reggie hid. "Ginnie, you can come out. I've caught the shooter."

Reggie peeked out from behind the rock, her brow forming a V. "That's a kid."

"I know. And he was shooting this." He held up the rifle. "Since he refuses to take me to his home, we're going to take him back to Eagle Rock and turn him over to the sheriff."

Abe fought to get away. "You can't take me to the sheriff. I gotta go home."

"Not if you don't take me with you," Sam said. "Those are your choices. You take me to your home, or I take you to the sheriff and let *him* take you home or to jail. It'll be up to him."

The teen glared at Sam for a long moment.

"Guess we're going to the sheriff." Sam pushed the boy toward the trail leading back the way he and Reggie had come.

"Okay, okay, I'll take you to my house," Abe said, a frown denting his forehead. "But can we take the deer with us?"

"Isn't that a little heavy for someone your size to carry through the woods?" Sam asked.

The boy again lifted his chin. "I can carry twice my weight as long as it's strapped to my back. Besides, it was a little deer."

Sam kept his grip on the teen all the way back to where the deer lay on the ground.

"You gotta let me go long enough to field dress it," the boy said. "I'm not carrying the whole thing back, just what's edible."

Sam couldn't believe he was going to let the young man loose to field dress the deer, but he suspected the deer was all the kid had to eat. So, he helped him dress the deer and strap what was usable to the boy's back.

"We gotta hurry. When it gets dark, the wolves come out. They'll take what's mine, if I let 'em." Abe led the way down the hill, picking his way across a ravine and through tall stands of pines and Douglas firs.

As they came to another clearing, Abe stopped and turned to Sam, his brow furrowing. "Look. You can take me to the sheriff, or whatever, just don't do it until Mama gets home to watch out for the young'uns." He glanced down at Grunt. "Does your dog bite?"

"No," Sam said.

"Well, keep him close. I don't want him causin' trouble." Abe descended a hillside into what was little more than an old deer camp, complete with shoddy camp trailers arranged in a semicircle around a native stone fire pit.

He stopped by the stone circle and let the deer carcass slide off his narrow shoulders onto the stones. "You all gonna stand there starin' or come help me get this meat cut up and ready to cook?"

Sam glanced around at what had, at first, appeared to be a deserted camp.

Then, one by one, children emerged from the shadows of the trailers and the brush surrounding the camp.

"They're just babies," Reggie whispered beside him.

Sam's gut clenched as he counted. One…two…three, four…five. The fifth was a female of maybe thirteen or fourteen, carrying a baby that couldn't have been more than six months old. All of them wore ragged clothing and needed a bath.

The teenaged girl handed the baby off to another girl a couple years younger and hurried forward. "Abe, what you doin' bringing strangers home with you? You know Mama doesn't like us talkin' to strangers."

Sam's lips twitched. So, the boy hadn't been lying when he'd said his name was Abe. "Who are all these children?" Sam asked.

Abe stood with his feet slightly apart, his shoulders back and his head held high. "These children are my family. Ain't no one gonna split us up or send us off in different directions. Our mama is takin' care of us. We don't need no stinkin' government ladies shipping us off to foster homes."

Sam held up his hands. "I'm not with the government. But is it safe for you all to be out here alone without adult supervision?"

"Mama's our adult supervision." The teenaged girl came to stand beside Abe. "We don't need anyone else."

"Where's your father?" Reggie asked.

Abe spit on the ground. "The bastard ran off after baby Jake was born. Damned drunk and coward. Beat up on Mama every chance he'd get."

The girl's lip curled back in a snarl. "We're better off without him. One less mouth to feed." She tipped her chin toward Sam and Reggie. "What do you want with us?"

Sam scratched his head. "I wanted to make sure Abe got home with his kill."

"Well, I'm home," Abe said. "You can leave now."

"I'd like to talk to your mother before we go."

Abe shot a glance at his sister. "She don't get home for a while. She works late at the tavern."

The teenaged girl nodded. "She'll pitch a fit if she knows we been talkin' to strangers."

"Well, I'm Sam, and this is Ginnie." He turned to Reggie and back to Abe. "You know our names, so now we're not strangers."

"Not falling for that load of bullshit." Abe crossed his arms over his chest. "You gonna turn me over to the sheriff?"

Sam shook his head. "No, but you can't be hunting out of season. Someone else might catch you who won't be willing to look the other way."

"Like I said, hunting season is dumb. We gotta eat all year long, not just in the fall." His gaze swept the faces of the little kids gathered around them, their eyes wide.

A tiny girl tugged on Sam's jacket. "Are you gonna take Abe to the sheriff?"

"No, ma'am." Sam squatted next to her and looked her square her bright blue eyes. "I just don't want him to get into trouble."

"The only trouble I'll get into is if you say anything to anyone about me and my family." Abe met Sam's gaze, his own intense.

Sam suspected the boy, as the oldest, was in charge nearly twenty-four-seven. He couldn't show any sign of weakness, or the others would have no one to guide them and keep them safe.

"I won't do anything to harm you or your family." He

didn't like it, but he and Reggie had to get back to the truck before the sun dipped below the ridge line. "We'll be going back the way we came."

"Do you know how to get back?"

"I'm pretty sure," Sam said, although the teen had taken them through the woods at a pretty quick pace.

Abe shook his head. He turned to the girl. "Lizzy, you and Josh cut up the deer and put some in a pot to boil. I'll be back before dark." He turned back to Sam and Reggie. "Let's go."

"You don't have to lead us back," Sam said. "You need to stay here."

"Lizzy can handle things while I get you back to where you came from." He took off toward the woods and stopped at the edge of the clearing to turn back. "You comin' or not?"

Sam grinned. "Coming." He took Reggie's hand and hurried her toward the teen. Grunt fell in step beside them.

As they walked through the woods, Sam asked, "You know these hills pretty good?"

Abe nodded without slowing his pace. "Lived here all my life."

Which couldn't be more than fourteen or fifteen years. Not much, but enough for a young man with a need to feed his family to find his way around the backwoods.

"Do you know of a place along the river where there are cliffs about twenty or thirty feet high?"

Abe glanced over his shoulder, still moving forward. "Yeah. But it's not on this branch of the river.

"What do you mean?" Sam asked.

"The river splits about a mile or two upstream and comes back together not far from here," Abe said.

"Which branch are the cliffs on?" Reggie asked.

"The north branch." Abe slowed and glanced back at Reggie. "Why do you want to know?"

"I heard it was really pretty and a place I should see," Sam said.

Abe came to a full stop. "Look, Sam or George, or whoever you are. We might be poor, but we're not stupid. What business do you have at the cliffs?"

Reggie's gaze caught Sam's.

Sam faced the boy. "Abe, some things are best left unsaid for good reason. For your protection, as well as ours. Kind of like not telling the sheriff about your hunting out of season."

Abe's eyes narrowed briefly. Then he nodded and continued through the woods until they came to the boulder where Reggie had been hiding. "I got you back here. You're on your own now."

Abe turned back the direction they'd come.

"Abe," Sam called out.

The teen stopped and looked over his shoulder, a frown on his brow.

"You're a good man, Abe." Somehow, someway, he had to help Abe and his family. But it would have to be after they found the house with the women. He dug his wallet out of his back pocket and extracted a one-hundred-dollar bill and one of the business cards Hank had made up for him. "Call me, if you and the kids run into any trouble. We have something to take care of, but we'll be back to check on you. So, maybe don't shoot before you check to see who it is."

When Sam held out the money, Abe's eyes widened, and he shook his head. "No, sir. I can't take that. We don't take charity."

"Abe, you worked for it. You gave us information we needed to know and led us back through the woods so that we wouldn't get lost." Sam took Abe's hand, laid the bill in it, along with the business card, and curled the boy's fingers around them. "You earned it. And keep the card in case you need anything."

The teen looked up at Sam. "Thank you, sir." Then he spun and ran down the hill, disappearing into the forest.

Sam gripped Reggie's elbow and led her along the trail paralleling the river.

"You think Abe and his family will be okay?" Reggie asked.

"They have to be. At least until we can find that house and free those women."

"We're coming back then, aren't we?" she asked. "I can't stand the thought of all those babies living the way they do. Their mother must be beside herself."

"If they even have one," Sam said through gritted teeth.

Reggie glanced his way, her eyes rounding. "You think he was lying about her working at the tavern? You think those kids are out there all alone?"

"I don't know what to think. But I don't like any scenario I can come up with." He kept moving. They had to get to the truck and contact Hank to let him know the cliff was on the northern branch of the river. If Kujo and Molly had taken the southern branch, they would have missed the cliffs. They'd have come close, but not close enough.

With the sun slipping low on the hilltops, they needed to get back to Hank's place and put the pieces they'd gathered together with whatever Hank's team had come up with in their investigation of the men from the Sexual and Violent Offenders Register and the county land records. Perhaps, that would help them narrow down the location of the house close to the cliff where Reggie had made her leap into the river.

CHAPTER 10

REGGIE FORCED HERSELF TO FOCUS ON THE PLIGHT OF the women being held prisoner in the Master's basement. She couldn't let herself be sidetracked by a group of children trying to make it on their own in the hills of the Crazy Mountains. Time might be running out for Beth, Kayla, Terri and Marly, whereas Abe had a handle on his siblings, for the time being. They had the deer to feed them for a week.

Already, a night had passed, and another full day, since Reggie's escape. Her mind played all the scenarios the Master could have enacted against those poor women.

By the time they reached the truck, her body was running on fumes. She was weak, and her knees shook so badly, she couldn't climb up on the running board.

Sam must have noticed, because he scooped her up in his arms and deposited her in the passenger seat without saying a word. He hurried around the other side of the truck, held the door for Grunt, and then climbed into the driver's seat. Soon, they were on their way back down the dirt road to the highway. The sun had sunk below the ridgeline, casting the road and hills into dark gray shadows.

So deep was she in her own thoughts about the women, the children and the Master, that they arrived in Eagle Rock before she realized they'd traveled that far. As they passed the Blue Moon Tavern, her hand shot out, as if of its own accord to touch Sam's arm.

He slowed immediately and pulled into a parking place beneath the wooden sign. "Are you thinking the same thing I am?"

She nodded. "You know we forgot to ask Abe what his mother's name was."

"That thought had crossed my mind, too." Sam shifted into park and got out. He snapped a lead on Grunt's collar and tied the line to streetlight pole, giving the dog just enough room to move around and lie down. "Stay," he commanded.

"Will he be okay out here by himself?"

"Yeah. I'd leave him in the truck, but he could stand some fresh air while we eat. I don't know about you, but I'm hungry, and we need to fuel our bodies for what comes next. Whatever that might be."

Reggie didn't argue. She didn't like being weak and knew a lot of her weakness was due to malnutrition for the past couple of weeks, as well as inactivity, due to being locked in a cell in the dark.

"Come on, Ginnie," he winked. "We need to eat and ask questions."

"As long as we don't out the kids to the authorities," she reminded him quietly. "We promised."

"I know what we promised." Sam's mouth drew downward into a frown. "I'm not too happy about that promise, but I understand why they don't want the government involved. With so many siblings, the only option would be to split them up into a number of foster homes."

Reggie nodded. "Abe has too much responsibility on his young shoulders."

"One crisis at a time," Sam said. "But we can at least solve one mystery while we're eating. Which we have to do anyway." He took her hand and led her into the tavern where they waited to be seated.

A pretty young brunette led them to their table. While they sat, the young lady gave them menus and told them about the night's specials. "If you have any questions, your server will be able to answer them." With a smile, she left Sam and Reggie to peruse the list of items offered at the tavern.

A waitress came to an abrupt halt beside their table and pulled a pencil from behind her ear and pad from her apron. "Hi, I'm Maggie, I'll be your waitress this evening. What can I get you to drink?"

"Feels wrong to not order a beer, but could you bring me a cup of coffee? Black?" Sam asked.

Maggie grinned. "I can do that." She turned to Reggie. "And you?"

After being held captive in the basement of a madman's house, sitting in a tavern with a perky young woman smiling at her and asking her what she'd like to drink suddenly seemed so surreal, it overwhelmed Reggie. "I'm sorry." She pushed back from the table and made a dash in the direction of what she hoped was the bathroom.

Behind her, she heard Maggie say, "Was it something I said?"

Reggie didn't care, she had to get away before she had a nervous breakdown in front of everyone in the tavern. Bumbling her way to the ladies' room, she finally made it through the door and into one of the stalls before the tears fell. Her heart raced and, her pulse pounded so hard against her eardrums, she couldn't hear herself think. Not that her brain was piecing together any coherent thoughts.

For several long moments, Reggie stood in the bathroom stall sobbing and trying to get a grip on the tears, her breathing and her messed up life. Would she ever feel normal again?

The door to the bathroom opened and closed.

Reggie swallowed hard on the sob rising up her throat and nearly choked. She stood still, praying whoever had entered would leave quickly, so that she could continue her panic attack in solitude.

"Reggie?" a male voice said from the other side of the stall door. "I know you're in there. Come out and talk to me."

The sob escaped her lips in a choking sound. Reggie couldn't move. Wouldn't.

In a softer tone, Sam said, "It's okay, it's just me. Unlock the door."

Reggie swiped at the tears streaming down her face and reached for the lock, pushing back the metal latch.

The door swung open.

Sam reached in and took her hand in his gentle grasp and drew her out of the stall and into his arms.

Reggie lay her cheek against his chest and let the tears flow.

He held her carefully, not applying too much pressure, but just enough to let her know he was there for her.

After a few minutes, the tears slowed, along with her pulse. "I'm sorry. I don't know what's wrong with me."

"You've been through hell. I'd think there was something wrong with you if you didn't fall apart sometimes." He tipped her chin up and stared down into her eyes. "Everything's going to be okay. We're going to find him and the ladies. No one will ever treat you like he did, ever again."

"How can you be...so sure?" she murmured between hiccups.

"Because I won't let anyone hurt you." He leaned toward her and pressed his lips to her forehead. "No man should ever treat a woman so badly. The bastard will pay." He brushed his thumb across her cheek, wiping away the traces of her tears. Then he kissed her cheek.

Reggie turned her face so that the lips kissing her cheek brushed across her mouth.

Sam captured her face in his hands and touched his lips to hers in a kiss so soft it felt like the flutter of butterfly wings.

She leaned up on her toes, wanting more, deepening the kiss on her own terms.

Still holding her cheeks between his palms, Sam let her set the pace and the extent of their kiss.

Conflicted by thoughts of what had happened at the Master's hands and what was happening now, Reggie didn't know whether she should pull away or grasp Sam's shirt and hold on. He wasn't forcing her, and he'd let go if she showed any sign of distress. Perhaps that's what made her lean closer, until her body pressed flush against his.

When she felt the hard ridge beneath the fly of his jeans, she was shocked out of the sensuous fantasy she'd fallen into and broke away. "I'm sorry. I can't. I shouldn't…" She pressed her knuckles to her mouth and fought more tears.

"No, Reggie." Sam took her hands in his and stared down into her face. "Don't be sorry. I shouldn't have kissed you. You've been through too much. Kissing you was uncalled for." He held her hands in his. "I won't do it again."

She shook her head and whispered, "What if I want you to?"

He smiled. "Then you'll have to initiate it."

She chewed on her bottom lip for a second, drew in a deep breath and let it go. "I just want to feel normal." Reggie leaned up on her toes and pressed her lips to his, closing her eyes as she did. When he didn't respond, she opened her eyes. "Only kissing you doesn't make me feel normal."

Sam chuckled and rested his hands on her waist. "I

don't know whether to take that as an insult or a compliment."

She stared up at him, willing her world to quit spinning out of control. "You make me feel better than normal." Again, she stood on her toes and pressed her lips to his.

This time, his hands tightened around her waist, and his lips covered hers, giving equal pressure.

Reggie sighed, opening to him, her tongue passing between his teeth, finding and caressing his.

His arms rose up around her, pulling her close until their bodies melted together.

Reggie slipped her arms around his neck, her fingers weaving through his hair. She wanted this kiss and didn't want it to end. It was nothing like what the Master had forced on her. Kissing Sam was everything a kiss was meant to be. Soft, hard, insistent, gentle, sultry and all-consuming. When she came up for air, she didn't feel dirty, abused or like she needed to rinse her mouth with bleach.

Sam was a real man who didn't need to force a woman to make love to him. She would come willingly.

The door to the bathroom opened and a middle-aged woman wearing a waitress uniform started through, spotted them and stopped. "Oh! Sorry." She backed out of the bathroom and the door swung shut.

Sam leaned his forehead against hers. "Guess we'd better get out of here before management kicks us out."

Reggie nodded. "I'll be a minute. I want to wash my hands and face."

"I'll be right outside waiting." Sam left her standing in the bathroom.

The woman who'd walked in a moment before entered as Sam left. She laughed. "For a moment, I thought I was in the wrong place." She frowned. "Are you okay?"

"Yes," Reggie responded and gave her a weak smile.

"Are you sure?" The waitress's eyes narrowed. "You've been crying. Was that man bothering you?" She glanced over her shoulder.

Reggie laughed, the sound catching a little. "Just the opposite," She stared down at the gold band on her ring finger. "He's my…husband."

"Okay." She propped a hand on her hip. "Then why were you crying?"

With a shrug, Reggie said, "I've had a bad couple of days. He was just checking on me."

"Honey, my name is Karen. Some would say I don't know a stranger, and I take that as a compliment." The woman stared at her a moment longer. "If you're in trouble, I'll help you in any way I can. Just say the word."

With a smile, Reggie nodded. "Karen, I appreciate that. But really. I think I'm going to be okay." And she really felt like she would be. "Maybe you could answer a question for me."

"Sure," Karen said. "Shoot."

Reggie wasn't sure how to ask, so she just did. "Is there a waitress here who has seven children?"

Karen's eyes widened. "The Blue Moose has a total of eight waitresses who work full or part time. I can't say that I know any of them who have more than two kids besides me. I have three. All are grown and on their own, thank the Lord." Karen's eyes narrowed. "Why do you want to know?"

"Asking for a friend," Reggie said, her chest tightening. "I probably have the wrong tavern." She knew she didn't. More so, she knew Abe had lied about his mother working there.

Karen tilted her head to the side. "The only other restaurant in town is Al's Diner, and I don't think any of the waitresses there have that many children."

"Thanks. Sorry to bother you with my drama."

"No bother. Two of my children were girls. Drama came with the territory."

Reggie prayed their drama wasn't as destructive as what had happened to her. "You're very sweet. They must be proud to call you Mom."

Karen snorted. "They are now, but there was a time they weren't so happy with me. Curfews and groundings helped to keep them in line." The woman entered a stall, closing it between them.

Reggie turned the water on in the sink and splashed her face with cool fresh water, hoping to lessen the ravages of her tears. When she'd done all she could do to reduce the redness, she dried her face and hands with paper towels, straightened her wig and left the bathroom.

Sam leaned against the wall in the hallway, his arms crossed over his chest. When he saw her, he dropped his arms to his sides and fell in step beside her as she walked back to their table.

"Abe lied," she whispered. "His mother doesn't work

here. No woman with seven children works as a waitress in town."

Sam's lips pressed into a thin line. "I figured as much."

Maggie appeared with the ordered coffee and another mug with hot water and a tea bag. "I thought you might like some hot tea," she said with a gentle smile. "It always helps me when I'm feeling low."

"Thank you." Reggie dipped the tea bag into the mug of hot water. When the water was dark enough, she removed the bag and stirred in a teaspoon of sugar.

Sam drank his coffee black. No sugar.

The waitress returned to take their orders of the night's special: chicken fried steak, mashed potatoes and green beans. She was back several minutes later with their food and a smile. *"Bon Appétit."*

"I can't eat all of this," Reggie said, guilt knotting her gut. "I find it hard to sit here like nothing is wrong in the world when I know there's so much that needs to be fixed."

"Eat what you can. We'll take the rest home."

Reggie knew he'd said home as part of their cover story, but the word from his lips gave her a warm safe feeling she wrapped around herself like a blanket. For the next half hour, they ate, making comments about the weather, comparing it to what it was like in San Diego. As if they'd just moved to Eagle Rock from there. Again, all part of their cover.

Occasionally, Sam reached across the table and caressed the hand with the wedding ring on it. A blast of electricity would zing through her system every time he touched her.

Reggie wondered, if they weren't putting on a show would Sam find her attractive. Or would he think, like she did… that she was too damaged and dirty to want to be with her?

She tensed, a terrible thought occurring to her. What if she was pregnant? What if that bastard had gotten her with child? And what man would want to take on the responsibility of being a father to a rapist's spawn?

Though she'd hate the thought of having a lifetime's reminder of her captivity, Reggie wouldn't terminate the pregnancy. It wouldn't be the child's fault the father was a criminal.

Sam's big hand covered hers. "Stop it."

She looked up, startled. "Stop what?"

"You're getting all worked up again. You can't change the past, but you're in full control of your future." He leaned closer and whispered. "Don't let him take one more minute of your life from you."

She nodded, realizing her pulse had picked up and her breathing had become ragged. "You're right." Willing her body to calm, she closed her eyes, drew in deep, steadying breaths and let them out slowly. Finally, she opened her eyes and gave Sam a tight smile. "I'm okay."

By then, several of the tavern's customers had risen from their tables and headed toward the exit.

Maggie came by with their check and laid it on the table. "Do you need anything else?"

"No, thank you." Sam handed her his credit card.

When Maggie turned toward the cash register, she bumped into one of the men on his way out, knocking into his arm.

The man dropped the jacket he'd been carrying and let out a stream of curse words.

His voice struck a chord in Reggie's memory. Her heartbeat went from zero to one hundred and twenty in a second. She fought between spinning to see who the man was and ducking beneath the table. She turned slowly, but all she could see was the man's back as he bent to retrieve his coat.

"Oh, I'm sorry," Maggie was saying as she bent to help.

"Damned clumsy woman," the man said loud enough everyone in the tavern heard and turned toward him. He straightened and stormed out, muttering more curse words

Maggie shot a glance around at the people staring at her and the door where the man had stormed out. "Sorry, folks."

A hand closed over Reggie's. "What's wrong?" Sam asked.

Reggie turned back to him, his voice one she would always associate with warmth and safety. She shook her head. "I had a déjà vu moment."

"Whatever it was, you're as white as a ghost," he curled his fingers around hers. "What brought it on?"

"That man's voice. The one Maggie bumped into." Her gaze captured his as the full import of what she'd just heard hit her. "He sounded just like the Master."

CHAPTER 11

Sam was out of his seat in the next second. "Stay here," he commanded and wove his way through customers to get out of the building. Once he was outside, he searched the darkness for the man who'd bumped into Maggie.

Unfortunately, that man had been one of about ten people who'd left the tavern at the same time. Several vehicles were pulling out of the parking lot at the same time. A sedan, two trucks and two SUVs. Sam couldn't tell into which vehicle the man who'd bumped into the waitress had gone. He tried but failed miserably at memorizing six different license plates. He gave up and hurried back into the tavern, afraid to leave Reggie alone any longer than he had to. What if the Master had doubled back to grab her and take her out the back?

Reggie met him in the front entryway, standing back in the shadows, out of sight of the street beyond the door. "Did you see where he went?" she asked, her voice shaking, her body trembling.

Sam shook his head. "No. There were too many people, and they were already driving away by the time I got outside."

Maggie found them by the door. "Oh, good, you're still here. I thought you'd left without your credit card." She held out Sam's card and a receipt. "I need your signature."

He scribbled his name at the bottom and added a sizeable tip. "Maggie, that man who bumped into you…"

"I feel so bad. I'm not usually so clumsy." She grimaced. "He did have a potty mouth though. I'm so sorry you had to hear that."

Sam shook his head. "I'm not worried about that. Do you know who he is?"

Maggie shook her head. "I've only seen him in here one other time. He sat by himself and didn't talk to anyone except to order his food."

"Did he pay with a credit card?" Reggie asked.

Maggie's brow creased. "I don't know. One of the other waitresses had his table tonight. I can ask. Why?"

"I'd like to know his name," Sam said. "He looked familiar, like someone I know."

Maggie stood on her toes, looking back into the tavern. "Wait here. I'll ask Janice if she knows him, or if he used a card to make his purchase. I'll be right back." She took off, weaving her way through the tables and people coming and going.

From where Sam stood, he could see her talking to the other waitress. They walked to the register by the bar and opened the bottom drawer. After a moment or two they both looked up, shaking their heads.

Maggie returned a moment later, her lips pressed into a line. "I'm sorry, but Janice thinks he paid with cash. She checked the register, but most of the receipts were people she knew. If you see the man, please let him know I'm super sorry for knocking into him." Maggie went back to work, waiting tables.

"God, I hope he wasn't here to target any of the women in Eagle Rock," Reggie said. She slipped her arm through the crook of Sam's elbow and leaned into him. "Let's get out of here."

Sam led her out the door and settled her into the passenger seat of his truck. He untied Grunt from the light post and held the back door open for him to jump inside, closing it behind him. When Sam climbed into the driver's seat, he cast a glance her way. Though her face was still pale, she'd stopped trembling. "Do you really think it was him?"

She shrugged and grimaced. "It could have been him. Or I could have been too sensitive to a similar voice." Reggie wrapped her arms around herself and looked at him, her brow twisted. "Is this how it's going to be? Me jumping at every voice or worrying that he's in the same room as me, and I can't recognize him?"

"No. We're going to find him and put him away for good." Sam shifted the truck into reverse, backed out of the parking space and headed toward the White Oak Ranch. "We're getting closer. I just know it's only a matter of time before we catch up to him."

Reggie didn't say it, and she didn't have to. It was only a matter of time before the Master hurt those women. Maybe even killed them. They had to hurry before it was too late.

"I feel like he's close," Reggie said, twisting the ring on her finger. "Like we could have been the ones to bump into him instead of Maggie, if we'd left a couple minutes earlier."

"We'll find out what Hank's guys came up with and put it together with what we learned today. Maybe it will lead us straight to him."

"God, I hope so." Reggie sat quietly for the rest of the drive to Hank's ranch.

No sooner had Sam hit the intercom button at the gate, then Swede's voice came over. "Sam, glad you made it here. See you in the war room."

The gate slid open, and Sam drove along the winding drive to the ranch house. He helped Reggie out of the cab and up the steps to the front door where Sadie and Hank met them.

"Come on in," Hank said.

"Have you had supper?" Sadie asked.

"We have."

"Good. Then we can get right down to business." Hank led the way down the stairs into the war room.

Sam squeezed Reggie's hand reassuringly as they descended into the basement and came to a halt behind Swede.

Three other people were in the room with him. A big man with a barrel chest, broad shoulders and a thatch of thick brown hair. A man with black hair and piercing blue eyes stood beside him, the same height, also broad-shouldered, but nearly as thick as the bigger guy. Beside him stood a woman whose head came up to his shoulders and had dark red hair.

As Sam and Reggie entered the war room, the redhead flashed her bright green eyes at them. "You must be Sam and Reggie." She held out her hand. "Molly Greenbriar. FBI."

Reggie shook her hand, a frown forming on her brow. "I'd forgotten you were with the FBI. I was just thinking that you were Kujo's woman, accompanying him on the river."

The black-haired man beside Molly stuck out his hand. "I'm Joseph Kuntz, affectionately known as Kujo." He rested a hand at the small of Molly's back. "Actually, I'm with Molly, aka Special Agent Greenbriar. She's the one with all the training."

Molly elbowed him in the gut. "Don't listen to him. He's prior Delta Force. And yes, we were on the river all day with a drone."

Sam held out his hand and shook Kujo's and Molly's. "I'm Sam Franklin, the new guy with the Brotherhood."

"Good to know you," Kujo said. He motioned toward the dog at his feet. "This is Six, retired military war dog extraordinaire.

The Belgian Malinois lifted his head briefly and laid it back down on his paws.

"I hear you adopted one as well," Kujo said.

"I did," Sam reached down and let Six sniff his hand. "Grunt's out on the porch keeping an eye on the squirrels."

Kujo turned to the big guy beside him. "Oh, and this is Bear."

"Nice to know I rank after the dog. Tate Parker," The big man engulfed Sam's hand in his larger one. "Glad to have you aboard. You can call me Bear."

Sam turned to Molly and Kujo. "Which way did you go at the fork? North or South?"

"We took the south fork. Why?" Kujo asked.

"We ran into a local who knows the area fairly well. He said the north fork has the high cliffs. Reggie jumped from the cliffs into the river. Did you see any cliffs beside the river on the south fork?"

Molly exchanged a glance with Kujo. "Not anything over a couple meters."

Sam turned to the man at the computer keyboard. "Swede—"

"Pulling up the contour map now." His fingers danced across the keyboard, and the monitor flashed an image of a contour map with squiggly lines depicting the elevation of the terrain. He scrolled across the map, following the blue line of the river to the point where it split into two around a long, broad island that stretched for several inches across the map. Based on the legend, the island was approximately a mile long and a quarter of a mile wide.

Swede zoomed in on a grouping of contour lines that converged into one with tick marks pointing toward the river.

Sam pointed. "There. Abe said it was on the north branch of the river. It has to be the one Reggie jumped off. Bring up the satellite map of that area."

"On it," Swede said. A moment later he had the satellite map displayed beside the topographical contour map. Matching the sizes, he zoomed in on the cliff then backed out slowly. "The problem is that there are so many tall trees, unless the houses have been cleared around them, you might not see them."

Sam studied the satellite image, his brow furrowing. Finally, he pointed to the image. "Isn't that the place where you said one of the registered sex offenders lives?"

Swede nodded. "Thomas. But his cabin was too small to have a basement big enough to hide five women in individual cells."

"I checked with the parole officer today, asking about Ogletree, Thomas and Knowles."

Reggie cringed. "What reason did you give them?"

Bear said, "I told him I was concerned about them being in this area as my fiancé was a rape victim. I wanted to know if they were reporting regularly to their parole office and if he'd had any issues with any of them."

"And?" Sam prompted.

"They are all playing by the books," Bear said. "So, I drove out to Knowles and Ogletree's houses while they were away at work in Eagle Rock and had a little snoop around." He shook his head. "Nothing. Like you said, the cabin at Ogletree's place was small with an even smaller basement beneath it. No women in there."

"You broke in?"

"Not really," Bear shrugged. "The place was unlocked. And Knowles's place was a mobile home. No basement and no outbuildings with basements. Just a veritable junk yard filled with discarded truck chassis."

"What about Thomas?"

Bear nodded. "I drove out near to his place and went in on foot to keep from being seen or heard. The man lives like a hermit. Just him. He lives in what I'd call a cottage. It has a cellar, but it's not on the side of a hill, and the cellar was really small from what I could see through a dirty window. Again. It wasn't on the side of a hill.

"Maybe we're focusing on the obvious people and not on the real culprit," Hank said. "Who owns the land directly north of the cliff?"

Swede brought up the county plat map of the area from the state website and scrolled over the areas slowly. "This is going to take some digging. I'll look into these owners and run some background checks. Likely, it will take into the night."

Sam shot a glance toward Reggie. "We could use showers and sleep."

"I'm okay," Reggie said, though her face was pale, and the shadows beneath her eyes had darkened.

"You might be, but I could use a few hours of sleep after tromping around in the woods." Sam held out his hand. "We should head back to the cabin."

"Nonsense," Sadie said. "It's late. You two can stay here. We can loan you some clothes to wear for the night and Swede will have information for you first thing in the morning." She looked to Hank.

"Sadie's right," Hank said. "There's plenty of room for all of you to stay."

"If you really don't mind, I'd like to do that," Reggie

said. "The cabin's comfortable but a little distant from the computer and the information it can generate."

"Agreed," Sam said. "But I was serious, you need some rest."

"I know my limits." Reggie squared her shoulders as if ready to fight. Then she gave him a twisted grin. "And you're right. I'm on the edge of them." She turned to Sadie. "I feel bad accepting anymore clothing from you when you sent over so much to the cabin."

"Oh, don't worry. I've got more clothes than I'll wear in my lifetime. Clothing designers send me stuff all the time, hoping I'll represent their lines. Come on. I'll find something suitable for sleeping." She turned to Hank. "Make sure your guys have what they need, will you?" Her gaze went to Molly. "Come on, us ladies have to stick together, or these men will run all over us."

Kujo laughed. "You obviously don't know Molly very well. She can hold her own."

"I'm sure she can," Sadie said.

Molly followed Reggie and Sadie up the staircase out of the basement.

Sam remained behind, not sure why he felt as if he was missing something important. Like the woman he'd been with fulltime for more than twenty-four hours. She was growing on him. So much so, that he didn't like it when she wasn't within sight.

"Hank, Reggie and I ate at the Blue Moose Tavern this evening. When we were finished and waiting to pay our bill, Reggie thought she heard the voice of the man who'd held her captive. He was on his way out the door when she heard him. By the time I got outside to check it out, he was gone. I'm not sure that information buys us anything since we didn't see him, but it might prove that he's from around here, if that was in fact the man who'd kidnapped all those women."

Hank's face set in grim lines. "All the more reason to catch this guy. None of the women of Eagle Rock or the surrounding areas are safe as long as he's running free. I'd like to issue a warning to the area."

"But we can't," Sam said. "Not until we find him and the women he's currently holding captive."

Hank nodded. "In the meantime, we can only hope and pray he doesn't kidnap anymore women."

CHAPTER 12

Sadie, carrying Emma in her arms, led Reggie and Molly up the stairs to the second level of the ranch house and into the massive bedroom she shared with her husband, Hank. She kept walking to the other side of the room where a door led into a walk-in closet larger than Reggie's apartment in Bozeman.

Molly whistled. "Holy hell, I could live in here."

Sadie blushed. "Hank went a little overboard designing the closet. He seems to think a movie star needs a closet big enough to house a small nation." She grinned. "I have to admit, I love it. And Emma likes playing in here while I'm getting ready in the morning.

Emma flapped her arms and leaned over.

Sadie set her on the floor and closed the door to keep her from wandering out. "Let's see. You both need something to sleep in." She shot a glance from Molly to Reggie with raised eyebrows. "Unless you sleep in the buff."

Molly shook her head. "I rarely sleep in the nude. My mother told me I should never go to sleep in anything I don't want to stand outside in, in case of a fire."

Reggie chuckled. "Same." Though she'd slept in the nude for over two weeks while being held in the basement of the Master's house, wrapped only in a threadbare blanket he'd sparingly provided. The memory brought her back to that bad place she never wanted to return to.

Sadie broke into her morose thoughts by handing her a soft pink, baby doll nightgown. "This should fit you. It's short, but it covers the bases." She gave Reggie's arm a squeeze. "And pink is cheerful and will compliment your strawberry-blond hair. You look like you could use a little cheering up. I can't imagine what you went through, and I won't pretend I do. But you're safe here, and Sam will make sure you stay safe."

Sadie handed Molly a mint green nightgown, also short and sassy. "Sorry, ladies, Hank likes me in baby doll nighties or nothing at all." She winked.

"Suits me," Molly said. "I don't like things that tangle up around my legs at night. I used to sleep in gym shorts and a T-shirt while at the academy at Quantico."

Sadie sifted through a drawer and pulled out silky bikini panties. "You'll need some of these." She added them to the top of the nightgowns the two women held. Moving to another drawer, she pulled out two loose cashmere sweaters, one in a deep forest green, another in powder blue, handing the green one to Reggie and the blue one to Molly. "I take it you're okay with the jeans you're wearing?"

Reggie nodded, grateful for anything. Until she returned from the dead and could visit her apartment in Bozeman, she was at the mercy and kindness of Sadie. "Thank you for putting me up in your home."

Sadie waved her hand. "Oh, please. I love having company out here. You're doing me a favor by staying." She wrapped her arms around Reggie. "I'm just so sorry we've met under such dire circumstances. But I'm not sorry we met."

Tears welled in Reggie's eyes. "Thank you." She stepped back and turned to admire the racks of dresses hanging behind her.

Emma had found her way in among the long dresses and tugged at their hems, playing hide-n-seek among the folds.

"Come here, you rascal." Sadie swooped in and gathered the happy child in her arms.

"Mama, play," she said in her little baby voice.

Reggie's heart squeezed hard at the love she saw in Sadie's eyes for the little girl.

One day…she hoped and prayed she would have a little girl like Emma to hold in her arms.

"Let's show these ladies to their rooms. I'm sure they're tired and could use a good night's rest, like you." She kissed her daughter's chubby cheek and led the way out of her closet and down the hallway to a door on the left. "Molly, you can have the blue room. It has its own en-suite bath. The bed is already made. If you need anything, just let me know."

"Lord knows, I need a shower after being on the river all day. I'm sure I smell like fish and sweat." Molly thanked Sadie and entered the room, closing the door behind her.

"Reggie, I'm putting you in the room near the end of the hall. Sam will have the room beside you, since he's in charge of keeping you safe. Not that you have anything to worry about here. Hank had the entire ranch wired with security cameras and alarms. No one can get in without triggering some really loud and annoying sirens. Seriously, I thought I'd lose my mind when they were testing them." She flung open a door. "You have the yellow room. It's one of my favorites. Yellow reminds me of sunshine and makes me happy. I hope it does the same for you."

"I'm sure it will. Thank you."

"Again, if you need anything, let me know." Sadie glanced down at Emma. "Say night-night, Emma."

The little girl waved her hand and gurgled, "Night-night."

Reggie waved at Emma as Sadie closed the door between them.

Left alone in the yellow bedroom, Reggie's body sagged with weariness. She'd held it together all day, because she refused to give up on finding the women. Now, alone in a stranger's house, the weight of the world seemed to settle on her shoulders.

Before she collapsed from exhaustion, she carried the clothing Sadie had equipped her with into the bathroom, started the water in the shower and stripped off the clothes she'd worn on their hike through the woods that day.

Naked again, she shivered and faced the mirror. She didn't look much different from the woman who'd had a life in Bozeman, working at the office she'd set up to manage the various businesses and investments her father had left to her and her mother in a trust. Maybe she was a little thinner, with darker shadows beneath her eyes, but not much had changed on the exterior.

Inside, she would never be the same again.

Reggie stepped beneath the shower's spray and let the water run down over her skin. She didn't try to scrub the filth of the Master from her body. No amount of scrubbing would ever get what he'd done to her out of her memory. Only time would heal that broken place inside. As Sam had said, she couldn't let him rob one more minute of her life from her. The best revenge would be to live a happy life, in spite of what he'd done—after she made sure he didn't hurt any other woman, ever again.

Reggie squeezed shampoo into her palm and worked it through her hair. It smelled like spring and wildflowers. She rinsed the suds from her hair and body, applied conditioner and rinsed again. By the time she left the shower, she was more relaxed and smelled like a completely new person.

After quickly drying with a large, fluffy white towel, she dressed in the soft pink nightgown and panties. Finding a new brush in one of the drawers, she ran it through her hair, smoothing the tangles. Feeling so much better, but tired, she walked into the bedroom and switched on the lamp on the nightstand.

That's when she noticed a door at the side of the room. She walked to it and pressed her ear to the panel.

Sounds of movement on the other side made her pulse quicken.

Sadie had said Sam would sleep in the room beside hers to keep her safe.

Warmth spread throughout her body at the thought of Sam on the other side of the paneled door. After spending the past twenty-four or more hours with him, Reggie found she missed him. He'd made her feel safe, even while they'd been tromping through the woods.

Perhaps he'd showered and was climbing into bed right now. Did he sleep in shorts and T-shirt? Or was he one of those men who didn't wear anything to sleep in?

Her core heated, desire pooling low in her belly. How could she be aroused when she didn't know the extent of the damage that monster had done to her? She could be infected with a sexually transmitted disease. She could be pregnant. If she hadn't had to play dead, she'd have had a rape kit run on her and reported directly to the police. They'd need every bit of evidence possible to convict the man and send him to jail for the rest of his life.

Reggie leaned her cheek against the cool panel. She wanted to be with Sam, to have him hold her in his arms.

A sharp rap startled her and made her cry out. Reggie jumped back from the door and pressed a hand to her chest.

The doorknob turned and opened. "Reggie?" Sam poked his head through the door. His chest was bare, and his hair was damp. Random droplets of water stood out on his shoulders.

Reggie swallowed hard but couldn't get words past the knot in throat.

Sam frowned and stepped through the door. "Are you okay?"

He wore black boxer briefs that did little to hide the ridge of his cock beneath the fabric.

She shook her head.

He entered the room, gripped her arms and stared down into her eyes. "Sweetheart, what's wrong?"

"I can't…" She shook her head again. She wanted to say she couldn't be with him until she had all the answers, but that would assume he wanted to be with her. Instead, she finished with, "I can't sleep."

"Do you want me to stay with you until you go to sleep?"

Her brow furrowed. "I'm not usually so wimpy."

"You're not wimpy at all." He drew her into his arms. "You escaped a madman. I'd say that took a huge amount of courage."

She lay her cheek against his bare chest, inhaling the clean, fresh scent of him. "Courage didn't get me out of there. I'm not that brave."

"Yes, you are." Sam tipped her chin up and stared down at her. "You knew what he'd do if he caught you digging, but you dug anyway."

"Because I was afraid of what he would continue to do to me, if I didn't get out of there."

"And yet, you're trying like hell to go back."

"I have to. I can't abandon the others." She rested her hand on his chest, her fingers curling ever so slightly into his skin. He felt so good, so right, she couldn't stop touching him.

"Come on. I'll tuck you in."

God, she didn't want to move. She wanted his arms to remain around her for as long as she drew air into her lungs. He was her lifeline in a sea of uncertainty.

When she made no move toward the bed, he bent, scooped her up in his arms, carried her across the room and laid her on the mattress.

She clung to him, her arms wrapped around his neck. "I can't let go. Please, don't make me."

He chuckled. "Okay, then. But let me lie down beside you."

She scooted over, making room for his big body on the bed.

He laid down and gathered her again in his arms. "You know you're safe here in Hank's house."

She nodded. "My brain tells me I'm safe, but my heart...not so much."

"I'll stay as long as you need me," he reassured her.

"And if that's all night?" she whispered.

He sighed. "If it's all night, I'll be here." Sam brushed a strand of her damp hair behind her ear. "Just know, it'll be a struggle."

She frowned. "I'm sorry. If you don't want to, you don't have to stay."

He snorted. "That's just the problem. I want to...too much." He kissed the tip of her nose and frowned.

"Sorry. I said I wouldn't initiate a kiss again, and yet, I did."

"Don't," she said, touching a finger to his lips.

"Don't what?"

"Don't be sorry." She cupped his cheek in her palm and pressed her mouth to his. "I want you to kiss me," she said against his lips. "I want you to hold me. But not because I want you to." She brushed her thumb across his lip. "Because you want to."

"Oh, baby, I want to hold you. I want to do more than hold you. But after what you've been through, I won't go beyond holding you. Not until we see this through and get you the medical attention you need."

She nodded, her heart swelling in her chest. "One good thing about all this is that I got to meet you." Reggie snuggled into his side and laid a hand across his chest. "I'll sleep for now, but tomorrow…we're ending this chase."

Sam laid a hand over hers. "Damn right, we are."

Though her pulse raced, and she wasn't in the least bit sleepy, she lay still next to him, knowing she could get up and leave whenever she wanted. Because she could leave, and Sam wouldn't stop her, Reggie had no desire to move. Her desire grew for this man, giving her hope that the abuse she'd suffered wouldn't affect her attitude toward her future sexuality.

Unfortunately, the women she'd wanted to help were being forced to spend another night with an insane man. She'd hoped that by escaping, she could get back to them with the help they needed to be free of the Master.

Hang in there, she prayed. *Help is coming.*

Eventually, her heartbeat slowed, and exhaustion claimed her. With Sam's arms wrapped around her, her ear pressed to his chest and the steady beat of his heart marking time, Reggie drifted into a troubled sleep.

She woke in a dark cell, the scent of damp earth and urine filling her senses. She felt her way around the walls until she came to the door. It had no handle on the inside. Only someone on the outside could open it. Reggie tried digging her fingers into the gap between the door and the doorframe, but the fit was too tight. Back around the room she moved, feeling for something, anything she could use to pry the door open. All she found was a thin blanket and a tin cup.

Sounds of someone sobbing drifted in beneath the door. Heart wrenching wails echoed down the hallway beyond the door, adding pressure to the weight of hopelessness on her chest.

"We'll never get out," a voice called. "We'll die here."

"No," Reggie said. "Help is on the way. Someone will come."

"It'll be too late," another female voice cried. "Too late."

No. It couldn't be. Sam and Hank would send help. They would get them out.

"They won't find us in time."

"Yes, they will." Reggie argued. "They're coming."

Footsteps sounded on the stairs leading down into the dark, dank cellar. The crackle of the cattle prod sent a flash of fear through Reggie's body.

"He's coming for you," a voice called out. "He's angry that you got away."

Reggie backed away from the door until she felt the cool damp wall of her cell against her naked back.

The footsteps stopped.

Her breath lodged in her lungs.

The door swung open, and a large man in a ski mask stood silhouetted against the dull yellow lantern hung on the wall behind him.

Reggie screamed.

CHAPTER 13

"Hey, Reggie." Sam sat up and smoothed a lock of strawberry-blond hair away from her forehead. "Sweetheart, wake up. You're having a bad dream."

She tossed her head back and forth on the pillow. "No…please…no," she cried, tears slipping down her cheeks.

Sam's heart constricted. He didn't like seeing her in pain. If he could, he'd take it all away from her. "Reggie," Sam said, more insistently. "Wake up. It's just a dream."

Her eyes popped open, and a whoosh of air left her lungs. "Sam? Dear Jesus. Sam!" She flung her arms around his neck and pressed her face against his bare chest. "I didn't think you'd get to us in time. He was there." Her words drowned in sobs. "He'd come to get me."

"Sweetheart, it was only a dream." He leaned against the headboard, holding her in his arms, his hand sliding up and down her back. "Just a dream."

"It was so real. The voices. The smell... Him." Her body shook.

Sam knew exactly what she was talking about. He still had dreams of battles where he'd lost friends. In his dreams, he could still smell the dust, hear the cries of his teammates and taste the blood. "I know, baby. I know just how real it feels. But you're not in that cellar. You're here in Hank's house, with me."

Her hand on his chest clenched and unclenched, finally smoothing over his skin. Reggie drew in a ragged breath and tilted her head up to look into his face. "Thank you," she said.

"For what?" He chuckled and pressed his lips to her forehead for a brief kiss. "I didn't do anything."

"You found me on the river. And you came in time to save me from my dream."

"Agreed, I was on the river at the exact right moment to find you. But I've been here all night. You just had to come back from your dream. I didn't save you then."

She snuggled closer, still staring up at him. "I'm afraid to close my eyes again. He's waiting for me. I can feel it."

"Then stay awake with me. We can talk or play cards."

She shook her head. "You shouldn't have to give up your sleep for me. I'll be okay. Please, go back to sleep." She started to pull away.

Sam tightened his hold, ever so gently. "I'm awake. I wasn't sleeping very well anyway."

She seemed reluctant to move any further away.

Sam was glad. He liked holding her. But that short pink nightgown was doing crazy things to him. The longer she pressed her scantily-clad body up against his, the tighter his groin grew. He'd be in physical pain before long.

"Why were you awake?" she asked, her head resting on his shoulder.

"I couldn't sleep. There was a beautiful woman in my arms, keeping me awake and aware." He smiled down at her. "I told you it would be a difficult night for me, but I'm here for you."

"I'm sorry," she said.

"Don't be. You didn't ask to have a man kidnap you. It's not your fault you're having nightmares because of what he did to you." He brushed his lips across her forehead. "I'm glad I could be here to help."

Her eyes narrowed, and her lips twisted. "Were you this kind as a Navy SEAL?"

Sam stiffened. "Only to my teammates, women, children and dogs."

"Do you have nightmares about the battles you fought?"

"All the time," he answered, his words barely a whisper.

She snorted. "Aren't we a pair. I'm a wreck, and you're kind of broken, too."

This time, he gave her a lopsided smile. "That's why we work well together." Settling back against the padded headboard, he sighed. "What do you want to do until daylight? Talk, sing, play cards? Although, I have to warn you, I can't carry a tune. My friends liken my singing voice to the braying of a donkey."

Reggie chuckled. "We can sleep," she suggested. "I think I can close my eyes now without seeing him."

"Are you sure?" Sam asked.

She nodded.

"Give it a try. I'll stay awake in case you slip back into that dream."

She nodded, took a deep breath and closed her eyes. For a moment, there was silence. "See?" she said. "No bad guys. No bad dreams." She slipped lower into the sheets, her nightgown riding up her thigh to expose a shapely hip covered in lacy pink panties.

Sam swallowed a groan and pulled the sheet and quilt up over her and him to hide the evidence of his growing desire. He slid lower in the bed and held her close until her breathing deepened, and she slept.

Sleep for Sam didn't come. He wanted to hold Reggie so much closer but knew he couldn't. Only time and patience would see her through the damage that bastard had done to her. To get his mind off the beautiful woman in his arms, his thoughts turned to what they had to do when the sun rose, and they could get out to the river and backtrack to the house Reggie had escaped. He hoped they weren't too late to help the women trapped beneath it. He figured freeing the others would go a long way toward helping Reggie recover from her own memories and lingering demons. They had to find them soon.

Sam curled his hands into fists.

They would.

. . .

He must have fallen asleep, because the next thing he knew, sunlight was pushing through the slits of his eyelids, urging him to rise.

Reggie lay with her head tucked into the crook between his shoulder and chest, sleeping soundly. The color had returned to her face, and the dark shadows had faded significantly.

Her eyelashes fluttered. She opened her eyes and stretched, her hand encountering his body.

"Hey," he said. "You seem to have slept pretty good."

She nodded and smiled up at him. "I did. No dreams that I can remember."

"That's a step in the right direction."

"Yes, it is. I'm ready to start this day and make it count." She sat up, remembered she was wearing a tiny pink nightgown and blushed. Her hands went to the sheet, and then paused. "I guess it's a little late to cover up, considering I slept with you all night."

"You do what makes you comfortable." He laced his hands behind his neck and winked. "You can think of me as furniture."

"You're anything but furniture, Sam Franklin." She settled back down beside him and slipped her hand over his chest. "Why didn't I meet you before…?"

"You didn't need me then," he answered. "And it's likely you won't need me after we wrap up this case." He lifted her hand and kissed the tips of her fingers. "Did you ever consider that? I mean, we barely know each other."

"I know enough about you to know I like you." Reggie frowned, her gaze on the hand he held in his. "Is it that I'm just a case to you? An assignment?" Her frown deepened as she gazed up into his eyes.

"No. Actually, how I feel is far from thinking of you as an assignment. I'm afraid I'm failing at my first job as a Brotherhood Protector."

"How so?"

His jaw hardened, and he looked at the window in front of him. "First, we haven't found the bastard who hurt you." When he glanced back down at her, his face and voice softened. "Second, I'm pretty sure that I'm not supposed to fall for my client."

Her cheeks reddened, and she swept her tongue across her lips. "And are you?"

"Going to find the bastard?" He nodded, purposely answering the wrong question. "You're damn right we are."

He liked it when the color in her cheeks deepened. "No," she said. "I meant are you falling for your client?"

He tilted his head as if considering her question. "Hmm. I'm lying in bed with her. She's beautiful. And I haven't tried to make love to her when my entire body and soul is begging me to." He nodded. "Yeah. I'd say I'm in grave danger of falling for her." He sat up and brought her to a sitting position with him. "You, or at least the idea of what we could be together, is the primary reason I left the military. I want a life. A wife. A passel of children and a place to call home." He gathered her hands in his. "I know it's too soon to hit you with all that, but that's what went through my head all night long while I held my client in my arms, watching her battle nightmares and PTSD."

She stared at their hands. "What if I'm not ready for all that?"

"I wouldn't expect you to be ready. Like a physical wound, the emotional wounds take time to heal. Sometimes, those take more time than the physical ones." He lifted her hands to his lips. "When I know what I want, I'm a very patient man. And I'm persistent. But don't let me scare you. You might not want what I want. It's my job to show you what a great guy I am. And if that doesn't work, no worries. I'll come up with another plan." He winked. "Now, let's get this day started. We have some women to free and a lunatic to catch and put away for the rest of his life."

Reggie snorted. "You make it sound like it's all by the numbers," she said swinging her legs over the side of the bed, a smile pulling at her lips. "Find the bad guy. Rescue the women. Put the bad guy away." She stood and clapped her hands together. "And done." Her smile faded. "God, I hope you're right. I hope we find him and bring him in without anyone else being hurt."

Sam stared at her standing in the soft morning light, the shape of her body silhouetted beneath the frothy pink nightgown.

His groin tightened. "The sooner we get started, the better," he said and got out the other side of the bed. He headed for the other room, his back to her so that he didn't embarrass or scare her with the jutting evidence of desire. "I'll be ready in less than ten minutes," he called out over his shoulder.

"I'll be ready in five," she responded.

Sam closed the door between them and groaned.

Ten minutes might not be enough time in a cool shower to bring his desire under control. He hurried to the bathroom, stripped and turned the water on cold. The shock of water that originated as snow on the mountaintops hitting his engorged cock brought him back to reality.

He couldn't think straight if he was always thinking about making love to Reggie's beautiful body. He had to focus on the other women whose dire situation was desperate and sobering.

Stepping out of the shower, Sam had renewed his determination to bring this manhunt to a close. Today was the day. It would be done.

Then perhaps he could get on with his life, and Reggie could start healing. Sam wanted to be there to help her through the process, but she had to be in a place to heal herself. With the Master still on the loose, she wouldn't have the closure she needed.

Reggie dressed in her borrowed jeans and sweater. She slipped the shoulder holster on and buckled it in place, then slid the .40 caliber into it. The weight felt unnerving at the same time as it comforted her. As soon as they found the Master and freed the women, she would return to her apartment and her own wardrobe. She'd buy her own pistol and get her concealed carry license.

Her life in Bozeman seemed so far away. Had it really only been a little over two weeks since she'd been kidnapped?

For the first time since that fateful night, she felt better. More like the old Reggie, though she knew the old Reggie would be no more. She couldn't go back to being the carefree young woman who couldn't conceive of being kidnapped and raped multiple times. For the rest of her life, she'd be wary of dark alleys, strangers and men she didn't know.

As soon as she could, she'd enroll in self-defense classes. If she ever had children, she'd have them trained in self-defense from the moment they could walk.

She shivered at the thought of having a child kidnapped and tortured as she'd been tortured. Knowing the kinds of monsters that existed, could she bring another child into this messed up world? She thought of Hank and Sadie's daughter Emma. That precious baby.

Reggie had always wanted children, but now…? She wasn't sure she could.

After she'd dressed, combed her hair and brushed her teeth, she pressed her ear to the door between her room and Sam's. She could hear the water in the shower still running. Rather than wait for him, she decided to go downstairs and help out in the kitchen. With extra guests in the house, there would be added work to prepare breakfast for them all.

When she arrived in the kitchen, she found Hank and Kujo in control of cooking breakfast. "There's coffee in the pot, milk and juice in the refrigerator," Hank said. "Help yourself. Sadie's changing Emma's diaper. She should be back in a second."

"What can I do to help?" she asked.

"How about setting the table with utensils and glasses?" Hank suggested. "Kujo and I have the cooking under control."

Kujo pulled piping hot biscuits from the oven and set the pan on a trivet.

Hank returned his attention to a pan of fluffy yellow scrambled eggs and a griddle lined with pancakes.

Sadie sailed into the kitchen with Emma in her arms. "Good morning, Reggie. I hope you slept well last night."

Heat climbed up Reggie's neck and suffused her cheeks. "I did. Thank you."

"After breakfast, we'll meet with Swede in the war room and bring you and Sam up to speed on what we've discovered during the night."

"Did you find the house?" Sam asked from the doorway to the kitchen.

Reggie's insides quivered at the sound of his voice, and warmth spread throughout her body. She'd never had that kind of reaction to any man in her life. Why was Sam so different? Was she experiencing some kind of hero worship because he'd saved her life? Would it fade after the Master was captured and rotting in prison? She turned to see Sam wearing his jeans like they were a natural part of his body. And the black T-shirt he'd put on to cover his gorgeous chest stretched over the muscles, leaving little of his impressive physique to the imagination.

Her body on fire with desire, Reggie turned to the refrigerator, opened the door and stood in the cool air, praying the heat would abate before she had to face the man again.

"What did Swede find?" Sam asked.

"Not a whole lot, but maybe something," Hank said. "Upon close inspection of the satellite images, he thinks he found the hard lines of a roof through the trees in a couple places near the cliffs and dirt roads leading in from the highway. They bear checking into."

"Is there an address from the road, leading into the property?" Sam asked.

"Not that we could find. We suspect it's an old abandoned house." Hank met Reggie's gaze. "Do you remember if there were electric lights in the house?"

Reggie closed her eyes and pictured the cellar, the stairs and the house above. It had the musty smell of an older home with dry rotted joists and moldy walls and furniture. "I remember there not being many lights and lots of shadows. It was really creepy. And there was a steady hum of an engine when the Master was there."

"Maybe a generator?" Sam asked.

Reggie nodded, opening her eyes. "He always hooked a battery-powered lantern on the wall outside our cells before he opened the door and took one of us up to the big house. And he left it there until he brought us back." A cold chill rippled down her spine as she shut the door to the other memories of being inside that house.

Sam took her hand. "Thanks."

"Does that help?" she asked.

Hank nodded. "It could mean he's off the grid. Which means, no registered address with the power company or the tax office. It also makes the house harder to find. Especially, if the trees and vegetation have grown up around it."

"But you said Swede found evidence of buildings out there," Reggie said.

"He did," Hank said. "Let's hope one of the buildings is the house we're looking for." He glanced at Sam. "The other alternative is that the rooflines are old deer camps or covered deer stands hunters placed in the trees."

Swede joined them for breakfast and discussed the potential of hidden buildings in the forest.

"There's another thought we might need to be prepared for. Montana has several active groups of survivalists. They live off the grid in remote locations."

Hank's face was grim. "And they don't like folks walking into their camps uninvited."

"That's right," Swede said. "They might shoot first and ask questions later. And they have plenty of places to hide the bodies."

When the conversation turned morbid, Sadie shooed them out of the kitchen and down to the war room, claiming she'd heard enough negativity for a lifetime.

In the Brotherhood Protectors' basement war room, the men continued the conversation. Two more men arrived, introducing themselves as Taz and Chuck. They joined in on the planning and potential outcomes.

The more theories they came up with, the worse Reggie felt. "If there's a chance those women are out there, I'm willing to risk running into a survivalist's camp to find them. As far as I could tell, there was only one man at the house where I was held. But he had two Rottweilers who'd just as soon rip you apart as look at you. So, whoever goes in with me needs to be prepared for them."

Sam was shaking his head before she finished speaking. "You're not going in."

Reggie lifted her chin and met his gaze. "I have to. I promised to get them out of there. I know the layout of the house enough to get to the cellar."

Sam frowned. "He could be armed. I can't put you at risk of being shot."

"You're not putting me at risk," she said. "I'd be putting myself at risk. And it's a risk I'm willing to take. Besides," Reggie lifted her chin higher, "if you don't take me, I'll go by myself. I have to see this through."

Sam started to say something, but Hank stepped into the conversation with, "We'll cross that bridge when we come to it. For now, we need to recon the areas Swede has identified. If we find a house on a hill, we report back. No one goes in until we have a team assembled. Understood?"

Sam, Kujo and Swede all nodded, used to taking orders.

Reggie slowly nodded. They were right. She couldn't go in alone. She needed Sam, Hank and his team to get those women out alive. And they needed the element of surprise on their side.

"I'm sending Bear, Taz, Kujo and Chuck out to scout the area. Molly, you're welcome to join them. But I wouldn't alert your counterparts in the FBI, just yet. We don't know if the kidnapper has connections. The rest of us will wait until we hear back from them. However, they'll remain in place until we have the team assembled and ready to make the move. Sam, you and Reggie can stay here, or head to town. I don't suggest you drive on the highway out to the locations. The fewer people out that way, the better. He might be watching the roads. They aren't major highways.

Hank had his team gear up with satellite phones, two-way radios, headsets and bulletproof vests. Each man selected his choice of weapon and ammunition.

"Reggie, I know we fit you with a .40 caliber pistol. Did you have a chance to test-drive it?" Hank asked.

She shook her head. "No, we didn't. Do you happen to have a taser or a stun gun?" she asked. "I might feel better about using something that won't kill me if I mishandle it."

"I do have a taser, and you might also like this." He held up a small canister that would fit easily in the palm of Reggie's hand.

"What is it?" she asked.

"Mace." He held it up. "All you have to do is point it in his face and press the top. It'll blind him long enough for you to get away."

Reggie shoved the canister into the pocket of her hooded jacket and placed the taser in the other pocket. She patted the .40 caliber pistol in the holster beneath the jacket and felt a little ridiculous at being armed to the teeth. Then again, she was going after the man who hadn't hesitated to deploy a taser on them, shocked them with cattle prods and kept them drugged so much that they couldn't fight back.

If she had to, Reggie would use the full force of every weapon she had to stop him from ever doing that to anyone ever again.

Everyone headed out of the ranch house. Hank walked with them. "I want you to take a trailer with you and several four-wheelers. Park the trailer a couple miles away from the locations identified by Swede. Split up and go in on the ATVs until you're within a mile of each."

"Got it," Kujo said. "And we'll move in on foot from there."

Bear drove the truck around to the barn where they hitched a trailer to the back of it. One by one, they loaded the four-wheelers onto the trailer. It was decided that Molly would ride double with Kujo. His dog, Six, would be able to run alongside them through the woods until they reached the point at which they'd ditch the ATV and continue on foot.

Reggie's pulse quickened as they finished loading the ATVs. Kujo, Molly, Bear, Taz and Chuck loaded up into the four-door cab of the pickup, and they left the barnyard with the coordinates Swede had given them of the places he'd identified from the satellite images.

"I have business in town," Hank said. "I'll be at the sheriff's office to talk to him about another case one of my guys is involved in. I'll keep my ears open for anything out of there and my satellite phone clipped to my belt. Where will you two be?" he asked of Sam and Reggie.

Sam turned to Reggie. "We'll be in town as well. Since the highway is on the other end of town from this ranch, we might as well be as close as we can get without actually driving out there."

Reggie gave a tight smile, glad Sam hadn't decided to leave her behind with Sadie.

"I'll get Reggie geared up with some of your communications equipment before we head into town," Sam said. "Should have done it when we got the others wired."

Hank nodded. "Good. I'll see you later." He kissed Sadie and Emma, and then climbed into his four-wheel-drive pickup and headed for town.

Swede and Sadie walked with Reggie and Sam back into the house, down the stairs to the war room and into the arsenal.

Sam gave Reggie a two-way radio headset and showed her how to use it. After she'd successfully communicated with him from the other room, he helped her fold it up and stuff it in the pocket with the mace. Then he filled a bag with two bulletproof vests, a couple of flashlights and night vision goggles.

Swede approached Reggie, carrying what appeared to be a necklace with a pendant hanging from the chain. "Wear this at all times. If for some reason you're separated from Sam, we can find you with this. It has a built-in tracking device we can follow using this." He handed a GPS tracking monitor to Sam.

"What if I want to keep track of Sam?" Reggie asked, arching an eyebrow.

"Trust me," Swede said. "He'll find you. And you're the potential target. Not him."

Swede made a good point, but Reggie would have

liked to be able to track Sam if she should lose sight of him. The mere thought of being out of Sam's sight made her knees weak and her body tremble.

Reggie squared her shoulder and fought the fear threatening to overwhelm her. She'd clawed her way out of that hell without any help. She would do whatever it took to get the others out alive. If it meant going in alone, she would. Her hand rested on the .40 caliber tucked beneath her jacket. This time, she wouldn't let him hurt her. And she'd kill him before she let him hurt anyone else. God, she wished she'd had time for Sam to show her the basics of how to use the gun. Somehow, she'd make it work.

CHAPTER 14

Reggie followed Sam out to his truck.

He held the door for Reggie, and then Grunt, and placed the equipment bag on the back floorboard. Once they were settled, he climbed in and drove to Eagle Rock.

As they passed the sheriff's station, Reggie noted Hank's truck parked there. If they ended up needing help, Hank was in the right place to get it. That was reassuring on a day when anything could happen. Or not.

Reggie sat silently in the seat beside Sam, her fingers twisting in her lap.

Near the opposite end of town from where they'd entered, a woman driving a minivan was parked at an odd angle in front of an antique store, the hatch on the back of her van open and several bags of groceries scattered across the ground.

Reggie could see immediately that the minivan's left

rear tire was flat, and the woman was struggling to lift a tire out of the back.

"We have time," Reggie said. "We should stop and help."

Sam had already put on his blinker and was pulling over.

"My father made sure I knew how to change a flat tire as soon as I was old enough to drive on my own. He said no woman should ever be stranded on the side of these Montana highways because she didn't know how to change a flat." Reggie glanced across at Sam. "Want me to do it?"

Sam smiled. "I'm sure you're amazing at it, but I'd feel better if you stayed in the truck with Grunt."

Reggie didn't argue. Sam had agreed to take her on the mission to find the Master. If he wanted her to stay with Grunt, she'd stay with Grunt while he changed the tire.

The lug nuts on the woman's flat tire proved to be a challenge. From what Reggie could hear through her open window, they'd been put on with a torque wrench, making it nearly impossible to dislodge. Fifteen minutes into changing the woman's tire, Sam only had half of the lug nuts off, and he'd worked up a sweat.

Grunt paced across the back seat of the pickup.

Reggie was getting anxious, thinking the guys might have reached the drop-off point by now and would be mounting the ATVs for the next leg of their reconnaissance mission. She glanced at the satellite phone, praying for it to ring. She crossed her fingers, hoping they found the house and reported in soon.

Then they'd be on their way to finally free the other women.

She stared out the window at the minivan, willing the lug nuts to loosen already.

Grunt whined behind her and paced faster, back and forth across the truck seat.

"I know. They're taking too long." Then she had another thought. "Do you need to go outside?"

The dog stopped moving and stared at her. Then he barked and went to stand at the door, waiting for her to let him out.

"I guess when you gotta go, you gotta go." Reggie glanced at Sam bouncing on the tire iron, working hard at loosening the lug nuts and making slow, painful progress. She didn't want to bother him. He needed to get done with the tire changing as soon as possible.

Which meant she'd have to take Grunt for a walk to relieve himself.

She grabbed the lead, straightened her wig and slipped out of the passenger seat. As soon as she opened the back door, she realized her mistake.

Grunt leaped to the ground and took off before Reggie could snap the lead on his collar.

Sam had just dropped the tire iron, the clatter covering the sound of Reggie's curse. She closed the truck door gently and ran after Grunt. The animal turned down an alley between the antique store and an insurance agency. He'd probably seen a cat and was hot on its trail.

"Grunt!" she called out. What was the word Sam used to make the dog stay? "Grunt, *bleib!*"

Too late, the dog had rounded the back corner of the building and disappeared out of eyesight and hearing.

A sharp yelp sounded from the back of the building.

Reggie ran after Grunt, afraid he'd tangled with the wrong cat and had gotten himself hurt. Running as fast as she could, she barely slowed to take the corner.

As she came around to the back of the building, she saw Grunt lying on the ground, motionless. "Grunt?" she called out and rushed toward him, her wig slipping off the back of her head.

A figure detached from the shadows, leaped out and flung a bag over her head.

Darkness blocked the daylight. Reggie couldn't see anything, and her arms were trapped by the coarse fabric of the bag and the strong arms wrapped around her. Hands reached beneath her jacket and relieved her of the .40 caliber pistol. They patted her sides and removed the taser as well. Then she was lifted off her feet, carried several yards, and then dumped into what could only be a trunk.

As soon as the arms around her let go, she shot up and tried to roll out of the back of the trunk, screaming as loud as she could. The sound was muffled by the sack over her head as she fought to push herself free from the back of the vehicle.

No. No No. This was not happening again.

"You shouldn't have run away," a voice said. The sound filtered through the sack but was no less familiar. He shoved her back into the trunk and tried to shut it on her.

Reggie fought even harder, bracing her feet on the

trunk lid, pushing up to keep him from lowering the heavy metal and locking her in.

She couldn't let him take her. She'd made a promise to herself that she would return to free the others, not to return to become a prisoner once again.

"Hey, leave her alone," a young voice called out.

Hope spurred Reggie on. She kicked at the trunk lid and aimed blindly at the hands attempting to close it.

The Master lurched as if he'd been hit broadside. He slammed the trunk closed before Reggie could get free.

Complete darkness surrounded her. She finally worked the fabric sack from her head and shoved it aside.

"Let her go!" the youth's voice sounded again.

Something hit the trunk hard, and then the sound of heavy footsteps pounded around the vehicle. A door opened and closed with a sharp slam. The engine revved, and the car jerked forward.

Reggie screamed as loud as she could and kicked the trunk lid, hoping to get the attention of anyone the car passed. At first moving slowly, the car picked up speed. Reggie assumed it had reached the edge of town and now sped along the highway, back to the big house, the dark, dank cellar and the end of her freedom—and probably her life. For surely, he wouldn't let her leave again. Not alive.

She didn't feel as sorry for herself as she did for the women she'd failed to free of this sociopath. When he stopped and got her out of the trunk, she had to make it count. He'd taken her taser and pistol, but he'd missed the little canister of mace. Reggie had one shot at escape. She needed to be accurate and deliberate. Most of all, she'd better make it count. If the Brotherhood Protectors were out there, she prayed they'd found the Master's house. She might be able to buy some time, but between the Master and his two Rottweilers, it wouldn't be much. Reggie doubted she'd make it to the river a second time.

She clutched the small canister of mace in one hand and the necklace with the GPS pendant in the other.

Come on, Sam. I've never needed you more.

Though she'd been raped and tortured, and it could happen again, Reggie wasn't ready to give up on life.

Sam had shown her that she wasn't just damaged goods. He found her attractive, even though another man had left his mark on her mentally and physically. He'd shown her that not all men were monsters like the Master.

Though she'd only known him for a short time, Reggie knew Sam was special. A man of honor and integrity. He would never hurt a woman or take advantage of her when she was broken. She wanted the chance to get to know him better, to learn to trust men again, because of him.

She wanted to have a man make love to her…when she was ready. And she wanted that man to be Sam.

A sob rose up her throat.

Reggie swallowed hard, forcing it back down. For now, she was on her own. She couldn't fall apart and wallow in the stench of fear. She had to keep her cool and fight back the only way she knew how. With every fiber of her being.

. . .

Sam had switched the tire and was tightening the lug nuts on the spare when a familiar voice called out behind him. "Sam!"

"Abe?" Sam turned to find Abe, the teenager, staggering toward him, his cheek bruised and blood running down his face from a cut over his eye.

"You gotta come quick." He staggered and fell into Sam's arms. "Your lady… He took her."

Sam's gaze shot to the truck where he'd left Reggie to wait for him with Grunt. The back door was open, and neither Reggie nor Grunt were in the truck.

Abe grabbed his arm and tugged him toward an alley. "Your lady, he took her. And your dog…" He shook his head. "I think he's dead." Tears blended with the blood on the boy's face. "I tried to stop him, but he was bigger. I couldn't…" He shook his head as he limped down the alley, hurrying to the other end.

Sam left him and ran ahead. When he reached the back of the buildings, the only sight that greeted him was that of the German Shepherd lying on his side as still as death and a brown wig.

"He was here. The man in the ski mask. His car was here." Abe stood near Grunt, turning in a three hundred and sixty degree circle, clasping his hands to his head. "He threw her in the trunk…and he got away."

Sam's heart slammed against his ribs. "What did the car look like?"

"It was dark. Black, I think. Four doors. But he put her in the trunk." Abe dropped to his knees next to the dog. "He's dead, isn't he?" He looked up at Sam. "I couldn't help either of them."

As Sam approached the dog, he pulled out his cellphone and contacted Hank. "The Master got Reggie. Call in the big guns. We have to find her before he kills her."

"I just heard from Kujo," Hank said. "He and Molly saw a dark sedan pass them on the highway, heading in the direction of their designated location to investigate. They were on foot with more than a mile to go, I'll let them know."

Sam ended the call, leaned over Grunt and watched his chest for any sign of life. After a few moments, he noticed Grunt's chest expand. Then it did it again. He was breathing.

Relief filled Sam. He scooped the dog into his arms. "Is there a vet nearby?"

Abe pointed. "A block that way. I used to hang out and walk the dogs there before Mom got sick." He led the way to the vet's office less than a block away. The vet was in and took Grunt into surgery immediately.

Sam said he'd be back, but he had to leave.

Abe followed him out. "Are you going to save Ginnie?" he asked running alongside Sam as he raced back to his truck and the satellite phone he'd left in the console.

"I'm going to do the best I can."

"I'm going with you," Abe said.

Sam shook his head. "Where I'm going could be dangerous. I need you to go home and take care of your siblings until I can get back to you."

"My sister, Lacey, has them. She can watch over them until I get back."

"No, you don't understand. If you come with me, you might get hurt. You might not get back to your family. And I know for a fact that they depend on you. You can't afford to have something bad happen to you." Sam put a hand on the young man's shoulder. "Your duty is to them. I'll take care of my lady. You've already been a big help. Please."

Abe nodded. "Okay. But I feel responsible for Ginnie, too. I should have stopped him."

"You couldn't, but you did your best. Now, I have to go."

Abe took a step back, squaring his shoulders. "You know where to find me if you need help."

"I do. And I'll be back. That's a promise." Sam climbed into the truck, shifted into drive and pulled onto Main Street, heading west into the Crazy Mountains and following the road that paralleled the north branch of the river. He pressed the accelerator to the floor, hoping to catch up to the sedan that was taking Reggie away from him. What if the Master didn't take her to the house where he'd been holding the other women? What if he killed Reggie and dumped her in a ditch along the side of the road? Sam might never find her.

Then he remembered the GPS tracker. Still blasting along the highway at an insane speed, he fumbled in the bag he'd packed to find the tracking device.

For a moment, he took his foot off the accelerator, allowing the truck to slow to a more manageable pace.

Switching it on, he waited for it to warm up and find Reggie in the vastness of the Montana landscape.

For what felt like forever, the screen remained dark. Then it blinked to life and displayed a bright green dot. It was moving. It had to be Reggie. She had to be alive.

Sam pressed his foot down hard on the accelerator. She wasn't more than five minutes in front of him.

He held the steering wheel in a white-knuckled grip as he maneuvered the curves, increasing his speed as he came out of them. If the master had shoved Reggie into his sedan alive, he hadn't had time to stop and kill her. As long as they were still moving, Reggie had a chance. Once they stopped, all bets were off.

All the more reason for Sam to catch them before that happened. He pushed harder on the accelerator, screaming around the curves, the bed of his pickup swinging wider, almost pushing him into a spin. He righted the truck, slowed slightly on the next turn and raced on.

The satellite phone rang in his lap. He fumbled with it to answer, keeping one hand on the steering wheel.

"You just passed Kujo and Molly," Hank said. "They're at their site. It's an old barn. They're high-tailing it back to the ATV and will continue on the road to catch up with you."

"I've got Reggie on the GPS tracker. They're still moving. I'm maybe four minutes behind them."

"Stay on them," Hank said. "Bear, Taz and Chuck haven't checked in yet. Wait. That's them now. I'll call right back."

A quick glance at the tracker assured him Reggie was still on the move, but they were slowing.

His pulse raced, and his heart squeezed hard in his chest. Reggie's life hung in the balance of a few short minutes.

If the Master stopped, he could kill her in less than a second. Sam could be too late.

He leaned into the steering wheel, urging the truck to go faster, the curves to be straighter and Reggie to live long enough for him to save her.

The satellite phone rang.

Sam grabbed it and held it to his ear. "Talk to me, Hank."

"Bear and Taz are on foot, closing in on a dilapidated two-story house that appears to have been abandoned."

"And?" Sam prompted, impatiently.

"They just saw a car drive into a lean-to on the other side of the structure. A dark, four-door sedan."

"Tell them to shoot the bastard," Sam entreated.

"They can't see him from their vantage point. They're moving around the perimeter now."

"They can't wait. He might kill her."

"They don't have a clear line of fire. Got your radio headset?" Hank asked.

"Yeah."

"Wear it. You don't want to shoot each other."

He reached for the earbud, fumbled to slip it into his ear and switch it on. "Got it on," he reported.

"Good," Hank said. "I'm not far behind you. Don't do anything crazy. Remember, we're better as a team. We can't let this guy get away because we were too hasty in our decisions."

Sam gritted his teeth. "I'm three minutes out, closing in. If they don't get to him first…I will. He will *not* get away."

CHAPTER 15

"Get out!" the Master said, his voice a menacing growl.

Reggie blinked at the flashlight beam shining down into the trunk and her eyes. Gripping the canister of mace in her palm, she waited, not wanting to blow her only chance because she couldn't see his face. The mace had to hit him square in the eyes to blind him long enough for her to make her escape.

She sat up and braced her free hand on the edge of the trunk

"Get out!" He reached a cattle prod into the trunk and hit her with the charged end.

A surge of 50,000 volts blasted through her, sending her falling back, her body jerking. The hand with the canister automatically opened, and the mace can rolled out.

"Hurry up, bitch, or you get it again."

"I can't move when you zap me with that," she said through clenched teeth, her hand patting the floor, searching for the little canister. Just when she thought she'd lost it, her fingers touched the smooth metal. Curling her fingers around it, she gripped the side of the trunk and pulled herself up.

Before she could get her balance, the Master grabbed her hair and yanked her out onto the ground.

She landed on her hands and knees, her knuckles slamming against the gravel. But she didn't let go of the little canister. And now that she was out of the trunk and her eyes had adjusted to the dim light of the lean-to he'd pulled the car under, she could aim and put her plan into action.

"Get up!" he yelled. He raised the cattle prod, swinging it toward her.

Reggie lurched to her feet, spun and faced the bastard. "Don't hit me again," she said, through clenched teeth.

"I'll do whatever the hell I want. You've caused me more than enough trouble. Now, I'll have to get rid of you and the others."

Before he could hit her again with the business end of the cattle prod, Reggie raised her hand and sprayed mace straight into eyeholes of his ski mask.

The man screamed and clutched at his eyes with his empty hand, while swinging the cattle prod in the air in a wild attempt to zap her.

Unfortunately, to make her escape, she had to either go through him to get out into the open or go into the house through the door behind her. Armed with the cattle prod, even if he couldn't see clearly, the Master could hit her in one of his wildly swinging moves.

Taking her chances on the house, she lunged for the door and yanked it open. Reggie dove into the kitchen, turned, closed the door and twisted the lock. Since the top of the door was a window, it wouldn't hold him long. Reggie ran out of the kitchen and through to the old sitting room.

The muffled sound of dogs barking came from somewhere else in the house. Reggie prayed they were locked in another room and wouldn't be able to come out at tear her apart.

What little light that filtered through the filthy windows cast shadows on the ragged furniture, making it difficult for her to weave her way through what once had been a happy home, but was now a house of horrors. She remembered the sagging, dusty sofa, the faded wingback chair and the fireplace that smoked whenever he chose to light a fire in the grate. She remembered the path he'd taken her from the stairs in the hallway, through the sitting room and into the bedroom where he'd raped her and the other women.

Her anger fought against fear. She wasn't drugged now. Her head was clear, and she'd be damned if he'd get away with hurting her ever again.

Glass shattered, and the door slammed open in the kitchen.

Her heart in her throat, Reggie searched the room for a weapon. She'd used as much of the mace as possible the first time around. It was only meant to be used once to allow her time to get away. The sitting room had no doors to the outside. Reggie passed through to a hallway that had once been a front entryway with a large wooden door. She ran to the door, gripped the handle and pulled hard. It didn't budge. Not even a little. She twisted the deadbolt and pulled again. Nothing.

The sound of boots hitting the wooden floor sent her across the hall into another room devoid of furniture, with moth-eaten curtains hanging on the long windows too thick with dust and dirt to see through. A broken wooden chair lay on its side in a corner, covered with cobwebs.

Reggie ran for the chair, grabbed it and swung it at the closest window.

The glass shattered, leaving razor-sharp shards jutting up from the window frame. Using the chair, she wiped at the shards, knocking them loose.

The footsteps sounded in the entryway, crossing the hall. From all the noise she was making, he'd know which room he'd find her in. Reggie threw down the chair, swung her leg over the windowsill and screamed.

Sharp pinpricks pierced her back and electrical shocks burned through her nerves.

She fell back on the floor, completely incapable of moving to defend herself.

No. No. No.

The Master entered the room, pulled zip-ties from his back pocket, rolled her over and secured her wrists together behind her back.

Reggie knew from having experienced being tased before that that the effects lasted between five and thirty seconds. If he didn't secure her legs, she still had a chance of getting away. Any chance was better than none. As long as he didn't carry her down the basement before the paralysis wore off...

One thousand and one. One thousand and two.

The Master, lifted her, flung her over his shoulder and took her to the hallway where he unlocked the door that led into the cellar below.

One thousand and three. One thousand and four.

Reggie could feel some of the feeling returning to her fingertips and toes, but she still couldn't move her arms or legs.

He descended the steps one at a time, slowed by the effort of carrying the deadweight of her body.

One thousand and five. One thousand and six.

Come on muscles. Work!

One thousand and seven. One thousand and eight.

At the bottom of the steps, he paused in front of a wooden door, fumbling with a key on a keychain clipped to his belt loop. A battery-powered lantern hung on a hook on the wall. Sobs sounded behind other doors along the narrow passageway.

They were still alive. Relief flooded through Reggie, and determination swelled in her chest. She had to get them out.

One thousand and nine.

Reggie could wiggle a toe, and then another. Her fingers tingled and moved.

One thousand and ten. One thousand and eleven.

The Master shoved the key into the lock and flung open the door to a dark, dank, earthen cell.

As if a veil lifted on her muscles, Reggie could feel when the paralysis lifted, and her legs would answer her brain's command to move. She kicked out, slamming her feet against the doorframe. She pushed so hard it took the Master off balance. The arm he'd had clamped around her legs loosened enough she twisted and fell out of his grip, crashing to the floor.

The Master reached for the door and tried to swing it closed.

Reggie rolled to her knees, bunched her legs beneath her and rushed him like a linebacker going for the quarterback. Her shoulder hit him in the gut, sending him flying backward. He landed hard on the floor. Without the use of her arms and hands, Reggie couldn't slow her momentum and crashed to the floor on top of him.

He lay for a moment, the wind knocked out of him, unmoving.

Reggie rolled off him, pushed to her feet and raced up the stairs.

"Bitch!" he yelled and came after her, clomping up the stairs in his boots.

Thankfully, the door was still open.

Reggie ran through and straight for the window she'd broken out. It was her only hope. He wouldn't have time to reload the taser. If she could get to the window first, she'd make it.

Down the hallway, into the empty room and across rotting wooden floor she flew. She didn't care that she would be going through the window headfirst or that she had no way of breaking her fall. All she knew was that she had to get away from him, or she'd die. She didn't slow but kept moving, using all her momentum to throw herself through the opening. Her body sailed through. And as if in slow motion she saw the windowsill pass by. Her head ploughed through an overgrown bush, and her legs had almost cleared the room. She was almost free when a hand reached out and snagged her ankle.

Her flight came to an abrupt halt, and she crashed down into the bush, the hand on her ankle feeling like an iron shackle.

Reggie kicked at it, but another hand captured her other foot, making it impossible for her to fight his hold. She was slowly dragged over the branches and the windowsill, back toward the house and into the room. Her only hope left was that Sam and the Brotherhood Protectors would find her. She drew in a deep breath and screamed as long and loud as she could.

SAM HAD the windows down in his pickup as he turned down the rutted path leading to the location where the green light designated on the GPS tracking device. When the ramshackle house came into view, he heard a piercing scream.

Rather than slow his truck, he raced toward the house and skidded to a stop at the foot of the rotted steps leading up to a front door. He drew his weapon from his shoulder holster, threw open the truck's door, leaped out and ran up to the front door of the dilapidated house. Boards had been nailed across the entrance. It would take him too long to pull them free. By then, Reggie would be dead. He ran around the corner to where a covered shed had been built, butting up against the side of the house. A dark sedan had been parked beneath the rickety shed.

Another scream sounded from inside the house.

"Sam, you copy?" Bear's voice sounded in his headset.

"Roger." He slipped between the car and the house. A door stood open, the window busted out of it.

"Taz is on the other side of the house. Our bogey just pulled Reggie in through a window. He's coming in from that direction. I just made it around the perimeter to the side with the shed. I'm coming in behind you. Don't shoot me."

"Roger. Going in."

"I'd say wait for backup," Bear said, "but it sounds like she's in trouble. Go!"

Sam stepped through the door. Glass crunched beneath his boots, but he didn't slow. Sounds of a struggle came from a room deeper inside the house. He hurried forward, his pistol in front of him.

He found his way through a kitchen and a sitting room, what little light left in the sky barely making it through the grimy windows. When he emerged into a hallway, he found Reggie, her arms trapped behind her, her back pressed up against a man wearing a ski mask who held a pistol pointed at her head.

"Come one step closer, and I'll shoot the bitch," the man warned.

Reggie's gaze was wild and piercing. "Sam. Don't listen. Shoot him. He's going to kill me anyway."

"You don't want me to kill her," the Master said, his mouth drawing up on one side beneath his mask in a sneer. "I saw you two together in the tavern. You're sweet on her. You don't want her pretty face splattered all over your hands."

"Sam," Reggie said, her tone calm, insistent, resigned. "Shoot him. If you don't, he'll kill the others."

Sam's heart pinched in his chest. "I can't. I risk hitting you."

She sighed and gave him a weak smile. "Please, Sam. You have to do it for the others. For me. I promised I'd get them out. And you can't let him get away."

"Shut the hell up," the man said and poked her temple hard with the tip of his pistol. "You've been nothin' but trouble. You weren't even that good to screw. Why, I should…"

"Shoot her?" Sam said, leveling his gun at the man's chest. He couldn't pull the trigger yet. If he did, the bullet would pass through Reggie before it hit the man in the heart. But he could be ready. If anything changed…if Reggie were to get away from him…he'd take that shot. The man had to die. He was pure evil. He didn't deserve to live, much less to breathe the same air as Reggie. "You know if you shoot her, you're a dead man. I'll take great pleasure in filling you with holes. But I'd hit you where it hurt a lot before you died. I'd make you feel every bit as much pain as you've inflicted on the women you've abused."

Sam's anger took him a step closer. "Men who prey on women aren't men. They're cowards who can't find a woman to love them because they're too weak and pathetic."

"Shut the fuck up," the man bit out. "Do you think I

care if she dies? I don't. She means nothing to me. Go ahead, like she said and shoot me. You're not going to let me live anyway. Think I care if I die?" He snorted. "I'm tired of hiding. Tired of living where people treat me like shit. Go ahead and shoot me. Go ahead." He tightened his hold on Reggie, his finger shaking on the trigger. "But I'm taking her with me."

Reggie shook her head. "You bastard. You don't deserve to get off that easy."

Just then, he saw Reggie shift. Sam wasn't sure what she was doing, but she dipped slightly, her arm flexing behind her.

The man behind her squealed and hunched over, the barrel of his weapon moving from the side of her head.

At the same time, Reggie bent in half, giving Sam the opening he needed to take the shot.

He did, hitting the man in the shoulder of the arm holding the gun. His arm jerked back, the weapon flying from his fingers to skitter across the floor.

Reggie let go of her captor's balls that she'd been squeezing and staggered forward into Sam's chest. He circled his free arm around her, his gun held steady on the man in the ski mask.

The Master grabbed his arm and dropped to his knees. "Go ahead. Kill me. You know you want to."

Sam felt his frame tremble. The urge to do just that was strong. "Oh, man, I do. But I want to see you suffer more. What's the going sentence for someone who has held a woman captive and raped her on multiple occasions? Multiply that by the number of women you've done that to." Sam snorted. "You'll be in prison until you die. And maybe someone there will use you as his bitch and rape you, too."

Bear entered the room, his gun drawn. "I see you got everything under control. Want me to take over?"

"Please," Sam said. "Reggie and I have more to do." He nodded toward the man in the mask. "Let's see who the bastard is who had to hide behind a mask to feel like a man."

Bear reached over and plucked the ski mask from the man's head.

The guy beneath had salt and pepper hair and appeared to be in his mid-forties.

Hank entered the room from the hallway, his gun drawn, followed by Taz, Molly, Kujo and Six. "I see you've found Timothy Thomas. I believe you've not only committed multiple violent crimes, but you've also violated the hell out of your parole." Hank holstered his weapon. "The sheriff is on his way out to collect his prisoner. Have you found the women? Are they alive?"

Reggie turned. "If you'll get me out of this, I'll lead the way."

Sam pulled his pocket knife out of his jeans and sliced through the plastic.

"First, give me your jackets," Reggie said.

The men stripped out of their jackets and handed them to Reggie. She motioned for Molly. "They'll be more comfortable seeing women first."

Molly nodded.

Reggie bent and ripped the keychain off Thomas then led the way down the stairs into the cellar, opening the doors one at a time.

The women inside fell into her arms, crying. Their naked bodies were bruised and dirty, but they were alive.

Sam watched as Reggie and Molly wrapped each one in a jacket and passed them over to the Brotherhood Protectors to carry out of the basement and the house, up into the fresh air.

Ambulances arrived along with several sheriffs' vehicles.

The ladies were loaded into the ambulances first and carried off to Bozeman, where they'd be evaluated, have rape kits run on them and be treated. Their families would be notified, and they'd start the long road to recovering from the horror they'd endured at the hands of their captor.

"You, too," Sam said, nodding toward the ambulance. "You need to be checked over by a doctor and have a rape kit done on you as well. Every voice needs to be heard. All the evidence needs to be collected. That man needs to stay in prison for the rest of his life."

"I'll go, but I'd rather you took me," she said. "That's if you don't mind."

"Sweetheart, if you wanted to ride in the ambulance, I'd ride with you." He pulled her into his arms and held her close. "I don't want to let you out of my sight ever again."

She laughed, feeling better by the minute. Then a thought occurred to her. "Grunt. What happened to Grunt?"

The sheriff chose that moment to walk up to Sam

and Reggie. "You must be Sam Franklin, Hank's new agent. I'm Sheriff Barron."

Sam shook the man's hand.

The sheriff turned to Reggie, his smile as gentle as the hand he held out to her. "And you must be Reggie McDonald. From what Hank tells me, you're quite the hero." He held her hand in his and patted it softly. "I'm sorry you had to go through what you did. But I'm glad you had the chutzpah to get yourself out of it and bring us to the others. It's an honor to meet you."

"Thank you," Reggie said, her eyes suspiciously bright. A single tear slid down her cheek. "I don't see myself as a hero, though. I only did what I had to."

"Well, you did a hell of a job." He let go of her hand and turned back to Sam. "I just got word from one of my deputies who knows the veterinarian. Your German Shepherd was stunned by a blow to the head, but he'll live. He's got him resting at his office until you can collect him. No hurry, if you want to see this amazing woman to Bozeman for a checkup."

Sam let go of the breath he'd been holding, a rush of emotion filling his chest. "Thanks for letting me know."

Reggie slipped an around his waist and leaned her cheek against his chest. "We should go. I want to be back in Eagle Rock before it gets too late. Grunt needs you."

Sam chuckled and held her close. "I came to Montana to start living my life and maybe find someone I cared enough about to share it with me, someone who might care enough about me to consider being a part of my life." He gave her gentle smile. "Here it's been less than a week, hell less than a few days, and I think I've found the woman of my dreams." He tipped her head up and stared down into her eyes. "Don't let me scare you off. I'm willing to wait until you're healed and ready to think about dating. But I hope I can be first in line when you decide you're up for it."

She laughed. "I'll pencil you in on my calendar." Reggie leaned up on her toes. "I wouldn't want to miss out on my very own hero."

"Oh, baby, you've got that all wrong." Sam shook his head. "The sheriff nailed it. Sweetheart, *you're* the hero. I was just along for the ride."

"Well, take me to the doctor. I want to know I'm okay physically." She cupped his cheeks in her palms and brushed her lips across his. "I'm thinking I might be recovering sooner rather than later."

"Darlin', no rush. I'll be ready whenever you are." He slipped her into the crook of his arm and escorted her to his pickup.

As they drove away from the house, Reggie looked back at the structure and shivered. "To think, someone used to call that home a long time ago."

"It's a shame that Thomas used it like he did. The best thing that could happen would be for someone to bulldoze it and plant a tree in its place."

Reggie turned to face the front. "That's how I will think of it. As if someone planted a tree there. No more looking back. The future is in front of me. I'm not giving another minute of my thoughts and memories to the past."

Sam reached across the console for her hand and held it on the hour-long drive to Bozeman.

He knew it would take more than a promise to let go of the past. Reggie would be plagued by flashbacks and bad dreams until they faded. But knowing her tormentor was locked away for good would bring a measure of closure to that chapter of her life and allow her to build a future.

Sam realized it was the same for him. He'd come to Montana weighed down with grief and regret over his last mission that had gone so badly.

Reggie was right. The future was in front of him. He couldn't change the past, and he wouldn't wallow in it. And if he had to wait a month or a year or two for Reggie to recover enough from what she'd gone through, he would. She was worth it. The woman would risk her life to help others, including him. The least he could do would be to help her find a new normal. Hopefully, with him.

CHAPTER 16

"Sam? Are you ready? Everyone is waiting in the van." Reggie stood inside the front door of the big old, drafty house they'd bought for a song three years ago and yelled up the stairs to her husband. She shifted her six-month-old baby girl to her other hip.

"I'm coming. I can't believe you wanted me to wear this old thing." He came down the steps dressed in his formal dress blues with colorful ribbons covering his left chest and a shiny gold trident flying above them.

Reggie's heart fluttered as it always did when she saw her husband coming toward her. He was as handsome now as the day he'd pulled her out of the river. And he was such a good father to their eight children.

He stopped in front of her and let her tug at his necktie.

"You know you wanted to wear it," she teased. "Abe's never seen you in your dress blues. He'll be so proud to have you there when he swears into the Navy."

"He should have gone into the Air Force," Sam muttered.

Reggie snorted. "As if you'd let him."

"It's not as hard."

"Abe's up for it." Reggie smiled. "He's going to be amazing at whatever he does. He's had you as a role model."

"That boy had it in him before he met me. We just gave him the opportunities he needed." Sam kissed the top of her head. "Did you hear from Hank?"

"Sadie called. They left fifteen minutes ago. They'll be in Butte before us, if we don't get a move on."

"Anyone else coming?" he asked.

"Swede, Bear, Boomer, Chuck, Trevor, Gavin. Hell, it would be easier to ask who's not coming." Reggie smiled up at him. "They're all so proud of Abe and want to give him a good sendoff."

"Well, let's get going. We wouldn't want Abe to be late for his swearing in." He reached for his daughter.

Reggie backed away with her. "No way. She'll burp up milk all over your jacket."

"I'll take my chances."

"No, you'll drive," she said.

"You know, you're a lot easier to get along with when you're naked." He swept her into his arms and planted a long, satisfying kiss on her lips.

"Sam! You're impossible." She laughed and swatted at his arm.

Samantha hooked her daddy's arm and made the transition to him like a little monkey.

Reggie shook her head, giving up. She could never

be mad at Sam. He was everything she'd ever wanted in a friend, lover and husband. They'd been in perfect agreement over adopting Abe and his six siblings when they'd finally found out that their mother had died of an overdose, leaving them orphaned. The state had had one condition—Sam and Reggie had to be married in order to adopt all seven of the children.

That hadn't been a problem at all. The Brotherhood Protectors had experience putting on weddings and were quick to pull it together. The wedding had been perfect with the children participating in the ceremony and agreeing to love honor and cherish each other for life.

With Timothy Thomas safely ensconced in jail for the rest of his life, and the women he'd terrorized free and recovering, life had only gotten better.

Abe had graduated from high school at the top of his class. He'd preferred to defer college in lieu of following his adopted father's footsteps into the Navy. He'd even been training seven days a week to Navy standards, borrowing the pool at Hank's to build his swimming skills and strength.

Sam was so proud. The rest of the Brotherhood Protectors had taken a personal interest in Abe's training, all volunteering to run, swim or weightlift with him.

Lacey was in her last year of high school and already had a full ride scholarship to Montana State University.

The other children had taken to Sam and Reggie as if they'd been starved for love and attention. And they'd all been ecstatic when baby Samantha had come along.

Reggie still had an occasional nightmare, but those were few and far between. She was happier now than she'd ever been in her life and wouldn't change a thing.

Sam tucked Samantha into her car seat and tightened the straps around her shoulders. He bent and kissed her forehead then straightened and pulled Reggie into his arms.

"Do you know how much I love you?" he asked.

"I have an idea," she said, gazing into his eyes.

"I'm thinking we're about the luckiest folks on the planet." He tilted his head at the twelve-passenger van Hank and Sadie had gifted them with at their wedding. "I always wanted a family. Now, I have one, and life couldn't get better."

"Oh, no?" Reggie winked.

His eyes narrowed as he stared down into her eyes. "You have that look on your face."

"What look?"

"The one you had when you told me you were pregnant." His eyes widened. "You're not, are you?"

"Not what?" she teased.

"You are!" Sam lifted her off her feet and spun her around. "You hear that?" he yelled into the van. "We're going to have a baby!"

A cheer went up from everyone in the van.

Sam set Reggie on her feet and smiled down at her. "I love you, Reggie Franklin, and the adventure we call our lives."

"I love you, too, Sam. And I wouldn't trade this menagerie for anything."

"Come on, we have a swearing in to go to. This is

Abe's day. Let's celebrate!" Sam gave a loud, piercing whistle and yelled, "Grunt!"

The German Shepherd came barreling around the side of their house and made a flying leap into the side door of the van.

Sam and Reggie climbed into their huge van, with their huge family and drove into the sunrise of another day in the Crazy Mountains of Montana.

Thank You for reading SEAL Justice. Interested in more military romance stories? Subscribe to my newsletter and receive the Military Heroes Box Set

Subscribe Here

RANGER CREED

BROTHERHOOD PROTECTORS BOOK #14

New York Times & USA Today
Bestselling Author

ELLE JAMES

RANGER CREED

BROTHERHOOD PROTECTORS

NEW YORK TIMES BESTSELLING AUTHOR
ELLE JAMES

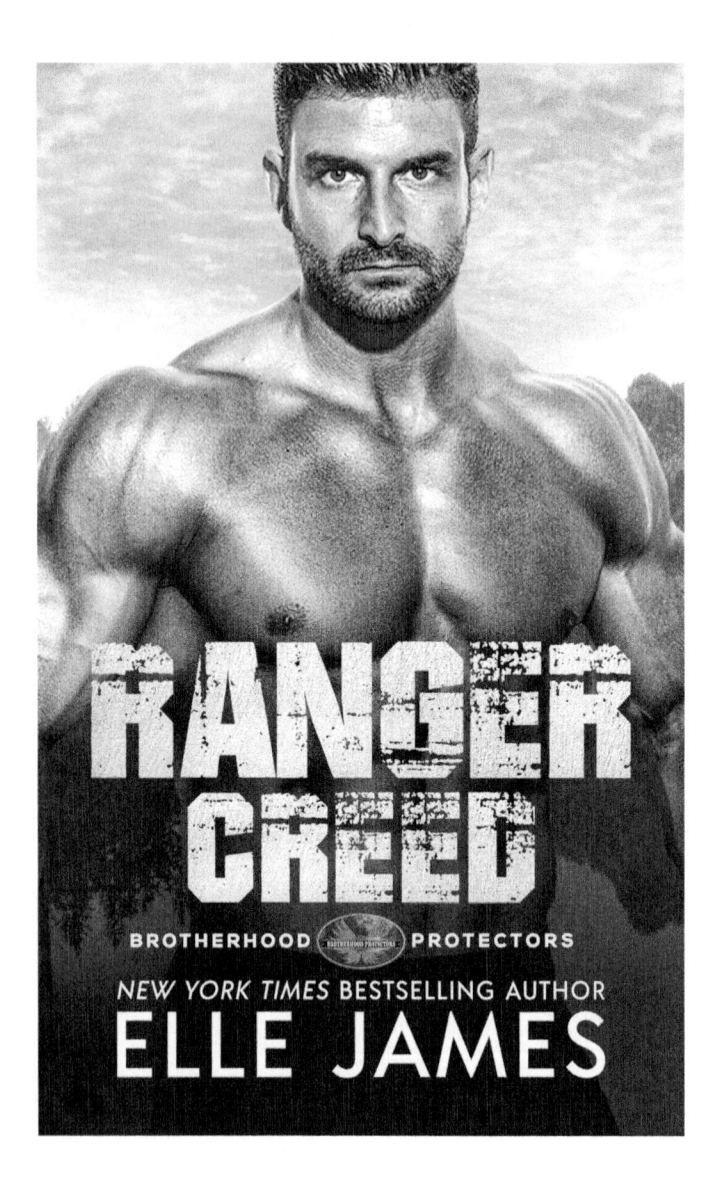

CHAPTER 1

"Running Bear, you copy?" Christina Samson, sitting at dispatch, asked.

Lani Running Bear keyed the mic on her radio. "I copy."

"We just received a call from Mattie Lightfoot. She needs you out at her place on Willow Creek ASAP."

Lani sighed. On her thirteenth hour of a twelve-hour shift, she was tired and ready to call it a night. Or, in this case, a morning. "Roger," she said, and turned her Blackfeet Law Enforcement Service vehicle around in the middle of the road and headed back the direction she'd come while on her way in for shift change.

Mattie Lightfoot lived in a mobile home next to Willow Creek with her grandson, Tyler. She'd raised Tyler since he was four years old, when his mother left the reservation to go make her fortune in Vegas. Her daughter, Stella Lightfoot, hadn't known who Tyler's father was. None of the men she'd slept with claimed him. Mattie's daughter had promised to send for Tyler when she'd made enough money to support them both.

Stella never sent for Tyler. She never came back to visit her son and, after a couple of years, she quit calling.

Mattie did what she could for Tyler. She worked at a convenience store in Browning, bringing in just enough money to pay utilities and groceries. Food stamps and food pantries had become a necessity. She made sure Tyler had food, even when she didn't.

A fiercely proud Blackfeet matriarch, Mattie was a respected member of the tribe. When she called for help, it was something very serious.

Lani could have refused the call and let the tribal police officer from the next shift take it. But, when she'd sworn in, she'd promised to respect and look out for members of her tribe, her family.

The drive to Mattie's place took fifteen minutes, traveling on a number of different gravel roads, until Lani finally turned onto the rutted path leading to Mattie's single-wide mobile home.

Several vehicles were parked in the yard next to Mattie's old red and white Ford pickup with the rusted wheel wells and bald tires.

Recognizing the new charcoal gray Denali, a full-sized SUV belonging to tribal elder Raymond Swiftwater, Lani tensed. In her opinion, Swiftwater was a pompous ass, full of his own self-importance. He liked to think he could make decisions for the entire tribe without consulting the other elders. And he bullied the others who were older and wiser than he was into agreeing with his way of thinking.

The man was accompanied by Stanley and Stewart Spotted Dog, his minions and the muscle he kept close for intimidation purposes. Stan and Stew had broad shoulders and thick necks and arms. They were effective visual deterrents, and strong enough to take down anyone who bothered their boss.

Swiftwater crossed his arms over his chest. "About time tribal police showed up."

Lani ignored the man and walked toward the trailer. "Where's Mattie?"

"Inside," Ray said. "It ain't good. Sure you have the stomach for it?"

Since she didn't know what *it* was, she couldn't say. Instead, she walked past Swiftwater, climbed the rickety stairs and knocked on the door. "Mattie, it's me, Lani Running Bear."

A woman's sob sounded from inside. "He's gone. My boy is gone."

Lani frowned, her chest constricting at the despair in the older woman's voice. "Mattie, may I come in?"

"Door's open," Mattie said, her voice muffled.

Lani entered through the narrow door into the dark interior of a mobile home that had seen more moons than Lani had been on this earth.

Mattie Lightfoot was on the floor beside the inert body of her grandson, Tyler. He lay on his back, his face smashed, his arms battered, his chest and belly slashed by what appeared to be multiple knife wounds.

Lani's chest tightened. She'd liked the kid. He'd been

going somewhere. Tyler had been committed to completing his degree and getting on with his life as soon as he could. But mostly, he'd been kind to everyone and never had anything bad to say about anyone, Native American or otherwise.

Mattie stroked Tyler's long, thick, black hair back from his forehead, tears streaming down her face as she rocked back and forth. "He's gone."

Lani didn't have to touch the base of his throat to know she'd find no pulse, but she did anyway. As she suspected, his skin was already cool to the touch, and no amount of searching would produce a pulse. "What happened, Mattie?" she asked softly.

Mattie closed her eyes and rocked. "I don't know. I don't know who could have done this to my Tyler."

Lani hated asking questions of the woman when she was deeply distressed. But she had to know as much as possible to help find who'd beaten the poor kid to death. "Did you find him here? Or did someone bring him here like this?"

"He was here when I came home from work," Mattie said. "I should have been here for him. Maybe none of this would have happened. If I'd been home, he wouldn't be dead."

"You don't know that. You could have been hurt as well."

"Rather me than him," Mattie said. "He had so much to live for."

Lani glanced around the interior of the single-wide mobile home. Though it was old, Mattie kept it clean. A mismatch of dishes was stacked neatly on a drainboard by the sink. Laundry lay neatly folded on the built-in couch. There was no blood pooling beneath Tyler's body, nor was there any broken glass or furniture in the vicinity of the body. The young man had been beaten and stabbed multiple times.

The crime hadn't been committed inside the trailer, which meant whoever had killed him had brought him there.

"Did you see anyone leaving your yard?"

Again, Mattie shook her head. "No one was here when I got home, and I didn't pass anyone on the road coming in." She stared at her grandson. "Who would have done this to Tyler? He was such a good boy."

"I'm sorry, Mattie. I don't know who did this, but I will find out. We'll find who did this to Tyler." She hoped she wasn't lying. Too often, crimes on the rez remained unsolved. "Mattie, the FBI will be involved in solving this crime. They have a lot of resources at their disposal that our own tribal police don't. They'll likely perform an autopsy and determine what weapons were used and what was the actual time of Tyler's death."

"Good. I want you to use whatever means possible to find Tyler's killer and bring him to justice."

Lani nodded. "When was the last time you saw Tyler...alive?"

Mattie's eyes filled with tears. "Yesterday afternoon. I had the night shift at the convenience store."

"Was he planning on going anywhere after dinner? Meeting anyone?"

She gave a hint of a smile. "He was going to see Natalie Preston, his girlfriend in Conrad. They had a date. He was going to take her out to the new diner for supper. He'd been working extra hours at the K Bar L Ranch so he could treat her to something special."

"Do you know if he made it to Natalie's?"

Mattie shook her head. "I had to work. I was looking forward to hearing all about their date." More tears slipped down the older woman's face.

Lani reached for Mattie's hand, squeezed it, and then pushed to her feet. "Did you call Raymond Swiftwater after you called the police?"

Mattie shook her head. "I didn't. He showed up a few minutes before you."

Lani's jaw tightened.

Swiftwater was known for showing up at reservation crime scenes.

"Could you make them leave?" Mattie asked, looking up at her.

Lani's lips pressed together in a thin line. "I'll do my best. In the meantime, I need to make some calls back at the station. I'll be back. Try not to disturb Tyler's body or any evidence. The FBI will want to look over everything very closely."

Mattie nodded and continued to stroke Tyler's hair, despite having been told not to disturb Tyler's body.

Lani left the trailer. As she descended the steps to the ground, Swiftwater approached her.

"So, what do you think?"

"I don't know what to think. A thorough investigation will have to be conducted."

"One of our people is dead," Swiftwater said. "What are you going to do about it?"

Lani squared her shoulders. "I'm going to do what I'm paid to do, and that is to investigate and find out who killed him. Now, if you'll excuse me, I need to get the FBI out here."

When she tried to go around Swiftwater, he stepped in her way, blocking her path. "Why must you call the FBI? This happened on the reservation."

"You know perfectly well the FBI has responsibility for investigating murders on the reservation." She lifted her chin. "You know we don't have the training or the resources to conduct a thorough investigation within Blackfeet Law Enforcement Service."

Swiftwater sneered. "Then what are you good for? Writing speeding tickets and giving rides home to drunks?"

"As you are also aware, we don't have the ability to perform autopsies. We need to know the cause of death and time of death."

"I can tell you how he died," Swiftwater said. "A white man crossed onto the reservation and killed Tyler Lightfoot."

Lani planted her fists on her hips. "And you know that how? Were you there? Did you see it happen? And if you were there and saw it happen, why didn't you do something to stop it, or at least call it in?"

Swiftwater's face turned a ruddy red beneath his naturally dark skin. "We don't need an autopsy to determine what happened. It's obvious. Tyler dared to date one of their own. White men don't like it when Blackfeet date their women. Check with his girlfriend's family. I bet you'll find the murderer there."

"We'll get the FBI involved to help us find the murderer."

Swiftwater shook his head. "We don't like the FBI crawling around the reservation."

She drew a deep breath, trying to hold onto her temper. "We don't have access to the resources available within the FBI. They have the resources and skills needed to solve this kind of crime."

Swiftwater's eyes narrowed. "And how often do they solve crimes on the reservation? I don't know why they can't leave it to our own people to solve the crimes."

Lani frowned. "You know we're always shorthanded. We barely have enough staff to man two shifts."

"I've offered my own men as contract labor to help with law enforcement efforts."

She wouldn't trust Swiftwater's men any more than she'd trust Swiftwater. She suspected they were all corrupt; she just didn't have the evidence to prove it. "They aren't certified police officers. They have no authority to enforce the laws."

Lani was tired of his harassment. She narrowed her eyes. "Do you know anything about Tyler's death?"

Swiftwater blinked. "No."

"Then how did you come to be here so quickly?" she asked.

The tribal elder lifted his chin. "As a tribal elder, I have access to the police scanner. As a man responsible for the welfare of his tribe, I like to know what's happening. I also like to know how fast our law enforcement officers respond in situations such as this."

Lani snorted and turned away.

"I will report to the tribal elders how long it took you to arrive on scene."

Not bothering to reply, Lani climbed into her service vehicle, requested assistance and asked dispatch to notify the FBI.

Lani returned to the trailer to wait with Mattie. While they waited, Lani used her cellphone to take pictures of the crime scene, Tyler's body and the many wounds that had been inflicted. She knew the FBI would conduct a thorough investigation but wasn't sure they would share the information with her.

Within the hour, many of Mattie's friends and tribe women arrived in support of Mattie. At the same time, the tribal elders arrived and formed a circle around Swiftwater.

Lani, with Mattie in tow, exited the mobile home, wanting to know what the elders were discussing, and needing the older woman out of the trailer when the women converged on her. They didn't need to contaminate the crime scene any more than Mattie already had.

She found out soon enough.

"Officer Running Bear," Chief Hunting Horse called out.

Lani stepped forward. "Yes, sir."

"As the FBI will be involved in this investigation, we want Police Chief Black Knife to be their contact. No others."

"That means you are officially off this case," Swiftwater said, stepping forward to stand beside Chief Hunting Horse.

At that moment, the chief of tribal police arrived.

Swiftwater nodded toward his vehicle. "Officer Running Bear, you can leave now."

Lani ignored Swiftwater and converged upon her head of law enforcement, Police Chief Black Knife. "Are you going to let the elders pull rank on you?"

Her boss frowned. "What are you talking about?"

"They just pulled me off this murder case."

He frowned. "What did they say?"

"That you will be the direct contact with the FBI investigation."

His frown deepened. "I'll find out what's going on." He left her standing by his vehicle and joined the tribal elders. A few minutes later, he returned, a scowl marring his forehead. "You're officially off the case."

"What? Why?" she asked.

Black Knife's face was set in stone. "There'll be no discussion. I'll see you back at the station."

When she opened her mouth to protest, he held up his hand. "No discussion."

Anger burned through her. She glanced toward the front of the mobile home where Mattie Lightfoot was being led away from the crime scene by Swiftwater.

Her gaze met Mattie's distraught one. The woman looked to her as if asking what was happening.

Lani started toward her.

A hand on her arm stopped her.

"You're off the case," Police Chief Black Knife reminded her.

"I just want to help Mattie."

"Go home. Your shift has ended." The stern look he gave her ended her arguments.

She wanted to go to Mattie and reassure her that she'd do everything in her power to find her grandson's killer, but she couldn't.

Maybe she couldn't do anything in an official capacity, but she could do something in an unofficial capacity, and she had an idea of who she could get to help her.

Lani took her service vehicle back to the station, climbed into her Jeep and headed to her cottage at the edge of the reservation. She hadn't gone five miles along the road home before a massive lump in the road forced her to slow to a complete stop.

She stared at the lump for a moment before her heart dropped to the pit of her belly. She pulled her service weapon out of her shoulder holster and stepped out of her vehicle, searching the roadside and ditches for any sign of movement. Nothing moved, including the lump in front of her.

She knew before she reached it what it was. The question wasn't so much what it was, but who.

Dressed in a gray hooded sweatshirt and sweatpants, the victim lay on one side, facing away from Lani. Her police training had her estimating height and weight. Based on how long the body was, it was either a man or a very tall woman.

As she rounded the body, she gasped. The man's face had been so badly beaten that she couldn't tell who it was. And just like Tyler, he'd been stabbed multiple times in the chest and abdomen.

Lani checked for a pulse. For a long moment, she rested her fingers on his battered neck, hoping she might find a pulse. When she finally gave up, she started to pull her hand away.

The man's body jerked, his hand came out and grabbed her wrist.

Shocked, Lani tried to pull away, but his grip was so strong, she couldn't break free.

The man's eyes opened, and he stared at her through quickly swelling eyes, his pupils dilated. "Hep ma," he groaned.

Lani forced herself to calm. The man was still alive, but for how long? "Who did this to you?"

The man made a sound like a hiss then collapsed back to the ground. His grip relaxed on her wrist, his hand falling to the ground.

Lani checked again for a pulse. Nothing. She searched his pockets for some form of identification but found none.

She hurried back to her SUV, pulled out her handheld radio and called dispatch. "Need an ambulance ASAP." She gave the location and information on the victim. Within minutes, the Blackfeet Emergency Medical Service arrived.

They were unable to revive the victim before loading him into the ambulance.

By that time, Police Chief Black Knife arrived, along with Swiftwater and his minions.

The chief listened to her account and made notes. When she'd finished, he tipped his head toward her SUV. "You can go now."

"Sir, with all due respect, I need to be there when the FBI does their investigation."

He shook his head. "You heard the elders. I'll be the only contact for this investigation. You're off duty. Go get some rest."

Lani snorted. "Two bodies in less than twenty-four hours. You think I'm going to rest? Do you even know who that man is?"

He nodded. "It was Ben Wolf Paw."

"Ben?" Lani's heart contracted. "Ben's one of the nicest guys on the reservation. Why?"

"I don't know, but we'll figure it out." He gripped her arm. "In the meantime, I need you to take a few days off."

She frowned. "Are you kidding me? Why?

"This has been a lot for you."

She frowned. What the hell was going on? Why were they freezing her out? "I've seen worse in Afghanistan. You can't put me on leave."

"I can, and I will." He gave her stern look. "Take the leave, or I'll have to fire you." He turned and left, not giving her an opportunity to argue.

Lani stood for a long moment after the ambulance left and everyone else cleared out. She stared at the place Ben had been lying on the road.

No blood. He'd been dumped after he'd been beaten and stabbed. Had he been murdered in the same location as Tyler, and then dumped here?

She didn't have the answers and, if the police chief had his way, she wouldn't get them.

Bullshit on that. She couldn't take a few days off and not do anything. Someone was killing good people on the reservation. And she intended to keep her promise to Mattie. These murders would not be left like so many on the reservation—unsolved. Not when she could do something about it.

As soon as she reached her cottage, she called an acquaintance she'd known from her days in the Army, Zachariah Jones. Though they'd butted heads while deployed at the same base in Afghanistan, they'd had enough in common to want to keep in touch.

Zach had just left the Army and come back to his home state of Montana. He'd taken a job with a man from Eagle Rock, Montana. A man who provided security services. What she needed now was someone who would have her back while she conducted her own investigation regarding what was happening on the reservation. She needed someone who could live with her on the reservation. Someone who was a member of the Blackfeet tribe.

Zach was her man.

CHAPTER 2

Zachariah Jones had been in Eagle Rock, Montana, for an entire week, familiarizing himself with the area, with his new position with the Brotherhood Protectors and with his boss, Hank Patterson, when he'd gotten the call from Lani Running Bear.

The woman had been, at first, a thorn in his side when he'd been at Bagram Air Base in Afghanistan. She'd been the MP who'd busted up the fight he'd gotten into with a Marine who'd tried to tell him that Army Rangers weren't nearly as effective as Navy SEALs.

Staff Sergeant Running Bear had taken him down and hauled his ass off to a temporary holding cell until his commanding officer came to collect him. Because his CO had been at a two-hour briefing, Zach had had enough time to get to know the hot MP who'd busted his ass.

Talk about a small world. He'd discovered she was from Montana, like him. And that she was Blackfeet, like him. Well, he was a watered-down version of Blackfeet, his grandmother having been one hundred percent Blackfeet. He'd been intrigued by her and impressed by her desire to return to Montana to help the people of her tribe.

When Zach had left Montana, he'd had no desire to return. However, after twelve years in the Army and too many deployments to count, he'd been ready to go home. He might not have been as eager to get back to Montana if he hadn't heard of the Brotherhood Protectors from one of his former teammates, Kujo, also known as Joseph Kuntz. He'd been with the Brotherhood for a couple years and spoke highly of his boss, former Navy SEAL Hank Patterson.

Having a job waiting for him after leaving the military had been a godsend. Too many of his compatriots who'd gotten out, thinking life was better as a civilian, had been gravely mistaken when they didn't find a place to fit in. The Brotherhood Protectors valued the skills they'd learned while fighting in the Middle East and other places around the world. They put those hard-earned skills to use protecting people who couldn't protect themselves.

But after a full week of getting used to being back in Montana, Zach was ready for an assignment, a purpose…some action.

When Lani's call had reached him, he'd been hesitant. He wanted to help her, but he had yet to prove himself to Hank and the Brotherhood.

He'd promised he'd help, but he had to clear it with his new boss first. Hank might have found an assignment for him, in which case, he'd have to assign one of the other men working for him to cover.

Zach drove out to Hank's place on the White Oak Ranch.

Sadie met him at the door, carrying their toddler, Emma, on her hip. "Zach, I'm glad you came. Hank's been talking about you."

Zach grimaced. "Has he found an assignment for me?"

She shook her head. "Not yet, but it won't be long. Seems the word has gotten out about the Brotherhood Protectors. Many of my fellow actors have asked for bodyguards. Once they have one of Hank's guys, they're hooked and spread the word. And, with so many people from California discovering the beauty of Montana, we have more and more opportunities to provide security here in the state."

"Zach," Hank's voice sounded from inside. "Come on in. Swede and I were working on something in the war room. Come on down."

"Yes, sir." Zach tipped his cowboy hat at Sadie and chucked Emma beneath her chin. "Good to see you, Mrs. Patterson."

"Oh, please, call me Sadie." She stepped aside to allow him to enter the house. "I'll bring coffee."

Zach shook hands with Hank and followed him into the basement headquarters of the Brotherhood Protectors.

"What brings you out?" Hank asked. "Not that you need a reason to come…"

"I had a call from an Army acquaintance I knew back

at Bagram Air Base," Zach started without preamble. "She needs help and wanted to know if I could come to her assistance."

Hank's brow puckered. "What's her situation? I like to know the right person with the right skillset is assigned to a job."

"She's working a murder investigation and needs someone to watch her back," Zach said.

Hank nodded. "And why does she think you're the right man for the job?"

"She knows I'm a prior Army Ranger," Zach said.

"So are Taz and Viper," Hank pointed out.

Zach smiled. "Is either one of them Blackfeet?"

"Blackfeet?"

"Lani Running Bear is a member of the Blackfeet Nation. To live on the reservation, you have to be Blackfeet."

Hank raised a brow. "And you are?"

Zach lifted one shoulder. "My grandmother on my father's side was one hundred percent. I'm in the Blackfeet registry as a quarter Blackfeet."

Hank grinned. "I guess that makes you the right man for the job."

Zach frowned. "Look, I'm pretty sure this isn't a paying job."

"She needs help, right?"

Zach nodded. "Sure sounded like it."

"Then it's a legit job." His brow furrowed. "You'll be on your own out there, but we're only a call and plane ride away should you need backup."

"Anyone need some coffee?" Sadie descended the

steps into the basement, carrying a tray of brimming coffee mugs.

Zach hurried over to take the tray from her. "I could use a cup."

"How are you going to arrive at the reservation?" Hank asked.

Setting the tray on the large conference table, Zach took one of the cups of coffee, frowning. "I could go, claiming my one quarter Blackfeet heritage."

"Won't you make them suspicious by showing up the day after a double murder?" Hank asked.

"You have a good point." Zach sipped the steaming cup of coffee. "Lani said they only allow Blackfeet to live on the reservation, and I'd need to be on the reservation to help keep her safe and find the killer."

"And how well do you know Lani?" Sadie asked, handing a cup of coffee to Swede.

"We met at Bagram Air Base in Afghanistan," Zach said. "We kept in touch because of our connection to the Blackfeet tribe."

"Is she married?" Sadie asked.

With a frown, Zach answered, "Not that I know of. She was single when we were deployed together."

"Then why don't you show up as her boyfriend." Sadie handed Hank a cup of coffee. "Or better yet, as her fiancé. That way, they would expect you to be with her and live in the same house."

"You think the tribal elders will buy that story?" Zach asked.

Sadie gave him a sassy smile. "Only if you make your engagement appear real."

"How do I do that?" Zach asked.

Sadie laughed. "You demonstrate your love, the reason the two of you are engaged," she said, her hand fisting on her hip.

Zach's brow twisted. "How do I do that?"

"Really, Zach?" Sadie shook her head. "You hold her hand in public. Kiss her sometimes, and put a ring on her finger. Do enough public displays of affection, and you'll have them fooled."

Zach frowned. "I don't know…"

"Do you have a better idea?" Hank asked, arching an eyebrow.

"No," Zach said, rubbing the back of his neck. He didn't know what Lani would think of that idea.

"I'll be right back." Sadie climbed the stairs and disappeared out of sight, reappearing a minute later. "What you need is a prop to help convince people you two are truly engaged." She held up what appeared to be a diamond ring.

Zach held up his hands. "I can't take your jewelry."

Sadie chuckled. "Oh, sweetie, this is a prop from one of my movie sets. It's not a real diamond."

Taking the ring, Zach stared down at the shiny solitaire. "It looks real," he whispered.

"It'll be as real as you make it seem, with a little acting to convince anyone who looks at it." Sadie smiled and handed the ring to Zach.

"Now, you have a reason to go to the reservation and stay there." Hank clapped him on the back. "Congratulations, man."

Still staring at the ring, Zach asked. "For what?"

"For taking on your new assignment," Hank said.

"And for your recent engagement," Sadie added.

"Lani doesn't know anything about this fake engagement. What if she doesn't go along with it?"

"Then you two will have to come up with another reason for you to be there two days after a murder," Hank said with a grin.

Sadie smiled and patted his arm. "Don't worry. If she called you, she needs the help and will be willing to go along with your ploy."

Zach slid the ring in his pocket.

"Now that you're armed with your undercover story, let's get you armed for hunting a murderer." Hank led the way into the room he called his armory. Inside, he had at least one of every kind of rifle, pistol and piece of electronics he might possibly need to run a covert or tactical operation.

Zach selected a nine millimeter pistol. "Anything more than this would be too easily seen." He slid a shoulder holster over his arms and tucked his gun inside.

Hank handed him a couple of magazines and two boxes of ammo.

"You really think I'll need that many bullets?" Zach asked.

"Trust me," Hank said. "If you don't need it to defend Lani and yourself from humans, you never know when you'll run across a pack of wolves or a bear. Consider this your first assignment."

Zach shrugged into his jacket and held out his hand to Hank. "Thank you, Hank. I'll do my best."

Hank gripped his hand and gave it a hard squeeze. "I don't envy you. The tribal police can be pretty cranky about anyone trespassing on their reservation and investigation. Whatever you do, don't let them know you're there to launch an investigation of your own into the murders."

"I should be able to convince them I'm with Lani. And we'll be able to move around on the reservation. Lani's been suspended from law enforcement for a couple of days. That should give us some time to get around and ask some questions."

Zach thanked the Pattersons, climbed into his truck and set off on the four-hour road trip to Browning, Montana, the headquarters of the Blackfeet Reservation.

As he passed through the small town of Eagle Rock, he tried to call Lani on his cellphone, but he didn't get an answer. Soon, he was out of town and in a dead zone of cellphone coverage. He'd have to fill her in when he reached her home. Hopefully, she'd go along with his cover.

His lips twitched. Seemed like a little turnabout was fair play—from Lani busting him in Afghanistan to needing his help in Montana. He liked being on the other end of this situation. Maybe he could prove to Hank, and to Lani, that he wasn't a screw-up. He had skills that would come in handy should anyone try to harm Lani.

. . .

Lani slept for six hours, knowing she'd need the rest in order to be her sharpest when she went out on her own to question some of the people who were closest to the victims.

By the time she awoke, the sun was on its downward trajectory toward the ridges of the Rocky Mountains less than a hundred miles away. Anxious to find out what had happened in the murder investigation, she called Black Knife.

"Black Knife," her boss answered.

"Chief, Running Bear here. What have you heard on the Lightfoot and Wolf Paw murders?" She held her breath, not knowing what kind of answer she'd get from the chief of police. Especially since he'd told her she was off the case.

"The FBI has transferred the bodies to the Glacier County Coroner for examination. That's all we have so far. Not that it's any of your concern." His tone was tight, his words clipped.

She wrinkled her nose. "I promised Mattie Lightfoot I'd do my best to find out who killed her grandson," Lani said.

"You shouldn't have promised anything," the chief said.

"Well, I did, and I'm not going to let her down."

"You're off until further notice. Don't let me or any of the tribal elders find you're asking about the murders."

"Are you telling me to stay out of it?"

"I'm saying…don't let me or anyone else find out

you're asking about the murders," Black Knife repeated, speaking slowly, as though to a dimwitted child.

"Yes, sir," she said and ended the call and stared at the phone.

That conversation was odd.

Had her boss given her roundabout permission to conduct her own investigation into the murders?

He hadn't said don't do it. He'd only said don't get caught.

She wondered what her boss really meant. However, whether he did or didn't want her snooping around, she was going to do it anyway. She'd made a promise to a friend, and Lani didn't break her promises.

She showered, blow-dried her hair and French braided it to get it out of her face. Since she wasn't working until further notice, she left her uniform hanging in the closet and pulled on a pair of jeans and a pale green, short-sleeved sweater that fit her to perfection. She was lacing up a pair of hiking boots when a knock sounded on the door to her cabin.

She rose from the chair she'd been sitting on, crossed to the entryway and pulled open the door.

Raymond Swiftwater stood in the doorway, flanked on either side by the Spotted Dog brothers.

"Ray," she said and dipped her head slightly. "What are you doing here?"

"The tribal elders are concerned you won't leave the murder investigations to the FBI and Police Chief Black Knife. I'm here to reiterate, you're not to work the case."

Lani crossed her arms over her chest. "I'm curious. Why are they so concerned about me?"

"The elders see you as a loose cannon. Ever since you returned from your stint in the Army, you've walked around like you own the place."

"I don't know what you're talking about. If you mean I'm a competent female law enforcement officer, then yes, I walk around with confidence. Does my self-assurance intimidate you or the other tribal elders?" She lifted her chin and met his gaze square on.

Swiftwater snorted. "Hardly. We think you're too full of yourself, and that you don't have any experience being a police officer on the rez."

"I was born and raised on this reservation. I spent ten years on active duty in the Army as a military police officer and survived six deployments." She squared her shoulders and met his gaze head-on. "I'd say I have the experience necessary to provide law enforcement to my people."

For a long moment, Swiftwater stared down his nose at her. "I only warn you to keep you from getting hurt."

Lani snorted. "Yeah. Well, thank you for your concern."

A truck pulled up beside Swiftwater's large SUV.

A man Lani barely recognized stepped out of the vehicle, his eyes narrowing at the men standing on Lani's porch.

It took Lani a full thirty seconds to place the man. As soon as he grinned, she knew. Her heart fluttered against her ribs, and heat climbed up her neck into her cheeks.

"If you're finished with your warning, I have better

things to do." She pulled the door closed behind her, stepped past Swiftwater and the Spotted Dog brothers and raced down the steps.

"Zach, I'm so glad you got here." She flung her arms around his neck and hugged him tight. "I didn't expect you for a few more days."

Zachariah Jones wrapped his arms around her waist and pulled her close. "I freed up sooner than I expected, and I thought I'd surprise you."

She pasted a smile on her face and leaned back in his arms. "I'm glad you did. It's been too long." He was going along with her ruse better than she'd expected. "Want to come inside?"

Zach set her at arm's length and shook his head. "Not until I say what I came here to say…"

Lani's brow dipped. "What is it, sweetheart?"

"I know it's kind of sudden, but I had a lot of time to think about it once I notified my CO I was leaving the military."

Lani wasn't sure what he was talking about, but she went along with it. "What have you been thinking about?"

"This." He stuck his hand in his pocket, pulled out a ring and dropped to one knee. "Lani Running Bear, you're the love of my life. Will you marry me?"

Lani stood in stunned silence. Of all things Zach could have said, *Will you marry me?* wasn't something Lani expected. "Uh…I don't know what to say."

He looked up at her and winked. "Just say yes."

She frowned. "Yes." The word came out more of a question than a commitment.

Zach stood, gathered her in his arms and kissed her soundly on the lips.

Lani didn't even try to stop him. She was too stunned to think.

Zach ended the kiss, pressed his lips to her ear and whispered, "Go along with it. It's my cover." He leaned back and grinned. "You don't know how happy you've just made me."

"Not as happy as I am," she said, falling into the ruse, even if her words were a little stiff.

Zach slipped the ring on her finger and smiled. "It fits."

"How did you know what size I wear?" she asked, staring down at the fat stone, twinkling up at her.

"I got it from your roommate in Afghanistan," he said.

"Tessa? You were thinking about this all along?" She shook her head and smiled up at him.

He chuckled. "Were you surprised?"

"I didn't think you even liked me," she said, thankful the statement was the truth.

"I didn't…at first." He lifted her hand and pressed a kiss to her ring finger. "No man likes it when a woman takes him down and hauls him off to confinement. But you grew on me, as I hoped I grew on you."

"Yes!" She flung her arms around his neck again, putting on a show for Swiftwater. Later, she'd tell him how brilliant his cover story was. Right now, she had to convince the elder of its truth. When she settled back on her feet, she turned with a smile toward Raymond Swiftwater and the Spotted Dog brothers. "Elder Swiftwater, this is Zachariah Jones, my...fiancé." She hooked her hand through his arm and drew Zach toward Swiftwater.

Swiftwater's eyes narrowed. "You do realize you have to be Blackfeet to live on the reservation."

Lani grinned and hugged Zach's arm. "That was one of the reasons we hit it off so well when we were deployed. When I told him I was Blackfeet, he let me know his grandmother was one-hundred percent Blackfeet. It was such a cool coincidence to meet one of my people in such a faraway land."

His eyes narrowing even more, Swiftwater harrumphed. "I'll have to check into that." He lifted his chin. "Your grandmother's name?"

Zach raised an eyebrow in challenge. "Margaret Red Hawk. She's in the registry, as am I. My mother was sure to add me as soon as I was born."

Swiftwater snorted. "Only a quarter Blackfeet."

"But he satisfies the quantum test. A quarter meets the requirement, allowing Zach to live on the rez," Lani said. She let her hand slide down Zach's arm to his hand. Gripping it firmly, she smiled up at him like she thought a newly engaged woman should. "Come on, I'll show you our home."

Lani walked past Swiftwater, up the stairs and into the house.

Once inside, she started to let go of his hand.

Zach held tight and led her toward the front picture window. "He's still standing there. We need to give him one more reason to believe." He positioned them in front of the window and pulled her into his arms. "Make it count."

She leaned up on her toes and pressed her lips to his.

He snorted. "That wasn't very convincing."

She stared up into his eyes and cocked an eyebrow. "You can do better?"

Zach wrapped one arm around her middle and pressed her body to his. With his free hand, he cupped the back of her head and claimed her mouth in a kiss that left her knees weak and her heart pounding against her ribs so hard she was certain he could feel it against his chest. Not to mention the flood of heat coiling low in her belly. Holy hell.

When he finally let her breathe again, she didn't want his mouth to leave hers.

"That ought to do it," he said, and smiled down at her.

Stunned and a little dizzy, Lani leaned back against the arm around her waist and looked around him to the front yard where Swiftwater still stood, staring at the house.

She waved at the man and grinned broadly.

The elder turned, marched to his Denali and climbed into the back, while the Spotted Dog brothers took the front two seats.

Lani waited until they had driven out of sight before she stepped out of Zach's arms and smoothed her hair out of her face. That kiss had thrown her off balance, more than she'd like to admit. Especially to the man she'd hauled off to confinement during her deployment. Still… "You don't know how glad I am to see you."

"Just so you know, my boss made you my first assignment." He pulled her into his arms and hugged her like a long-lost friend. "But don't worry, I was coming anyway. How could I ignore a call from my favorite MP?" He winked. "I'm almost certain you saved me from an ass-whipping with that Marine."

"I doubt that. You were on top of him." She fought the urge to touch her throbbing lips with her fingertips. When he let go of her, she ran her gaze over him. "You've lost weight."

"My last deployment was tough on me. I got really tired of MREs."

"So, you quit eating?" Lani shook her head. "I guess the least I can do is feed you while you're here. But that'll have to be later." She glanced again out the window. "Now that Swiftwater is gone, I'd like to go talk to a few people. Are you ready to jump in with both feet?"

"I'm ready," he said. "You can fill me in on the way."

They exited the little house together.

When Lani started toward her SUV, Zach snagged her arm and turned her toward his vehicle. "Let's take mine. Not everyone knows it yet."

She nodded. "Good point," she said, and climbed up into the truck and fastened her seat belt.

Zach slid in behind the steering wheel and backed out of the driveway. "Where to?"

"Conrad," Lani said. On the way to Conrad, she filled him in on Tyler Lightfoot and Ben Wolf Paw's murders. "We're going to Conrad to talk to Tyler's girlfriend."

And in the meantime, Lani would try her darnedest to forget that kiss. It had all been for show.

On Zach's part, at least.

Lani had felt something she'd never felt before—a spark, a flame…hell…*an inferno*—when Zach had kissed her so thoroughly.

That's what she got for going so long without dating. She really needed to get out more often. And she would…after she caught the murderer.

CHAPTER 3

Zach listened to Lani's detailed description of the deaths of Lightfoot and Wolf Paw and cringed at the horror and pain they'd experienced. He chose to focus on the investigation, rather than the kiss that had started as part of his cover and ended as so much more.

Yeah, he'd been attracted to the black-haired, sexy MP when she'd taken him down and held him until his CO could claim him. He remembered her light, curvy body pressed against his as she'd nailed him to the ground in a pretty impressive move. Not only was she built the right way, she was strong and athletic, something he admired in a woman. He figured, if she was asking for help, she had bigger problems than wrestling with a couple of testosterone-heavy guys.

"What exactly do you want me to do?" he asked, when she'd finished outlining the situation.

"I'm going to be poking my head into an investigation where I've been told to butt out. I need you to watch my back. Someone has violently murdered two people already. When I start asking around about who could have done it, I don't want someone sneaking up on me. You're to be the eyes in the back of my head, as well as a second set of eyes on the evidence."

Zach nodded. "Okay, but I'm not an MP. I don't know how investigations go."

"No, but you're trained in combat. You might need that training if something goes wrong. And who else can I trust, if I can't trust an Army Ranger?" She gave him a lopsided grin.

"I've got your six," he said, feeling the weight of responsibility and accepting it. He was in an entirely different environment from his deployments in Iraq, Afghanistan, Syria and other places all over the world. Use of deadly force was something he had to keep to a minimum. Civilians didn't like it when people came through their hometowns guns ablazin'.

When they pulled up to the address she'd given him, Lani glanced over at him. "We need to keep up our cover. We're just here to express our condolences to Natalie, and I'll ask a few questions."

Zach nodded. "You're the cop. Take the lead."

She didn't wait for him to round the truck but got out and met him at the front fender.

Zach took her hand in his and gave her a hint of a smile as they walked toward the door of a white clapboard house with royal blue shutters.

Lani drew in a deep breath and knocked on the door.

A few moments later, the door opened, and an older man appeared, frowning.

"Mr. Preston?"

"Yeah." His eyes narrowed. "If you're here to talk to Natalie, she's not here."

"I'm sorry to hear that," Lani said. "We're friends of Tyler's family and only wanted to come to express our condolences. Could you please let her know Lani Running Bear, the officer who was first on scene, stopped by?"

Zach saw movement behind the man he assumed was Natalie's father. From the brief glimpse he caught, it appeared to be a young woman with blond hair. He squeezed Lani's hand.

She squeezed back and gave a nod to the man. "Thank you, Mr. Preston."

Zach turned with Lani and headed back to the truck. Once inside, he turned to Lani. "I saw someone behind Mr. Preston."

Lani nodded. "It was Natalie. Go slowly around the corner."

Zach shifted into drive and inched around the corner. Even as slow as he was going, he had to slam on his brakes when a young woman ran out in front of him. It was the blonde he'd seen behind Mr. Preston.

Lani opened her door and started to get out. "Natalie?"

The woman ducked low and ran around to the passenger side of the truck. "Let me in," she said.

Zach popped the locks.

Natalie yanked open the back door and slid onto the seat, keeping her head down. "Go, go, go!" she urged.

"Before I do, are you eighteen?" Zach asked.

"Yes. I turned eighteen last month." Natalie sobbed. "Tyler took me out to my favorite restaurant for my birthday." Her words came out garbled as she fought and lost against the tears.

Zach pressed his foot to the accelerator and sped away from the Prestons' home.

When they'd gone a couple of blocks, he noticed a city park and pulled into an empty parking space.

As soon as Zach stopped the truck, Lani climbed out of the passenger seat and into the back with Natalie.

The young woman fell against her and buried her face in Lani's shirt.

Lani held her for a long time, stroking her hair and saying soothing words in the Blackfeet language.

When Natalie had spent her tears, she raised her head.

Zach handed her a napkin from his console.

She blew her nose and finally met Lani's eyes. "What happened? Why did Tyler die?"

"First of all, who told you he died?" Lani asked.

She drew in a shaky breath. "I had a visit from Police Chief Black Knife and an agent from the FBI. They said Tyler was…dead." She stopped, the tears flowing again.

Zach passed her another napkin.

Natalie wiped at the tears and blew her nose again. "I can't believe he's gone. I loved him so much. We were going to get married when he finished his schooling. We were going to move to Bozeman, away from the reservation, and have a lovely home and a couple of kids. All I had to do was wait." She stared at Zach. "Now, I have nothing."

"I'm so sorry," Lani said and continued to hold the woman in her arms, letting her cry until the sobs slowed to a stop.

"How...how did Tyler die?" Natalie asked.

Lani looked over her shoulder at Zach.

He held her gaze until Lani set Natalie at arms' length and looked her square in the eye. "Are you sure you want to know?"

Natalie nodded, tears trembling on her lashes.

Lani inhaled and let it out. "He was beaten and stabbed multiple times. Then he was left inside his grandmother's trailer."

The young woman pressed her hands to her mouth, fresh streams of tears flowing down her face. "Why?" she wailed.

Lani shook her head. "I don't know. But I promised Mattie I would find the killer. I'll need your help."

Her brow wrinkled. "Isn't that what Police Chief Black Knife and the FBI are going to do? Do you work for the reservation law enforcement, too?"

"They pulled me off the case. I'm not supposed to be working right now." Lani squeezed Natalie's hands. "I made a promise to Mattie. I won't let her down. I won't let Tyler's death go unpunished."

"Who would do that to him?" Natalie whispered. "Tyler never hurt anyone."

"Natalie," Lani held the woman's hands in hers. "I need you to tell me everything you know down to the smallest detail that might have anything to do with you and Tyler."

"I told the chief and agent everything I knew." She

shrugged. "What more could I say? What does it matter? It won't bring him back."

"Please, be patient if I repeat questions," Lani said. "Had Tyler had an argument with anyone recently?"

The young woman shook her head. "No. Everyone who knew him loved him. He was always so kind to everyone, even when they weren't kind to him."

"Were there people who were unkind to Tyler?" Lani asked.

Natalie's brow furrowed. "A couple months ago, some of the guys from my high school ganged up on him when we were at the Orpheum Theater. They didn't like the idea that he was from the reservation and dating a white girl." Natalie's lips thinned. "I told them to get lost and that I'd date Tyler before I dated any of them."

"Who were they? Can you give me their names?"

She nodded. "Russell Bledsoe, Dalton Miller and Brent Sullivan. But that was months ago. They haven't bothered us since I graduated from high school in June."

Lani pulled a pad and pen from her shirt pocket and jotted down the names. "You were with Tyler last night?"

Zach watched as Lani continued her questioning, calm and empathetic. If he were Natalie, he'd have spilled every detail to the capable and caring cop. She was as competent now as she'd been on the base at Bagram.

Natalie nodded. "He brought me home about ten o'clock." She dipped her head. "My father insists on a curfew, even though I'm old enough to make my own decisions. And since I still live with my parents, I have to live by their rules. Tyler walked me to the door and…everything."

"How did your father feel about Tyler? Did he have issue with him being Blackfeet?" Lani asked.

"At first. But, like I said, anyone who knew Tyler… really knew him, loved him. Even my father." She gave a crooked grin that turned downward with more tears. "My father helped him apply for college. He wanted any man who married his daughter to be able to support her."

"Did they have any harsh words or arguments that you know of?"

Natalie shook her head. "No."

"Did you visit the reservation often?" Lani asked. "Do you know who his friends are, where he likes to hang out?"

Natalie gave her a watery smile. "He took me to some of the events on the reservation. He was so very proud of his heritage. We went horseback riding with some of his friends and had picnics. Tyler was always careful to take good care of me. He wanted me to be happy."

Lani sat silently, waiting for Natalie to give her details.

Zach admired her unflappability. He doubted he could be so patient.

Natalie closed her eyes. "His best friend is Jonathon Spotted Eagle. His other friends are Ashley Morning Star and Jesse Davis."

"Where were his favorite places to hang out?" Lani asked, her voice low, persistent, but gentle.

"He liked to go to Jonathon's place. Jonathon's mother works late at a bar in Browning. He'd go there after dropping me off. He and Jonathon either watched television or played video games late into the night. He'd text me when he'd head home to his grandmother's place."

"Tyler was attending college, wasn't he?" Lani asked.

"Yes, ma'am. He was going to the community college in Browning. He was awarded a scholarship to attend based on his grades in high school. He was going to do two years close to home, and then transfer to Montana State in Missoula to finish out his degree. He had everything going for him. He was studying to be an engineer. I was going to start at Montana State this fall. He was going to join me in a year." Her voice caught on a sob. "He was so smart and had everything going for him." She buried her face in her hands and cried.

Lani gave her a moment before she asked, "Was Tyler out of school for the summer?"

Natalie scrubbed the tears from her face and sat up. "Yes. He worked during the summer to have money for the fall and spring semesters, so that he could concentrate on his studies."

"Where did he work?" Lani asked.

"At a ranch near Cut Bank…the K Bar L Ranch. It's a pretty large ranch, over a hundred thousand acres. The owner is also the owner of some sports teams." Natalie's brow dipped. "The ranch foreman he worked for is Patrick Clemons."

"Did he do any other odd jobs in or around Browning?" Lani asked.

"On weekends, he helped clean Mick's Bar," Natalie said. "He was supposed to work there this morning. When he didn't text me, as usual, I called Mick's to see if he'd left his phone at home. He never made it there."

Zach glanced at the clock on his dash. They'd been sitting there for over twenty minutes. "Natalie, will your father be worried about you?"

Natalie looked up. "How long have I been with you?"

"About twenty minutes," Zach said.

"Oh, dear." She started to get out of the truck. "I need to go home. Daddy will be beside himself."

Lani laid a hand on her arm. "We'll get you close faster than you can walk."

The younger woman nodded.

Zach pulled out of the parking lot and turned back the direction they'd come.

Lani's voice continued in the back seat. "Natalie, if you can think of anything else. Anyone Tyler might have had contact with last night, an argument he might have had, anything, call me."

In the rearview mirror, Zach saw her hand Natalie a business card.

"The number on the back is my cellphone number. I don't care what time of day or night you call," Lani added.

Natalie clutched the card in her hand. "Thank you for caring about Tyler. I hope you find who did this."

By then, Zach was one block away from the white clapboard house with the blue shutters.

"Stop here," Natalie said.

Zach pulled to the curb and waited as Natalie climbed down from the truck.

"Be careful," Lani said. "We don't know who did this, or who he'll go after next."

"Don't worry. My father won't let me out of his sight for long." Natalie hurried back to her house and entered through the back door.

Zach waited until she was inside, and the door was closed.

Lani slipped out of the back seat and climbed up into the passenger seat.

"Where to?" Zach asked. "Want to interview the boys from the theater?"

Lani shook her head. "Not yet." She hit some keys on her cellphone. "Christina, Lani Running Bear here. I need a favor. I need Ben Wolf Paw's next of kin's address. Then I need you to look up addresses for the following people in Conrad, Montana—Russell Bledsoe, Dalton Miller and Brent Sullivan. Yeah, I'm not supposed to be involved in the investigation, but I'm off for a couple of days and need something to keep me occupied. If you could keep this between you and me, I'd appreciate it."

Zach listened as Lani did what she did best.

He was impressed and inspired by her dedication and determination to find who had killed Tyler and Ben. What she was doing was gathering the pieces of a puzzle. Zach was already caught up in the investigation and was just as eager now to get to the bottom of the murders.

. . .

ONCE LANI HAD the address for Ben Wolf Paw's next of kin, she gave Zach the information and sat back, thinking through everything Natalie had said.

"What I'm not seeing yet is the connection between Tyler Lightfoot and Ben Wolf Paw. They didn't run in the same circles. Ben was at least fifteen years older than Tyler. But whoever killed Tyler also killed Ben. The murders were too similar to be a coincidence. And they were dumped, rather than being left where they were murdered."

"Did they find the victims' vehicles?" Zach asked.

"I don't know." She dialed Christina again, kicking herself for not thinking about the victims' vehicles.

Her friend answered on the first ring. "Lani, you're going to get me into trouble," she whispered.

"Are Police Chief Black Knife and the FBI agent in the office right now?" Lani asked.

"Yes," Christine said, her voice cryptic.

"Can you tell me if they found the victims' vehicles?" Lani asked.

"Yes."

"Thanks. That's all I need for now." Lani ended the call.

"You didn't ask where they found them," Zach said.

"She couldn't talk. The police chief and FBI agent were in the office. Besides, I know who to ask." Lani pointed to the next road ahead. Before we leave Cut Bank, we'll go there first, then to Ben's family."

Zach followed her directions to the Glacier County impound lot where the vehicles had been delivered.

When they arrived, Lani climbed down out of Zach's truck and headed for the office at the center of the lot.

Zach followed, giving her a feeling of reassurance. Not that she felt any sense of danger at the impound lot. It was nice that she didn't have to ask him to follow her. He did it on his own.

"Pete?" she called out as she neared the office door.

An older, grizzled man emerged from the building. "Officer Running Bear, what brings you to my lot?"

"Good to see you, Pete. How's your wife?" Lani held out her hand.

Pete took it and gave it a firm shake. "She's getting over a cold. Otherwise, we're doing okay. The kids are coming up from Bozeman this weekend."

"I know that will make Betty happy to see them." Lani dropped his hand and turned to Zach. "This is my fiancé, Zach Jones."

Pete shook Zach's hand. "Congratulations."

Zach nodded. "Thanks."

Lani asked, "Did you get a couple of vehicles in from the rez today?"

Pete frowned. "I did." He nodded toward a corner of the lot where an older model, blue Ford truck sat. Lani recognized the vehicle as Tyler's. Beside it was a black SUV.

"Mind if we take a look?" Lani asked.

Pete shrugged and started toward the vehicles. "Your boss and an FBI agent were here an hour ago to look them over. I wouldn't actually touch them until they've had a chance to dust for prints and whatever else they do."

"We won't touch. We just want to look." Lani followed Pete. "Who brought them in?"

"Whitegrass Towing. Dan and Isaac brought them in a few hours ago." Pete shook his head. "Sad to hear about the two murders on the reservation. I don't suppose you know who did it...?"

Lani shook her head. "Not yet. We're working on it."

Pete frowned. "Why aren't you working with the Chief of Police and the FBI agent?"

"I'm not officially on the case," Lani said. She touched Pete's arm. "I'd appreciate it if you didn't mention my visit to anyone."

Pete's eyes narrowed. "You asking me to lie?"

Lani shook her head. "No. But if no one asks..."

The old man's lips twitched. "Gotcha."

Her jaw tightening, Lani said, "I promised Mattie Lightfoot I'd find her grandson's killer."

"I'm glad there are good cops out there," Pete said. "The media gives them a bad name. Thank you for being one of the good guys."

Lani circled Tyler's old truck, careful not to touch it. The crime scene experts would dust for fingerprints and search for any other evidence they might find.

From all outward appearances, Tyler's vehicle appeared normal. Lani couldn't see any blood on the outside or inside through the windows. As violent as the murders had been, if the victim had been in or near his vehicle, there would have been some blood spatter.

Unless the murderer cleaned the vehicle after performing his heinous crime.

After she'd looked over Tyler's truck, she moved to Ben's SUV. An older model vehicle. It had more trash inside it, including old food wrappers, empty soda cans and junk mail. Again, just by looking through the window, Lani couldn't see any blood or signs of struggle. The trash appeared to be scattered, but not like it would have been had the driver been attacked inside the SUV.

"See anything that helps?" Pete asked.

Lani shook her head. "No."

Pete nodded. "That's pretty much what the chief and FBI agent said."

"Thanks for letting me take a look." Lani held out her hand to the older man. "Say hello to your wife. I hope she feels better."

"Will do," Pete said. "And you be careful out on the reservation. Hate to think there's a killer loose."

Lani followed Zach to his truck and climbed in, unease tugging at her belly. She waited until he'd pulled onto the highway until she spoke. "Did you notice anything about those two vehicles?"

Zach shrugged. "I didn't see anything out of the ordinary. Did you see anything I missed?"

Lani shook her head. "No. That's just it. If they were driving when they came across the murderer, they stopped the vehicle and got out before the confrontation occurred."

"It would help to know where their vehicles were found," Zach said.

"Right. If they were found on a deserted road versus at a convenience store, it will tell us a little more about the murderer."

"Like?" Zach prompted.

"If they were found on a deserted road, the victims could have stopped to help someone supposedly stranded. It's quite possible they knew the person who murdered them, especially if the vehicles were found on the rez."

"What do the two victims have in common? Why were they targeted?"

Lani frowned. "Other than they are both from the reservation, I don't know. They don't have the same friends or work at the same location."

"There has to be a connection."

"Agreed. But so far, I don't have one in mind," Lani said.

Zach pulled out onto the road. "Where to next?"

"Whitegrass Towing. We need to know where those vehicles were found." She gave him the directions to the towing company located in Browning.

To fill the silence and because she was curious, Lani, asked, "So, what's your story? Why did you get out of the military? I would have thought you'd stay until you at least hit twenty." She looked across the console at him. "Were you medically retired? Or had you had enough?"

Zach gave her crooked smile. "I'd had enough deployments. I guess when you busted me in Bagram, you reminded me of home." He snorted softly. "Up to that point, I'd never thought I'd come back to Montana."

Her lips twitched on the corners. She'd felt much the same. Joining the military had gotten her out of Montana. Once out, all she could think about was going back and helping fix some of the things that were broken on the rez. Too many of her people were on a slow path to nowhere. The military had shown her that she had choices in life. Every person was the master of his or her own destiny. She didn't have to wait for life to happen. She could make the changes necessary to be healthy and happy. It was all about attitude and the right choices. Lani hoped she could instill some of her positivity into the local youth and help them find a path that led them to success.

As part of her determination to help, she'd signed on with the Blackfeet Law Enforcement Services and volunteered at the local high school to help the teenagers with career planning. In some cases, she'd been helping them study for college placement exams and applying for universities. Her parents hadn't known how to help her along those lines, never having been to college themselves. Lani's platoon sergeant had used his down-time to take online college courses. He'd encouraged all the members of his platoon to do the same. He'd taken Lani under his wing and helped her fill out the necessary forms to enroll and request her high school transcripts.

He'd helped get her started taking college courses while she was on active duty. Using the GI bill, she planned on finishing her undergraduate degree. Then she'd either teach or join the Montana State Police. She had options. The reservation children needed to know they had options as well.

"What about you?" Zach asked. "Why did you come back?"

Lani shrugged and stared out the window. "I missed Montana. Don't get me wrong. The Army was good for me. It got me off the reservation and taught me there was more to life than the rampant unemployment you find on the rez."

Zach's brow twisted. "And you came back anyway?"

She gave him a crooked grin. "Yeah. I wanted to do what I could to help others who might be feeling hopeless."

Zach chuckled. "Another do-gooder?"

Lani frowned. "Another?"

"Your victim, Tyler. From what you said about him, he was good to others." Zach's smile faded.

Lani frowned. "Tyler was a good young man. Always doing things for his grandmother and anyone else who needed help." Was that the connection? Was the murderer targeting nice people? Lani shook her head. At that moment, they arrived at the outskirts of Browning.

"Turn at the first street to your right," Lani directed. She hoped the location where the vehicles were found would give her a clue.

CHAPTER 4

Zach turned at the first street in Browning and parked in front of a building with a tow truck out front. The lettering on the tow truck read Whitegrass Towing.

Lani hopped down out of Zach's truck.

He joined her in front. Together, they walked into the building.

Inside, the air smelled of old oil, grease, rubber and cigarettes.

A dark-haired man sat in a dilapidated swivel chair, his booted feet propped on the counter in front of him. He blew a stream of smoke into the air and stared over the tops of his boots at Zach then Lani. "Running Bear, who's your friend?"

Lani tipped her head toward Zach and gave the man an easy smile. "Isaac Whitegrass, this is Zach Jones... my...fiancé." She slipped her arm through Zach's and turned her smile up at him. "I just got engaged."

Isaac's feet slipped off the counter and dropped with

bang on the floor. He pushed to his feet and held out his hand. "Nice to meet you." He nodded toward Lani. "You got a good one there. Her heart's in the right place. Not sure I would ever cross her though. I hear she can throw down a man twice her size in the blink of an eye."

Zach nodded. "I've been the recipient of just such a throw." He chuckled. "I completely underestimated her."

Isaac grinned. "I bet that was a mistake."

"Not at all. You could say that she swept me off my feet. I fell in love at first body slam." He slipped his arm around Lani and pulled her close. "Isn't that right?"

Lani pinned a smile on her face that was as fake as a wooden nickel. "Yes, that's right."

Isaac glanced from Lani to Zach and back to Lani. "You here about the two vehicles we towed to Cut Bank earlier today?"

Lani nodded. "We are. Would you mind telling us where you found them?"

Isaac scratched his dark head. "Got the same question from your boss and the FBI agent earlier."

Lani's smile relaxed. "I figured as much. I also figured it doesn't hurt to have more than a couple sets of eyes on a case in case someone misses something important."

"True." Isaac nodded. "I was sick over Tyler and Ben's deaths. They were some of the good guys."

Lani's lips twisted. "I promised Tyler's grandmother that I'd do my best to find his killer."

Isaac studied her for a long moment, before opening his mouth again. "Rusty Fenton called in an abandoned vehicle at the turn-off to Kipps Lake. Dan and I had been listening to the police scanner at the moment when Tyler's grandmother called in about Tyler. When Rusty notified us of the abandoned vehicle, we thought nothing of it...until we realized it was Tyler's old truck."

Another man, who looked remarkably like Isaac appeared in the doorway at the back of the shop, rubbing his greasy hands on a shop rag. "Who wants to know about Tyler's truck?" Dan Whitegrass asked. He frowned at Zach. Then his gaze went to Lani, and his frown deepened. "Who've you got with you?"

"Lani's got herself a man," Isaac said with a grin.

"He ain't Blackfeet," Dan said, his tone low.

"Actually, he's a quarter," Lani said.

Isaac and Dan both turned to Zach, eyebrows raised.

Zach squared his shoulders and lifted his chin, meeting their challenge. "My grandmother was one hundred percent," Zach said. "You can look her up. Margaret Red Hawk."

"I will," Dan said, but his frown lessened. "This is the second round of law enforcement personnel sniffing around, asking about Tyler and Ben's vehicles. You and the chief aren't working together on this case?"

Lani glanced away. "I wasn't assigned to it, but I promised Tyler's grandmother I'd make sure I found his killer."

Dan and Isaac nodded as one.

"I didn't like the FBI guy, anyway," Dan said. "Not Blackfeet."

"Yeah, but you know it's standard procedure for the

FBI to help with murder investigations," Lani said. "I just want to be a second pair of eyes and fulfill my promise to Mattie."

"What do you need to know?" Dan asked.

"Where you found the two vehicles," Lani said.

Isaac answered. "I picked up Tyler's out by the turn-off to Kipps Lake."

"And I collected Ben's after the FBI agent and the police chief called us to a street a couple blocks away from the elementary school."

"Thanks," Lani said. "That's all I needed to know for now."

Zach slipped an arm around Lani's waist. "Ready to go?"

She leaned into him and smiled up into his eyes. "I am."

He liked the way she felt against him.

She turned her smile toward Isaac and Dan. "Thank you."

"We hope you find who did it. Tyler and Ben were good people," Dan said.

"And we have more faith in you than in the FBI," Isaac said. "They have yet to find Angel."

Zach turned her toward the door and walked with her out into the sunshine. "Who is Angel?"

"A missing teenaged girl. The last time she was seen or heard from was four months ago. She was on her cellphone talking to her boyfriend when she was cut off. No one has seen her since. The FBI were called in via the Bureau of Indian Affairs, but they weren't able to locate the girl. There are far too many missing or exploited women from the reservation."

"You think these cases are related?"

"No. Angel's body was never found. This murderer *wanted* Tyler and Ben to be found." Lani shook her head. "It doesn't make sense. Especially Tyler's murder. Why would he have been out by the lake so late at night? And there was no blood or sign of struggle inside or outside his vehicle."

"Unless he picked up his murderer and drove out to the lake with him in the vehicle," Zach suggested. "Then, when they reached the remote location, his attacker got him out of the vehicle before he stabbed him."

"In that case, Tyler had to have known the man," Lani said.

"And it had to be a man," Zach said, "to lift, drag or carry another full-grown man and shove him into a truck or the back seat of a vehicle to deposit him elsewhere."

"And he had to have staged his car at the lake." Lani's eyes narrowed. "We need to find the vehicle he used to stash the bodies as he moved them from the murder location to their final resting places."

Zach's eyes narrowed. "How many people live on the reservation?"

"A little over ten thousand."

His brow puckering, Zach shook his head. "That's a lot of vehicles to investigate."

"It all goes back to what Ben and Tyler had in common." Lani stared out the window. "Or were they just in the wrong place at the wrong time? Damn, it can't be that random."

Zach stopped before pulling out onto the road. "Where to?"

"We need to talk to Ben's brother." She gave him directions to Ben's house. "Ben lived with his older brother, Mark. Mark wasn't the best role model. He's been in and out of jail for possession of drugs and public intoxication. Ben bailed him out whenever he had the money to help. Mark was his only family."

"Where are their parents?"

"Long since passed," Lani said.

As he drove through Browning, Zach shot a glance toward Lani. "You like police work?"

She nodded. "I don't do it to be a pain, like a lot of people think about law enforcement personnel." Her lips twisted into a grimace. "I do it because I hope I can make a difference."

Zach chuckled. "Like saving two dumbasses from breaking each other's bones?"

She frowned. "Yeah. I didn't haul you in because I was on a power kick." Her lips quirked upward on the corners. "Although, I did get a kick out of taking you down."

"I let you."

She snorted. "Believe what you want. As far as your buddies are concerned, a woman got the better of you."

Zach lifted one shoulder and let it fall. "Yeah, I have to admit, my ego was bruised that day, along with my backside. My teammates gave me hell later, after the CO chewed me out." But he'd admired her strength and ability. He'd found it extremely sexy, not that he'd tell her and suffer another takedown.

He looked her way again.

Hell, he might just tell her and enjoy the takedown.

She turned, her eyes narrowing. "What are you smiling about?"

Zach quickly refocused on the road ahead. "Nothing. I just didn't realize how much I missed your intensity." Out of the corner of his eye, he could see her studying him, her brow puckering.

Then she glanced forward. "Turn here."

"Here?" he asked.

"Yes, here," she said.

With only seconds to respond, he stomped on the brakes and turned the steering wheel in time to leave the pavement and pull onto a rutted dirt road, leading up to a ramshackle mobile home with old tires on the roof, holding down a tattered tarp. A junk car stood in the drive with the hood up, the wheels removed and the chassis resting on concrete blocks. An old washer lay on its side to the right of the house and the steps leading up to the front door were faded wood, possibly rotten.

The truck was still rolling when Lani cursed, yanked open the door and leaped to the ground.

"What the hell?" Zach yanked the truck into park. Before he could get out of the vehicle, Lani had disappeared around the back of the trailer.

As they'd driven up to the trailer, Lani spied Mark Wolf Paw staring out the window of the trailer. His eyes widened, and he twisted the blinds closed. He was going to run.

Lani didn't wait for the truck to come to a full stop. She shoved the door open and jumped down, hitting the ground running.

If Mark got away, they wouldn't be able to question him about his brother. Mark was known to get lost for weeks at a time, if he thought he might be in trouble.

Lani really needed to talk to him. He could be the key to identifying the killer. She couldn't let the bastard run. He owed it to his little brother to stick around and answer a few questions.

As she ran around the side of the trailer, the back door slammed open.

The man who jumped to the ground raced away without looking back.

Lani gave chase, running as fast as she could.

Before she could get close enough, he hopped onto an old dirt bike, revved the engine and spun in the dirt before the threadbare tires engaged and shot the motorcycle forward.

Lani didn't slow; she kicked up her pace and ran after him.

She flung herself at the man, her hand catching on his jacket.

Mark jerked backward but kept his grip on the handlebar. The bike spun to the side. Mark regained his balance, shrugged off her grip and goosed the throttle, sending it speeding away.

Still running when Mark forced her to let go, Lani stumbled and fell forward. Tucking her body, she hit the ground, rolled to her side and was on her feet again within the next second. But it was too late.

Mark was a plume of dust rising up from the dry prairie.

As she stood watching the man disappear in a cloud of dry soil, hands descended on her shoulders.

Zach spun her toward him. "Are you all right?" he asked, his breathing coming in short gasps.

Dragging in a steadying breath, Lani nodded. "I am. But he got away, dammit."

"Please," Zach said, his fingers tightening on her upper arms. "Don't do that again. At least, warn me before you jump out of a moving vehicle."

She gave him a sheepish grin. "Sorry. I saw him looking at us in the window. I knew he'd make a run for it." Lani tipped her head toward the settling prairie dust. "And he did. I'd hoped I could catch him before he got away."

"You asked me to watch your back." He pulled her into his arms and rested his chin on top of her head. "How can I do that if you're running off without me?"

"I'm sorry." She leaned her cheek against his chest and listened to the wild beating of his heart. Had she scared him? Or was it just exertion from trying to catch up to her? Whatever it was, she liked the way his arms felt around her. She liked it too much. Lani inhaled the scent of Zach. He smelled the same as when she'd tackled him in Afghanistan. All male and sexy as hell. She'd spent more time with him when he'd been cooling his heels in the camp holding cell than she'd spent with any other soldier she'd yanked out of a fight. Though she hadn't admitted it to herself, she'd been intrigued with him, with his scent, with his heritage. And she'd been disappointed when his commanding officer had finally come to claim him. Yeah, she'd seen him around the camp, and had even spoken to him several times, but it hadn't been as intimate as when she'd thrown him to the ground and held him down with her body.

Having him hold her now was an entirely new experience and one she didn't really want to end.

What was she thinking? He was there to cover her six, not to tempt her into his bed. Not that he'd asked. But if he did...

Lani blinked, stiffened and forced herself to place her palms on the hard planes of his chest. At that point, she should have pushed him away. But she didn't. Instead, she let her hands absorb the warmth of him through his black T-shirt.

"Are you okay?" Zach asked. "You took a tumble chasing after Ben's brother."

She shook her head, feeling a little dizzy, but not from her fall. Lani raised her head and stared up into Zach's eyes.

Warning bells went off in her head.

"I was worried about you," Zach said. "He could have dragged you across the ground or run over you." Zach smoothed his thumb across her cheek and tucked a strand of her hair behind her ear. "See? You must have hit your head when you went down." He brushed his thumb against her right temple. "You have a small scrape there."

She shook her head, mesmerized by the concern

pulling his brow low on his forehead. "I don't feel it," she murmured.

He smiled down at her. "I'm not surprised. You're bound to be hopped up on adrenaline." Then he did something amazing. He leaned forward and pressed his lips to her forehead. "Promise me you won't go all badass cop on me and run off on your own. He might have been carrying a weapon. You could have been shot."

"I'm a cop. I go after the bad guys."

"Yeah, but you have backup. Use me." Again, he pressed a soft kiss to her forehead. "Please."

"Don't," she said, shaking her head.

"Don't what?" he asked.

"Don't do that."

"Do what?"

Her cheeks heated. "Nothing." Finally, she found the strength and mental capacity to pull out of his arms and stand on her own. Maybe he was right. Maybe she'd hit the ground too hard and scrambled her brains.

Zach glanced at her once more before tipping his head toward the back door of the trailer that stood wide open. "Should we look inside to see if there's anything incriminating?"

Lani squared her shoulders and nodded. "Yes, we should."

"Do you have to have a warrant or anything?" he asked.

"The door was open. I assume he left it that way for me to go in." She turned away from Zach and strode toward the trailer. The backside was no better than the front side, with an array of old tires, car parts and trash lying in the dirt. The back steps were rickety wood, split and weather-worn. Lani mounted each step with caution, placing one foot at a time, testing each riser before entrusting her weight to the damaged wood. At the top, she ducked her head through the door into the dark interior, her nose wrinkling.

The window blinds had been drawn. Some of the windows had no blinds at all but were covered in a variety of old sheets or worn blankets. On a table against a wall were several plastic bags of white powder, syringes and other drug paraphernalia.

"He didn't appear to be too concerned about the death of his brother," Zach observed, his voice coming from over Lani's shoulder.

Lani's jaw firmed. "Mark wasn't concerned about anything but his next fix. Ben took care of him on more than one occasion when he was stoned out of his mind. Ben begged Mark to give it up. He even had him committed to a rehab facility against Mark's wishes. He only wanted his brother to be healthy and live to see his fortieth birthday. Why does it seem only the good die young?" She shook her head. "I'm going to leave the investigation to the chief. He needs to know what's going on here."

"I'd say." Zach frowned. "Do you think he might have killed his own brother?"

Lani shrugged. "It's possible. Ben put him into rehab before. He might have threatened to put him in rehab again." She tipped her chin toward the drugs. "Especially based on what's on that table. But what reason would he have had to kill Tyler?"

"Could the two murders be unrelated?" Zach asked.

"They could," Lani said, "but consider this: they occurred on the same night, each one was killed in a similar manner and in a location other than where his body was found. This leads me to believe they were killed by the same person or persons."

Zach nodded. "Make sense."

Lani pulled out her cellphone and glanced down at the screen. "No service out this far." She eased down the stairs and rounded the trailer.

Zach followed. "I can stay here while you take my truck back to town for potential cellphone reception."

She glanced back at the trailer. "I don't want to leave the place unprotected. Mark might return and clear the evidence. The other option is for you to go back to town, and I'll stay here." Her eyes narrowed. "I actually think that's the better option. That way you're making the call. Not me. Since I'm off the case."

Zach's gut clenched. "I don't like leaving you here. What if Mark comes back?"

"I can handle him." Lani patted her jacket, beneath which she had her gun. "And I have my own protection, if he gets stupid."

"Why didn't you use it when he took off?" Zach asked.

"I wanted to question him." Her lips quirked. "Kinda hard to get answers out of a corpse."

Zach would rather she'd shot the bastard than get torn up being dragged behind the druggie on his motorcycle. "Still, how can I protect you, if you're here and I'm halfway back to town?"

"I'll take my chances." She motioned with her head. "There's not much a person can hide behind out here. I can see anything coming. If I feel threatened, I'll shoot first, ask questions later." She winked. "Please. Go. Call 911 and ask the dispatcher to send the chief."

Not happy about leaving her, Zach climbed into his truck and drove down the rutted path as fast as he could without tearing up his truck. Once on the paved road, he hit the accelerator and pressed it to the floor, watching his cellphone and the reception indicator on the screen. He was almost all the way to Browning before a single bar showed. Immediately, he slowed and dialed 911, passing on the information just as Lani had asked.

"Your name?" the dispatcher asked. Her voice sounded female.

"Zach Jones."

"Are you Lani's fiancé?" the dispatcher asked.

Hesitating for a second, he responded. "Yes."

"Congratulations. I hear you're a hunk."

He didn't know what to say to that. "You'll pass the word on to the chief?"

"I will. Keep my girl safe, will ya? She's the best thing to happen to the rez in a while."

Zach relaxed. Apparently, Lani had allies on the police force, even if she'd been pulled off the murder case. "I'll do my best."

Before he ended the call, he was turning his truck around, bumping onto the shoulder and down into a ditch before he regained the pavement. As quickly as he'd come, he was on his way back to Lani, his heart in his throat, his hands gripping the steering wheel so tightly his knuckles turned white. With as much product as had been left on the table, Zach wouldn't be surprised if Mark returned, ready to claim it. Even if he had to go through Lani to get to it.

CHAPTER 5

Lani circled the trailer several times while waiting for the chief or Zach to return. She didn't want to disturb the interior in case there was any evidence pertaining to the murders inside. At the very least, Mark could be brought in on possession charges, at which time, they could question him on his whereabouts at the times of the murders. The man could have killed his brother in a drug-induced rage, but her gut wasn't ready to believe it.

The two murders had to have been committed by the same person. They were too much alike. Lani couldn't come up with a single reason why Mark would have killed Tyler. They weren't related like Mark and Ben, and they didn't run in the same social circles. It didn't make sense.

And, based on the other vehicles outside the trailer, the only one operational had been the one Mark had escaped on. A man couldn't load and carry a corpse on a motorcycle. Not far, anyway. Like Tyler's vehicle, Ben's hadn't seemed disturbed, as if he'd been killed in it, and then carried to an alternate location to be dumped.

She needed to see the coroner's report on the two victims. Had they fought back? Were there any signs they'd struggled, scratched or bruised their opponent before being beaten to death? If they had gotten in a punch, the murderer would have some marks. The sooner they found him, the better. Bruises and scratches faded after too much time.

With her attention on the plains around her, she heard the engine before she saw Zach's truck pull onto the rutted path leading up to the isolated trailer. She hated to admit it, but she was glad to see him. Had Mark returned, he might have been hopped up on whatever drug he'd left on the table. He could have come after her full of aggression and desperate to get his next fix. A bullet wouldn't necessarily stop him in his tracks.

Zach pulled into the littered yard and slid to a stop in the loose dirt.

Lani approached his truck as Zach dropped down.

He met her at the front fender and pulled her into his arms. "He didn't come back?"

She chuckled and rested her hands on his chest. "No. I didn't even have to take out my gun."

"Thank God," Zach said. "I was worried."

"I think you were gone all of five minutes. Not much can happen in that short time," she said. But she didn't pull out of his embrace. She liked how solid he felt against her.

The sound of another engine caught her attention.

Zach must have heard it too. His body stiffened, and he turned toward the rutted path he'd just come in on.

Her hand on her pistol, Lani watched. Not until she saw the lights on top of the vehicle did she relax slightly.

The chief's Blackfeet Law Enforcement vehicle came to a stop beside Zach's truck. Police Chief Black Knife climbed out of the front seat, frowning. "I thought I told you that you were off the case," he said without preamble.

Lani stepped away from Zach's arms. "I heard you," she said. "I was just checking on Mark to see how he was after hearing of his brother's death."

"And?"

Lani waved her hand toward the trailer. "See for yourself. He took off before I could ask."

Black Knife's frown deepened. "If he took off, what's there to see?"

"He left the back door wide open." Lani raised an eyebrow. "What he left inside is in plain sight."

The police chief rounded the trailer and climbed the rickety back steps.

Lani followed and waited at the bottom of the steps. "Neither of us went inside. We didn't want to destroy any evidence."

"Good thing," the chief said. "I can get him on possession."

"Do you think he could have killed Ben?" Lani held up her hands. "Not that I'm investigating or anything. Just a concerned citizen with a valid question."

The chief shot a glance her way before disappearing

inside the mobile home. A few moments later, he came to the door, shaking his head. "I didn't see anything he could have used to inflict the blunt force trauma both Tyler and Ben endured. But I have a reason to haul his ass in and question him."

"If you can catch him," Lani said. "He took off on a dirt bike. Knowing he'll be busted on possession, he might not come back."

"I'll put out a BOLO on him." He nodded toward Lani. "I have a stash of evidence bags and a camera in my vehicle."

"I'll get it." Lani turned and hurried around the trailer to the chief's service vehicle. In the glove compartment, she found the bags and the camera. When she returned to the back door of the trailer, Black Knife was inside opening cabinet doors.

Lani stepped past Zach, brushing against him on the steps. Her heart fluttered against her ribs, sending blasts of electricity through her senses. She hurriedly entered the trailer, carrying the items her boss had requested.

He held out his hand. "You shoot while I collect," he said.

Lani nodded and handed him the bags. As she snapped photos, Black Knife collected the drugs and paraphernalia. The table wasn't the only place with contraband. Several cabinets contained more blocks of white powder and bags full of pills.

Bedrooms at either end of the trailer were as different as night and day. One had a neatly made bed with carefully hung clothing in a small closet. Shoes were lined up on the floor and towels were folded on a shelf. At the opposite end of the trailer was what appeared to be a pile of filthy blankets shoved up against the wall. Lani wasn't sure the mattress had ever had a protective sheet on it. Empty beer cans lay amongst the blanket folds, along with an old pizza box, with a half-eaten pizza in it. The filthy room smelled as if someone had urinated in it and hadn't cleaned it up.

Lani pinched her nostrils. The scent was overwhelming. "Are you about done?" she asked.

"Almost." He lifted the mattress and looked beneath the bed. A large compartment contained even more of the white powder bricks. "There's no way this was for personal use. The bastard was selling." He held up the mattress while Lani clicked away. Then he propped up the mattress and bagged the remaining drugs. "There's going to be a lot of unhappy people when they don't get their stuff."

"You need to send it on up to the state headquarters. If you keep that much product in the office, someone is liable to shoot up the place trying to get to it."

"Good point." He handed her several bags. "Let's get this into the trunk of my vehicle."

Lani helped carry the bags of evidence out to the chief's service vehicle and settle them into the trunk.

When all had been collected and stored in his trunk, the chief closed it and stared at Lani. "I know you're conducting your own investigation," he said.

Her gut clenching, Lani could only nod. She wouldn't lie to the man who'd taken a chance on hiring her. A man whom she looked up to and admired.

"Don't...stop," he said. "Don't stop. We need all eyes

on the search for who did this. I don't give a damn if we anger the elders. They're getting to be yes-men to Swiftwater. He has some hang-up with you, but I'm not buying it. Do your thing, while we're doing ours. If you need backup, let me know. I'll be there."

Lani let go of the breath she'd been holding. "Thank you. I wasn't sure where you stood. It helps to know you haven't lost faith in me."

His eyebrows rose. "Are you kidding? You're the best thing to happen to BLES. We needed fresh blood. Too many of us have gotten complacent. Now this…" He shook his head. "We've had people go missing, but never blatant murder. It's as if the killer wants us to find him but is leading us on a wild goose chase in the meantime. Why else dump the bodies where they can be easily found?"

"Agreed." Lani frowned. "So far though, I've not come across enough of a clue to feel like I'm heading in the right direction."

"Then dig deeper. I will be. Along with my shadow, the FBI agent," he said, wrinkling his nose.

"I'm going to follow Mark. Any idea where he might run to? Or does he have a favorite hangout?"

"I've seen him at the local bar on more than one occasion. You might try Mick's Bar and Grill. But don't bother getting there until after nine o'clock. That's when the hardcore drinkers congregate."

"Will you and the agent be there?" Lani asked.

"No. Everyone knows I'm on the case." The chief tipped his head toward Zach. "You and your fiancé could get in on the pretext of showing the new guy the local haunts." He grinned. "By the way, congratulations on your engagement. I didn't even know you had a boyfriend."

Neither had she. Lani's gut twisted. She didn't like lying to her boss. He'd given her a chance when others might have passed her over, since she was a female. "Thanks," she said. "I'll do my best."

The chief glanced over at Zach. "I trust you'll have her back?"

Zach nodded. "I will." He slipped an arm around Lani. "She can take care of herself but, sometimes, it helps to have eyes in the back of your head." He winked down at her. "I'll watch her back."

A shiver of awareness rippled across Lani's skin as she stared up into Zach's eyes. She'd like him to watch her back. Her *naked* back.

As soon as that thought popped into her head, her cheeks burned.

Zach's lips turned up on the corners.

Could he read her naughty thoughts? More heat spread up her neck and into her cheeks.

Her boss chuckled. "You two don't do anything I wouldn't. And if you do, use protection." He winked and slid into his service vehicle. "And let me know if you find anything we could use in our investigation."

Lani swallowed hard, turned to the chief and touched two fingers to her temple. "Yes, sir."

Chief Black Knife drove away, his SUV bumping across the road leading toward the highway and pavement.

"Ready?" Zach asked.

Oh, she was ready...but he didn't need to know for what. Her thoughts were headed into dangerous territory. Territory she had no business wandering into. Zach was on a temporary assignment.

Her.

He wasn't there to scratch the itch he'd created the first time she'd tackled him in Afghanistan.

Zach held the truck door for Lani, though he knew she could do it herself. She was the tough cop who could take down a felon twice her size and pin him to the ground. Still, she was all woman beneath the badge.

She'd sparked his interest in Bagram. He'd thought it was a passing desire. After redeploying to the States, he'd found himself thinking about the Blackfeet beauty and wondering what she was doing. Had she redeployed? Had she gotten out of the military and returned to Montana as she'd said she would? Though he'd given her his cellphone number, Zach hadn't expected to hear from her ever again.

When her call had come through, he'd been more excited than he'd thought he could be over a woman he'd met while deployed. It wasn't as if they'd slept together, or even kissed. He'd found her fascinating. Her background similar to his and her dedication to helping others made him want to know her even more.

"Where to?" he asked as he drove away from the dilapidated trailer.

"The diner." She glanced his way. "I don't know

about you, but I'm hungry, and we have time to kill until going to the bar tonight."

"Is the diner like most diners in a small town?" Zach asked.

"You mean, places where everyone eventually goes, and coffee and gossip flow freely?" She grinned and nodded. "Yes. We might learn something more while we eat."

Zach loved it when Lani smiled. Her entire face brightened. She went from the focused, consummate professional cop to a young woman who was approachable and very desirable.

By the time they'd reached the asphalt road, all Zach could think of was how much he wanted to kiss Lani's full, luscious lips.

He had to shake himself as a reminder he was on a mission to protect this woman, not make love to her.

And, just like that, the thought of making love to Lani filled his head. When they'd been at Bagram, he'd seen her jogging in her PT shorts. Her long, slender legs with their well-defined muscles had made his mouth water and his groin tighten. The memory was just as impactful. He could imagine those legs wrapped around his waist. It was just as well they were headed to a public place, not back to her little cottage where they'd be alone.

Coffee and food would help get his mind off Lani's tight body and kissable lips.

At least, he hoped it would.

Minutes later, they were back in Browning. Zach pulled into the parking lot of the diner and turned off the engine. The lot was packed with vehicles. He glanced at the clock on his dash and noticed it was already six-thirty. "I didn't realize it was getting so late. We completely missed lunch."

Lani snorted. "I miss lunch more often than I remember it."

Which accounted for the fact she was slim, almost too skinny. "Remind me to get groceries when we're done here. I'm pretty good in the kitchen."

"The man can cook, fire an M4A1 rifle and rescue a damsel in distress." She nodded, a smile tugging at her lips. "I'd say you hit all the qualifications of a knight in shining armor."

"I haven't rescued you yet," he reminded her. "And shiny armor makes too easy a target."

"No, you haven't rescued me yet, but you're keeping me safe and helping me investigate the murders. I'd say that checks that box."

He shook his head. "Hold your judgment until I prove myself…in the kitchen, on the range and having your back. In the meantime, let's get some chow. I'm starving." He dropped down from the truck and rounded the front fender.

Lani met him there. So much for chivalry. He'd open her door for her, but she was quick and opened her own damned doors.

Zach found himself a little irritated. He wasn't a knight. He hadn't done anything extraordinary for her, and he didn't like taking credit for anything he hadn't accomplished. The best he could do, for now, was make certain she didn't get hurt and help her find the killer.

Only then could he prove his worth as her protector and a valuable asset to Hank Patterson's Brotherhood Protectors.

He beat her to the door of the diner and opened it for her, giving him a smidge of satisfaction.

Inside, a waitress with dark eyes and a long black braid hanging down the middle of her back yelled out, "Find a seat. Menus are on the table. I'll be with you in a moment."

Lani led the way, selecting a booth in a corner. She sat with her back to the wall, her gaze on the door.

Zach fought a grin. The woman was Old West. He bet that if she played poker, she'd have her pistol on her lap, her hand on the grip.

Zach sat across from her, turning slightly sideways in the seat to give him more of a view of the rest of the diner's interior. He could also keep an eye on the door in his peripheral vision. He lifted a laminated menu from where it was wedged between the napkin holder and the salt and pepper shakers.

"Hi, Lani." The waitress who'd yelled at them arrived at the booth, a pot of coffee and two mugs in her hands. "Coffee? Or does it keep you up at night?"

"I'll take a cup," Lani said.

"Make that two," Zach seconded. He'd need it to stay awake later that evening at Mick's Bar and Grill.

The waitress plunked the mugs on the table and filled them with coffee.

The heavenly scent filled Zach's nostrils. He inhaled deeply.

"Cream?" she asked.

"Black," Lani said at the same time as Zach. She laughed as she met his gaze. "I learned to drink it black when I was deployed. Faster, easier and more consistent. We couldn't always get cream."

"I started drinking coffee at the age of seven. Always black, no sugar." He lifted his mug and sipped the hot liquid.

"Careful," the waitress said. "It's hot."

He swallowed the steaming brew. "It's perfect."

She smiled. "You must be Lani's fiancé. I'm Rebecca."

"Zach," he offered.

"Nice to meet you," she said. "And I hear you're Blackfeet."

"A quarter," he corrected. "My grandmother was one hundred percent."

"Welcome to Browning." She held out her hand.

Zach set his mug on the table and shook the waitress's hand. "Nice to meet you, Rebecca."

The woman's cheeks pinkened. She pulled her hand free and fished a notepad and pencil out of her apron pocket. "What can I get you two to eat?"

"I'll have the usual," Lani said.

"One serving of pot roast." Rebecca jotted notes on the pad then looked at Zach. "And you?"

Zach slid the menu back in its slot. "I'll have the same."

The waitress left to place their order with the kitchen, deliver plates of food to another table and refill water glasses on other tables.

"Rebecca is raising two children on her own and going to college part time," Lani said, her gaze following the other woman around the restaurant. "She has a big heart and a lot of determination. She'll realize her dreams, while setting a great example for her kids."

"She's a woman to be admired," Zach said. "My mother raised me on her own. She worked a couple jobs to make ends meet and keep a roof over our heads."

"Where is she now?" Lani asked, her attention shifting to Zach.

His lips thinned, and he stared down into his half-empty coffee mug. "She died of breast cancer, right after I graduated from high school."

"I'm sorry."

He shrugged. "It was a long time ago."

She reached across the table and took his hand. "It's hard to lose a parent at such a young age."

He curled his fingers around hers, liking how warm and strong they were. "I joined the Army after the funeral. I couldn't stay in my hometown."

"Where was your hometown? I know you said you were from Montana, but where in Montana?"

"I grew up in Great Falls," he said.

"About two hours from here."

He nodded. "Your determination and desire to return inspired me to come home. I figured it was time to come back and see if there was anything left to keep me here."

She squeezed his hand. "I hope you stay. The state needs its children to come home. Only those who were born and raised here understand how deep the rivers run, how blue the skies are and how tall the mountains stand."

"I hadn't been back since my mother's passing." He smiled across the table and curled his fingers around hers. "And you're right. This place is still in my blood."

"I've found it to be more than just a place. It's the air I breathe, the beat of my heart and my state of mind." Her gaze met his. "No matter the people who aren't here anymore. It's home."

"You two are too cute," Rebecca's voice jerked Zach out of the depth of Lani's eyes and back to the diner. "I can come back while you share a moment..." The woman held two plates of steaming hot roast beef, potatoes and carrots.

Lani pulled her hand free of Zach's, her cheeks flushing a warm red. She leaned back. "No, please. We're starving."

Rebecca chuckled. "I get that, but I'm not so sure you're starving for food." She winked as she laid the plates in front of Lani and Zach. "I'll be right back with your dinner rolls and a refill on the coffee."

Zach used the time it took for Rebecca to duck back into the kitchen to gather his wits and focus on the food in front of him. For a moment, he'd completely lost himself in Lani.

Her passion for and commitment to life in Montana were as infectious as her smile and laughter. He couldn't help but feel the same when she was around. Thus, his decision to return to Montana, a state he'd associated with loss and sorrow. It was if she'd thrown off the pall of death and opened the curtain of life so that he could once again see the big blue skies and the frosted tips of the mountains in the distance. Suddenly, he remembered the good times of his youth, the camping trips, canoeing the rivers and fishing in the lakes. His mother had loved Montana as much as Lani. She'd taken him across the length of the state, showing him the beauty of the plains to the stunning mountains and the ancient glaciers.

Rebecca returned with a basket of dinner rolls and the pot of coffee. She topped off their mugs and stood for a moment, smiling at them. "It's good to see young people in love."

Lani's cheeks pinkened again.

"Have you picked a date yet?" she asked.

Zach shook his head. "I only just asked her."

"Show me the ring," Rebecca held out her hand.

Lani twisted the ring on her finger and held out her left hand, her gaze shooting across to Zach.

He winked.

"Wow. That's a big rock." She held Lani's hand in hers and studied the ring. "He must love you a lot."

Zach nodded. "Yes, I do. She's everything I ever dreamed of. I still can't believe she said yes."

Rebecca cocked an eyebrow. "Seriously? Have you looked in the mirror lately?" Then she chuckled. "Lani, sweetheart, he's a keeper. If you decide to ditch him, give me a little head's up." Her smile faded. "Really, you two look like you're made for each other." She let go of Lani's hand. "We needed a little happiness around here after what happened last night."

Lani nodded, tucking her hand in her lap. "You heard?"

"About Tyler and Ben?" Rebecca nodded. "I can't

believe they're dead. They were good people. They didn't deserve to die like that."

"I stopped out at Ben's place to give my condolences to Mark," Lani said, lifting her fork, her gaze on her food.

Rebecca snorted. "Was Mark even lucid enough to understand what you were saying?"

Lani shook her head. "I didn't get to say anything to him. He lit out like his tail was on fire."

"Idiot. Probably cooking meth or something," Rebecca said, shaking her head. "Ben tried to get him to quit the drugs. He was fighting a losing battle with that one."

"He left so fast…" Lani shook her head. "I worry he'll hurt himself. I wish I could find him and make sure he's okay."

"He'll probably head back to their trailer when he sobers up," Rebecca said.

"I doubt it. Black Knife confiscated his stash. He's probably afraid he'll be picked up for possession with the intent to sell."

"Serve him right. Might do him some good to spend some time in jail. He could stand some solitude to detox," Rebecca said.

"Besides the trailer he shared with Ben, does he hang out anywhere else?" Lani asked. "I'm really worried about him."

Zach almost grinned at the concern on Lani's face. After Mark had knocked her down, she was probably more concerned about taking the bastard down and forcing some information out of him.

"You gonna haul him in if you find him?" Rebecca asked.

"Not unless he wants me to," Lani said. "I want to make sure he's okay. Losing his brother had to hit him pretty hard."

Rebecca shook her head. "Ben tried so hard to get him straight. Doesn't make sense that Ben died, and Mark is still alive."

"I know what you mean," Lani said. "Any idea where I can find Mark. I think Ben would want someone to check on him."

"If he's afraid to go home, he might have holed up with one of his druggie friends. I think some of them hang out at the old abandoned warehouse. You know, the one on the north side of town, out toward the grain silo."

Lani nodded. "I've chased teens out of there. Sometimes, they go out there to drink and raise hell."

"Damned dangerous, if you ask me," Rebecca said. "They say the floors are rotting, and when the wind blows through the cracks in the wall, it sounds like screaming banshees." The waitress shivered. "Wouldn't catch me out there after dark. Place gives me the creeps."

A customer called for the waitress.

Rebecca grimaced. "Duty calls. Let me know if you need anything." And she was away to help her other customers.

Lani dug into her food and lifted a forkful up to her mouth. "Lou makes the best pot roast in Glacier County." She popped the bite into her mouth and moaned. "Amazing."

Zach's groin tightened. He could imagine that same sound coming from her mouth in the middle of making love. Shifting in his seat, he forced a chuckle. "You make eating so interesting."

She tipped her chin toward his plate. "You haven't tried it."

Lifting his fork, he placed a bit of the roast in his mouth. The explosion of flavor left him moaning as well.

Lani laughed. "Told you."

He was entranced by her laugh as much as he was by the melt-in-his-mouth roast beef. "I concede. You're right. The roast is out of this world. I can't believe I had to come all the way to Browning, Montana, to find it."

"See? It's not all boring on the rez," she said. "We have our perks."

"Like Lou's pot roast." Zach glanced toward the kitchen where he could see a man with his hair pulled back in a ponytail, placing a plate on the ledge for the waitress. "Remind me to compliment the chef."

"He'd like that," Lani said and popped a bite of potato into her mouth.

After another mouthful of the delicious meal, Zach asked, "Where did he learn to cook like that?"

Her lips lifted on the corners. "In the Navy. He cooked for the crew of an aircraft carrier."

"That's a tough audience."

Lani nodded. "He was selected to cook for the President of the United States, but Lou chose to return to Browning, instead."

"That he was selected was a huge honor," Zach said. "I'd heard they sometimes take the best of the Navy's best cooks to function as chefs for the White House."

Lani nodded. "Instead, Lou came home, bought the diner from the previous owner and started cooking for his people. He also volunteers on his days off doing home repairs for some of the families living in substandard housing."

"He and Rebecca better watch out. If the killer is targeting do-gooders, they might be next on his list."

A frown pulled Lani's brow downward. "They are good people. And there are so many more." She laid her fork on the table, her food only half-eaten. "We have to find the killer before he targets someone else."

"Agreed. And to do that, you need energy to keep you going late into the night." He tipped his head, indicating the food on her plate. "Eat."

Slowly, she lifted her fork and pushed a cooked carrot around on her plate. "I feel like I should have been there for Tyler and Ben."

Zach shook his head. "Lani, you didn't know someone was going to kill them. You can't be everywhere, all the time."

"I know, but it happened on my shift."

"You didn't kill them. You can't take the blame."

"But I've sworn to protect the people on the reservation." Again, she set her fork down next to her plate, her brow furrowing.

Zach tried another tactic. "If you don't eat all your food, you're going to upset Lou."

"I'll take it to go and finish it another time." She looked up, her gaze searching the diner.

Rebecca hurried over. "What's wrong? Did the food get too cold? I can warm it up for you."

Lani gave Rebecca half a smile. "No. It's good, as usual. I'm just full. Can I get a box to take it home in?"

"Sure." She turned to Zach. "You too?"

He nodded. Though the roast was good, he too had lost his appetite. "Please."

The waitress left, returning with the boxes and their check.

Zach pulled out his wallet and paid the bill before Lani could.

Rebecca took the money to the register.

"But you're working for me. I should be paying the bill," Lani insisted, keeping her voice low so that Rebecca couldn't hear her protest.

"You introduced me to the best pot roast since my mother's." He grinned. "It's on me."

Rebecca returned with his change and a smile. "It was really nice meeting you, Zach." She gave him a quick hug.

"Nice to meet you, too," Zach said, surprised by the outpouring of warmth from a veritable stranger.

The waitress brushed a tear from the corner of her eye. "You make me believe in love again. I don't think I've seen Lani happier."

CHAPTER 6

Rebecca leaned forward, wrapped her arms around Lani and squeezed her tightly. "I wish you two a wonderful life together. You deserve to be happy."

"Thank you, Rebecca." Lani's cheeks burned. She hated lying to Rebecca about her engagement. The woman was her friend and deserved all the happiness she was wishing on Lani and Zach. "You deserve the same."

Rebecca laughed and looked to Zach. "You don't happen to have a brother, do you?"

Zach lifted his shoulders and let them fall. "Sorry. I'm an only child."

"It doesn't hurt to ask," Rebecca said. "Have a good night."

"Be safe," Lani said. "Have someone walk you to your car after work, and don't stop to pick anyone up on the road."

Rebecca frowned. "You think I might be a target?"

"We haven't found the killer yet," Lani said. "I'd

advise everyone to do the same. Until we find him, don't trust anyone."

The waitress nodded. "I hate that we have to be so distrustful."

Lani squeezed Rebecca's arm. "Me, too." She gathered the two boxes of food and turned toward the door.

Zach slipped an arm around Lani's waist and guided her to the exit.

She liked the way his arm around her felt so natural and exciting at the same time. She found herself wishing he really was that into her and would continue to wrap his arm around her, but because he wanted to. Not because it was part of their cover.

Outside, he opened the passenger door of his pickup and took the boxes from her. Once she'd climbed in and fastened her seatbelt, he handed her the boxes.

"We have enough time to take this food to my house," Lani said.

Zach left the diner and started to turn toward Lani's house on the southern corner of town.

"Before we go to my house," Lani said, "let's swing by the abandoned warehouse. I want to see if anyone's hiding out there."

"You mean Mark?" he asked.

Lani sighed. "Or anyone. We don't know that Mark is the killer. But I'd really like to ask him questions about who Ben might have had contact with."

"Which way?" Zach asked.

She turned her head toward the right. "Head north."

Zach pulled out onto the main street, cutting through Browning and heading toward the north.

Lani scanned the streets, searching the faces of people standing on corners, sitting on their porches or strolling in the evening dusk as the sun sank below the mountain peaks in the distance. It should have been a picture of an idyllic life. Instead, she tried to see behind their stares or casual waves. Was one of them the killer, hiding behind a friendly façade?

"I hate thinking any one of them could be smiling as they plot the death of his next victim," Lani murmured.

"Until we find the killer, you have to think that way. If you don't, you might be the next one on his list."

Lani nodded. "I know. And I'm keeping vigilant. But I don't have to like having to treat every person in town like a potential killer." She looked over at him. "I mean, what if it was Rebecca or Lou? I would be just as surprised as Ben and Tyler. I saw their bodies. Neither had any defensive wounds on their hands or arms. They didn't know they were about to die."

"I doubt it was Rebecca. Although she looks physically fit, she couldn't have lifted Ben or Tyler into a vehicle, and then carried Tyler up steps into a trailer to dump his body."

"True. But Lou is certainly strong enough to do all that." She shook her head. "I just can't see some of these people being cruel enough to kill. Most of them are just trying to eke out a living to feed their families." She raised her hand. "And before you ask, both Tyler and Ben still had their wallets in their pockets, with all their money and credit cards intact."

Zach's lips twitched. "I wasn't going to ask. But thank you. At least, now, I don't have to wonder."

"Sorry." She gave him a crooked grin. "Sometimes, I jump ahead and anticipate questions." She looked at the road ahead. "Turn left here."

He made the turn and drove several blocks. The road ended at an abandoned warehouse that rose two stories. Some of the siding had been stripped away, and several sheets of metal roofing were either missing or peeled back by the wind.

"Some of the building's materials have been removed by people who live on the reservation to patch exterior walls of the homes they live in," Lani explained. "The reservation council had a fence built around the site to keep people out because it was just too dangerous. And it was less expensive to put up the fence than to tear down the building." She nodded toward a gap in the fence. "Fences don't always keep people out."

Zach shifted his truck into park.

Lani set the food boxes on the console and climbed down from the truck, meeting Zach at the barrier in front of them. She slipped through the gap someone had cut in the chain link fence and walked toward the warehouse.

Zach ducked through the fence and caught up to her, pulling his gun from the holster beneath his jacket. "I don't like this."

Lani drew her weapon as she neared the building. "You don't have to go in. I just want to see if anyone has been squatting here or is using the building to deal drugs."

"Let me go first…?" he asked.

"I'm a trained law enforcement officer. I can handle this," she insisted.

"I was hired to protect you," he argued. "Let me go first."

"I need you to cover me from behind. I don't want you killed because you were helping me."

Zach frowned. "This is messed up."

"Because I'm female?" She shot a glance his way, her eyebrows raised. "If I were Chief Black Knife, would you insist on going first?"

He hesitated before answering honestly, "No."

Her lips turned upward. "Then let me do my job."

His lips pressed into a thin line. "Then be careful."

"Always," she said and approached a gap in the exterior siding panels, waving him to get behind her. With her back to an existing panel, she peeked around the edge into the darkened interior, giving her eyes a chance to adjust to the limited lighting inside. When she could make out shapes in the shadows, she slipped into the building, sinking into the shadows. One step at a time, she carefully placed her feet in front of her, making her way across a wooden floor that had long since weathered and lost its rigidity. In several spots, the floor sank beneath her weight. She'd been told the warehouse had a basement beneath the original floor.

The wood creaked behind her.

"Zach?" she whispered.

"Right behind you," he said.

"Don't get too close. I'm not sure how much weight this floor can hold."

"Then don't go any further," he urged.

"Stay where you are. I'll be right back," she said and moved forward, pulling her cellphone out of her pocket and hitting the flashlight button on it. Holding it high, she shined it front of her and into the far corners. Nothing moved.

"No one here," Zach said behind her.

"I want to look for evidence of occupation. Depending on what I find, it might tell me how long it's been since someone has been here."

"These floors are dangerous," Zach said. He must have taken another step because the boards creaked.

"Seriously, you weigh more than I do. Don't come any deeper into the building," Lani warned.

"If I'm not close to you, I can't help you," he said. "Please, come back out."

"I need to know if anyone's been in here." She continued across the floor. In the far corner, she saw what appeared to be some kind of blanket or tarp, wadded up on the floor. As she neared it, she held her gun in front of her. Again, nothing moved.

Lani nudged the fabric with her foot. A rat scurried out from beneath it.

Startled by the creature, Lani gasped.

"What?" Zach called out. "Are you okay?"

She pressed a hand to her chest, where her heart beat so hard and fast she felt as though it would jump out of her ribs. "Sorry," she said, swallowing hard. "I disturbed a rat."

"Rats can be rabid," he said. A loud crack sounded from the vicinity of where Zach stood.

"What was that?" Lani asked, standing perfectly still, her heart lodged in her throat.

"The floorboards cracked beneath my weight."

"Please," she begged. "Don't come any further."

"Trust me, I won't. I almost fell through," he said. "I see another door around the side closer to you. You might want to come out that way. The floor on this side has been exposed to the weather for too long. I don't think it will hold up under much more weight. I'm backing out. See you around the other side." The floor on that side of the building creaked and groaned as Zach edged his way back out the way they'd come in.

Left alone, Lani swallowed a sudden rush of panic. She was a cop. A professional. She had a gun and her wits.

Squaring her shoulders, she brushed the blanket aside and stared down at crumbled food wrappings, a discarded syringe, cigarette butts, an empty green and white cigarette package and crushed beer cans. She picked up the cigarette package. They items appeared fairly recent. If not days then within the past week or two. She held her hand over the cigarette butts, but felt no warmth, nor did she smell lingering smoke.

She poked around more, looking into discarded crates and beneath a broken pallet for any signs of stashed drugs. When she'd satisfied herself that no one had been there that day and no drugs remained in sight, she headed for the door Zach had indicated. As she reached for the handle it shimmied beneath her light.

"Lani?" Zach called out, shaking the door though it didn't open.

"I'm here," she said, the reassuring sound of Zach's voice chasing away the residual panic she'd felt a moment before. Lani twisted the lock on the door handle and pushed open the door.

Zach reached in and pulled her out and into his arms. "Next time, I go in first," he said, holding her close, his chin resting on top of her head.

She wrapped her arms, her hands still gripping her gun and cellphone, around his middle and rested her cheek against his chest, listening to the rapid beat of his heart. "Were you scared for me?"

"Damn right, I was," he murmured, his breath stirring the hairs at her temple.

"I can take care of myself." She tipped her head up and looked into his eyes. The sun had long since set, leaving the sky a dull, dark gray as the fading light extinguished.

"I didn't like being so far away from you," he said. "I can't protect someone if they don't stay close."

"I'll remember that," she said. "I didn't get to explore the basement, but I did find some signs the place had been used fairly recently, if not today." She held up the cigarette package. "This looked fairly recent, along with some beer cans and a syringe."

"We can come back when we have more light to work with."

"I'll bring a flashlight next time," Lani agreed. "Let's go to my house."

Zach slipped his arm around her waist as he had done at the diner and led her back to the truck.

Lani didn't mention that there weren't any people

around. They didn't have to pretend to be in love. But she kept her mouth shut and reveled in the way his arm felt all warm and strong at her back. She could get used to having it there. She could get used to having him around on a permanent basis.

Too bad his assignment was temporary.

He helped her up into the truck and climbed in beside her.

Without having to be told, he made his way back through town and out to Lani's house.

Lani sat in silence, stealing glances toward Zach. She was looking at him when he pulled up to her house.

"What the hell?" Zach said, a frown pulling his brow low.

Lani turned to see what had caused him to curse and gasped.

Her cute little white cottage was marred with blood red paint sprayed in giant swaths over the siding, windows and door. Among the random slashes of red were huge letters, spelling one word.

NEXT.

ZACH CAUGHT her arm before Lani could get out of his truck. "Stay."

"It's my home," she said.

"Whoever did this might still be here." He gave her a stern stare. "Please. Just stay."

She frowned heavily and opened her mouth. Then she closed it and nodded. "Be careful."

Zach slid out of the truck, pulling his weapon free of

the shoulder holster. He hurried toward the house. The front door had been forced open, the doorframe split into jagged edges. Easing it wider with the barrel of his gun, Zach entered.

As an Army Ranger, he'd been trained in clearing an enemy-infested building. Drawing on experience, he moved through the small house, going room to room, searching for intruders. The living room had been tossed, the sofa cushions ripped and tossed across the room. The refrigerator had been tipped over and lay on its side. The mattress on her bed had been slashed and red paint sprayed across the walls in broad strokes. The clothes from her closet had been ripped from their hangers, strewn across the room, and were also covered in paint.

Zach kept moving. When he'd ascertained there were no lingering threats inside the house, he exited through the back door, scanned the surrounding tree line and circled back around the front.

Lani pushed the passenger door open.

"All clear," he said.

"Good. Because I wasn't waiting any longer." She dropped down from the truck and walked toward the house, her pace increasing the closer she got, her eyes shining in the light from the porch. "Son of a bitch." Color rose like red flags in her cheeks.

Zach's blood boiled for her. He wanted to erase all the paint across her home.

Her house had been vandalized. The safe place she went to find peace and relaxation had been violated.

Lani scowled at the writing on the wall and entered the house without slowing.

"Damn it. Damn it all to hell," she yelled.

Zach followed her inside, cringing at what he'd already witnessed but feeling her pain at having her things destroyed.

"Lani, they're just things. They can be replaced."

"I got some of those *things* on my travels. I might never go back to some of those places."

"They're just things."

"Damn it. They were *my* things." Her voice trembled as she held a uniform blouse doused with red pain and stared at the clothes strewn across the room. "He even ruined my uniforms."

"Grab what clothes that aren't ruined. You can't stay here."

"I have nowhere else to go," she said, her voice fading. "This was my home."

"When we're done at the bar tonight, we can go to Cut Bank or Conrad and rent a motel room."

She shook her head. "It's too far away from my people. I won't be here to protect them."

Zach gripped both of her arms. "Sweetheart, did you read the word on the front of the house?"

She nodded.

"*Next*. He's targeting you next. You can't stay here. He might come back to finish the job." He kissed her forehead. "I'm *not* going to give him the opportunity."

"If he can't come after me, who else will he take his anger out on?" She shook her head. "I can't leave. I have to stay here."

Zach wasn't going to win the argument. She was determined to stay on the reservation. "If you insist, we'll figure it out." He'd stand guard while she slept. He'd gone without sleep before. It wouldn't hurt him to do it again.

Lani tipped her head back and looked up into his eyes. "You don't have to stay."

"I'm going to ignore that comment." He kissed the tip of her nose, and then let go of her arms. "Okay, then. We only have about an hour before we need to get to Mick's Bar."

Lani dropped the uniform top. "What do you suggest we do?"

"Call your boss," Zach said. "Report this crime."

Lani pulled out her cellphone and dialed the chief of police.

A couple hours later, after Black Knife and several of Lani's counterparts had been through her house, dusting for fingerprints and taking pictures of the damage, Zach and Lani watched as they drove away.

Chief Black Knife frowned as he walked out on the porch. "I don't like this."

Lani snorted. "And you think I do?"

He gave her a stern stare. "Be extra vigilant." He glanced over her shoulder at Zach. "Watch her." And he left.

Silence fell over the little house.

"What now?" Lani asked.

Zach clapped his hands together. "First, you need to help me get your refrigerator upright."

They worked together to set to rights what they

could and piled the destroyed items on the porch outside. Her bed was a complete loss, as were her sofa and chairs. Zach found a hammer and nails and did what he could to repair the damaged doorframe until he could get lumber to replace the split wood.

With a nail in one hand, he held the hammer ready to slam it into the broken doorframe.

Lani stood by watching.

He hoped he didn't hit his thumb instead of the nail head. He smiled at her. "Without a bed, where do you plan to sleep?"

"I can sleep on the floor," she said.

He wouldn't let her sleep on the bare floor. "I have a sleeping bag I keep behind the back seat of my truck," Zach said. "You can sleep in it."

Lani frowned. "What about you?"

He would love to share that bag with her but knew that if he did, he wouldn't be sleeping that night. And he wasn't sure she'd want him to sleep with her. His desire could all be one-sided. He'd be watching over her, making certain no one slipped past him to harm one hair on Lani's head. "Let's worry about that after we hit Mick's Bar." He hammered the last nail into the front door frame and tested the locking mechanism. It held. He glanced at her.

Lani standing nearby, holding a jacket draped over her arm. "We'd better get going."

"I'm ready." He unrolled his sleeves, shrugged into his jacket and held the door for her.

She hesitated before walking through. "You don't think he'll come back while we're gone, do you?"

Zach shrugged. "If he does, we won't be here. And I'll clear the house before we go back inside."

With a nod, she walked through the door and waited for Zach to close and lock it before walking out to his truck in the light from the porch.

The drive to Mick's Bar didn't take long.

"I hope the killer is here tonight," Lani said, her lip curling up on one side. "I'd like to thank him personally for redecorating my house. I always hated that sofa. And the bed was as hard as a rock. I needed a new mattress."

"I hope he does, too," Zach said. "I'd like to end this game of cat and mouse, once and for all." He didn't like that Lani was the next target. He'd do everything in his power to keep her safe, but they still didn't know who they were up against. Plus, he didn't have any idea from which direction the attack would come. What if he was focused on the wrong direction?

He slipped his arm around her and guided her through the door of Mick's Bar, praying he would be there for her, no matter what direction the attack came from.

CHAPTER 7

Lani stepped into the bar, blinking to let her eyes adjust to the dim lighting. She wished she could shine a spotlight through the interior to help her look at all the faces. She searched everyone she could see, hoping to spot Mark. All the while she looked at familiar and unfamiliar faces, she wondered if one of them was the killer.

Her hands bunched into fists. If the killer was there, she'd be ready. He'd been clear in the message he'd painted on her house. She was next.

Good.

At least others would be safe, and she would be ready when he struck.

All the tables were taken by customers drinking beer or whiskey or shooting the breeze with friends.

Gazes swung their way as Lani and Zach wove through tables and past booths.

With his hand at the small of her back, Zach urged her toward the far corner of the bar and the only empty stool they could find. From that vantage point, they should be able to see everyone in the establishment and anyone coming through the door.

"Sit," Zach said into her ear.

When she hesitated, he leaned closer and pressed his lips to her temple. "Make it look like we're on a date." He smiled and asked her in a louder voice, "What do you want to drink?"

"Whiskey on the rocks," she said.

His lips curled in a smile that made her knees weak, and warmth heated her core. She took him up on the offer to claim the stool and slid onto the smooth wooden surface, turning her back to the bar. Lani wished the smile wasn't just for show. If they weren't on a mission, would he smile at her like that? If he did, she'd melt into a puddle of goo. The man was sexy as hell. She'd recognized that fact the first time she'd taken him down and pinned his body beneath hers.

Her heart fluttered at the memory. Did he think about that day? Lani had. Often.

Mick, the bartender and owner of the bar and grill, took Zach's order of one whiskey and one draft beer. A moment later, he had both drinks on the bar in front of Zach.

Lani lifted her glass to Zach. "To...us," she said.

He touched the rim of his to hers. "To us," he repeated, firmly, his gaze locking with hers.

Lani downed a healthy swallow of the clear amber liquid, feeling the burn all the way down to her stomach. Moments later, she felt her muscles relax slightly. Not so much that she'd be useless in a bar fight. Her focus became clearer. She smiled and set her glass on the bar. She didn't need another swallow. "I'm ready," she whispered.

Zach chuckled and took a long draft of his beer. "For what?"

"Anything."

Zach set his beer on the bar and draped an arm over her shoulder, leaning into her. "Have I told you how sexy you are when you go all cop?"

Butterfly wings erupted in her belly. Electricity shot through her where Zach's arm rested on her shoulders, his hand falling to hover over her breast. If she moved just a little, or drew in a deep breath, his fingertips would touch her there.

She caught herself drawing in a deep breath and let it out before her chest swelled. What was she thinking? They were there to find Mark and catch a killer. This was not a real date.

If it was, they wouldn't be in a seedy bar. They'd be at a nice restaurant, staring across a table at each other, probably holding hands. She'd like that. After a satisfying meal, they'd end up at her place where they'd close the door and make love against the wall because they couldn't wait to get to the bedroom.

Her pulse quickened at the mental picture she'd created. With Zach standing so near, she could smell his aftershave, the same brand he'd used in Afghanistan. She hadn't forgotten how much she'd liked it then. It was even more enticing now.

Focus.

Lani shook herself and forced her gaze to scan the

room, searching for Mark. As she looked, she paused on each of the familiar faces, wondering if a killer lurked behind smiles and laughter.

Zach brushed his lips against her earlobe. "Do you know all these people?"

She smiled and nodded. "Most of them. Take the man with the long black hair tied back in a ponytail. That's Teddy Hunting Horse. Not only is he Chief Hunting Horse's brother, he also raises cattle and works part-time at the feed store. He has a wife and four kids. He's always there when someone needs a helping hand. The man beside him is James Matson. He works for one of the large ranching conglomerates outside the reservation. They share ranching tips and tricks."

"What about the three men at the table beside them?" Zach asked.

"David Two Ponies, the man with the Seattle Seahawks baseball cap, runs an auto repair shop in Browning. The two men with him are mechanics who work for him. They come here to blow off steam after a long day." She nodded toward a young man, wearing a hooded sweatshirt and jeans, sitting at a small table by himself. "The guy in the hoodie is Alan Swiftwater."

Zach frowned. "Wouldn't happen to be related to the tribal elder, would he?"

Lani nodded. "His son. He's been in and out of trouble all his life. I'm not sure what's going on with him, but he seems to think he's above the law because of his father's position. Either that, or he's pushing all of Daddy's buttons, trying to get his attention. He was suspended from school so many times his father finally let him finish by taking his GED. Ray sent him off to Great Falls to start college but quit funding him when he didn't show up for classes for an entire semester. Without money, he had to return to the reservation."

"Or get a job."

"He didn't have any real skills. His father was able to get him on at the feed store part-time." Lani sighed. "It's young people like Alan I'm trying to get through to. There are jobs and career paths if you're willing to put in a little work to get them."

A movement out of the corner of her eye brought Lani's attention to the front entrance. She stiffened.

In response, Zach's arm tightened around her shoulders. "What?"

"Mark," she said softly. "He just walked in. Block me a little. I don't want him to see me until he's well inside the bar, and I can get to him quickly." Lani leaned back enough that Zach's big body stood in the way of her and Mark who hovered at the door, his gaze scanning the room.

The man had dark circles beneath his eyes, his dark hair hung lanky and dirty around his shoulders, and he looked like he'd slept in his clothes…in a pig's sty.

"He looks awful," Zach said.

"That's what drugs will do to a person." She sighed. "I've seen it all too often. It broke Ben's heart that he couldn't convince his brother to get clean."

"He's moving," Zach said.

"Which way?" Lani braced herself, ready to run after the man if he decided to make a break for it.

"Toward the other end of the bar." Zach turned sideways enough that Lani could see Mark lean against the counter and request a drink.

While he waited for his order, Mark turned his back to the bar and studied the occupants of the room, his gaze sweeping through until it came to the other patrons at the bar.

Lani ducked behind Zach. "I'm positive he didn't see you when we went to his trailer. Hopefully, he doesn't know you're my fiancé."

Mick set Mark's drink in front of him. As the bartender turned away, Mark leaned toward him, spoke and tipped his head toward Lani's end of the bar.

Zach stiffened. "They appear to be looking this way."

Mick said something to Mark.

Lani slipped off the bar stool, ready to sprint for the exit.

Mark's eyes narrowed. He slapped a bill on the counter, took one long draw from his drink, set it back on the counter and bolted for the door.

"He's running," Zach said.

Lani had already seen what was happening. She pushed past Zach and dashed for the door.

At the same time, David Two Ponies and his mechanics rose from their table.

Working her way around the three men, Lani continued on toward the door, only to be slowed again when Alan Swiftwater decided it was time to leave as well. He pushed his chair out from the table, effectively blocking Lani's way. "Officer Running Bear, I didn't expect to see you here. What brings you out this late? Are you working?"

"No," she answered, trying to look around him without being obvious. Mark was almost to the door.

"She's on a date," Zach said behind her. "If you'll excuse us, Lani isn't feeling well."

"Oh, sure."

When Lani stepped one direction, Alan stepped that direction. "Oh, sorry."

Again, Lani chose the other direction.

Alan sidestepped again, blocking her path. "There we go again. Tell you what…" He pointed to her right. "You go that way, and I'll go the opposite."

Mark had left the building by the time Lani finally made her way around Alan. She bolted for the door, having to weave her way through more tables and people.

Zach was right behind her as she blew through the door and out into the cool night air.

Stars shined down on the town of Browning, making it easy to see movement, but no matter which direction Lani looked, she didn't see Mark anywhere. She could barely hear the distant whine of a motorcycle engine. It was too far away to tell in which direction it had gone.

Lani blew out an exasperated breath. "Well, that was a bust. Next time, I'll have to find a place to stand that's closer to the door."

Zach nodded. "The place was pretty crowded."

David Two Ponies and his gang piled out of the bar, laughing and joking. David nodded a greeting to Lani and climbed into his truck. His mechanics climbed in with him.

Alan Swiftwater ambled out of the building, shaking a cigarette out of a green and white package. He placed it between his lips, glanced her way, and then turned and walked toward his bright red, beautifully restored 1967 Ford Mustang, his shoulders hunched, his hood pulled up over his head, likely to block a cool northerly breeze. He climbed in and spun his wheels, leaving the parking lot and kicking up gravel in his wake.

"We might as well call it a night," Lani said. "I'll check Mark's place again in the morning. Maybe he'll have gone home by then."

Zach helped her up into the truck and climbed into the driver's seat. He turned the truck south and covered the short distance to her house in silence.

When they pulled into the driveway of her home, Lani sighed again. Nothing had changed. The paint was still splashed across the siding and her car. The pile of debris remained on the porch, untouched, a cruel reminder of the devastation they'd found inside the walls.

Feeling beat and a little discouraged, Lani dropped down from the truck and walked toward the house.

Zach got out, grabbed a rolled-up sleeping bag from behind the back seat of the truck and joined her before she reached the porch. He was first up the steps. Before she could get her key out, he tried the lock.

Lani was relieved the door was still in place, the lock having held. She used her key to let them in.

Zach dropped the bedroll on the floor, pulled out his gun and made quick work of clearing the rooms. He was back in no time. "It's just as we left it," he assured her.

Glancing around the room, Lani wanted to cry. And she wasn't a weepy kind of female. She really must be tired to feel that way. "We still haven't established where you're sleeping," she reminded him.

"I'm not." Zach moved into the kitchen, flipped on the light switch and checked the interior of the refrigerator. "It's working."

Lani frowned. Zach was ignoring her concern over his sleeping arrangements. "You have to sleep sometime."

"I can go without sleep," he said. "I've done it many times."

Her lips pressed together in a tight line. "Maybe so, but you're not staying up all night on my account. If it makes you feel better, we can split the shift. I'll sleep the first four hours. Remember, I'm a cop. I've been working night shift. I'm used to being awake in the middle of the night."

"Okay." He gathered the bedroll and looked around. "Where do you want this?"

"Right here in the living room."

"You don't want it somewhere you can close the door?"

She shook her head. "Much as I hate to admit it, I feel safer when I'm in the same room as you." She glared at him. "Don't let that go to your head. I'll be fine once we catch this killer. In the meantime, I like the company and the clear avenues of escape." She motioned toward the front and back doors.

And she liked him.

Now that they were alone, all the sexy thoughts she'd had about being with Zach came flooding back.

How was she supposed to sleep when all she could think about was getting naked in the sleeping bag with her protector?

ZACH SMILED. He was glad she'd chosen to sleep in the living room. "Good decision. I'd rather keep you within eyesight anyway." He untied the strings holding the roll tight and unfurled it onto the carpet.

Lani scrounged through a closet in the guest bedroom and found an undamaged pillow. She lay in the bag, turned onto her side and punched the pillow, wadding it up beneath her head. A moment later, she rolled to her other side and performed the same punching ritual. Then she lay still for an entire minute.

Zach held his breath. Had she really gone to sleep this time? He prayed she had, because he wasn't sure how long he could watch her wiggle and squirm without dropping down on the bag and holding her spooned in his arms.

Lani's eyes popped open, she sat up on the sleeping bag and wrapped her arms around her legs.

Zach chuckled. "You won't get much sleep sitting up."

She gave him a crooked grin. "I'm still wound up."

He did what he shouldn't have even considered and dropped down behind her. "Come here." He pulled her up against his body, stretched his legs out on either side of hers and massaged the back of her neck. "Better?"

"Mmm," she moaned. "Much."

Better for her, but not for him.

With her bottom rubbing against his crotch, his groin tightened, his cock pushing hard against the zipper of his jeans. Zach paused his massage to shift, trying to adjust for his purely physical reaction to being so close to this woman.

She leaned her head back and to the side to look up into his eyes. "Why did you stop?"

"There are some things better left unsaid." He grimaced and shifted again in his jeans. "You're doing crazy things to me."

"What do you mean?" Lani's brow puckered.

He moved forward, nudging her backside with the hard ridge beneath his jeans. "That's what I mean. I'm not a saint. And you're a very desirable woman." He bent to press a kiss to her forehead. "I think this is a very bad idea." He started to get up, but a hand on his thigh stopped him.

"Don't go," she said. She turned, facing him, still sitting between his outstretched legs, one hand resting on his thigh. "Did you really mean what you said?"

"What? That I'm not a saint?" He laughed. "You know from experience I'm not. You dragged my ass into confinement for fighting with that Marine."

"No, did you mean what you said…about me?" Her gaze captured his, and then lowered to his mouth.

"Oh, sweetheart, the part about you being desirable?" He drew in a deep breath and let it out slowly, trying to get his pulse in check. She had him tied up in a tight little knot of lust that could leave him completely unraveled. "Every word. You're a beautiful woman."

She looked at him as if he'd lost his mind. "I'm far from it. I'm plain. And I don't wear makeup or do my hair."

"You're not plain." Zach brushed his knuckles along her jaw. "Your skin is so soft and smooth. It makes me want to touch you all over."

She leaned into his hand.

He opened it to hold her cheek in his palm, and then swept his fingers through her hair. "And your hair is so silky and dark, like midnight." He cupped the back of her head. "Hell, I'm not a poet. All I know is that I haven't gotten you out of my head since you knocked me off my feet in Afghanistan."

"Seriously?" She chuckled. "I would have thought you'd be angry at having been bested by a female."

"I was, a little," he admitted. "But I deserved it. And meeting you was the best part of that entire incident." Zach brushed his lips across her forehead and down to her cheek. "Spending those few short hours with you changed my life." He raised his eyebrows. "I mean, I'm here, aren't I? I wouldn't have been able to answer your call if I'd remained on active duty. If I hadn't met someone as passionate about the state as you, I wouldn't have come back to Montana." His mouth skimmed across hers. "You reminded me of what I missed most about the state."

She tipped her head back, her eyes half-closed. "And what was that?" she whispered.

"The people, the beauty, the life." His mouth came down on hers, claiming her in a single kiss that burned through him like a brand.

Ever since he'd left the state, Zach had been searching for meaning for himself. He'd joined the Army to give him time and purpose on his journey. That experience had helped him to mature and make friends who were more like the brothers he'd never had growing up. But eventually, they were transferred to other units, deployed to other lands, separated from the military or killed.

He'd found a temporary home in the military. What he'd needed was a place to lay down roots. What he hadn't realized was that his roots had already been established. Right there in Montana. He'd needed to live away from the state to understand what he'd left behind.

Being with Lani, there on the reservation that was her passion to serve and protect, made him aware of what he'd lost when he'd left the state. A part of himself.

He held her close, his tongue sweeping across the seam of her lips.

When she opened to him, he thrust past her teeth to claim her tongue with his in a long, sensuous caress.

Her arms wrapped around his neck, her fingers weaving into the hair at the back of his neck.

God, she felt good against him. Her long, lithe, muscular body fit perfectly with his.

Zach ran his hands over her shoulders and down her arms. He swept across her back, and lower, to cup her bottom in his palms. Then he laid her out on the sleeping bag and stretched out beside her, propping himself up on one elbow to better stare down at her and drink in her swollen, pouty lips.

"You're beautiful," he repeated.

When she opened her mouth to protest, he covered her lips with his own. "Don't argue. Accept that in my eyes, you are magnificent."

When he raised his head, she slipped a hand behind his neck and brought him back down to her, taking charge of the kiss, rising up to press her breasts to his chest.

He wasn't sure who started it, but one button loosened, leading to more, and soon, their clothes were flying off to the far corners of the living room until they both lay naked, the sleeping bag crumpled beneath them.

"I didn't mean to start something," he whispered against her ear as he leaned over her, nudging her knees open with his thigh.

She chuckled. "Too late to turn back now." She gripped his buttocks and guided him to her center.

When she increased the pressure, urging him to enter, he paused, a nagging voice in the back of his head making his brain engage. "Wait."

"Wait?" Lani moaned. "I can't wait." Her grip tightened.

"Protection," he said through gritted teeth. It was all he could do to hold back and think with his head, not his dick. He leaned over, snagged the jeans he'd tossed to the side and dug into the rear pocket, unearthing his wallet. After rummaging through the various slots inside, he gave a triumphant cry. "Thank God." Zach held up a single foil packet of protection.

Lani grabbed it from him and tore it open with her teeth.

"Hey, careful there, I only have two of these."

She grunted as she rolled it over his stiff erection, her fingers gliding down his length to cup his balls. "Don't make me wait any longer."

Zach laughed "Or what?"

"Or, I'll cuff you to my bedpost and have my wicked way with you," she said, her voice a low, sexy growl.

"Promises, promises," he murmured, his lips skimming across hers as he slid between her legs, his cock nudging her wet entrance.

Lani wrapped her legs around his waist and dug her heels into his backside, forcing him into her in one swift thrust.

"So much for taking it slow," he said as he eased back out.

Again, she clamped her heels into him and brought him back home, his cock filling her channel, sinking in the full length of him.

"Foreplay is overrated," Lani said. "I want you. Fast, hard and now."

Zach increased his speed, thrusting deep and hard.

Lani's legs unwrapped from around his waist and dropped to the floor, her heels digging into the carpet. For every one of his thrusts, she rose up to meet him.

The more he met her, the tighter his control stretched, until a burst of sensations jettisoned him over the edge. One last thrust, and he buried himself deep inside her, his shaft throbbing against the tight walls of her channel.

For a long moment, he held his breath, letting the force of the orgasm wash over him. When he came back to earth, he dropped down on top of her and rolled her to her side, facing him. "Your turn."

She laughed. "I thought that *was* my turn."

"Oh, baby, you ain't seen nothin' yet. I'm going to make you roar like a lion before we're done."

Her brow puckered. "I'm not sure that's possible. Besides, I'm sleepy."

"Uh-uh." He traced a finger along her cheek and down the length of her neck. "It's your turn." His finger drew a path from the pulse beating wildly at the base of her throat down to the tip of her right breast.

"What if I can't…roar," she said, her voice fading.

Zach leaned up on his elbow and frowned down at her. "You've orgasmed before, haven't you?"

She shook her head. "Only when I've pleasured myself."

"No man has made you come?"

Her lips twisted. "Is that a bad thing?"

"Sweetheart, you deserve better." He smiled down at her. "Challenge accepted."

CHAPTER 8

Lani had loved every minute of having Zach inside her. Long ago, she'd believed the only way for a female to orgasm was to do it herself. None of her previous lovers had gotten her there. Not for lack of trying. They just never seemed to hit the right spot.

Lani lay back, fully expecting to be disappointed, yet again. But she didn't mind. Having Zach trail his fingers, lips and tongue over every inch of her would be just as satisfying. Wouldn't it?

He started with a kiss that set her world on fire. Then his mouth left hers and seared a path down the length of her neck to the pulse thumping against her skin at the base of her throat. He sucked and flicked that spot before moving on to her collarbone and lower to the first of her breasts.

When he flicked the tip of the beaded nipple, she felt a tug deep down in her core. "Mmm. That's nice," she said.

He flicked it again, and then rolled it between his teeth.

It wasn't enough. Arching her back, she rose up, offering more of her breast.

He took it into his mouth, sucking hard. Again, that tug deep in her core made her writhe beneath him.

An ache grew, swelling inside.

Zach moved to the other breast and treated it to the same teasing nips and flicks, sucking it between his teeth.

He lay between her legs, his cock pressing against the inside of her thigh.

Lani wanted him inside again. She raised her hips, hoping he'd take the hint.

"Uh-uh," he said and abandoned her breast to burn a path of kisses into the skin over her ribs, down to her bellybutton. "Not until you get there, too."

Lani's breath caught as his hand cupped her sex and a finger found her wet entrance, pleasantly sore from his thorough lovemaking. He dipped a digit into her and swirled around, while his tongue flicked into her bellybutton then slipped lower to the curls hiding her clit.

He wasn't the first to go down on her. But she'd never been quite so keyed up at this point. That ache that had started when he'd made love to her breasts had grown with each flick of his tongue.

She closed her eyes and willed him to continue, to take it a step further and touch her where only she had been able to ignite that flame.

He brought that wet finger up from her entrance,

parted her folds and slathered the juices over that little strip of flesh all packed with a million little nerves just waiting to be set alight.

Then he stroked her with the tip of his finger.

Lani's hips rose automatically. He'd touched that spot. That incredibly elusive spot that lit her world.

He left her clit and dipped into her channel again.

Lani drifted back down, a little disappointed that the brief flick of his finger hadn't fully awakened her senses.

He was back with a wet finger and another attempt to get it right.

Zach swirled and tweaked with that magical finger, but he couldn't get it at just the right spot.

Lani shifted her hips, hoping to help him find it, but to no avail.

"Hey," he said, his breath warm against her sex. "Leave it to me."

She relaxed, determined to enjoy whatever he managed to inspire.

He moved lower between her legs, until his face was where his fingers had gone before. Parting her folds with his thumbs, he blew a warm stream of air over her heated flesh.

Lani sucked in a breath and waited. She had to watch, had to see him take her with his mouth.

And he did.

The first flick of his tongue tapped against the very tip of her clit.

A shock of electricity shot through her body.

She gasped, her body stiffening.

The second time his tongue touched her there, she

slammed her palms to the floor and lifted her hips. "Please," she moaned.

He chuckled. "Please what?"

"Please, do that again."

He flicked her again. This time, he ignited that flame that exploded like a firestorm, sending heatwaves and electric shocks all the way through her and out to the very tips of her fingers and toes.

She would have been happy if he'd stopped there, but no. He increased his attack on her senses, laving, flicking and sucking her clit into his mouth until she was moaning, roaring his name in an attempt to capture the moment and save it for all eternity. Her release poured over her in waves, her body pulsing to the rhythm of his tongue moving against her.

When she thought she might never breathe again, she finally came back down to earth, the sleeping bag and the floor where she lay.

Zach climbed up her body, slipped a fresh condom over his shaft and pressed it against her entrance. "Are you too sore to do it again?" he asked.

"No. Oh, no. Please." She tossed her head from side to side, still in a fever from the best orgasm she'd ever experienced. "I want you. Inside me. Now." She gripped his ass, guided him to her center and slammed him home.

He took her again, this time riding on the waves of her exquisite release.

Lani had never felt anything quite like it. She met his thrusts with her own, wanting him so deep that she couldn't remember where she ended, and he began.

When he came this time, his body shuddered inside hers, every one of his muscles so tight they were like steel bands.

Then he fell on top of her, rolled her onto her side and held her without breaking their intimate connection.

Lani lay in his arms, exhausted but replete, a smile curling her lips as she drifted into sleep.

"I love you," she whispered in her dream.

Zach lay for a long time, holding Lani in his arms, cherishing the moment, memorizing every curve of her delicious body. Somehow, he'd known it would be good with Lani. Never in his wildest dreams could he have known just how good.

The woman was as passionate making love as she was about everything else in her life.

As she'd drifted off to sleep, she'd murmured three words that had shaken him to his very core.

I love you.

He shook his head, even as he held her in his arms.

She'd been asleep when she'd said the words. They'd been part of a dream, not reality.

The words had poured over him like melted butter over pancakes, absorbing into every pore of his skin. If only she really did love him. What a life they could build together.

Images of a cottage with a picket fence and half a dozen dark-haired children running around the yard emerged in Zach's head. He'd never thought about settling down and raising a family. Hell, he'd only just gotten used to the idea of living in Montana again.

Lani shifted against him, nuzzling her cheek against his chest.

He liked the way she felt, how warm her skin was against his. He wanted that feeling to last.

A very long time.

As the air temperature decreased in the room, Zach knew he'd have to let go of her and wrap her in the sleeping bag. If he lay beside her much longer, he'd fall asleep. He couldn't let that happen. Not when Lani's life was at stake. That one word written on the exterior of the house had been seared into Zach's memory. He couldn't let anything happen to this woman.

She had quickly found a way into his heart, and he wasn't ready to let her go.

Except to wrap her in the warmth of the sleeping bag, which he did, careful not to wake her.

He rose, dressed and checked the pistol in his holster. His gaze returned to the woman lying in the folds of the sleeping bag. She'd rolled to her back, the edge of the bag slipping low, exposing a full, luscious breast.

His groin tightening, Zach bent to cover the breast. He had to be vigilant. If anyone was going to attack, it would be in the dead of night, after they were both asleep.

Zach left Lani in the living room and made a cursory check of the other rooms, testing the locks on the windows. Back through the living room, he checked the lock on the back door and left the house through the front.

He checked his watch. Despite Lani's desire to take the second shift, Zach had let her sleep. It was nearing five o'clock in the morning. The sun would rise soon, and another day would begin. Another day of chasing leads. Why couldn't they catch a break on this guy? Who had it out for Tyler, Ben and, now, Lani?

Zach made a pass around the entire house, checking for movement in the tree line or down the road leading up to the house. Other than a stray cat lurking in the woods, nothing moved. Clouds moved in, blocking the light from the stars, making the darkness even more complete, the only light now coming from the single bulb burning over the front porch.

He climbed the steps and had just reached for the doorknob when the door opened and Lani stood there, wearing only a T-shirt, her long legs bare in the light shining down over her.

She pushed the hair from her face and stared up at him. "You were supposed to wake me."

As she raised her arm to shove the hair back from her forehead, the hem of her shirt rose, exposing the curls over her sex.

Zach swallowed a groan. "Sweetheart, go back to bed. You're making me crazy."

She draped her arm over his shoulder. "Come with me."

"Someone has to keep an eye open for danger."

"Seems like we've made it through the night. What more could happen between now and sunrise?"

He backed her into the house, kicking the door shut behind him. "I'll tell you what could happen…"

Gripping her bottom, he raised her up, wrapping her legs around his waist. Then he leaned her back against the door and pressed into her.

"Mmm. I'm liking your scenario already." She leaned away from him, enough to reach down and unbutton the waistband of his jeans.

Zach took over, lowering his zipper.

His shaft sprang free.

"I don't have another condom," he said, nudging her entrance.

"That's okay," she said. "I have another idea. Put me down."

He lowered her until her feet touched the floor.

She didn't stop there but dropped to her knees and took him between her palms. "Your turn," she said with a smile.

Lani touched the head of his cock with the tip of her tongue.

The sensations shooting through him were so strong, he flinched.

Her chuckle sent heat through his soul. Lani wrapped her hand around him and stroked him all the way to the base of his shaft then rolled his balls between her fingers.

His groin tightened. He didn't think he could get any harder. "I won't last long with you doing that."

"I'm not done yet." She leaned forward and took him into her mouth, pressing his buttocks until he bumped against the back of her throat.

Zach gripped her head, his fingers threading through her long hair.

When she leaned back, his grip tightened, bringing her to him.

She took all of him again.

He couldn't just let her please him. He wanted to touch, feel and taste her, too.

Zach gripped her arms and raised her to her feet.

Lani frowned. "You didn't like that?"

He smiled through gritted teeth. "More than you can imagine. But I want to touch you, too."

"This was your turn."

"Why not make it both of our turns?"

"But you don't have another condom."

"We don't need one." He bent and swung her up into his arms.

Lani squealed and wrapped her arm around his neck. "Where are we going?"

"You'll see." He carried her to the living room and laid her on the floor. Then he stripped out of his clothes, pulled her shirt over her head and laid on the floor on his back.

His cock jutted straight out ready for more.

Sitting on the floor beside him, Lani wrapped her fingers around him and bent to claim him in her mouth.

"That's a start, but I want to taste you, too."

Zach positioned her hips over his face, one of her knees on either side of his head, and spread her legs until she'd lowered herself to within range of his mouth.

While she sucked his cock, he pleasured her clit.

Zach flicked and teased that highly sensitive area,

sliding a finger into her channel. At the same time, he pumped upward into her mouth, her warm wet tongue swirling around him.

It wasn't long before he felt the surge of his release, and he fought to hold it in check.

Lani stiffened and sank lower over his mouth, her body bucking with her orgasm.

When he could hold it no longer, Zach pulled her off him and let go.

Lani stroked him, milking him until he was empty.

"Wow," she said. "That was better than coffee for waking me up." She rose to her feet and stretched her beautiful body. Then she reached down, extending a hand to him. "Come on. I'll wash your back, if you'll wash mine."

"Deal." He leaped up, slapped her bottom and raced her to the bathroom. Soon, they were laughing and covered in suds.

When they had thoroughly soaked the bathroom floor and used all of the hot water, they spent a long time drying every inch of each other's bodies, kissing and touching along the way.

After sopping up the water off the floor, they left the bathroom, dressed and threw the damp towels into the washer.

Zach was rolling up the sleeping bag when Lani's cellphone rang.

She was in the kitchen when she answered it. "Running Bear." She paused. "At home…" Lani listened. "He was at Mick's last night. No, I didn't get a chance to talk to him. He left in a hurry, why?" Her face paled. "Seriously?" She stared across the room at Zach. "At Kipps Lake? What time? Six? Where did they take him?" Lani nodded. "Yes, sir. I'll be there in five minutes." She ended the call, her gaze capturing his, her face pale and her eyes rounded. "They found Mark Wolf Paw's body in Kipps Lake this morning. It appears he drove his motorcycle into the lake and drowned."

Zach tightened the string holding the bedroll together and stood. "Suicide?"

"That's what it looks like." She frowned. "But as they pulled his body out of the water, Chief Black Knife noticed injuries to his forearms, as if he'd been blocking an attack. And there was a bruise at his temple."

Zach shook his head. "He was probably dead when he was thrown into the lake."

Lani nodded. "If he was murdered, at least we know for sure that Mark wasn't our killer. Someone might have killed him and staged it to look like suicide to make us think the killer is now dead."

"And we're back to square one," Zach concluded.

"Exactly." Lani pulled their dinners from the night before from the refrigerator and popped them into the microwave. "I need to get to the police station. The chief wants me fully engaged in the investigation again. He got the tribal elders to agree, finally."

"I don't have to eat. We can go right now," Zach offered.

Lani's lips twisted. "You might not be hungry, but that was quite the workout last night. I'm starving." The microwave beeped, and she pulled the food out, slapped the roast beef from her box between two slices of bread, grabbed a fork from a drawer, shoved her arms in a jacket and headed for the door. "I'll drive. You eat. I can eat mine on the way. I'm really good at eating on the go."

Zach took his food box from her, tossed her the keys and followed her out to the truck.

She climbed into the driver's seat and started the engine. After shifting into reverse, she took a bite out of her sandwich and backed out into the street. Then she shifted into drive and drove to the Blackfeet Law Enforcement station where several police and civilian vehicles were parked in the lot.

"Looks like we're late to the party," Lani said, taking another bite out of her sandwich.

Zach set his box on the dash, untouched. "Let's find out what we've missed."

"I wish we could have caught Mark last night. I just bet he knew something."

"Yeah. And he took that something to his grave." Zach met her at the front of the vehicle.

Lani was just eating the last bite of her sandwich.

He grinned.

She frowned. "What?"

Zach brushed a crumb from her chin. "I've never seen someone polish off a sandwich as fast as you just did."

Lani snorted. "You learn to eat and run. Hell, I learned that in Basic Combat Training. If you didn't get it down in three minutes, you didn't eat."

"I remember." He laid a hand at the small of her back. "Let's do this."

Though she was a cop in the middle of a murder investigation, Lani still liked that Zach opened the door for her and touched her like she meant something to him. She hoped last night was an indication of just how much he was beginning to care for her. If it wasn't...she was in for some major disappointment.

Once the killer was caught, Zach had no reason to stick around. It would be a shame to lose the only man who'd ever managed to get her off. A real shame. Besides, she liked having him around. He was strong, protective and didn't mind that she was a cop. Not many men would be okay with her being in law enforcement. Zach had only known her in that capacity. And he didn't seem to mind. In fact, he seemed to admire her strength and the fact she could take him down.

Who was she kidding? Not many men would tolerate that part of her.

Why should Zach?

CHAPTER 9

Zach followed Lani into Blackfeet Law Enforcement station where a crowd of people stood around, some in uniform. Some not. He recognized the police chief, the FBI agent and Raymond Swiftwater, the elder who had an attitude about Lani.

Lani pushed her way through the people standing around until she reached her boss. She kept hold of Zach's hand, dragging him in behind her. "What's going on?"

Chief Black Knife tipped his head toward the elders. "We're dealing with the death of Mark Wolf Paw. The elders are concerned that no progress has been made on the first two murders, and now we have another."

"What are you doing about it?" Chief Hunting Horse approached her. "Why don't we have more people on this case?"

"If you recall," Black Knife reminded him, "the elders asked that I work with the FBI agent in charge of the murder investigation. No others from the BLES force were to be involved."

"Aren't we short-handed on the force?" Hunting Horse asked. "Isn't that why we asked that only the chief of police and the FBI get involved?" The chief turned toward Raymond Swiftwater. "Wasn't that the reason you asked to limit our own personnel's involvement?"

Swiftwater frowned. "That hasn't changed. We're still short manpower."

"And you've had me bench one of my best from the investigation," Black Knife said. "Officer Running Bear has taken it upon herself, on my authority to continue investigating the murders of Tyler Lightfoot and Ben Wolf Paw. On her own time."

Elder Swiftwater glared at Lani. "She was not to be involved in this case."

"Why?" Chief Hunting Horse asked. "Seems we should have as many people as possible looking for this guy. Instead, we've had another murder take place. We cannot continue to lose people. These were our brothers, our friends and the future of our people."

"Then I have your permission to bring Officer Running Bear back on the case?" Black Knife asked.

Swiftwater's lips pressed into a thin line as if he wanted to say something but was holding his words in check.

"Yes," Hunting Horse said. "Officer Running Bear should be included in the investigation. We cannot afford to lose another member of our tribe." The older man turned and left the building, followed by his entourage of elders and assistants.

When they were gone, Black Knife faced Lani. "Something I didn't tell the elders is that the station was broken into last night."

Lani gasped. "Was anyone hurt?"

The chief shook his head. "No, but they tried to get into the evidence room."

"And did they?" Lani asked.

"No."

"Did you store the confiscated drugs in that room?" Lani started around him.

The chief snagged her arm. "I sent most of it on to the state crime lab. I kept a small amount here, hoping to smoke out those desperate enough to make a move on it."

"Good thinking." Lani raised an eyebrow. "And did you catch him?"

"I had a camera on the evidence locker, but whoever broke in sprayed the camera lens with red spray paint."

Lani gasped. "Just like my house."

The chief nodded. "Like your house."

"So, you didn't even get an image of your thief?" Lani's shoulders slumped.

Zach wanted to pull her into his arms and hold her. He was as disappointed as she was, and it wasn't even his job to protect the people of the reservation. He'd been hired to protect her, alone.

"No images."

"Fingerprints?" she prompted.

Again, Black Knife shook his head. "No. And he got away with the little bit of drugs I had stored in the evidence locker. He cut the lock and forced open the door. No one saw him coming or going."

"Damn," Lani said, her shoulders falling.

"What do you know about Mark Wolf Paw?" the chief asked. "Besides the fact he had a lot of drugs hidden in his trailer. Who were his friends? Who did he hang out with?"

Lani shook her head. "I haven't been here as long as you have, sir."

The chief grimaced. "And I haven't been nearly as observant as I should be about the young people on the reservation, a fact I plan to rectify as soon as possible."

"As I told you," Lani said, "we saw Mark at Mick's last night. As soon as he saw me, he made a run for it. I didn't catch up to him before he disappeared."

"The FBI agent and I haven't made much progress on solving the murders of Tyler and Ben." Black Knife sighed. "I believe we've interviewed the same people and gotten nowhere. And you heard the elders, they want answers. Now."

"We can't give them answers if we don't have them ourselves."

"How did the guy get into the station?" Zach asked.

"The man on desk duty made a trip to the bathroom," the chief shook his head. "The thief jammed the door shut on the bathroom, sprayed the camera and broke into the evidence locker. He was out in under the five minutes it took for Payton to contact one of the officers on duty using his cell phone and get him there to unblock the door and let him out."

"Were there any tire tracks at the lake where Mark was found?" Zach asked.

"Other than his motorcycle's tracks...?" Lani added.

Black Knife shook his head. "It appeared as if someone swept the dirt leading up to the entry point into the lake. Not even a shoe print remained."

Lani pressed her lips tightly together, her brow furrowing. "I'd like to go back out to the Wolf Paw home and see if I missed anything, a list of names, a cellphone, anything. I'd also like to check with the coroner and compare the bodies of the deceased."

Zach realized how gruesome that sounded, but he was also interested in the similarities and differences in the three attacks. "Ready?" he asked, wanting to get started on the day's investigative activities. He was worried about Lani. If the killer made good on his threat, he would be looking for his opportunity to get to Lani.

Zach wasn't going to let her out of his sight for a minute.

They left the station and walked out to his truck. He scanned the buildings and shadowy alleys for movement. Just because the killer had beaten his victims to death didn't mean he wouldn't consider a less hands-on death for Lani. A well-placed bullet would take her out faster and more efficiently. Not that Zach was eager to see her murdered. He worried he wouldn't be fast enough, or ahead of the killer's thought process.

"I'll drive." He slipped into the driver's seat and shifted into reverse, pulling out of the parking space. "Where to first?"

"The Wolf Paws' place," Lani said, her gaze on the road ahead.

They drove through town and out the other side, taking the road where the isolated trailer was parked.

As they turned onto the ragged road leading up to the trailer, Lani gasped. "What the hell?"

Small puffs of smoke rose from the Wolf Paw brothers' home. Nothing was left but the caved-in siding, the melted tire that had been on the roof and a smoking pile of rubble.

She climbed out of the truck and circled the wreckage. "What the ever-loving hell?"

Zach joined her in front of the truck.

"It must have burned during the night," she said. "It was far enough out of town, no one saw it."

"There's nothing here, let's move on to the coroner's office," he suggested. "Which way?"

"The Glacier County Coroner's office is located in Cut Bank. On our way back through Browning, I'll call in this fire. While we're in Cut Bank, we can run down those kids who threatened Tyler while we're there." Lani held her hands out, palms up. "What else do we have to go on?"

Zach could hear the frustration in her voice. He felt it himself. What did it take to bust a case wide open and nail a killer? He wasn't a detective, and neither was Lani. She was working on a promise she'd made to a grieving grandmother.

The case had to break soon. He and Lani were living on the edge of disaster. It was only a matter of time before the killer made his move on Lani. Through every battle, Zach's instincts had proven themselves over and over. He could feel it in his bones. That time was coming soon.

After Lani gave Zach directions to the coroner's office in Cut Bank, she sat back in the passenger seat, running everything she knew through her thoughts but coming up with nothing. Not a damned clue that would lead her to Mark, Tyler or Ben's killer. Bodies were stacking up in Browning, Montana, and she didn't know where to turn next.

They pulled into the parking lot at the coroner's office and got out.

Lani had been there before on one other occasion. A dog had dug up bones by the river. They'd been taken to the coroner for identification. When they couldn't identify them, they'd turned the bones over to the FBI. A forensic scientist had determined the bones dated back to the late eighteen hundreds.

Inside the office, Lani asked to speak to the medical examiner. Martha, the woman at the front desk, asked her to wait while she asked whether he was available. He already had someone with him.

When she opened the door behind her to walk into the back room, Lani heard voices, one of which she recognized as Raymond Swiftwater.

Without waiting for the woman to clear their entry, Lani followed her through the door to the examination room where three bodies lay on stainless steel tables. Swiftwater stood beside one with the

Medical Examiner. They both glanced in Lani's direction.

Martha spun and glared at Lani. "You can't be back here without the M.E.'s okay."

"I'm here for the same reason as Mr. Swiftwater," Lani said. "I want to know the status of Mark Wolf Paw's examination." She met Swiftwater's gaze with a direct one of her own.

The M.E. waved at Martha. "It's okay. Officer Running Bear can stay."

"What about him?" Martha tilted her head toward Zach.

"Are you with Officer Running Bear?" the M.E. raised an eyebrow at Zach.

Zach nodded. "Yes, sir."

"You can stay, too."

Martha huffed and left the room, giving Lani the stink-eye for not following the rules.

"Don't let Martha bother you," the M.E. said with the hint of a smile. "She's like a bulldog and runs interference for me when I'm really busy."

"Thank you for letting us stay," Lani said.

"No problem," he said in his soft voice. Lani had met the M.E. before. He'd been a family practice doctor before he'd left his practice and "retired" to the position of medical examiner and coroner of Glacier County. As he'd told her before, it was a lot less stress.

Lani and Zach joined the two men at the table.

Swiftwater shot a venomous glare at Lani and Zach before schooling his expression into one of disinterest.

"I was just getting started explaining what I've found

so far," the M.E. said. "From what I can tell, Mr. Wolf Paw didn't die from drowning. I found no water in his lungs." He pulled the sheet back and lifted the deceased man's arm, turning it so that they could see the underside of the forearm. "You see these bruises? They were made before he died." The M.E. held his own arms up in front of his face. "Most likely, he was defending his face and head from an attack with a blunt weapon." He slid his gloved hand down to Mark's fingertips. "I also found skin and blood underneath his fingernails. In the struggle, he got a piece of his attacker. Whoever it was should have a pretty significant scratch on an exposed portion of his body, like his arm, face or neck." He lowered the arm and pointed to the side of Mark's head. "Most likely, he was killed by blunt force trauma to his skull here," he touched the man's temple where a blue bruise stood out, "or here." The M.E. parted Mark's dirty hair and pointed to a large lump on the man's scalp. "He was dead before he went into the lake."

"So, it wasn't suicide," Swiftwater stated.

"No," the M.E. said. "Either it was murder, or he had a big fight with someone and lost."

Swiftwater stared at the man lying on the table without displaying an ounce of emotion. "Thank you for your time," he finally said, turned and left the room.

Lani followed the man. "Excuse me, Elder Swiftwater."

The man stopped and turned. "Yes, Officer Running Bear?"

Lani crossed her arms over her chest. "Why are you here?"

Swiftwater lifted his chin. "As a tribal elder, I consider it my responsibility to know what's going on with the people of the Blackfeet reservation."

Lani's eyes narrowed. "Isn't visiting the coroner taking your responsibilities a little far?"

"My concern is for my people. Since the tribal police and the FBI can't seem to find the man responsible for now three deaths on the reservation, I've taken it upon myself to conduct my own investigation." The passion in his voice faded, and he added in a flat tone, "Someone has to stop the killer before he takes yet another life. Now, if you'll excuse me, I have work to do." Swiftwater's cellphone chirped in his pocket. He reached in and pulled it out, answering with a curt, "Swiftwater." He listened, frowning. "How the hell do I know?"

Lani observed the man's face go from no emotion to instant anger. "I told you…I don't know. He's a grown man; he has the schedule. It's up to him to get to work on time. Call his cellphone and leave me out of this." Swiftwater closed his eyes, a muscle ticking in his jaw. "I know it was a favor. I know you need the help, but I have no control over my son. Fire him, if that's what you need to do." Swiftwater pulled the phone away from his ear, jabbed his finger at the button ending the call and stuffed the device into his jacket pocket. He shot a glare at Lani, turned and left the coroner's office, letting the door slam closed behind him.

"Is he always that angry?" Zach said beside her.

"I don't know about others, but he always seems angry around me or his son." She couldn't imagine growing up around a father with such a sour disposition. She'd been fortunate to have a loving mother, who had supported and encouraged her to follow her dreams, wherever they led.

Zach touched his hand to the small of her back.

For a moment, Lani leaned into that hand and against Zach's shoulder. She missed her mother, and she was tired. Tired of hitting brick walls and tired of dead ends. "I wish the killer would attack me. At least then I would know who it was and could do something about it."

"I, for one, hope he doesn't attack you." His hand slipped around to hook her hip, pulling her closer. "He knows you don't know who he is and will have the advantage of surprise on his side. I suspect it's someone each of his victims knew and never suspected would attack them."

Lani glanced up into Zach's face. His jaw was firm, his gaze on the door that had closed a moment before. He was glad he was with her. Having another pair of eyes watching her back made her feel a little safer.

"I want to stop by the homes of the guys who bullied Tyler at the theater. I don't think they could have been on the reservation without being noticed, but it doesn't hurt to cover all the bases."

Zach nodded. "Let's do this."

Lani looked up the addresses of the three young people and typed the first into her map application on her cellphone. They arrived a few minutes later outside of a white house with antique blue shutters that looked as if it had been built in the early nineteen hundreds.

"This is where Russell Bledsoe lives, or at least, where his parents live," she said.

Lani climbed out of the truck and headed for the front door.

Zach caught up as she rang the doorbell.

After several seconds, she heard a male voice inside yell, "I'll get it."

A young man with blond hair, blue eyes and broad shoulders like a football linebacker opened the door. "Yeah?"

"Are you Russell Bledsoe?"

He frowned. "I am. Why do you ask?"

Lani pulled her wallet out of her jacket pocket and flipped it open to her BLES badge. "I'm Officer Running Bear from the Blackfeet Law Enforcement Service. This is my assistant, Zachary Jones. Could we ask you a few questions?"

Bledsoe's frown deepened. "I don't know anything about the reservation. I haven't been on it since I was a little kid."

"We'd like to ask you about your relationship with Tyler Lightfoot."

He shook his head. "Was he one of the people who was in the news report?"

"What news report are you referring to?" Lani asked.

"The one about the three men murdered on the reservation?" Bledsoe offered.

Lani nodded. "Yes, Tyler was one of the victims."

"I never knew him or any of the others, personally."

"But you knew of them?"

Bledsoe shrugged. "I might have run into Lightfoot a

couple of months ago here in town. And everyone knew Wolf Paw."

Lani's eyes narrowed. "Why did everyone know Wolf Paw?" She suspected the reason but wanted to hear it from someone other than a member of her tribe.

The young man shifted his weight from one foot to the other. "Well, everyone who wanted drugs knew him." Bledsoe held up his hands. "Not me. I'm clean. I've got a football scholarship. I'm not going to screw that up." He dropped his hands. "Wolf Paw was the guy everyone went to for their fix. He was dealing. In a big way."

Lani circled back to her original reason for coming. "Did you and your friends, Dalton Miller and Brent Sullivan, threaten Tyler Lightfoot outside the Orpheum Theater a couple months ago?"

The young man stiffened. "I don't know what you're talking about."

"Did you and your friends threaten Tyler Lightfoot because he was dating Natalie Preston?" Lani asked.

He started to shut the door. "I'm done talking here."

Lani placed her hand on the door. "Russell, where were you two nights ago around midnight?"

A woman appeared behind Russell. "He was here at home in bed. I can vouch for that. He'd been out with his friends earlier, but he was home early that night. You can subpoena his phone and social media records. He was in this house all that night."

"Mom, I can handle this," Russell said.

His mother shot him a narrow-eyed look. "You've said enough. Anything else will have to be with an attorney present." She stepped in front of her son. "Now, unless you have a warrant, I suggest you leave."

"Thank you, Russell," Lani said, capturing the young man's glance over his mother's shoulder. To his mother, she said, "For what it's worth, I don't think your son committed the murders. I just needed to ask him some questions so that I could cross him off my list of suspects."

The woman responded by closing the door in Lani's face.

"Well, that was productive," Lani said, her tone dripping sarcasm. "I imagine talking to his two friends will be just as useful."

"He's probably on his phone now, warning them," Zach said.

They climbed into the truck.

Lani sighed. "We might as well head back to the rez. The other two guys won't be home."

"What about hitting up some of Mark's customers?" Zach suggested.

"It's not like they'll just walk into the station and confess to buying drugs from Mark," Lani said.

"No, but you have to have arrested some of them for public intoxication or something," Zach suggested.

"Let's head back to the station where I can ask my chief who is most likely to open up about his drug dealing with Mark."

Zach nodded and helped her up into the truck, his hand resting on her leg for a little longer than necessary.

When she settled into her seat, she looked over at

Zach as he slid behind the steering wheel. "Thanks for coming along on this ride with me."

"I don't feel very useful."

"You are. I know that I don't have to watch my back when you're around. Especially now that I've been warned that I'm next on the killer's list."

"Seems he jumped the gun with Mark."

"Maybe he hadn't intended to kill Mark. He didn't stab Mark like he stabbed Tyler and Ben."

"Yeah, and he tried to make it appear as if Mark committed suicide."

Lani shook her head slowly. "To me, it almost appears that Mark's attack was committed by a different person from the one who committed the first two murders." As soon as she said the words out loud, the idea made more sense.

"Holy hell," she murmured. "We have two killers loose on the reservation."

CHAPTER 10

Zach chewed on Lani's words, not feeling any better about the situation with every passing minute. When they arrived at the station, he held back. "You go on in. I need to touch base with my boss. He might have some insight or maybe provide some help looking into the backgrounds of different people."

"I'd like to know more about Ben and Mark Wolf Paw, as well as Russell Bledsoe."

Zach nodded. "I'll see what he can do. I know his computer guy has some special skills when performing background checks."

"Good." Lani slipped out of the seat onto the ground. "I'll talk with my boss and see if he's familiar with any other drug busts and who was involved. Some of those people might have been Mark's customers. They might have taken exception to Mark losing all their product."

"Giving them a motive to kill," Zach finished.

She nodded. "Exactly."

"I'll see you inside, after I talk with Hank."

Lani gave him a brief smile and entered the station.

Zach scrolled through his cellphone contacts, found Hank's number and placed the call.

The head of the Brotherhood Protectors answered on the first ring. "Hey, Zach, how's it going?"

"Not great," Zach responded.

"I got that feeling when I saw your call come through," Hank said. "I haven't heard from you since you left here, but I understand there was another murder last night."

"There was," Zach said. "The local drug dealer. The body was dumped in the lake, along with his motorcycle. We think the killer tried to make it look like a suicide." He explained his visit to the coroner and the evidence of a struggle visible on the body.

"The killer's body count is up to three," Hank said. "Need some help?"

"Maybe." Zach went on to explain Lani's theory that the first two murders were different than the third. "We might have more than one killer. And someone trashed Lani's house and left a message. The word 'Next'."

Hank whistled. "Look, I can send more help. All you have to do is say the word."

"Right now, I'm living on the reservation with Lani as her fiancé. No one is questioning my right to be here. The elders aren't that keen on outsiders poking their noses into reservation business. I get a free ride since I'm with Lani. The best you could do for me now is run some background checks on the following people: Russell Bledsoe, Mark Wolf Paw, Ben Wolf Paw, Tyler

Lightfoot, Mattie Lightfoot and..." he hesitated, then added, "Raymond Swiftwater."

"I'll get Swede right on it," Hank promised. "And, Zach, don't hesitate to call if there's anything else you need. I have access to aircraft that could get me and half a dozen of my guys to you in less than an hour."

"That's good to know." Zach smiled into the phone. "I'll let you know if I need that kind of assistance." He liked that Hank was willing to throw everything he could at a situation, no matter the cost. How often had he gone into battle without backup? Too many times, he hadn't even had the full buy-in from his commanding officers.

Hank Patterson was everything he'd heard about and more. He cared about his people and was there if they needed him.

Zach rang off and entered the police station.

Lani was deep in conversation with the chief. She motioned him over and continued. "I'm telling you, Mark's murder was different. Either it was another killer, or the killer got sloppy."

"Could it be he killed Mark for different reasons?" the chief suggested. "Mark was the reservation drug dealer."

"Which leads to my next question..." Lani drew in a deep breath. "Who were his clients?"

"It might be easier to ask who wasn't one of his clients." The chief ran a hand through his hair. "We've picked up a number of people who've been strung out on drugs. We suspect they were using some of the illegal substances we found in Mark's trailer.

"Why would Mark have all that stuff out on his kitchen table?" Zach asked.

"I'm betting he was getting ready to move it," Black Knife said. "Or he'd just moved it to the trailer after his brother's death, and he was just starting to pack it away when Running Bear showed up."

"He had to know someone would be out to the trailer to ask him questions about his brother's death." Lani shook her head. "It doesn't make sense."

"Maybe his former hiding place was compromised, and he had to move it in a hurry," the chief said. "We might never know, since Mark can't answer any of our questions. The FBI agent went back to Great Falls. He'll be back after he does some research on his database back at his office. In the meantime, I have three dead Blackfeet and a group of elders breathing down my neck."

"Would it help for me to go back out to the lake and look again for evidence?" Lani asked.

"We combed that area," the chief said. "Whoever dumped Mark was good at covering his tracks."

"He had to have missed something," Lani said.

Black Knife snorted. "Yeah, like he missed at the Lightfoot home or Ben's place."

"Oh, and speaking of elders," Lani said. "You'll be happy to know Swiftwater is conducting his own investigation."

The chief swore. "What's he up to now?"

"He was at the coroner's office when we got there. He stayed while the coroner gave us his preliminary findings."

"Great, just what we need…an elder mucking up our investigation. I never did like Swiftwater. Why he's one of the elders, I'll never know." The chief scratched his chin. "He can't stay out of our business, and yet he can't keep his son employed. Not the best qualifications for an elder, if you ask me."

"What's wrong with his son?" Zach asked.

"He didn't show up for work this morning." The sheriff's brow furrowed. "I had coffee with his boss. He was complaining about the fact Alan hadn't come to work, nor had he bothered to call to explain why."

Lani recalled Swiftwater getting the call about his son missing work while he was at the coroner's office. "Do you think something happened to his son? Maybe the killer targeted him as well."

The chief shook his head. "That boy has never had to live up to his responsibilities. His daddy keeps bailing him out whenever he fails to meet expectations. His job at the feed store…?" Black Knife jerked his head. "Ray got him that job by putting a little pressure on the owner. And what does the owner get in return? A deadbeat employee. I'd fire his ass. But he can't, or Daddy Swiftwater will make his life miserable."

"Sounds like a winner," Lani said

"Granted, the kid has been sick lately, but no one knows whether it's real or due to substance abuse." The chief shrugged. "Either way, the least he could do is call in to his employer. Not showing up is rude and inconsiderate. Any employer would be within his rights to fire him. He'll be lucky to get another job anywhere near here without a decent reference."

Lani frowned, her thoughts going to the bar and her run-in with Alan Swiftwater. "Was Alan Swiftwater one of Mark's clients?"

The chief tilted his head considering her question. "If Alan is doing drugs, he could well have been."

Zach met her gaze. "He was at the bar when Mark came in."

Lani nodded. "He blocked my attempt to go after Mark."

"He was there to buy product from Mark," Zach concluded.

"Mark didn't have anything to sell, unless he had another stash outside his home," the chief said.

"Who knows what a man desperate for his next fix will do?" Lani said.

"He might have been angry when his dealer didn't come through for him," Zach said.

Lani drew a sharp breath. "Angry enough to beat him to death?"

The chief's brow formed a V on his forehead. "It's worth bringing Alan in for questioning. Since he didn't show up for work, we'll have to get creative about looking for him."

"We should start by going to his house," Lani said. "He lives with his father."

"If he were at his house, his boss would have gotten hold of his mother," the chief said. "She would have said something about him being there or not."

"Unless he's hiding out in his room and not answering his mother's calls," Lani said. "I'll swing by.

Then I'll make a pass through town, looking for his red Mustang. It ought to be easy to spot."

"If he's in town at all. If he killed Mark Wolf Paw, he might be miles away by now," Zach said. "He could have crossed the border into Canada."

"Great." The chief planted his fists on his hips. "We could be dealing with a fugitive who has gone international. It'll take time to wade through the red tape of extradition."

"We can't worry about that now," Lani said. "First, we have to make certain Alan hasn't left the county, much less the country."

"Right," the chief said. "I'll put out an all-points bulletin on him. If anyone sees him, they're to proceed with caution and bring him back for questioning. We don't have any evidence that he was responsible for Mark's murder. We won't be able to hold him long."

"I still don't think the same man who killed Tyler and Ben killed Mark." She rubbed her arms. "It doesn't feel the same. It didn't fit the M.O. While we're chasing Alan Swiftwater, who may or may not have killed a drug dealer, the other killer is laughing at us and eyeing his next victim." She jabbed a thumb against her chest. "Me. He said I was next. Not Mark Wolf Paw."

"Good point," the chief said. "You should stay home and arm yourself. I'll get one of the other officers on duty to bring Alan in."

"I don't want to sit at home and wait for the killer to come to me," Lani said. "I just want to remind you that he's still out there. We have to keep open minds and eyes while we're out looking for Alan Swiftwater."

"Will do, Running Bear. Now, get your ass out there and find our killers," he said, pointing at the door. "I'll be out there doing the same. You got your radio?"

Lani patted her jacket pocket. "Got it."

"Good. Call me if you find them. Or if you get into any trouble. I'm going to check out the Swiftwater residence on the off-chance Alan's hiding there."

"We'll head out to the lake and look for anything you might have missed."

"I guess it doesn't hurt to have another pair of eyes on a crime scene," the chief said. "Be careful."

"Yes, sir." She popped a salute and turned to leave the building.

Zach chuckled when they reached his truck. "I thought for a moment the chief was going to pull you off the case again."

"He can't," Lani said and climbed into the passenger seat of the truck. "We're too shorthanded, and he needs all the people he can get looking for our killers."

"I would prefer to go back to your house and wait for the killer to show up. At least then, we'd have a defensible position."

"Yeah, but we don't know how long he'll take to make his move. I can't sit that long. I'd have to save him the bullet and shoot myself." She winked down at him as he closed the passenger door for her.

Lani's gaze followed him around the front of the truck, admiring the way he held himself. The man might be out of the military, but he hadn't lost an ounce of his military bearing. He held his broad shoulders back and squared. His torso narrowed to a slender waist and hips. The man walked with all the confidence of someone in charge of his own body and mind.

Damn, he was good looking. She'd much rather go back to her house and make love to him on the sleeping bag until the next day dawned, or longer. That just couldn't happen. Not with a killer on the loose and gunning for her. They'd taken chances the night before by making love and not paying attention to their surroundings. Sure, Zach had fixed the door frame and locked the door securely.

Still, the killer could have tossed a Molotov cocktail through the window and set the place on fire, burning them to crisps inside. Of course, he hadn't, and they'd explored each other's bodies thoroughly more than once.

The idea of repeating that exploration was so tempting, Lani almost threw her hands in the air and agreed to the chief's recommendation that she go back to her house and wait for the attack. At least then, she'd be alone with Zach. They might pick up where they'd left off and make love again. She stopped short of telling him to stop at the grocery store for more condoms. She didn't want to miss out on anything that might happen between them when they finally did retire to her house.

Before she could open her mouth to ask, they'd passed the grocery store and headed north toward the edge of town, moving slowly through the buildings. She focused on finding Alan's red Mustang. "If he was Mark's killer, and he thought he'd gotten away with passing it off as suicide, why would he hide? If I thought I'd gotten away with murder, I'd be out in the open."

"Remember, the M.E. said Mark got a piece of his killer. He scratched him." Zach slowed at a corner and looked left then right. "He might be hiding until the scratch heals."

"That could take days."

"Yeah, but how else would he explain it? And if his skin is as dark as yours, even after it heals—"

"It'll leave a pink or white mark for a lot longer." She nodded. "He'll have to hide for a while. Which is a good reason to avoid working in a public place. And he wouldn't be making any money, so he can't afford to go very far. He'll stay someplace where no one else goes." She looked across the console to Zach.

He nodded. "The abandoned warehouse." Zach goosed the accelerator, sending the truck shooting forward to the edge of town. Slowing slightly, he took the corner at the road leading out to the derelict building surrounded by chain link fence.

Lani leaned forward, her pulse racing, her hands clenched into fists. Excitement made her eyes shine and her cheeks darken.

Zach prayed they were on the right track. They had to be. He wasn't familiar with the area. He didn't know another place to look. Then he remembered Alan leaving the bar, shaking a cigarette out of a pack. A green and white pack. Just like the crumpled one Lani found in the warehouse. Swiftwater had used the site before. Surely, he'd use it again.

As they approached the abandoned warehouse, Zach slowed to a stop, two blocks before they reached the fence.

Lani's brow dipped, and she shot a quick glance toward him. "Why are you stopping here?"

"We're better off going the rest of the way on foot. If he's in there, we don't want him to hear the sound of my truck's engine. He might make a run for it."

Lani nodded. "You're right. We need to sneak up on him. If we see his car, we need to do something to disable it so he can't get away as easily as Mark did." She got out of the truck and started toward the old building.

Zach caught up with her and snagged her arm. "One thing."

"Yeah?" she asked her gaze on the building ahead of them.

"I go in first."

She turned back to him, her brow furrowing. "I'm the cop. You're—"

"Going in first. He wants to kill you. Not me."

"But he might kill you to get to me." She shook her head. "I can't let you go in first. This is my responsibility."

"If I have to handcuff you to the fence, I will. I'm going in first." His jaw set in a firm line. He wasn't going to let her go a step further until she agreed to his terms.

Lani looked from him to the building and back. "Okay. But I'm coming in right behind you." She punched his arm lightly. "Don't go and get yourself shot." Lani lifted up on her toes and pressed her lips to his in a brief kiss. "I kind of like having you around. Alive."

Zach wrapped his arms around her and kissed her thoroughly. "The feeling is mutual. I think we have chemistry, and I don't want to lose that anytime soon." He set her back on her feet. "Don't get yourself killed."

She stared up at him for a long moment. "You mean that?"

He locked his gaze with hers. "Every word. I've been thinking about you since Afghanistan. If you hadn't called me when you did, I was going to look you up."

Her face split in a grin. "Let's get this over with. I want to explore the possibilities with you more. When we're not hunting a killer."

"Deal." He led the way to the gap in the fence and went through first. He waited for her to follow, and then hurried toward the building, ducking into the shadows on the eastern side. As he rounded the corner of the building, Zach spotted the bumper of the red Mustang, parked behind a stack of pallets. He waited for Lani to catch up to him then pointed to the car.

She nodded. "Disable it," she whispered.

He nodded and headed for the car first, moving in the shadows until he reached the stack of pallets.

Zach stopped and listened for sounds of movement from the other side of the stack. Nothing indicated the car was occupied. He inched his way around the pallets and peered into the back window of the sports car.

It appeared to be empty.

Lani slipped up beside him. "Look at the trunk," she said.

Deep scratches marred the previously pristine paint job. It was as if something heavy and metal had been dragged across the paint. Maybe a dirt bike being shoved into the trunk?

Zach slipped up beside the vehicle. On the back seat lay a tire iron. The murder weapon?

The front driver's window was down, and the key was in the ignition.

Zach reached in, plucked the key out and slid it into his pocket.

Then he moved past the old car, heading for the door on the side of the building where they'd exited the last time they'd been there.

Lani kept up with him, moving silently, placing her feet carefully so as not to make a sound.

When he reached the door, he knew that if Alan was inside, he'd hear the door opening. Their cover would be blown, and they'd have to move fast to catch him. Based on the location of his car, he had to have used this door to enter the building.

The last time he'd tried that door, it had been locked from the inside. Lani had unlocked it. If it was locked this time, they'd have to retrace their steps and swing around to the other side of the structure and enter through the missing panel.

Zach drew in a deep breath and held it. Then he gripped the handle and slowly turned it.

The knob turned, and the door opened.

Zach stood to the side, out of range, and let the door float open.

He leaned close to Lani and whispered in her ear. "Give me a second before you follow."

She nodded, her gun in her hand, her knees bent, and her stance ready.

Zach held his pistol in front of him as he slipped

around the edge of the door and into the building. Immediately, he ducked to the side, out of the wedge of light shining on the floor.

He moved deeper, hunching low, his ears straining to hear even the slightest sound. A noise behind him made him glance back.

Lani had ducked through the door and now clung to a shadow close by. She was inside, following him. A chill slithered down the back of Zach's neck. He prayed she wasn't following him into danger. He had vowed to protect her, not get her deeper into trouble. Lani would be the first to jump in feet first. She had a duty to protect the people of her tribe, and she wouldn't quit until she found the killer or killers.

Zach faced forward, allowing his eyesight to adjust to the darkness. He searched shadows for movement. Taking a step forward, he felt the boards beneath him give, the wood crackling and creaking. Splinters of wood snapped. He didn't linger in one spot, afraid that if he did, the whole floor would give way, and he'd plunge to the basement level below.

Behind him, he heard the snap and crackle of tired boards, groaning beneath the weight of one slender woman. He wished he had a flashlight to illuminate the vast room to help him find the man they were looking for. But a flashlight would make him a target, giving a shooter something to aim for. He had to go with the faint glow from the open door on the side of the building. The deeper he moved into the building, the less light he had to work with. Soon, he couldn't see the hand in front of his face.

The key in his pocket reminded him that he had Alan's means of escape.

"Alan," Lani's voice echoed in the vast blackness. "We know you're here. We just want to talk to you."

Silence reigned.

"You're not going to get away," she said. "We have the keys to your car. The only way you're getting out of here is on foot." She paused.

Zach listened for a voice, the sound of movement, anything.

Nothing.

Lani continued. "I was a star runner on my track team in high school," she said. "And I always aced the run on my fitness test in the Army. You won't get far. And even if you get away from me, you won't get away from my fiancé."

Still, no response.

Zach drew in a deep breath and added his plea. "Alan, we know what you did to Mark. He didn't commit suicide. He fought hard to survive. And he has the DNA beneath his fingernails to prove who hurt him. You might as well save some time and turn yourself in."

The creak of a floorboard sounded ahead of Zach. He hurried toward the sound, intent on catching Alan before he ducked out an exit they had yet to discover.

Zach took another step. The floor beneath him suddenly gave way, a gaping maw opening up to swallow him. He fell through the jagged-edged boards and rotted timbers. He didn't stop until he crumpled to the solid concrete floor of the basement below. For a moment, he lay gasping for air, the breath having been knocked from his lungs when he hit bottom.

"Zach!" Lani cried out. "Zach! Where are you? Are you all right? Please, tell me you're all right."

Zach lay on his back staring upward, the only light coming from above through the hole in the floor he'd just fallen through. The glow was barely a lighter gray in the pitch blackness.

When he could fill his lungs again, he called out, "Go back, Lani. The floor isn't safe. Go back."

"Not without you," she said. "Where are you?"

"In the basement. I fell through the floor." He pushed to a sitting position, testing his muscles and bones. So far, nothing felt broken. Running his hands over his legs, he felt warm wetness on his right thigh. His fingers encountered a tear in his jeans and the flesh beneath stung when he touched it. One of the boards must have ripped a hole in his thigh. It didn't feel that deep. Thankfully, he wouldn't bleed out. But he was stuck in the dark, and he had to find his way out soon. Lani was alone above him. And she was next on the killer's agenda.

"Zach? Talk to me," she said. "Are you okay?"

"I'm okay. But I need you to get out of here. Now."

"I'm not leaving you."

"You have to. You're not safe on your own."

"I'm with you."

"Not when you're up there, and I'm down here." He pushed to his feet and winced at the pain shooting through his thigh. "You have to get out of here."

"I'm turning on a phone's flashlight," she said.

"No, Lani. You'll only make yourself a target."

"I can't help you, if I can't see you," she argued. "I'm following your voice."

"Don't," he cried out.

At that moment, the boards above snapped, and the warehouse floor caved in, bringing Lani down with a resounding thud.

"Lani?" he called out, feeling his way across the floor to where he hoped to find her.

A moan echoed against the walls around him.

"Lani, sweetheart, talk to me," he begged.

CHAPTER 11

"I'm okay," Lani said, though every bone in her body had been jolted hard in the fall, especially her tailbone.

"Can you move?" Zach asked.

She couldn't see him, only hear him, as he shuffled through the debris, his voice moving steadily toward her.

Lani pulled her cellphone from her jacket pocket and tried to turn on the flashlight app. She slid her finger across the screen, feeling the sharp lines of a huge crack. "Damn," she said. "It's broken."

"Dear, sweet Jesus, Lani," he said. "What's broken, babe? Does it hurt bad?"

She laughed. "No, no. I'm not in pain, except my sore tailbone," she said. "My cellphone is broken. I can't switch on the light."

"Oh, Lani, baby," Zach said. "You're going to be the death of me."

"That's where you're wrong," a voice said from above. A beam of light shined down on them, moving from Zach to where Lani lay among the rubble of the broken floor. "You shouldn't have come. You should have let Mark's death be what it was...suicide. Because he might as well have committed suicide when he let all his drugs get confiscated by the police. The jerk was so strung out on them, he didn't even try to take them with him. He ran, wasting everything. All he had left was a tiny baggy not even half full." Alan paused. "A tiny baggy. I paid for a lot more than that, yet he wasn't willing to give me even that pathetic amount."

"So, you took it from him using force," Zach said. "Isn't that right?"

"I had no choice," Alan said, his voice shaking. "I had no choice. I couldn't go another day without it."

"So, you killed him," Lani prompted.

"It doesn't matter," Alan said. "Everything is going to hell, and you're going with me." He set the flashlight on the ground, the beam shining at his feet. He leaned over and hefted a large can in his arms. "It's over. It's all over," he said, his voice breaking on a sob. Tipping the can, he poured liquid onto the floorboards above them.

Some of it splashed down on the concrete near Lani. An acrid scent filled her nostrils and made her blood run cold.

Gasoline.

Lani pushed to her feet. "Alan, you don't want to do this."

"Yes. I do," he said. "I can't go to jail. They won't give me what I need. They can't fix what's broken, and they can't save the dying. I won't be here to watch it happen. I won't care."

"Alan, you're not making sense. Help us out of here. Let us get you the help you need. Killing us won't make things better. I promise you," Lani said.

"Maybe not, but if I die with you, they will blame me for all five deaths. No one will look further. No one will learn the truth."

"The truth about what?" Zach asked. "That you didn't kill Tyler or Ben?"

"Alan, we know you didn't kill Tyler and Ben," Lani said.

"You'll take that knowledge to the grave, along with me," Alan said. Sloshing gasoline over the floor above, he moved away from the gap in the floor.

Zach flicked on the flashlight in his phone. "Come on, we have to find a way out of here. Now." He took Lani's hand and helped her pick her way through the boards and trash on the basement floor, alternating between shining the light at their feet and pointing it at the walls.

"There has to be a staircase around here somewhere." Zach turned in a three-hundred-sixty-degree circle, shining the little phone flashlight around the huge expanse of basement beneath the warehouse. When the light fell on stairs leading up to the next level, he stopped. "Bingo." Gripping Lani's elbow in his hand, he hustled her toward the stairs.

"We might only have seconds before Alan lights a match and sets our world on fire. If we don't get out of here before that happens, we'll be trapped in the basement as the rest of the warehouse burns down around us," Lani said.

"You're not dying on my watch," Zach muttered, increasing their speed until they were running.

"Who said I was dying?" Lani reached the stairs first and climbed to the top, only to find a door blocking their exit. She pulled on the handle, giving it every bit of strength she could muster. It didn't budge.

"Move." Zach pushed past her, braced his foot on the wall beside the door, grabbed the handle and yanked hard. The door shook but didn't open.

"Again," Lani yelled, the scent of gasoline filling the air, making her gag.

Zach braced his foot again and pulled with all his might.

The door slammed open, nearly sending Zach flying down the steps.

Holding onto the doorknob, he regained his balance and held the door wide, allowing Lani to go through first.

"Get outside as quickly as possible," he said and pushed her through the door. He followed right behind her, still shining the phone's light over her shoulder at what lay in front of Lani, so she didn't step on any more rotten boards.

As they neared the door they'd come through, Lani realized it was closed. They'd specifically left it open when they'd come through minutes before. She hurried forward and tried the handle. It didn't work. She twisted the locking mechanism, only to find it had been broken. The metal door had been jammed and locked permanently.

"Let me try," Zach said.

Lani moved out of the way.

Zach hit the door with his shoulder. The door didn't budge.

He hit it again and bounced back. Rubbing his shoulder, he drew in a deep breath and would have slammed into the door again, but Lani laid a hand on his arm.

"Don't," she said. "Alan jammed the lock. It's not going to open." She turned toward the interior of the warehouse. "We have to find another way out."

"There is no other way out," Alan shouted from across the floor.

Lani and Zach turned toward the sound.

Alan struck a match, held it up for a second, lighting his face in an eerie glow. Then he tossed it into the warehouse through the gap in the exterior siding. Flames erupted on the gasoline-soaked wooden floor, shooting toward Lani and Zach.

Her heart stopped as Lani watched the flames racing toward her, lighting the interior of the old building.

Zach gripped her arm. "Move!" he shouted and dragged her away from the oncoming flames to a place on the floor where the wood was dull and dry.

Flames grew around them, consuming the gasoline Alan had sloshed sporadically throughout the structure.

"We have to make our way to the other side through the areas that aren't soaked in gasoline," Zach said. "And fast. It won't be long before the boards catch fire."

Lani nodded and followed him through the maze of flames, ducking low to avoid the rising smoke.

Between the fire and the rotten floor, they made

painfully slow progress. Lani pulled her shirt collar up over her nose and picked her way over the dangerously unstable floor, praying they made it to the gap in the wall before the fire took root in the dry wood flooring and consumed it like tinder.

She coughed and sucked more smoke into her lungs, causing her to cough uncontrollably.

Zach grabbed her hand and dragged her through the smoke and flames.

At one point, he stepped on a board that cracked and splintered. He would have fallen through had Lani not jerked him back in time.

He changed direction and kept moving, pulling her along until they were within ten yards of the opening. Alan Swiftwater stood in the gap, a gun in his hand. "No way. You can't leave. I won't let you. They have to believe it was me all along."

"That you killed Mark?" Zach called out. "They'll know…" he coughed, "soon enough, when the DNA under his fingernails is analyzed." Covering his mouth again, he continued forward despite the gun pointed at his chest. "Don't add to the murder count, Alan. You don't want to kill us. They'll put you away for life."

"You don't understand. My life doesn't matter. I'm already dead. Everything and everyone I ever cared about is dead or dying."

Lani dropped the hand holding her shirt up over her mouth. Smoke stung her eyes and lungs. "What are you talking about?" She coughed, desperate to breathe fresh, clean air. "You have your father. He cares."

Alan shook his head. "No. He's dying. Can't you see?"

"No, Alan. I can't see," Lani said, blinking to help her see the man through the smoke. "What do you mean your father is dying?" Her lungs burned with each breath she took. If they didn't get out soon, the smoke would kill them before the flames could.

"If you continue your investigation," Alan said. "then everyone will know. He'll die in disgrace. I won't let that happen."

"Enough!" A deep voice shouted.

Another man stepped into the gap in the wall. A man of equal height to Alan but with broader shoulders and a more commanding presence.

Raymond Swiftwater glared at his son. "How dare you?"

"I couldn't let them take you away," his son said. "They don't know what I do."

"Shut up. You have no right to fight my battles. You can't. This is mine, and only mine to fight." He shook his head. "You fool. You would have had it all. My business, my money, my life after my death. Yet, you chose to throw it all away on drugs, and then murder." Raymond shook his head. "Why?"

"I wouldn't have had it all. I wouldn't have had you. And I couldn't survive without the drugs. I mean, look at me." He held out his gun, his hand shaking uncontrollably. "I killed a man because he couldn't give me what I needed."

"You shouldn't have done it," Raymond said.

Alan glared at his father. "*I* shouldn't have done it?

What about *you*? Why Tyler and Ben? What did they ever do to you?"

"They had what I didn't, damn it," Raymond ground out.

"And what's that?" his son demanded. "A long life ahead of them?"

"Yes!" Raymond shouted.

Zach knelt on the wooden floor of the warehouse and drew his gun from his holster.

Shocked at Raymond's revelation, Lani dropped to her knees searching for better air to breathe, her hand going to her weapon as well.

"We have to get out of here," he said softly. "I'll distract them. You go. Slip up to the wall and wait for my signal. Then make a break for it."

She shook her head. "I won't leave without you."

"Just do it," he urged. "I'll get out after you're safe."

"No."

He cupped her face in his hands and kissed her lips in a brief but tender kiss. "I think I'm falling for you, Lani Running Bear. Live, so that I can find out if what I'm feeling is love." He nodded his head toward the gap and the two men blocking their escape. "Now, go."

"But—"

"Go!" Zach pushed to his feet and staggered to the right, away from Lani, but in the general direction of the Swiftwater men.

Lani darted in the other direction, moving toward the exterior wall and the shadows that would hide her until she could reach the gap. Her heart hammered against her ribs, and her lungs strained to pump oxygen into her system. She was dizzy, her chest burned and heart swelled with the knowledge that Zach might be falling in love with her. Living was the only option. For both of them.

When she arrived at the wall, she crept along the metal siding until she was within a couple yards of Alan and Raymond Swiftwater. She glanced toward the spot where she'd last seen the man she was quickly coming to love and gasped.

Zach rose out of a wall of flame, his arms extended like a phoenix rising from the ashes. He was bold, larger than life and magnificent. "Let us go free…or kill us now!" His announcement was then followed by coughing.

The two men stopped arguing and stared at Zach.

Alan raised his gun and aimed at Zach.

No!

While the Swiftwaters' attention was on Zach, Lani charged toward Alan.

The pop of gunfire sounded. One shot, then another.

Before she reached the younger Swiftwater, he slumped to the ground and lay still.

Lani stumbled and fell to her knees. She scrambled around to face the inferno and the position where Zach had made his stand. Who had fired the shots? Where was Zach?

Her gaze swept the raging fire to no avail. If he was there, he was down.

Beside Lani, Alan lay on the ground, unmoving. Raymond stood with his gun to his jaw. He stared down at her. "He was my son. I only wanted to know he would be okay when I died." His lips firmed. "Now, it doesn't matter." He pulled the trigger.

At the same time, an earsplitting crack sounded, followed by a deafening rumble. The roof of the warehouse swayed, and then fell, crashing inward.

As her world imploded around her, Lani screamed and fell to the ground. A cloud of smoke and dust consumed her.

When Zach had raised his arms, he'd cupped his weapon in his palm. With the flames behind him, he'd banked on the fact he'd be nothing but a silhouette to the men standing in the door. They wouldn't see that he had his gun. Given the circumstances, he would be forced to use it. He had to make sure Lani wasn't hurt when she made her move.

As Alan pointed his gun, Zach knew he had to shoot first or die in the flames.

He didn't get the chance to pull the trigger first. Alan's gun went off at the moment Zach ducked, lowered his weapon and pulled the trigger.

He dove toward a black spot on the floor where the flames had already consumed the gasoline. Rolling to his feet, he was running for the opening when the roof shimmied, groaned and came down. As smoke and dust exploded outward, Zach held his breath and focused on getting the hell out of the building before he was crushed beneath the debris.

He ran blind, the air too thick to see through, his lungs burning from smoke and dust. He prayed he was still heading in the right direction as he sprinted, running as far and fast as he could.

Zach didn't stop until he cleared the cloud of dust and smoke and witnessed blue sky overhead. Only then did he stop and drag in a breath of clean, fresh air. He blinked to clear the grit of smoke from his eyes and stared back at the billowing cloud rising up from what was left of the dilapidated warehouse. Nothing moved out of the cloud. No one moved.

Lani.

Taking a deep breath of smoke-free air, he ran back into the cloud. "Lani!" he shouted. "Lani!"

The roar of the flames and the rumble of struts and timbers crashing in drowned out his calls.

Smoke made his eyes burn and tears form, washing the grime from his eyes. "Lani!" he called out.

He found the side of the building and felt his way along the wall, trying and failing to find the woman who'd shown him what a beautiful place his Montana was. The woman who'd brought his heart to life and given him hope for the future. A future in the state he thought he'd left forever. A future that might include a strong, beautiful woman.

"Lani!" When he came to the gap in the wall, he dropped to his knees and felt his way along the ground, searching for life. Searching for her.

His fingers encountered a lump. A body. Zach waved a hand over it in an attempt to identify who it was. The smoke cleared enough, Zach could see the face beneath him, and he let out a cry of disappointment and relief.

It wasn't Lani.

Alan Swiftwater lay in a pool of his own blood, his eyes staring up into the dirty cloud.

Zach moved past him to another dark figure lying in the dirt.

Raymond Swiftwater. He couldn't tell by the man's face, as it had been blown away and was nothing more than a bloody mess. But he'd been the only other man out there. It was him. And he was dead.

Knowing the smoke would kill her if the Swiftwaters hadn't already, Zach pushed past the deceased men and almost cried when he found her body, lying in the dirt.

Scooping her up in his arms, he walked in the direction he hoped would take him away from the fire and smoke. Soon, the cloud thinned, and he stood beneath the clear, blue Montana sky, sucking clean air into his smoke-filled lungs.

He kept walking until he was certain the smoke wouldn't shift in his direction. Then he laid Lani on the ground, pulled his cellphone out of his pocket and dialed 911.

Even before the dispatcher answered his call, he could hear the sound of sirens wailing. In the next few minutes, fire trucks arrived, and emergency medical technicians gathered around them and took over.

While one paramedic slipped an oxygen mask over Lani's face, another handed one to Zach and commanded, "Breathe."

He brushed the man's offering aside. "Not until she does."

"She will. But you're no good to her, if you don't do the same." Again, he handed the mask to Zach.

Taking it, he placed it over his nose and mouth and breathed in the oxygen. When he dissolved into a fit of coughing, he flung the mask aside and dragged in more air, feeling as if he would suffocate behind the mask.

The paramedic lifted the mask back up to his face. "Keep breathing the oxygen. Though you're out of the smoke and fire, your lungs might be damaged. You need this." He tipped his head toward Lani. "She needs it."

Zach covered his nose and mouth again. "I'm riding with her to the hospital." It wasn't a question. He would go, whether they wanted him to or not.

Chief Black Knife arrived in his service vehicle and ran to where the emergency technicians were loading Lani into the back of an ambulance. "Is she okay?" he asked.

"I don't know." Zach shoved a hand through his sooty hair, more exhausted than he'd ever felt after a battle. "She's not dead."

But she could still die. Smoke inhalation could claim her even after they'd removed her from the fire.

"What happened?" the chief asked.

Between hacking coughs, Zach gave the chief a digest version of what had occurred.

"Swiftwater?" the older man shook his head. "No wonder he didn't want too many people digging into the murders. But his son?" He sighed. "I guess the apple didn't fall far from the tree."

The firefighters had tamped down the flames, and

the smoke had begun to clear, exposing the two bodies lying near the building.

"I'd like to think I was the one who killed Alan Swiftwater," Zach said. "Based on the direction of his wound, I think his father did. Not from my lack of trying. I was inside the building facing him when I fired my weapon. He was aiming at me; however, his wound was in his side. I suspect his father shot him."

"They'll conduct an autopsy," the chief said. "I assume you'll be sticking around?"

Zach nodded and climbed into the ambulance with Lani. "Damn right, I will."

The door shut between him and the chief, and the ambulance raced toward Cut Bank, the reservation not having sufficient medical facilities to handle a severe case of smoke inhalation.

Zach sat beside the paramedic, holding Lani's hand, willing her to get well and be her usual, smart, strong and sassy self. If he hadn't known it before, he knew now that he loved this woman, and he wanted her to be all right, even if she didn't love him back.

CHAPTER 12

Lani woke the next day in the hospital. Her throat was sore, and her lungs felt like hell, but the sun shone through the window. She was alive.

"About time you woke up," a voice said.

She turned her head toward the door where a nurse in blue scrubs pushed a cart with a computer perched on top. "I'm Arianna, your nurse. I'm here to get your vital signs."

"How long?" Lani whispered, her words barely making it past her vocal cords.

"They brought you in yesterday afternoon. The doctor gave you a sedative to help you rest. You were fighting everyone when they tried to get you into that bed." She held out a thermometer. "Under your tongue, please."

Lani opened her mouth, allowing the nurse to stick the thermometer under her tongue. She wanted to ask but was afraid of the answer.

Where was Zach?

"From what I understand, you're lucky to be alive. That fire on the reservation flared and burned into the night. They say there wasn't anything left but melted metal siding and a concrete basement when it finally burned itself out. Some people died." She shook her head as she wrapped the blood pressure cuff around her upper arm. "Yes, ma'am, you're lucky to be alive."

Tears welled in Lani's eyes. When the nurse plucked the thermometer from her lip, Lani mustered the courage to ask. "What about…" she croaked. Clearing her throat, she started over. "What about my…fiancé?" She held her breath, crossed her fingers and prayed.

The woman had her stethoscope in her ears, listening to Lani's heartbeat. When she looked up, she frowned. "Did you say something?"

"Yes," Lani gushed, letting go of the breath she'd been holding. "What about my fiancé, Zach Jones?"

Her words came out loud and clear.

"Did someone say my name?" a deep, raspy voice said from the door to her room. Zach entered the hospital room, carrying a huge bouquet of daisies in a clear glass vase and a small duffel bag. He dropped the duffel bag, plunked the vase on the rolling table, bent and pressed a kiss to her forehead. "Hey, beautiful."

Lani flung her arms around his neck and pulled him down in a hug so tight, he had no choice but to let her have her way with him. "Oh, Zach. Thank God. Thank God," she said. Tears flowed down her cheeks, making gray spots of residual soot on the white hospital sheets. "I thought you died in the fire. The roof, the smoke. How the hell did you get out?" She laughed and let him straighten, a smile permanently affixed to her face. "Oh, who cares? You're alive. That's all that matters."

She felt like hell, probably looked like it, but she couldn't stop grinning. "You're alive."

He nodded, a smile spreading across his face. "And so are you. For a while there, I thought it was touch and go." Zach lifted her hand and kissed the backs of her knuckles, his brow dipping low on his forehead. "With all that smoke and dust blanketing the building and the areas surrounding the warehouse, I didn't think I'd find you in time. I have to admit…it scared years off my life."

She brought his hand to her cheek. "You found me."

"Yes, I did. And you're going to be fine. The doctor said so. In fact, he's signed your discharge papers. I get to take you home." He reached for the bag he'd dropped on the floor and dropped it on the bed. "You'll find shampoo, a hairbrush, clothes and unmentionables in there. Enough to get you cleaned up and ready to go home."

"Really?"

The nurse winked. "Really. You can use the shower in the bathroom. I put clean towels in there this morning."

Lani threw back the sheets and swung her legs over the side of the bed. "I'll be ready in two shakes." She stood, swayed and would have fallen if Zach hadn't been there to catch her.

"Whoa, take a baby step at a time. You were on death's door a short time ago."

"I'm okay," she assured him. "I just got up too quickly." Lani squared her shoulders and met his gaze. "See? I'm okay."

"Maybe I should help you into the bathroom to make sure you don't pass out and drown," Zach said with a wicked grin.

"Do you want to get out of here, or stay a little longer?" she asked, her brow rising.

"Tough decision." He glanced toward the bathroom. "How big is that shower?"

"Seriously?" the nurse said, frowning. "Let the woman get cleaned up. This is a hospital, not a hotel."

Zach laughed out loud. "Go on, get your shower…alone."

Lani hesitated, chewing on her bottom lip.

He gave her a twisted grin. "Don't worry. I'll be here when you get out."

She walked toward the bathroom.

"Uh, Lani?" he said.

She turned to see him smiling. "What?"

"That gown opens in the back." He winked.

Heat burned her cheeks. She dove for the bathroom and slammed the door between them. He was right, the gown was open, and she wasn't wearing anything beneath it.

Lani yanked the gown off, turned on the water and didn't wait for it to warm before she stepped beneath the spray. She needed the cooling effect of the water to tamp down the fire raging at her core. Once she got back to her house, she'd roll out the sleeping bag and make love to him until neither one of them could stand. Then she'd make love to him again.

Using a significant amount of soap and shampoo, she scrubbed at the soot covering every inch of her body. When the gray water ran clear down the drain, she turned off the water, dried her body, brushed the tangles from her hair and rummaged through the bag of clothing.

She didn't recognize any of it.

"Um, Zach?" she called out.

"Yes, dear?" he answered as if he were standing on the other side of the door. "Are you all right?"

"I'm fine. Are you sure you grabbed the right bag? Not someone else's?"

"A friend of mine helped me pack it. Ray Swiftwater destroyed all of your clothing with spray paint. The items in your bag are new, donated by Hank Patterson's wife. She assured me they would fit. She had me check the sizes on your ruined clothes, so she'd know what to pack."

Lani lifted a sunny yellow cashmere sweater out of the bag and held up to her chest, looking at it against her skin in the mirror. The color complemented her coloring beautifully.

A white lacy bra and matching panties fit her perfectly. She pulled on the yellow sweater and a pair of cocoa-colored trousers and a pair of slim, black flats for her feet. "Could I hire Hank's wife to clothes shop for me again?" Lani said as she opened the door and stepped out.

Zach's smile faded, and his eyes rounded. "Wow."

"I know, right?" She turned around to give him a full perspective of the outfit. "She's amazing."

"*You're* amazing." He drew her into his arms and kissed her soundly on the lips before setting her at arm's length. "Ready?"

She laughed. "Yes. But I want to go shopping with Hank's wife again. Think she would take me?"

"You'll have to ask her. She's pretty busy between her job and their baby."

"What does she do?"

"Movies," Zach said. He gathered the plastic bag full of her sooty clothing and the duffel bag he'd brought with him containing the toiletries and clothes.

"Movies?" Lani asked, following him out the door of the hospital. "Have I seen her in anything?"

"Most likely."

"Patterson…" She shook her head. "I don't remember an actress with the last name of Patterson."

"She doesn't go by Patterson. She goes by McClain. Sadie McClain."

Lani stopped in the middle of the hallway. "*The* Sadie McClain?"

He looked back, frowning. "Yes, of course."

Lani squealed. "Sadie McClain picked out my clothes?" She looked down at the outfit and shook her head. "How can you be so nonchalant?"

Zach shrugged. "They're just clothes."

"Clothes picked out by Sadie McClain." Lani slipped her hand into his and hugged his arm. "That's the second-best thing to happen to me today."

"What was the first?" he asked, smiling down at her as they walked toward the exit.

She hugged his arm again, the smile slipping from her lips. "Waking up to find you alive."

Zach stopped in the middle of the hallway, dropped the bags and gathered her into his arms. "You were the best thing to happen to me in my entire lifetime." He crushed her lips in a kiss that curled her toes and left her breathless.

"Yowzah," a nurse murmured as she passed them. "You're making me jealous. My husband doesn't ever kiss me like that."

Zach retrieved the bags and hurried Lani out of the hospital. He filled her in on his conversation with the police chief and what they'd found in Alan and Raymond's vehicles. The tire iron in Alan's Mustang had hairs from Mark's scalp. Raymond had hidden the knife and baseball bat he'd used to kill Tyler and Ben under the mat in the back of his SUV. The police chief was certain they'd find enough DNA on both to be certain Raymond had killed them.

"And Hank's computer guy, Swede, hacked into Raymond's home computer and found emails and reports confirming Raymond had been diagnosed with pancreatic cancer." Zach shook his head. "The man was dying. He'd saved his suicide note, explaining his reasons for killing Tyler and Ben. They had everything going for them: they were well liked and set for a long, happy life, something Raymond wouldn't have. Apparently, he was jealous and angry and decided if he had to go, he was taking them with him."

Knowing who killed Tyler and Ben wouldn't bring

them back, but Tyler's grandmother would have closure.

"I have a little surprise for you," Zach said as they drove through Browning and turned onto her street.

There were several cars parked against the curb and a couple alongside hers in the driveway. But that wasn't what caught her attention. "My house!" she cried out. "The paint's gone."

"Not only is the red paint gone," Zach grinned, "the entire exterior and interior of the house has been repainted."

Lani shook her head. "How?"

"Did I tell you that I work for the Brotherhood Protectors?"

She nodded. "I know that."

"Well, when they heard what happened here, they piled into their vehicles and drove the five hours from Eagle Rock to Browning and worked all night and morning to paint and repair what was damaged. They even hauled off the broken furniture and trash to the dump."

Lani's eyes filled with tears.

Zach dropped down from the truck, hurried around to her side and helped her to the ground. "That's not all."

"What do you mean? Not all?" She laughed. "Isn't that enough?"

He shook his head. "They all pitched in," he said, guiding her up the steps to the front entrance. The door opened and a smiling Sadie McClain stood there, larger than life and as beautiful in person as she was on the big screen. "Welcome home, Lani."

Behind her were at least a dozen other people, male and female, holding cans of beer and glasses of wine. A man carrying a small child on his arm slipped a hand around Sadie. "Lani, I'm Hank Patterson. This is my wife, Sadie, and our baby, Emma. I hope you don't mind that a few of us made ourselves at home." He stepped back and let Lani walk into the room.

The place had been transformed from a disaster to a place that belonged on the cover of a home design magazine. A new sofa and easy chair stood in the living room on a bright, clean area rug. Beautiful artwork graced the freshly painted walls.

Broad-shouldered men filled the space with lovely women at their sides. A large German Shepherd leaned against one of the men's legs.

Zach leaned close. "The dog's name is Six. Don't worry, he won't bite."

Lani looked up at the man with the dog. "Can I pet him?"

The man nodded.

Lani, in a state of shock, held out her hand for the dog to sniff before she reached out to scratch behind his ear.

He nuzzled her hand, his tail thumping against the floor.

"Come see your bedroom," Sadie said. "If you don't like the furnishings, you can tell me. It won't hurt my feelings. It was all I could get delivered overnight."

Lani entered her bedroom, stunned at the gorgeous

wood furniture and the soft white comforter spread out over a brand-new mattress. "This is too much," she said. "I can never repay you for all you've done."

"No payment required," Hank said. "It was worth it to see Sadie in action, ordering all of this and getting the store owners to ship it overnight. Not only is the woman a phenomenal actor, she knows how to get people motivated."

Sadie blushed and took the baby from her husband's arms. "Don't let him kid you. Hank got all these men and women to paint the house inside and out in less than twelve hours. That's what I call amazing."

Lani walked back into the living room, her head spinning and her legs growing weaker.

"Sweetheart, you need to sit," Zach said. "You aren't yet fully recovered." He walked her to the sofa and insisted she sit.

"We would have left before you got here, but we had a few finishing touches to do to the exterior," Hank said.

"And we wanted to see your reaction," Sadie said with a smile. "But we're all heading back to Eagle Rock tonight. Emma sleeps best in her own bed. Although she did well camping out in her playpen overnight while we worked." Sadie kissed her baby's chubby cheek and hugged her close. "We have a long drive back, or we'd visit longer. If you're ever down around Eagle Rock, please come stay with us."

"Thank you," Lani said. "Thank you all for everything. I don't know what else to say." She stood again and walked with the men and women who'd given so much of their money and time to put her place back together so beautifully.

Hank and Sadie were the last two to say goodbye.

Hank turned to Zach. "Now that this case is closed, when can I expect you back in Eagle Rock?"

Lani shot a glance toward Zach, her eyes wide. She wasn't ready to lose him. She suspected she'd never be ready to lose this man she'd come to love the first time they'd met in Afghanistan.

Zach glanced down at her and smiled. "Sir, if it's all right with you, I'd like to base my work out of Browning. Now that I've found my roots, I want to stay and explore my heritage."

Hank's lips twisted. "Roots? Is that what they're calling it now?" He winked. "I wish you both all the happiness together." He hugged Lani. "I hope you feel better soon. The Blackfeet Law Enforcement team has a gem in you. If you ever decide it's not enough to keep you busy, I'd be happy to have you join my team of Brotherhood Protectors."

Lani's heart swelled at the compliment. "Thank you. I'll keep that in mind. Right now, I just want to do what I can for my people. I like to think they need me."

"Oh, they need you all right," Hank said.

Sadie leaned close with Emma and gave Lani a hug. "Remember, come visit. We love having guests. Especially, if they're like family."

"I suspect all your Brotherhood Protectors are like family," Lani said.

Sadie grinned. "They are. I love them all." She led the way to their truck, strapped Emma into her car seat and soon they were driving away, leaving Zach and Lani alone in her beautiful home.

"You need to sit. Having all those people here when you got home was too much."

"It was perfect," Lani said as she walked back into the house that twenty-four hours before looked like a war zone. "I don't deserve all this. It's too much."

"Everyone pitched in. They all wanted to help." Zach urged her to sit on the sofa, and he sat beside her. "Now that the murders have been solved and you're safe, you don't need me anymore. Say the word, and I'll leave."

She reached out and took his hand. "These past few days have made me realize something."

He lifted her hand to his lips and kissed her fingertips. "Yeah?"

"Yeah," she said. "It's made me realize what I've been missing in my life."

"Your own personal bodyguard?"

She chuckled. "That and more. You're like the mirror to my soul," she said softly. "I've never been one to get all soft and squishy, but you bring it out in me. I like having you around. All these years, I thought I was fine on my own. Independent, never needing anyone."

"And now?" he asked, kissing her knuckles and pulling her closer.

"Now, I know I need you. I need you like I need air to breathe."

He laughed. "And we've both been short of air."

She nodded. "When I woke up in the hospital, all I could think about was you. I had to know if you were okay. When you showed up, carrying that huge bouquet of flowers, I could breathe again." She leaned into him, pressing her cheek to his chest, listening to the beat of his heart that matched hers. "Is it crazy to think I could fall in love with you after such a short time?"

"If it is," he said, "call me crazy, too. I thought I'd lost you." He pulled her into the shelter of his arms and held her close and tight. "I've never felt so desperate and devastated when I thought you were gone. And when I found you..." He pressed his cheek to the top of her head. "My world became complete."

"Will it always be this good?" she asked.

"No. I'm sure there will be times when we don't even like each other."

"But we'll always love each other," Lani said. "And that's all that counts."

"Yes, ma'am." He kissed the top of her head and stood. "With all the wonderful things they brought to your house, they tried to get rid of some things they thought you might not need anymore." Zach reached beneath a new end table and pulled out his neatly tied sleeping bag and held it up. "Do you want me to put it back behind the seat of my truck?"

Lani's lips curled and heat coiled at her core. She lifted her hand to Zach.

He took it and pulled her to her feet.

"You're not getting rid of that." She took it from him and hugged it to her chest. "We still have need of this."

"You have a perfectly fine bed now, complete with sheets and blankets.

"I do." She canted her head to one side. "But wouldn't it be even more comfortable if we had a sleeping bag on top of it? You know…so we can pretend we're camping out in a ravaged home, celebrating the fact that a killer didn't succeed in getting to his next victim."

"I'm all for a little role playing." He scooped her up in arms, sleeping bag and all, and carried her to her new bed, where they made love in his old sleeping bag.

Life was good. The spirits smiled down on them, and Lani knew she'd found what she'd never known she was searching for.

She'd found love.

DELTA FORCE RESCUE

BROTHERHOOD PROTECTOR BOOK #15

New York Times & USA Today
Bestselling Author

ELLE JAMES

DELTA FORCE RESCUE

BROTHERHOOD PROTECTORS

NEW YORK TIMES BESTSELLING AUTHOR
ELLE JAMES

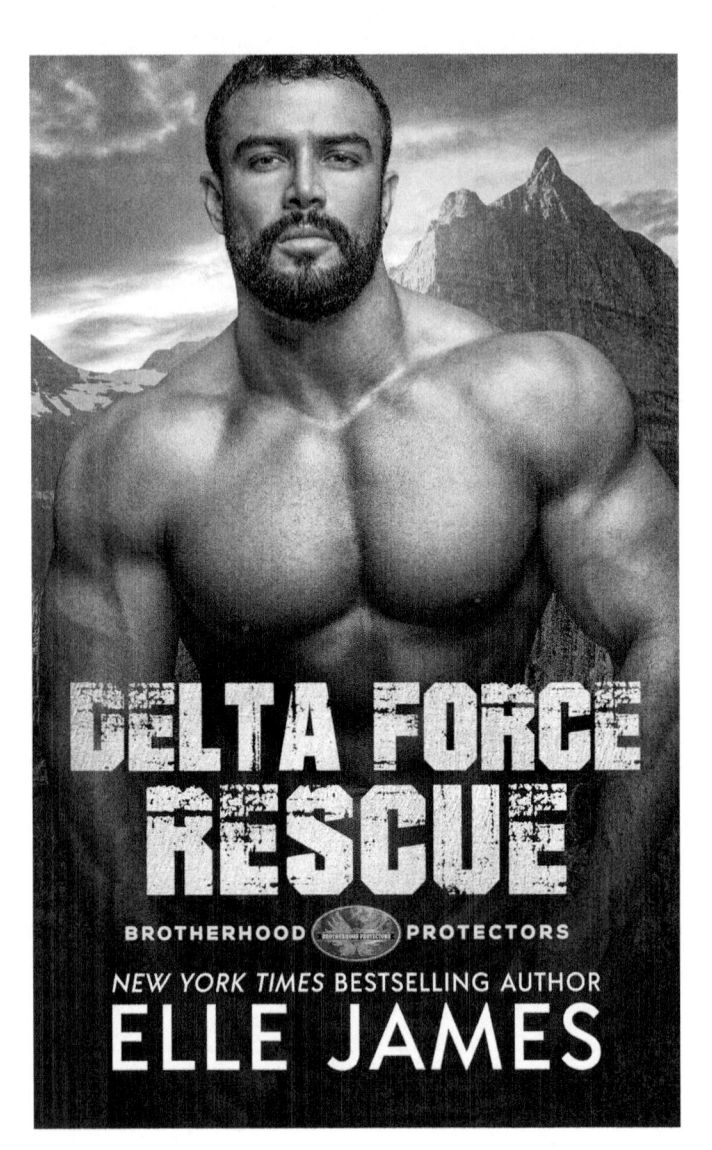

CHAPTER 1

Briana Hayes hitched up her leather satchel, resting the strap on her shoulder as she walked down the stairwell of the rundown apartment building. The day had been long and depressing. She'd already been to six different homes that day. Two of the parents of small children had threatened her. One child had to be removed and placed with a foster family after being burned repeatedly with a cigarette by the mother's live-in boyfriend. Some days, Briana hated her job as a Child Welfare Officer for the state of Illinois. Most days, she realized the importance of her work.

Her focus was the safety of children.

Thankfully, the last home had been one in which the mother seemed to be getting herself together for the love of her child. Because of drug abuse, she'd lost her baby girl to the state. After rehab treatment, she'd gotten a job, proved that she could support herself and the baby and regained custody. Briana prayed the woman didn't fall back into old habits. The child needed a functioning mother to raise her.

The sun had slid down below the tops of the surrounding buildings, casting the streets and alleys into shadow. A chill wind blew dark gray clouds over the sky. The scent of moisture in the air held a promise of rain. Soon.

Briana picked up her pace, hurrying past an alley toward the parking lot where she'd left her small nondescript, four-door sedan. A sobbing sound caught her attention and she slowed. She glanced into the dark alley, a shiver of apprehension running the length of her spine. This part of Chicago wasn't the safest to be in after sunset. Though she didn't want to hang around too long, she couldn't ignore the second sob.

"Hello?" she called out softly.

The sobbing grew more frequent, and a baby's cry added to the distress.

Despite concern for her own safety, Briana stepped into the alley. "Hey, what's wrong? Can I help?"

"No," a woman's voice whispered. "No one can." Though she spoke perfect English, her voice held a hint of a Spanish accent.

Briana squinted, trying to make out shapes in the shadows. A figure sat hunkered over, back against the wall, holding a small bundle.

"Tell me what's troubling you. Maybe I can help." Briana edged nearer, looking past the hunched figure for a possible trap. When nothing else moved in the darkness, she squatted beside a slight woman, wearing a black sweater and with a hood covering her hair. She looked up at Briana, her eyes red-rimmed, tears making tracks of her mascara on her cheeks.

The baby in her arms whimpered.

"What's your name?" Briana asked.

"I can't." The woman's shoulders slumped.

"My name is Briana," she said. "I just want to know your name."

For a long moment, the young mother hesitated. Then in a whisper, she said, "Alejandra."

"That's a pretty name," Briana said, in the tone she used when she wanted to calm someone who was distraught. "And the baby?"

The woman smiled down at the infant in her arms. "Bella."

"She's beautiful." Briana couldn't leave them alone in the alley. "Do you need help getting home?"

She shook her head. "I can't go there."

"Has someone hurt you?" Briana asked, pulling her phone out of her pocket. "I can call the police. We can have him arrested."

"No!" The woman reached out and grabbed Briana's wrist.

Alarm race through Briana. Instinctively, she drew back.

The woman held tightly to Briana's wrist, balancing the baby in the curve of her other arm. "Don't call. I can't... He can't know where I am."

"If he's threatening you, you need to let the police know," Briana urged, prying the woman's hand free of her wrist. "They can issue a restraining order against him." When the woman shot a glance around Briana,

Briana looked back, too. A couple walked past the end of the alley without pausing.

"Are you afraid to go home?" Briana asked.

"I have no home." The mother released Briana's arm and bent over her baby, sobbing. "He had it burned to the ground."

Briana gasped. "Then you *have* to go to the police."

She shook her head. "They can't stop him. He doesn't even live in this country."

"Then how…?"

"He has people," she said. "Everywhere."

Briana sank to her knees beside her. "Why is he doing this to you?"

The woman looked from the baby in her arms up to Briana. "He wants my baby. He won't stop until he has her."

Briana studied the woman and child as the first drops of rain fell. "You can't stay out here. You and the baby need shelter." She reached out her hand. "Come. You can stay at my apartment."

"No." Alejandra shrank against the wall, drawing the baby closer to her. "It's too dangerous for you."

"I'll take my chances," Briana reassured her.

"No. I won't do that to you. He will kill anyone who interferes with his attempt to take my daughter."

"Is he the father?" Briana asked.

Alejandra choked on a sob. "Yes. He is. But he's a very bad man."

"How so?"

"He is *El Chefe Diablo*," Alejandra whispered. "The head of the Tejas Cartel from El Salvador."

Though the word *cartel* sent a shiver of apprehension across Briana's skin, she couldn't ignore the woman and child's immediate needs. "I don't care if he's the head of the CIA or the Russian mafia, you and Bella can't stay out here in the rain. If not for yourself, you need to find real shelter for the baby." Again, she held out her hand. "Come with me. If you won't stay with me, we'll find a safe, anonymous place for you to stay."

Alejandra shook her head. "Anyone who helps me puts themselves in danger."

Briana firmed her jaw. "Again, I'll take my chances. And I know of a place where you won't be found. It's a privately run women's shelter where they don't take names and they don't ask too many questions."

Alejandra looked up, blinking as rain fell into her eyes. "I won't have to tell them who I am?"

"You won't," Briana assured her. She reached out again. "Come on. I'll take you there."

The woman clutched her baby closer. "You…you… aren't working for him, are you?"

"What?" Briana frowned. "No. Of course not. My job is to help children. Your baby needs protection from the rain. *You* need protection from the weather. If you don't come with me, I can't leave you. I'd have to stay here with you." She gave her a twisted smile. "Then we'd all be cold and wet."

"He always finds me. No matter where I go." Alejandra took Briana's hand and let her pull her to her feet. "I can't get away from him."

"We'll get you to the shelter. No one else has to know where you are. Just you, me and baby Bella."

"The people at the shelter?" she asked.

"Won't know who you are. You can tell them your name is Jane Smith."

Her eyebrows rose. "They won't require identification?"

"No. They've even helped immigrants who had nowhere else to turn." Briana slipped an arm around the woman and helped her to her car. "Come on. Get into my car. I can crank up the heater. You two will be warm in no time."

Briana helped Alejandra and the baby into the back seat of the car. "Hold on. I have a blanket I keep in my trunk." She rounded to the rear of the vehicle, popped the trunk lid and reached into the back where she kept a blanket, a teddy bear and bottles of water. She grabbed what she needed and closed the trunk.

Alejandra had buckled herself in and raised her shirt to allow the baby to breast feed.

Briana draped the blanket around the two, handed the woman the plastic bottle of water and laid the teddy bear beside her. "The shelter is about thirty minutes outside of Chicago. You might as well settle in for the ride."

Alejandra nodded and leaned her head back against the headrest. "Thank you." She closed her eyes, her arm firmly tucked around the baby nursing at her breast.

Briana climbed into the driver's seat, shifted into gear and drove out of Chicago to the shelter she knew that didn't require government assistance, therefore wasn't run with all the background checks or identification requirements. Alejandra and Bella would be safe there. Once she had them settled in, she could go home to her apartment, knowing the two were safe from harm and out of the weather, at least for the night.

Traffic was heavy getting out of the city. Eventually, she turned off the main highway onto a secondary highway, and then onto a rural Illinois county road.

A glance in her rearview mirror made Briana smile.

Alejandra, Bella lying in her arms, slept, her tired face at peace except for the frown tugging at her brow.

The wife or girlfriend of the leader of a drug cartel... Briana had run into women who had been on the run from drug dealers, mafia or gang members. Each had been terrified of being found, of their children being taken from them, or murdered. Their fears were founded in truth. Briana had witnessed the aftermath of a gang member's vengeance, and the memory still haunted her. She found it incomprehensible that a man could murder a woman and child out of sheer hatred.

The shelter was located at what had once been a dairy farm. The huge old barn, where the cows had come to be milked, had been cleaned out and converted into living quarters for women and their small children who needed a place to hide away from brutal and abusive relationships. The foundation was funded by a celebrity who preferred to remain anonymous. The rumor had it that the celebrity had once been a woman in need of assistance and a safe house to live in.

Manned by licensed psychologists, social workers and occupational specialists, the shelter was there to provide a place to live and to help the residents learn new skills and, ultimately, become independent and able to take care for themselves. They also had an attorney on retainer to assist the women in getting the restraining orders, separation agreements and divorces they needed in order to start new lives away from toxic situations.

When they arrived at the shelter, Briana parked at the rear entrance, where the people who ran it preferred potential residents to enter. Though they were out in the county, the fewer people who knew of the comings and goings, the better they were able to keep women hidden from their abusive significant others.

As soon as they drove beneath the overhang, a woman emerged from the entrance, a smile and frown of concern on her face. She started to open the passenger seat door but quickly changed to open the back door. "Hello, I'm Sandy. Welcome to Serenity Place."

Briana smiled as she climbed out of the vehicle and stood beside Sandy. "Hi, Sandy. This is…Jane and her daughter, Jill. They need a safe place to stay."

Sandy held out her hand. "You've come to the right place. We're very discreet here. Our primary concern is for the safety of our residents, both big and small."

Alejandra took her hand and let her pull her and the baby out of the car. "Thank you."

In the next few minutes, the woman had Alejandra and Bella assigned to a room with a full-sized bed, a crib and a package of disposable diapers. Once Alejandra had changed Bella's diaper, Sandy took them to a dining room where she helped Alejandra make a sandwich.

"Would you like one, too?" Sandy asked Briana.

She shook her head, though her stomach rumbled. "No, thank you. I need to get back to the city before it gets much later." Briana hugged Alejandra and slipped a business card into her hand. "If you need anything, call me."

The young woman's eyes filled with tears. "You've already done so much."

Briana gave her a gentle smile. "Nothing more than anyone with an ounce of compassion would have done. Take care of yourself and your little one." She brushed a finger beneath the baby's chin then turned to leave.

Sandy followed her to the exit. "We'll take very good care of them."

Briana turned to Sandy. "She's scared. From what she's told me, some very bad people are after her. The baby's father has some connections. If they find her, it won't be good for her or the people harboring her."

"We've dealt with similar situations." Sandy touched her arm. "We'll be on the lookout."

"Thank you, Sandy," Briana said. "You have my number. Call me if you need anything or have any concerns."

She nodded. "Be careful driving back into the city."

Briana climbed into her car and headed for Chicago. All along the way, she thought about Alejandra and her baby. The desperation in the woman's eyes had struck a chord in Briana's heart. She'd seen that look before in the faces of young mothers she'd visited. Too often, they stayed in bad situations, thinking they had no other alternative. Alejandra had taken the step to get away from the man who'd threatened her and her child. It took a lot of courage to leave an abusive man. The least she deserved was a safe place to hide until she could get back on her feet, maybe change her identity and start a new life somewhere else.

Back at her apartment, Briana climbed the stairs to the second floor and let herself in.

"That you?" her roommate, Sheila Masters, called out from the kitchen.

"It's me," Briana answered as she dropped her keys on the table in the entryway.

"You're late getting home. Did you have a hot date?" Sheila stepped out of the kitchen and handed Briana a glass of wine.

"You're a godsend," Briana said, accepting the offering with a heavy sigh. "I need this and a long soak in a hot tub."

"Go for it. I'll be out here watching some television. I had a busy day at the office. I had to train the new hire." She carried her own wine glass toward the living room, talking as she went. "I don't know why I always get stuck training the new folks."

"Because you have the most patience of anyone in that office. Who else could do it?"

Sheila turned, her lips pinched together. "You're right. Sherry is short-tempered, Lana is too into Lana and Trent is too busy to train anyone himself."

"Which leaves you." Briana touched her friend's arm. "That's why I love you so much. You're the best friend a girl can have. And you have the patience to listen to me vent every day."

"Girl, I don't know how you do it. I'd be a wreck every day." Sheila hugged her. "Go, get that bath. I'll be out here."

Briana nodded, too tired to think beyond the bath and the wine. She took a sip. "I'll be out shortly."

"Take your time. I'll watch the news until you're out."

Once in the bedroom, she dropped her purse on the nightstand, fished out her cellphone and checked for any missed calls. None. Hopefully, Alejandra and Bella were settling into the shelter.

Briana knew she was too sleepy to take a long, hot bath. Instead, she opted for a quick, hot shower, more interested in the wine and propping her feet up than falling asleep in the tub. After her shower, she dried off, stepped into a pair of leggings and was pulling her T-shirt over her head when she heard a loud banging sound from the other room. She'd just stepped out of the bathroom into her bedroom when she heard Sheila scream.

Her heart raced, and her breath hitched in her chest as she ran through her bedroom. She hadn't closed the door all the way earlier. As she reached for the knob, her hand froze.

Through the crack, she saw a man wearing a ski mask, standing over Sheila's crumpled body. He had a gun in his hand with a silencer attached to the end.

Sheila lay motionless on the floor, her eyes open, red liquid pooling beneath her arm.

Please, let that be wine.

Briana's gaze went to the coffee table where Sheila's full glass of wine remained unfinished. Her heart sank.

The man nudged Sheila with his boot.

She didn't move, didn't blink her wide-open eyes. Sheila lay still as death.

Briana swallowed hard on a moan rising swiftly up her throat and backed away from the door. Looking toward the window, she shook her head. She'd never get through it without the man hearing her, and the two-story drop could lead to broken bones or death. The bathroom was out of the question. He'd look there next. With nowhere else to go, Briana grabbed her cellphone from the nightstand, dropped to the floor and slid beneath the bed. She dialed 911 and prayed for a quick response, pressing the phone to her ear.

Footsteps sounded, heading into the other bedroom, fading as he moved away.

"You've reached 911. State the nature of your emergency."

"My friend was shot," she whispered.

"Is the shooter still there?" the dispatcher asked.

The footsteps grew louder as they moved toward her bedroom.

"Yes," Briana whispered and gave her address. "Hurry, please." She ended the call, switched the phone to silent and lay still, her gaze on the door as it swung open.

Black boots and black trousers were all Briana could see of the man as he entered the room, stalked to the en suite bathroom and flung open the door.

Briana watched as he disappeared through the doorway. She heard the sound of the shower curtain rings scraping across the metal rod. The boots reappeared, coming to a stop beside her bed. The man's legs bent, and his heels came up as if he was lowering himself into a squat.

Her heart racing, Briana scooted silently across the floor toward the other side of the bed.

The faint sound of a siren wailed in the distance.

The legs straightened, and the boots carried him out of the room. A moment later, silence reigned in Briana's small apartment. She lay for a long moment, counting the seconds since she last heard the sound of footsteps.

The whole time, Briana worried about her friend Sheila. Was she still alive? Had that blood only been a superficial wound? Should she get out from under the bed and find out?

Finally, Briana rolled out from under the bed on the side farthest from the door. She crawled across the carpet and peered through the open doorway into the living room. Sheila lay where Briana had last seen her. Her eyes still open, her face pale, the blood beneath her arm making a dark stain on the white shag area rug they'd purchased together last spring.

Briana glanced toward the entry. The door to their apartment hung open, the doorframe split as if someone had kicked the door in.

Nothing moved. No footsteps sounded on the tile entry.

Still on her hands and knees, Briana crawled toward her friend, tears welling in her eyes, blurring her vision. She had to blink several times to clear them before she could reach for Sheila's neck. Pressing two fingers to the base of her throat, she waited, praying for a miracle.

No pulse. No steady rise and fall of her chest. Nothing.

"Oh, Sheila," Briana whispered, the tears falling in earnest now.

The hole in Sheila's chest told the story.

Briana sat on the floor beside her friend, holding her hand, crying.

Sirens she'd heard moments before now blared loudly outside of the apartment. Soon, several policemen entered, weapons drawn.

Briana looked to them, her heart breaking. "You're too late."

They helped her up and started the interrogation, asking questions she didn't have answers to. Her thoughts went to Alejandra and her baby, but she couldn't say a word about them without giving up their location.

When they were finished, they told her she couldn't remain there. Her apartment was now a crime scene. She would have to find another place to stay. They let her grab her purse and keys but nothing else.

"Do you need someone to drive you to a hotel?" the officer in charge asked.

She shook her head, amazed it didn't fall off as fast as it was spinning. "No," she said. "I can drive myself."

"We can provide an escort, if you'd like," he offered.

"No. I'll be all right," she said, though she knew she was lying.

Walking out of her apartment, she didn't look back.

She couldn't. What had happened was inconceivable. Her mind could not comprehend it.

Briana climbed into her car and started the engine out of sheer muscle memory. When she reached for the shift, her cellphone rang.

She dug in her purse for it and pulled it out, praying it was Sheila claiming it had all been a hoax. *Come back up to the apartment. I'm fine. Everything's fine.*

The phone didn't feel right in her hand, but nothing felt right at that moment. When she swiped her finger across the screen to answer, a voice came across, speaking a language she didn't understand. It took her a moment to realize it was Spanish. "You have the wrong number," she said and started to end the call.

The voice switched to English with a strong Spanish accent. "Who is this? Where is Alejandra?"

Briana pulled the cellphone away from her ear and stared down at it. It had a black case like hers, but the phone wasn't hers. "You will tell me where she is now," the man's voice said. "If you do not, I will find you, and I will make you tell me, if I have to beat the information out of you. Do you hear me?"

"You did this?" Briana asked. "You had my roommate killed in your effort to find Alejandra?"

"I will do whatever it takes to bring her back to El Salvador," the man's voice said.

Anger and raw hatred burned hot inside Briana, bubbling up her throat. "You can rot in hell before I tell you anything." She ended the call, lowered her window and flung the phone out onto the pavement. "Hell, you hear me?" she yelled. Then she shifted into reverse, backed up a few feet, shifted into drive and ran over the cellphone.

The gesture wouldn't bring back Sheila, but it cut off the man who'd sent his thug to find Alejandra and who had killed her roommate in the process.

As she drove away from her apartment building, Briana knew the man wouldn't stop until he found Alejandra and her child. Briana was the only one who knew who Alejandra was and where she was staying with her daughter, Bella.

If *El Chefe Diablo* was as bad as Alejandra had indicated, he would send his killers after Briana.

She needed help. The police didn't have time to guard her, and they wouldn't do it unless she told them why *El Chefe* was after her. Briana needed someone discreet, someone she could trust implicitly. She pulled out her cellphone and dialed her brother Ryan's number. He was the only man she trusted.

"Hey, Sis," Ryan Hayes answered. "Can't talk long, I'm boarding a plane as we speak and will be out of touch for the next seventeen hours."

A sob escaped her, and she swallowed hard, trying to get words to pass her vocal cords. "Ryan."

"What's wrong," he asked, his words instantly clipped.

She couldn't speak for a full minute.

"Briana? Are you there?" he demanded. "Talk to me. Damned connection."

"I'm here," she said. "I need help."

"Oh, Bree, I'm not even in the States. What's the problem?"

"Sheila's dead," she said, her voice catching. "And I think her killer is coming for me next."

"What the fuck?" Ryan cursed. "I can't be there for another seventeen to twenty hours."

"Don't worry," she said. "I'll figure out something."

"No, wait. I know who you can call until I get back."

"Who?"

"Hank Patterson. Prior Navy SEAL. He has a security service."

"I don't know Hank."

"I have it on really good authority that he's the real deal. He and any one of his guys would lay down their lives for whomever they're protecting. I'll text you the number. Call him. No, never mind. I'll call him and have him contact you."

Briana drove down the street, away from her apartment building, not knowing where she was heading. Headlights in her rearview mirror blinded her until she shifted the mirror. "I don't know where I'll be."

"Don't worry, Bree. Get to somewhere safe. He'll figure it out," her brother said. "And Bree?"

"Yeah," she answered, on the verge of more tears.

"I love you," he said. "Stay safe. You're the only sister I have."

"I love you, too." She ended the call, turned a corner and glanced into the rearview mirror. Were those headlights the same ones that had followed her after leaving her apartment?

Increasing her speed, she rushed to the next corner and turned left, taking the turn as fast as she dared.

Again, the vehicle behind her turned and sped up.

Her heart leaped into her throat. Briana slammed her foot onto the accelerator, shooting her little car forward. She didn't slow when she took the next right turn, the rear end of her car fishtailing around the corner. Punching the gas, she raced to the next intersection where the light had just turned red. Ignoring the light, she shot through right before another car had pulled out.

The driver honked and kept moving forward, blocking the path of the vehicle following her, slowing him enough she was able to speed up and get through the next two lights and turn right then left, zigzagging through the streets until no headlights followed her.

She couldn't stay in Chicago. Briana didn't know where she could stay that would be safe. Going to a friend's house was out of the question. As Alejandra had predicted, being associated with her put others in danger. That was now true for Briana.

Briana had to find a place she could hunker down until help arrived.

CHAPTER 2

Rafe Donovan was just climbing into his truck after getting fuel at a gas station, when his cellphone vibrated in the cupholder. He noted the name on the screen and answered, "Yo, Hayes, miss me already? I thought you guys were tapped for a mission?"

"We're on our way back. Otherwise, I'd handle this myself," his friend, Ryan Hayes, said. "I just boarded a plane and won't be in contact for at least another seventeen hours, so listen up."

Rafe tensed at the urgency in his friend's voice. "Shoot."

"My sister is in trouble. I spoke with Hank Patterson out in Montana. He says you're the closest asset he has to Chicago, where she lives. He's going to send you to manage this case. You'll get a call from him any minute. I just wanted to give you a heads-up before I go silent in transit."

"What's happening?" Rafe asked.

"I'm not sure, but she needs protection. Her roommate was murdered, and whoever did it is after her now. Where are you?"

"I stopped in Kansas City to visit a buddy of mine on my way out to Montana. I was just about to look for a hotel for the night, but I can be in Chicago in seven hours."

"That's a long time."

Rafe frowned. "It's the best I can do without breaking speed limits."

"I get it," Hayes said. "It would take that long for anyone to fly commercial. My sister's smart enough to find a place to hide out, until then. I'll send her number to you. Expect a call from your new boss as soon as I end this call."

Before Hayes finished talking, another call made Rafe's cellphone vibrate. "I have an incoming call."

"That must be him now," Hayes said. "I gotta go. Take care of my sister. She's the only family I have left. I'm counting on you."

"Will do," Rafe said. "Safe travels, my friend. You're your sister's only blood relative. But you have a shit-ton of brothers who give a damn, too. So, don't fuck up."

Hayes chuckled. "Love you too, bro. Out here."

As soon as Hayes ended the call, Rafe answered the incoming one from Hank Patterson, the owner and founder of the Brotherhood Protectors security agency based out of Eagle Rock, Montana.

"Donovan, here." Rafe started the engine, and the call switched to his truck's speaker.

"You heard?" Hank asked.

"Hayes's sister. Chicago. Yes, sir," he answered, keying Chicago into the map on his cellphone.

"Anything you need, you let me know. If you need a safe house to bring her to, I can't recommend any in Illinois, but I have a couple places here in Montana, if you can get her here."

"Yes, sir. I'll let you know what I find when I get to Chicago." Rafe buckled his seatbelt and pulled out onto the road.

"Anything you require in the way of support, you let me know," Hank said. "Are you armed?"

"Yes, sir." He had a 9mm Glock in the console and an AR15 behind the back seat.

"Good. Let me know when you reach Miss Hayes."

"Yes, sir," Rafe responded. "Out here."

Rafe pulled out of the gas station and onto the interstate highway heading northeast toward Chicago. He could be there by early the next morning, if he didn't run into any construction delays.

A text came through from Hayes with his sister's cellphone number.

Rafe immediately called.

It rang several times before voicemail picked up.

"You've reached the voicemail of Briana Hayes. Please leave a message, and I'll get back to you as soon as possible." Her voice was soft, a little gravely and sexy as hell.

"This is Rafe Donovan, your brother Hayes—" he paused and added, "Ryan, and my boss Hank Patterson said you could use some help. Call me." He ended the call and waited impatiently to hear back from her.

Fifteen minutes passed. Rafe caught himself pushing faster and faster on the interstate and had to slow down to within five miles an hour of the limit. Getting a ticket would be a stupid waste of time, when he needed to get to Chicago as soon as possible. Seven hours stretched in front of him like an interminable amount of time.

Why hadn't she called back? Was she in that much trouble that she couldn't pick up her cellphone and call? Was he too late? Questions rattled around in his mind, and his foot rested heavily on the accelerator. Once again, he had to back off and slow to the limit.

Damn. Why hadn't she called? Twenty minutes passed.

His cellphone chirped through the truck's sound system. Her number appeared on the screen.

Rafe hit the talk button. "Donovan, here."

For a long moment, silence met his greeting. Then that slightly raspy voice sounded through the speakers. "This is Briana."

Rafe let go of the breath he'd been holding. "I've been assigned to protect you, but it'll take me six and a half hours to get to Chicago from Kansas City. Can you wait that long?"

"Guess I'll have to," she said softly. "I'm not in Chicago anymore."

"No? Then, where are you?"

She laughed softly, the sound almost like a sob. "I don't know. Give me a minute. I'll look for a sign."

"You're driving?" he asked.

Again, another sobbing laugh. "I have nowhere else to go. The police kicked me out of my apartment." Her voice hitched. "It's cordoned off as a crime scene." She paused. "Joliet. I'm passing through Joliet."

His chest tightened. The pain in her voice was evident. Apparently, whatever had happened had affected her so much she didn't know where she was going. "What highway?"

"Interstate 80," she said. "I'm coming up to Interstate 55."

"I'm on my way. If you stop, let me know where, and I'll meet you there."

"I'm not stopping. I can't." Another soft sob sounded. "I'm scared."

"Okay. Are you on a handsfree device?"

"If you mean, is my phone connected to my car…it is."

"Good. If you're going to keep driving, take 55 south," he said. "I'm coming across on 72 and will hit 55 in Springfield, Missouri."

When she didn't respond, he prompted, "Can you do that?"

"Yes." Silence stretched between them for several heartbeats. Then she whispered, "Will you stay with me? On the phone?"

"Yes, ma'am," he said, glad she would be in communication all the way. She sounded distraught. If he could keep her talking, he might get her to pull into a hotel and wait for him.

"Just got onto 55," her words came across his speaker.

"Good, just keep going. When you get close to

Springfield, Illinois, we'll see how far out I am. We can meet up there or somewhere close to that."

"Okay," she said. "I'm sorry. What did you say your name was?"

"Rafe Donovan."

"Rafe," she said, as if rolling his name across her tongue. He liked the way she said it.

"So, Miss Hayes…do you mind if I call you Briana?" he asked.

"Please. Miss Hayes makes me sound old."

He chuckled. "You don't sound old to me." He'd never been good at chit-chat, but he wanted to hear her voice. It made him feel connected. If she ended the call, he wouldn't know where she was or how she was doing. If she ran off the road, he'd have no idea where to look. "How old are you? Or is that one of those questions a man's not supposed to ask?"

"No. It's okay. I'm twenty-seven," she replied. "How old are you?"

"Old," he said. "I'm thirty-four."

"That's not old."

"Tell that to my body," he said. "It's seen better days."

"How do you know Ryan?" she asked.

"He's one of my teammates." Rafe frowned. "*Was* one of my teammates."

"Was?"

"I separated from the Army a week ago. Your brother and I worked together."

"Delta Force," she stated.

"That's right." He set his cruise control to keep from speeding up and slowing down.

"Ryan and his teammates are pretty tight," Briana said in that soft, gravelly tone.

"It happens when you go through some of the shit we've gone through. Hayes—Ryan—saved my ass on several occasions."

"And I'm sure you returned the favor," Briana said. "My brother calls his teammates his brothers. They're as much a part of his family as I am. Maybe more."

"Don't sell him short. He cares about you. He was on the phone with me right after he hung up with you and Hank. If he hadn't been on a mission, he would've been there for you."

"I know. I hated calling him, but I didn't know what else to do." Her words faded off.

"What happened?" Rafe asked.

"A m-man broke into our ap-partment…and k-killed…my roommate." He could hear the tears in her garbled words.

"Do you need to pull over?" he asked.

For a long moment, she didn't answer.

He worried that she would run off the road because she couldn't see through the tears she must be shedding. "You must have loved your roommate very much," he said in a soothing tone. "What was his name?"

"*Her* name was Sheila," she answered. "He killed Sheila. And yes. I loved her like a sister."

His gut knotted, and his fists tightened around the steering wheel. He'd lost close friends in battle. No amount of words made it better. He didn't begin to think anything he could say to her would make the pain any easier to bear. "I'm sorry."

"She did nothing to deserve what he did to her. Sheila wouldn't hurt anyone."

"Did the homicide detective have any clue as to why he did it?" Rafe asked.

"No. But I think I know why," she whispered.

Not wanting to push her, he waited for her to continue in her own time.

"I helped a woman and her child find shelter. She was running from the child's father. H-he sent the man who broke into our apartment and killed Sheila. He was looking for the woman and the child."

"How do you know this?" Rafe asked.

"I didn't know that I had the woman's cellphone. Her baby's father called it. I answered thinking it was for me. When he didn't get his woman on the line, he demanded I tell him where she was and threatened to come after me." She sniffed. "After what his man did to Sheila…"

"You did the right thing to ask for help."

"I had nowhere else to go. I don't know who works for him or how deep his contacts might be." She drew in a shaky breath. "Someone followed me from my apartment. When I tried to lose him, he remained on my tail, until I ran a stoplight and he was blocked by traffic."

He could hear the terror in her voice. "So, you're the only one who knows where this woman and her child are hidden?"

"The only one who knows who and where she is. The people at the place she's staying don't know her name. I know." She snorted softly. "Sometimes, I wish I didn't. But she's safe for now. I don't know how she lived with the man or how she got away from him with her baby. He's evil. I'm not scared easily, but he has me terrified."

"Hang in there. I'm on my way."

Several minutes passed in silence.

"Still awake?" he asked after a while.

"Barely," she admitted.

"Do you want to pull over at the next hotel?"

"No," she said. "I'm afraid to slow down. He might catch up to me."

"Then talk to me. It might help to keep you awake," he urged.

"About what?"

"Tell me about you," he said. The interstate highway stretched in front of him as he sped across Missouri.

"There's not much to tell."

"From?" he prompted.

"Born in Germany. Dad was in the Army, always deployed. Mom raised us," she said.

"How did you end up in Chicago?"

"My father retired to Bloomington, Illinois. I guess the military was in our blood. As soon as Ryan graduated high school, he joined the Army."

Rafe smiled. "You didn't want to?"

"My father and my mother encouraged me to go to college after Ryan joined the Army. I knew I wanted to work with children, so I studied social work."

"You like children?"

"I do. I wanted a younger brother and sister, but Mom and Dad were happy with just the two of us. We were enough to handle when we had to move so often. I wrote a research paper on causes and the number of cases of child abuse in the state of Illinois. I was appalled by how many were from Chicago and how undermanned the Child Welfare Department was. When I graduated from the university, I applied to the Children and Family Services of Illinois based in Chicago. I've worked there for the past five years, trying to help as many children as I could."

"How's that worked out for you?" he asked.

After a long pause, she said, "I do the best I can to protect children in abusive situations."

"I hear a 'but' in there," he said.

"But sometimes my best isn't good enough to save a child."

"That's got to be tough." He couldn't imagine coming face to face with an adult who repeatedly abused children. He'd put his fist in his or her face for every time they hit, kicked or punched a child.

After a pause, he asked, "Married?"

"No."

"Boyfriend?"

"Once I started work, I never had time. There was always one more child who needed my help." She sighed. "What about you?"

"What about me?"

"Why the Army? Why did you get out?" she asked. "You're not old enough to retire."

He'd agonized over his decision to leave Delta Force. "I didn't come from as stable a family environment as you." He drew in a deep breath and let it out slowly. "My father left when I was only two. My mother raised me alone. No brothers or sisters. She drank. When I was a senior in high school, she got so drunk she wandered outside in the dead of night, in the middle of winter. They didn't find her body until the next morning. She'd passed out in the snow and died where she lay. No one knew. I was asleep in my warm bed." He remembered that morning when the police came to his house, banged on his door and told him his mother had been found.

"You blamed yourself, didn't you?" Briana asked in her soft sexy tone.

Yes, he had. "If I hadn't gone to bed that night, I might have gotten her to put down her whiskey and sleep. She wouldn't have been out wandering around in the freezing temperatures."

"You couldn't have known she would do that," Briana said.

"No, but I should have done more." Rafe had agonized over what he should have done so many times in the years since. Nothing could undo what had happened. His mother was dead. She wouldn't be coming back.

"So, you joined the Army?" Briana spoke softly, reminding Rafe he was in a truck, headed toward a woman he'd never met but spoke so easily with that he felt as if he'd known her for a lifetime.

"I was due to graduate high school at the end of the month when she died. I was already eighteen, so the child welfare people didn't get all in my face about going to foster care. I ended up staying with a friend until school was out. During that time, I met with a recruiter, signed the papers and waited until I received my high school diploma. Then I shipped out to Basic Combat Training the following week. The rest is history."

"Married?"

"For about a week," he admitted.

She laughed. "I'm sorry. I shouldn't have laughed, but a week?"

He liked the sound of her laughter and wished he could make her laugh more. "We met in Basic Training, married as soon as we graduated and realized it was a mistake when we were shipped to different locations for our advanced training."

"You must have been in love."

"We were in lust or in love with the idea of having someone permanent in our lives." He snorted. "It didn't work for us. We keep in touch through social media and are still friends. She since left the military, married an accountant and has three kids."

"I'm sorry."

"Don't be," he said. "She's happy. I'm happy for her, and her husband seems to be a really nice guy and great father." He shrugged though she couldn't see him. "I realized when I joined Delta Force, I wouldn't have much of a life. I accepted that and swore off long-term relationships. They just don't work."

"They do for some. If you find the right person. I really hope my brother finds the right one for him, someday. He deserves happiness. And he'd make a great father, like our dad."

"You're lucky you had him," Rafe said.

"I know." She sighed. "I wish he would've lived long enough to get to know his grandchildren."

Rafe frowned. "What happened to him?"

"My father took my mother to Chicago for their anniversary. The weather turned cold and icy. They were killed in a twenty-car pileup on the way back. So, you see, Ryan really is all I have left, now that Sheila is gone." Her voice faded out.

"I'm sorry."

"I worry about my brother."

She had every right to worry about him. "I won't lie to you," Rafe said. "Each mission could be his last."

"I know," she said. "But he loves what he does. He feels like he's making a difference."

"Do you?"

"I hope I make a difference in the lives of the children under my supervision," Briana said. "I just wish I could do more to keep them from having to be under my care. So many of their parents didn't have good examples to teach them how to be good parents. A lot of the women had babies in their teens. They were babies themselves."

"You can't save them all," he reminded her.

"I have to remind myself that all the time," she said. "I can't save them all, but if I can save some, it's better than saving none of them."

Once again, silence stretched between them.

"Huh?" her voice came across slightly strained.

"What?"

"I'm just punchy."

Rafe's foot settled on the accelerator, pushing the

speed up above the limit by ten miles per hour. "What do you mean? Did something spook you?"

"Yeah, that's it. I'm spooked."

"By what?"

She laughed, the sound tight and unconvincing. "I saw a set of headlights in my rearview mirror."

His hands tightening around the steering wheel, Rafe leaned forward, inching the speedometer up another couple of notches. "Is he catching up?"

"Yes. But I'm sure it's just another motorist trying to get somewhere. There are a few out here. Mostly big rigs."

"Keep an eye on him. When do you stop for gas again?"

"Probably in the next thirty minutes. When I left Chicago, I didn't have a full tank." Her voice crackled.

"Are you hitting a dead zone?" Rafe asked. "You're breaking up."

"Must be. Down…one bar."

"Keep talking," he urged, his chest tight. "You might be able to hear me, even if I can't hear you."

For the next five minutes, he didn't hear anything. He kept talking for the first minute, until his cellphone disengaged from hers. He tried to call her. No answer. Again, he tried.

No answer.

The more time that passed, the more nervous he got. Had she really run into a cellphone dead zone? Or did the headlights following her belong to someone who was after her?

His foot pressed harder on the accelerator. Speed

limit be damned. At his best guess, he was still four hours away from her. Not nearly close enough to help if she got in trouble.

Fifteen minutes turned to twenty, and then thirty.

He called repeatedly, praying for an answer, wishing he'd gotten her last location before she'd faded out.

About the time he was ready to give up hope, she answered.

"Briana?"

"It's me," she said, her voice pure music to his ears.

"Thank God."

She laughed. "At first, I realized I was in a short dead zone. Then my battery died on my cellphone, and I didn't have a charger in my car. I had to pull into a truck stop for gas. While I was there, I bought a charging cable."

Rafe eased his foot off the accelerator, dropping from ninety miles per hour to seventy. "Good to hear your voice again. I was worried."

"Sorry. I thought you might be, but I couldn't do anything else."

"Any trouble at the truck stop?" he asked.

"No. I stayed in the well-lit areas, got out to put the pump handle into the car and got back in, locking the door. When it was done, I pulled up to the building before getting out. There were enough people inside to help, if I needed it. Anyway, I'm back on the road and should be in Springfield in an hour and a half."

"I should be there about the same time, maybe a little later."

"I'll continue through to find Interstate 72 and meet you on your side when you get there."

"Sounds like a good plan," he said.

"It's good to hear your voice," she said. "I know it's silly, but I feel safer when I'm talking with you."

"And I feel better about you when I can hear you."

She laughed. "It's strange, isn't it? I feel like I know you already. Like we've known each other for a long time."

"We have. For at least a couple hours," he said, smiling.

"How often do people really take the time to listen to each other? We're all so busy with our own lives, we don't have time to really get to know each other."

Rafe chuckled. "And here we are…strangers…getting to know each other."

"Thanks for taking the time to talk to me when you really didn't have to," she said. "Or is this part of your job, to protect me by keeping in touch?"

"Does it matter?" he asked. "For the record, I'm glad we're talking. It'll make it easier when we meet in person."

"None of that awkward getting-to-know-you stuff, right?" she said. "Tell me a little more about you."

"You know my life history. What more is there?"

"A lot. Like, do you prefer mountains or beaches? What's your favorite color? Dogs or cats?"

"You first," he countered. "Mountains or beaches?"

"Mountains," she said. "I like beaches, but there's something so serene and peaceful about the mountains. I always dreamed of going back to the Rockies. We vacationed there as a family when I was a teen. Now, you."

"Mountains. You can get lost in the mountains and find yourself there. I did that once. Spring break one year, I drove out to Colorado with a friend. We hiked so many trails and never saw another soul. The air was so crisp and clean, unlike the pollution and light noise of Minneapolis where I lived with my mother."

"Minneapolis, huh? And you're going to work for Hank Patterson? He's based out of Montana, from what my brother told me. He's told me he wants to work for Hank when he leaves the military."

"It's a good choice, from what I hear from other men I know who've gone to work there. He hires former Special Forces soldiers, SEALs and marines. Gives them work that suits the skills they learned on active duty."

"Sounds like a good gig," she said.

"I'll let you know after my first assignment," he said, his lips quirking upward.

"Me." She sighed, the sigh sounding more like a yawn at the end.

"Are you getting sleepy?" he asked. "You can pull over. I'll get there as soon as I can."

"No. I don't want to stop. I can stay awake, if we keep talking. My favorite color is blue. The blue of the sky after a summer rain. And though I like all cats and dogs, I prefer dogs, though it's been a long time since I've had one. And they like me for whatever reason. What about you?"

He smiled at her words. "I like blue for the same

reason. The blue of the skies I saw in Colorado make me want to head back to the mountains."

"Cats or dogs?"

"I had a cat and a dog growing up. I like the independence of cats but prefer the pure affection and loyalty of a dog."

They talked for the next hour, learning more about the places they'd been—Briana as a military brat, Rafe during his assignments with the military. They shared items on their bucket lists. They both wanted to see Devil's Tower Monument, the Tetons and Yellowstone.

As they neared Springfield, Rafe could tell Briana was getting sleepier. He looked at the hotels on the east side of the city then, put Briana on hold for a few minutes, called ahead and reserved a room with two beds. When he got there, he'd insist on them sleeping for a few hours before they decided where to go next.

"I've sent you a map pin of the place we'll meet. You should be there in twenty minutes. I'll be there about the same time, give or take a few minutes. Wait for me there. Stay in your car until I arrive. I'm in a black four-wheel-drive pickup."

"I'm in a small, silver four-door Nissan," she said. "I'm looking forward to meeting you in person."

"Me, too." He said and meant it. "None of the awkward stranger greetings."

"That's right," she said. "We're practically old friends."

"That's right," he said.

"Old friends meeting at a hotel." She laughed. "That's

not awkward at all. If I wasn't so tired, I might think it strange and a little weird."

"But not awkward," he finished.

"Right," she said. "I'm pulling off the interstate now."

"Me, too." Rafe exited the interstate. He could see the hotel sign clearly. His pulse quickened. After being on the phone for hours with Briana, he'd finally get to meet her. No, he didn't feel awkward. Yes, he was excited.

CHAPTER 3

Briana parked beneath the overhang at the entrance to the hotel and waited inside her car. Headlights flashed behind her. When she glanced in the rearview mirror, her heart fluttered. The big shiny grill of a pickup came to a stop behind her. A door opened, and a tall, muscular man wearing jeans and a black T-shirt climbed out.

All the time she'd spent on the phone with Rafe Donovan, she'd had an image in her mind of what he'd look like.

Her heart beat faster as he stepped into the light and walked up to the driver's side window.

Rafe Donovan was all she'd imagined and so very much more. Yes, he was tall, broad-shouldered and built like a brick wall. In addition, the man was hot enough to melt her bones.

If she hadn't been so distraught by all that had happened, she would have groaned at her own appearance, meeting the man for the first time in person. But her looks meant nothing in light of having lost her best friend.

Briana was just glad Rafe was there. Already, she felt better and more secure. She unlocked her door.

He opened it and held out his hand. "Briana?" he asked.

She nodded and laid her hand on his. "You don't even know how glad I am to finally see you."

He helped her out of the vehicle.

Her legs shook, and she would have fallen, but he wrapped his arm around her middle.

"I know you've been through a lot, but let's get inside and into a room before we relax," he said with a crooked smile.

She nodded, holding back ready tears. She swallowed hard on the lump blocking her throat and let him guide her into the building to the front desk.

"I have a reservation for Rafe Donovan," he said.

The clerk had him sign a card, handed him a key and pointed to the elevator. "Check out is at ten, but since you two are arriving so late, I'll make a note to hold the cleaning until one."

"Thank you," Rafe said. "I'll be back in a few minutes to move the vehicles."

With his arm around her, Rafe led her to the elevator and up to the third floor.

She walked in a daze, leaning into his solid form, glad for his strength and presence. She wasn't alone.

Once they were inside the room, he nodded toward the two beds. "I know we just met, but I can't keep an eye on you if you're in a different room. I promise to keep my hands to myself."

She stared at the two beds then turned her gaze to him. "Thank you. I'm just glad you're here." She bit her bottom lip to keep it from trembling. She could feel the waterworks welling in her eyes. The dam that had held back the tears was crumbling quickly.

"Come here," he said, opening his arms.

Briana fell into him and buried her face against his chest. The emotions she'd kept at bay throughout the long drive refused to be contained a moment longer. Tears streamed down her face and soaked his dark T-shirt. "I'm sorry. I just can't stop."

"It's okay. You've been through a lot."

For a long time, she stood in his arms, letting the tears fall.

Rafe held her throughout, smoothing a hand over her hair, murmuring soothing words Briana couldn't make sense of.

"I can't..." she whispered, "...can't get Sheila's face out of my mind. She was staring at me, and she was...dead."

"Not long ago, I held one of my best friends in my arms as he'd bled out in the back of a helicopter. His name was Freestone. Justin Freestone. He looked up at me, square in the eye, and asked, "Am I going to die?"

Briana stilled, Rafe's words cutting through her own grief. She could hear the torture in his own tone. She raised her face and looked into shadowed eyes. "Did you know?"

Rafe nodded. "He'd taken a hit so bad, he wasn't going to make it back to base."

"What did you say?"

His lips twisted. "No, buddy. We're going to get you a first-class ticket home to your wife and family. Hang in there. Freestone, you're going home."

"I'm so sorry." She pressed her palm against his cheek and leaned up on her toes, brushing her lips across his.

Rafe's arm tightened around Briana. He stroked her hair, cupped the back of her head and lowered his mouth to hers. His lips hovered over hers.

"I didn't get to say goodbye," she said.

"I know. Shhh," he said, his breath mingling with hers. "You're tired. You need sleep."

"I am," she said. "But I need this more." She leaned up on her toes, just enough to press her mouth to his.

What started as her move changed halfway through the kiss. He pulled her closer, until their bodies were flush up against each other and his hand swept up beneath her hair.

His mouth claimed hers in a kiss that pushed all other thoughts from her mind. All she could feel, think, hear or see was this man who'd spent the last few hours getting to know her over the phone.

Never had she felt so safe, so warm and protected. As the kiss continued, her feelings changed from safety to longing to need. She needed to be closer. The kind of closer that included skin to skin contact.

Briana slid her hands up his chest and locked them behind the back of his neck. She didn't need to breathe when she had him. She could die in his arms and have no regrets.

Alas, Rafe lifted his head and brushed back a strand of her hair from her forehead. "You need rest. We have to make some decisions in the morning about what's next, but for now…sleep."

He was right. She'd had a long day, and it was already three in the morning. The next day didn't promise to be any shorter. If she wanted to have functioning brain cells to solve the problems of her current situation, she needed rest.

"I don't have any clothes," she said.

"I do. You can borrow shorts and a T-shirt to sleep in. I'll go get them out of my truck and move the vehicles to a parking space."

When he turned to leave, her heart leaped up her throat, and she grabbed his arm. "You're coming back, right?"

He smiled and cupped her cheek. "I won't be gone but a couple minutes. Lock the door with all the locks after I leave, and don't open the door for anyone but me."

Briana nodded. Her pulse pounded so loudly against her eardrums she could barely hear herself think. "I will." She let go of his arm and stepped backward, her hands clutched in front of her. Now that she was with him, she didn't want him out of her sight. But that was silly. What could go wrong in a few short minutes?

"You can shower while I'm downstairs."

Her heart hammered against her ribs. The last time she'd showered, she'd only been in the bathroom a few minutes. Long enough for someone to break into her apartment, kill her roommate and change her life forever. She shook her head. "I'll wait until you get back."

He nodded and turned toward the door. He checked through the peep hole before opening it. "Lock up behind me," he said as he left the room.

Briana twisted the bolt on the door and threw over the metal latch. When she checked through the peephole, Rafe still stood outside the door.

"Did you turn the lock?" his muffled voice sounded through the thick door.

"Yes," she answered.

"I'll be right back." And he left the door, walking toward the stairwell.

Briana stood at the door for the next minute, staring out at the empty hallway. The other guests would be sound asleep.

Not Briana. Her body was tense, her pulse jumping, her breath caught and held in her lungs until she had to draw more in.

What was probably only five minutes felt like hours.

Briana knew staring through the peephole wouldn't make the time pass any faster. She stepped away and paced across the room. At every sound, she hurried back to the door to look out through the tiny hole.

When at last a soft knock sounded at the door, she raced to answer, looking first through the peephole to verify it was Rafe.

She quickly unlocked the door and jerked it open.

He stepped in, dropped a duffle bag on the floor and turned to lock the door behind him.

When he faced her again, she threw herself into his arms.

"Hey." He chuckled. "I was only gone five minutes, tops."

"I know. But if felt like forever." She clung to him for another moment before loosening her hold around his neck.

His hands gripped her around the waist. "Not that I mind a beautiful woman throwing herself at me. It's kind of nice. You know…helps the old ego."

"You're not old," she said, her cheeks heating. "I'm just…grateful." And a whole lot more emotions she wouldn't care to admit to a man she'd just met.

He lifted the duffle bag and carried it to the bed where he unzipped it and pulled out a T-shirt and a pair of gym shorts. "Sorry, but this is about the extent of my wardrobe. No robe. But I do have a comb, and I brought a spare toothbrush from the front desk." He handed her a comb, toothbrush and a travel-size tube of toothpaste.

"It's all perfect," she said. Gathering the items, she entered the bathroom and stared at the shower. Her body started trembling.

"What's wrong?" he asked, coming up behind her.

"N-nothing."

"Remember? We're old friends," Rafe slipped his arms around her from behind and crossed them over her belly. "You can tell me anything," he said, his warm breath stirring the hair beside her ear.

"I had just gotten out of the shower and dressed when the man broke into our apartment."

His arms tightened briefly. Then he let go, moved around her, swept back the curtain, switched on the water and stood back. "Get in. When you're ready, let me know. I'll open the door a crack and talk to you the whole time, if you like."

She thought about it for a moment, and then nodded. "It's silly to be afraid."

"No, it's not." He smoothed a strand of her hair back from her forehead, tucked it behind her ear, and then rested his palm against her cheek. "You had something terrible happen to a good friend of yours in your own home. You *should* be afraid. And if it helps to leave the door open, we'll leave the door open. I'm here. I'm not going to let anything happen to you."

She captured his hand and turned it over, pressing her lips against his lifeline. He was her lifeline. "Thank you." Briana entered the bathroom, closed the door and leaned her ear against it.

"I'm still here," he said through the door.

She smiled, quickly stripped out of her shoes, leggings, T-shirt, bra and panties. After adjusting the temperature of the water, she stepped behind the curtain. "Okay," she called out.

A draft of cool air ruffled the shower curtain.

"I'm right outside the door if you want to talk," he said. "You can pretend you're still in your car, which is now parked outside beneath a bright light."

"Thank you for moving it," she said. "And thank you for being patient with me." She squirted some of the hotel-supplied shampoo into her palm, wet her hair and rubbed the soap into it, trying to come up with a topic to talk about. It felt as if they'd talked about so much already. "What kind of music do you like to listen to?"

"I like country and jazz, but I'm a big fan of rock and roll. What about you?" His voice sounded close, as if he were standing in the bathroom beside the shower.

Briana peeked around the side of the curtain, suds slipping down her cheek.

Rafe leaned his back against the doorframe, facing into the bedroom, his arms crossed over his chest. He wasn't looking her direction. Instead, he was giving her the privacy she needed, while providing the comfort of knowing he was nearby. A gentleman. Who knew they still existed?

She ducked behind the curtain and tipped back her head beneath the water. "Rock and roll, pop and country. I do like jazz and R&B, as well."

"What about books?" he asked. "Fiction? Non-fiction?"

"Fiction. I like to escape when I read," she said. "You?"

"Non-fiction. I studied a lot of history and biographies. I'm interested in how people lived through the centuries. I also like books on how things work."

Briana squeezed conditioner into her palm and worked it into her hair. With only a comb to work with, she'd have to be careful not to get too many tangles. When they left the hotel, she'd ask Rafe to stop at a store so that she could buy a few necessities, like a brush, underwear, another shirt and, maybe, a pair of jeans. She wasn't sure how long it would be before she got back to Chicago, and if the police would allow her back into her apartment anytime soon. "I'll need to call my boss and let her know I won't be in for a few days."

"We'll need to talk about where we're going from here."

The thought of making a decision left her cringing in the shower. "Could we do that after we sleep?"

"Absolutely," he replied.

She washed her body with soap, her thoughts going to Rafe's strong arms and big hands. A shiver of awareness ran over her. The man was steps away from her naked body. If she knew him better…if they were dating…she'd invite him in to share the shower with her.

Heat built inside, pooling at her core, followed quickly by guilt. Her friend had died, and she was thinking of getting naked with a stranger.

But she and Rafe weren't strangers. They were practically old friends.

All the more reason for her to stop thinking about showering with the man.

After rinsing thoroughly, she switched off the water. "I'm done."

"I'll just close the door." His deep voice filled the bathroom.

She waited to hear the soft snick of the door closing before she pulled back the curtain and stepped out onto the mat.

Minutes later, she'd dried, pulled his large T-shirt over her head and let it fall down around her thighs. The shorts were too long, covering her knees, and she had to roll the waistband a few times to keep them from falling off her hips. She rinsed her panties in the sink and hung them to dry on one of the towel racks. Then she plugged in the blow dryer and worked the tangles out of her hair with the comb, blowing it dry at the same time. Satisfied she was clean of the smell of fear and death, she stepped out of the bathroom wearing Rafe's T-shirt and shorts.

He lounged on one of the beds with his hands laced behind his head. He smiled when he saw her. "That T-shirt looks better on you than me." His brow wrinkled as his gaze shifted lower. "The shorts, not so much."

"Thanks for the loan. I'm just glad to have something to wear." She padded across room and stared at the other bed.

"You can have this one," he offered. "I thought you'd want me to be closer to the door."

"This one is fine," she said, but she couldn't force herself to get under the covers. Images of her apartment, Sheila's lifeless body lying on the floor, and the EMTs loading her onto a stretcher all flooded back to her.

Rafe's hands settled on her shoulders.

Briana hadn't even heard him get out of the bed to come stand behind her.

"What's wrong?"

"How do you turn off the images? My mind is like a movie film on an infinite loop. It keeps replaying the man in my apartment, him standing over Sheila and then searching the rest of my place. I see him standing beside the bed I hid beneath."

Rafe eased her back against him. "You need to sleep."

"How?" She shook her head. "How do I turn it off?"

"I can't tell you that. I've never been able to do that myself. Especially right after the event happened. At the very least, you need to lie down and rest."

She looked over her shoulder into his face. "I'm afraid to close my eyes."

"Then lie on the bed and keep your eyes open. Relaxing has to be of some help. And maybe, you'll fall asleep."

She nodded and took a step toward the bed and stopped. "I'm afraid."

"Get in and scoot over. I'll hold you until you go to sleep." He pulled back the comforter and waved her toward the bed.

Briana slipped between the sheets and moved over to allow him to slide in beside her.

He'd kicked off his boots and changed into shorts while she'd been in the shower. He smelled faintly of a musky aftershave, and his body was warm and reassuringly solid beside her.

Once he was settled in the bed, she rolled into his side and rested her head on his shoulder. "Do you mind?"

He hesitated. "No. But don't be alarmed if I like this too much. It's been a while since I've been with a woman."

"I'm sorry." She leaned away from him. "Am I bothering you?"

He chuckled. "Only in the best way," he said. "Lie still

and stare at the ceiling. It's boring enough to put you to sleep. Light on or off?"

"On, please."

"On, it is." He pulled her close, his arm around her shoulder, his hand resting on her side. "Rest, Briana. We'll tackle the world when we wake."

For the longest time, she lay awake in Rafe's arms, staring at that boring ceiling. Rafe was right. She stared at it long enough it lulled her into a dreamless sleep. Briana woke several hours later spooned into the curve of Rafe's body. The sun had yet to rise, but the gray light of pre-dawn crept into the room around the edges of the blackout curtains.

She lay there, listening to the sound of Rafe's breathing. He'd been patient with her when she'd been scared, and he'd talked to her for the hours it took for them to finally meet in person. He hadn't had to do all that. She was an assignment to him. But he was going above and beyond what she would expect of a bodyguard.

She pressed her back into his front, laid her head on his thickly muscled arm and allowed herself to close her eyes. The disturbing images remained floating in the back of her mind but pushed way back. At that moment, Rafe's presence dwarfed any other thoughts, and soon, she fell asleep and slept through the remainder of the night without dreams. When she woke, light streamed through the window, and she was alone in the bed.

Briana sat up straight, her heart pounding. "Rafe?"

CHAPTER 4

When he heard Briana's cry, Rafe stepped out of the bathroom, barefooted, rubbing a towel over his wet hair.

She was finally awake, but the fear in her eyes tugged at his heart.

"Hey," he said with a smile, hoping to calm her. "Glad you finally decided to wake up. We're due to check out in thirty minutes. You all right? Or do I need to ask them to put us up for another night?"

"No. I'm awake. I can be ready by then." She blinked, the fear fading from her face, though the shadows remained. Flinging aside the comforter, she swung her legs over the side of the bed and stood, staring at him, her shoulders slumped. "I was hoping I'd wake in my own bed and everything that happened yesterday was all part of a horrible nightmare." Tears welled in her eyes. "She's gone, though, isn't she?"

Rafe's heart squeezed hard in his chest. He didn't

have words that could help her through the pain. Instead, he opened his arms.

Briana walked into them. "I know crying doesn't help." She sniffed, drew in a deep breath and wrapped her arms around his waist, resting her cheek against his chest. "I promise I'll pull myself together. Soon."

"You're allowed to grieve," he said. "You wouldn't be human if you didn't."

For a long moment, she remained in his arms, her body warm from the bed, her hair smelling of the shampoo she'd used the night before.

Rafe could have stood there forever. Briana, the stranger who wasn't such a stranger, fit perfectly in his arms and felt so right.

She lifted her head and stepped back. "Thank you for your patience." Her shoulders squared, and her jaw firmed. "I'll be ready in five minutes."

"You have thirty," he reminded her.

"I need to call my boss and let her know what's going on. I should have done it hours ago." She reached for her cellphone, hit her boss's number and waited.

Rafe studied her as she told her boss she wouldn't be in and why. His heart hurt for her as she spoke of the murder. When tears slipped down her cheeks, she wiped them away with the back of her hand. "I need the next few days off. No, I don't know how long. For now, consider me off for the next two weeks. I'll let you know if I'm coming back sooner." She ended the call, wiped her wet cheeks and pasted a weak smile on her face. "Now that that's over, I'll just duck into the bathroom. I won't be long."

His brow furrowed as he looked down at her. "Are you sure you're okay?"

She nodded. "I might not be now, but I will be. I want to call the shelter where the woman and her baby are hiding, but I'm afraid any contact with them will only lead others to them."

"I might be able to help. My boss, Hank Patterson, has a team of people with various skills. One of them is supposedly good at anything to do with computers and communications equipment. We could have him contact the people at the facility. That way, if your phone is being tracked, the call wouldn't be coming from you."

She nodded. "That makes sense. And I really need to know they're okay." Briana grabbed her clothes and shoes and entered the bathroom, pausing at the door. "You'll be here when I get out?"

He raised both hands. "I promise. I'm not going anywhere without you."

She nodded and closed the door.

As promised, she was out a few minutes later, her hair neatly combed, wearing her own T-shirt and leggings. The shirt and shorts she'd slept in were neatly folded in her hands.

He took them from her and packed them in his duffle bag. "Might need these again. I'm not sure where we're going from here."

"Maybe we should go back to Chicago. At least, there, I might be able to get into my apartment for some of my own things."

"That's a possibility, but I'm not convinced it's safe."

"Whoever is after me wouldn't know your truck. I could drive my car to the edge of the city and park it in a commuter lot," Briana suggested.

"We could do that," he said. "I'd like to get my boss's take on it first."

"Okay." Her stomach rumbled, and she grimaced. "I need to eat something. I haven't had anything since lunch yesterday."

"Then let's go find food. While we're eating, we can discuss where to go from here." He slung the duffle bag over his shoulder, checked the hallway through the peephole and opened the door. The corridor was empty except for the rolling cart filled with clean linens, towels and toiletries.

"Come on," he said, waving her through, his hand on the strap of his backpack, the other on the gun in the holster beneath his jacket.

He hadn't worn it into the hotel the night before but had brought it inside hidden in his duffle bag. His gut told him things could be different today, and he needed to be prepared for anything.

When Briana turned toward the elevator, Rafe blocked her path. "Let's take the stairwell. It's only two flights, and we control when the door opens."

Her brow puckered. "You think we're in danger here?"

"I'd rather not take any chances on my first assignment." He winked, and then his jaw hardened. "Seriously, until we know what we're up against, we can't take anything for granted."

She nodded. "I'm leaving it up to you."

He led the way to the stairwell, descending at a pace she could easily keep up with. When they arrived at the ground floor, he went through first and out into the parking lot, checking all directions before he went back to get her and led her out to his truck, using his body as a shield for hers.

He'd opened the passenger side door and was waiting for Briana to climb in, when she glanced around him and her eyes widened. "Sweet Jesus!"

"What?" He spun to see what she was talking about.

A black and white border collie ducked between vehicles parked in the lot. A car leaving nearly hit the animal and honked.

Briana flinched and started around Rafe. "He's going to get hit."

He gripped her arm, holding her back. "Forget the dog. You need to get into the truck."

She tugged at the hand restraining her. "We can't leave the dog. He could wander out onto the highway and get hit."

"If you don't get into the truck, you could be targeted by the people who killed your friend." He urged her toward the open door of his truck.

Her eyebrows lowered. "I will, but we need to do something about that dog."

Rafe sighed. "Will you at least stand behind the door for protection, while I go after the dog?"

She nodded. "I'll stay. Just grab him before it's too late."

Rafe was torn between going after the dog and staying at Briana's side. If he didn't save the dog, the woman would do it herself. Either way, she would be exposed.

He pointed to her. "Stay." Then he walked toward the dog. "Hey, big guy," he spoke softly, holding his hand out to the border collie.

The dog edged toward him, his nose out, sniffing. He whined and wagged his tail. Before he reached Rafe, the dog dropped to the ground, his entire back end wagging along with his tail.

As Rafe dropped to his haunches, the crack of gunfire sounded. Something whizzed over the top of his head and hit the stone façade of the hotel, kicking out fragments of rock.

Rafe dropped to the ground, shouting over his shoulder. "Briana, get down!" He low-crawled on his elbows and knees toward the closest vehicle.

The dog dove beneath the chassis.

Rafe came up on his haunches between two cars and glanced toward Briana.

She'd dropped to the ground and scooted beneath the truck, her head up, eyes rounded.

Rafe pointed toward her and mouthed the word "stay".

Briana nodded and scooted even further beneath the truck chassis, hiding behind one of the wheels.

Rafe gauged the trajectory of the bullet, turned and edged toward the back of the vehicles. A dark SUV parked on the other side of the street pulled away from the curb, made a U-turn in the middle of the road and barreled into the hotel parking lot, heading directly for Rafe's pickup and Briana.

Hunkering low, Rafe ran behind the backs of the vehicles toward Briana, pulling his gun out of the holster beneath his jacket.

The passenger door of the SUV opened. A man dressed in black clothes and a black ski mask started to get out.

Rafe's heart leaped. He leaned over the hood of a vehicle, sighted his weapon on the man and pulled the trigger.

The window beside the man exploded in little shards of glass. The man jumped back into the vehicle, and the SUV raced directly for Rafe.

Rafe dove away from the car he'd leaned on and rolled out of the path of the speeding vehicle.

The SUV plowed into the spot where Rafe had been standing, pushing the car into the one next to it. The barrel of a military-grade rifle poked through the shattered window, aiming toward Rafe where he lay on the ground.

He rolled beneath a minivan and out the other side as bullets pelted the ground he'd been lying against a moment before.

Leaping to his feet, Rafe aimed and fired at the passenger door where the rifle poked through. The rifle clattered against the glass and disappeared inside. The SUV's driver backed out of the mangled car, shifted into drive and raced out of the hotel parking lot.

Rafe remained where he was, a minivan hood between him and the disappearing SUV. When the SUV was out of rifle range, Rafe ran to his truck and held out his hand. "Come on, we need to leave before he decides to return and finish one or both of us off."

Briana crawled out from beneath the truck and took his hand.

Rafe pulled her to her feet and into his arms, crushing her to his chest. Her body trembled against his. "You're shaking."

"Give me a break. It's not every day my friend is murdered, and my bodyguard is shot at."

He tipped her head up, kissed her hard and lifted her up into the seat. "Stay low as we drive out of here."

She nodded and buckled her seatbelt.

Before he could close the door, a black and white streak of hair dashed between him and the door. The dog he'd leaned down to pet leaped into the truck and settled on the floor at Briana's feet.

Rafe started to tell the animal to get out.

Briana, hunching over in the front seat, ruffled the hair around the dog's neck. "Let him stay. He has a collar with a tag on it. We can call the owner after we get out of here."

He ran around to the driver's side, jumped in, revved the engine and took off in the opposite direction from their attackers.

As they pulled away from the hotel, Briana, lying on her side on the console, keyed the phone number from the tag on the dog's collar.

"Hello, this is Briana. We found your dog in a hotel parking lot." She listened, her brow knitting. "Yes, that's the hotel... There is?" Her frown deepened. "I'm so sorry to hear that." Her gaze went to the border collie.

"How do you want us to get the dog to you? We're kind of in a hurry to get back on the road."

Rafe leaned closer to her, trying to watch the road and eavesdrop on the conversation. He couldn't hear what the dog's owner was saying.

"Are you sure? I mean, she's beautiful and obviously well taken care of. Okay. We'll make sure she goes to a good home. Thank you and my condolences." Briana ended the call. "Is it safe for me to sit up? I'm getting a crick in my neck."

Rafe had been watching as he drove toward the interstate. "Yes, if you keep fairly low."

She sat up, sliding low in her seat. "Apparently, we've just adopted a dog."

"What?" He shot a glance her way.

"The man I talked to just lost his father. His father's border collie, Lucy's her name, keeps escaping the son's backyard and coming to the cemetery behind the hotel to visit his former owner." Briana leaned forward, smoothing her hand over the collie's head. "She misses him. The man's son has children, a full-time job and his wife works. They don't have time to keep chasing down Lucy and bringing her home. And they're afraid she'll get run over, which would have broken his father's heart."

"What are we going to do with a dog?" Rafe asked, thinking of the complications a dog could add to the job of keeping Briana safe.

"I guess we'll need to stop for a few essentials, like a leash, bowls, food, water and toys." Her lips twitched at the corners. "And don't even think we'll drop her off at the nearest shelter. She's been through so much already."

"You're running from a killer. We can't afford the distraction." Rafe frowned at Lucy. "No offense."

"Yeah. I get that," Briana said. "I also know that we aren't leaving her in that hotel parking lot. It was only a matter of time before she was hit by a vehicle."

Rafe wasn't going to talk Briana out of keeping the dog. He sighed and cast a worried glance at the border collie. "Give us any trouble and your ass is getting booted out of this truck." He pointed his finger at the dog. "Got it?"

Lucy barked and licked his pointed finger.

Briana laughed. "I think she gets it."

"Border collies are one of the most intelligent breeds of dogs." Rafe's brow dipped as he changed the subject. "What worries me is how those guys found you."

"Couldn't they have followed me from Chicago?"

"Maybe, but I doubt it. I'm betting they've tapped into the GPS on your cellphone. They followed you to your apartment because you had the woman's cellphone. They figured out who you are once they realized they murdered your roommate." He held out his hand. "Give me your cellphone."

She frowned. "You think they followed my cellphone? How?"

"Hacking into phone records."

"So quickly?"

He nodded. "They probably have connections with hackers on the dark web." He wiggled his fingers. "Your phone."

She laid her cellphone in his palm.

Rafe turned the truck into a gas station, rolled down the window and started to toss the phone into the trash.

Briana grabbed his arm before he could throw it and pointed to a truck full of furniture and household items with a sign painted on the side that said GEORGIA OR BUST. She smiled, took the phone from Rafe, lowered her window and dropped the phone into the bed of the pickup.

Rafe chuckled as he left the station and drove up the ramp onto the interstate headed west. His gaze took in every direction, searching for the dark SUV with the busted window.

"Have we decided where we're going?" Briana asked.

"I figure our current location has been compromised." Rafe's jaw tightened. "We need to get somewhere safer than the interstate. Safer than Illinois."

Briana looked to him. "You have a place in mind?"

"I didn't. But Hank Patterson sent me the location of a place that will work for us. We just have to get to Montana."

Her eyes widened. "We're going to Montana?"

He nodded, the idea resting well with him. He didn't know what they'd do once they reached the hunting cabin in Eagle Rock, but Hank had assured him the cabin was remote, hard to find and he'd have the guidance and help he'd need to keep Briana safe.

"You might as well settle back." He set the cruise control for five miles per hour over the posted limit. "It's a long way."

"How long?" she asked, her gaze seeking his.

"About twenty hours."

"Wow, that is a long way from home." She stared out the front windshield at the road ahead, the corners of her mouth turning downward. "But then, what home do I have? I can't go back to my apartment. I need clothes, but I can buy those. I have no family in Illinois." She gulped back what sounded like a sob. "My boss doesn't expect me back anytime in the next couple of weeks." Briana shrugged. "Might as well go to Montana." She gave him a weak smile, her hand buried in Lucy's fur. "Hear that, Lucy? We're going to Montana. I just hope the guys who attacked us don't decide to follow."

Rafe felt the same way. He could be taking the problem with them. At least, in Montana, he'd have backup.

CHAPTER 5

Numerous times during the long journey, Briana asked Rafe to let her drive to give him a break. He'd refused, stating he was used to being up for long hours and didn't fall asleep in vehicles.

He might not sleep in vehicles, but once the sun set, *she* did, and she slept hard until morning light. She yawned and stretched, amused to find Lucy lying half on the floor, half across her lap, the dog's head resting in her palm.

Briana smiled softly down at the dog who had been grieving for her former owner. "Poor baby. You miss your guy. I miss my friend. We're a pretty sad pair." She glanced up, blinking back some pesky tears. "Where are we?"

Rafe drew in a deep breath and let it out. "Montana. We're about an hour and a half from Eagle Rock."

"Is Hank expecting us? I thought I heard you talking on the phone a little while ago."

He nodded. "About an hour ago, I called Hank to let

him know we were on our way in. He said we could crash there for a day if we wanted, until we can get a better handle on who is after you and how to stop them. However, I think it would be better if we go straight to the hunting cabin he has lined up for us. I don't want to put Hank and his family at risk by our staying with them."

"Agreed," she said. She wished she'd known Alejandra's phone had been in her purse when she'd entered her apartment. Had she known, Sheila might not be dead. Then again, she'd had no idea how far *El Chefe* would go to find his woman and child.

"We'll need to give Hank more information about this guy who's threatening you, so that his computer guru, Swede, can run some checks, maybe find out who he's hired to do his dirty work. Also, so that he can check on the woman and her baby."

"I can tell you the name of the man she said is after her and the baby. He's from El Salvador. His name is *El Chefe Diablo.*"

Rafe's head jerked around, and the truck slowed. "Who did you say?"

"*El Chefe Diablo* from El Salvador. Apparently, he's a very dangerous man."

"You've never heard of him before now?" Rafe asked.

Briana shook her head. "I've been so focused on saving abused and neglected children, I haven't had time to immerse in international news. Why? What do you know?"

He gave a low whistle. "Holy hell. If the woman you helped find shelter is *El Chefe*'s woman, he won't give up until he takes her back to El Salvador or kills her. He won't hesitate to kill anyone who gets in his way."

"How do you know this?" Briana asked, rubbing her arms.

"I swear I read that once he sent a squad of men to his neighbor's house to shoot the neighbor, the children and the servants in that house because he got tired of listening to the dog bark, and the people never did anything to make it stop. He killed the family and had the dog brought to his place where he beat it until it didn't bark anymore."

Briana rubbed her hand across Lucy's shoulder, a frown pulling at her brow. "All because a dog barked?"

Rafe nodded. "I remembered the story because it seemed too bizarre to be true. I researched the issue and, sure enough, it was true. The guy's a sadistic bastard. He murdered an entire village because one man in that village skimmed a batch of the drugs they were producing and sold it to another cartel leader. Women, children…it didn't matter to him. He killed them all and burned the village to the ground."

Cold dread washed over Briana. "I'm glad we came to Montana. Surely, he won't have his men follow us here."

"If he does," Rafe said, "it'll be easier to see them coming than on a city street."

"What can I do to keep safe?" she asked, staring out the window at plains. "You can't always be around."

He frowned. "I plan on being around until the threat is neutralized."

"I know you will. But what if something happens to

you? What if that bullet had hit you in front of the hotel? I had no way of defending myself."

Rafe glanced her way. "Do you know how to use a gun?"

She shook her head. "Dad took me to the gun range, once, before I went to college. He offered to buy me a gun, but I didn't feel comfortable enough to carry one."

"While we're out here, I'll teach you how to use one. You'll carry it and get to the point you feel better about having it near."

Her fists clenched. "I hate this. I hate that I've lost someone who meant so much to me. A senseless murder. They were after me. Now, I hate that I'm afraid. My daddy taught me to be cautious, not afraid. To be strong, not weak." She shook her head. "I hate this."

Rafe reached across the console and took one of her fists in his large hand. "One good thing out of this, is that we're getting to know each other. We might have made new friends."

She unclenched her fist and wove her fingers into his. "There is that."

"We might never have met, otherwise," he said. "Not that I would've wished any of this to happen to you or your roommate."

She lifted his hand to her cheek, fighting back the ready tears. "Thank you for coming to my rescue. I don't know what I would've done if you hadn't."

"You probably would've kept driving." He chuckled. "You might have been in Texas by now, instead of Montana."

She smiled. "Probably. Not that I know anyone in Texas."

"Your brother is stationed there."

"Yeah. I guess I was headed that direction. But he wouldn't have been there."

"He cared enough to get you the help you needed." He brought her hand to his lips and brushed a kiss across her knuckles. "See the mountains ahead?"

She nodded, her gaze taking in the snow-covered peaks ahead.

"Those are the Crazy Mountains," Rafe said. "That's where we're headed."

"Why are they called the Crazy Mountains?" Briana asked.

"Legend has it that a family of settlers were attacked by Blackfeet in the early eighteen hundreds. After her husband and children were killed, the mother went crazy and ran into the mountains. From that point on, the white settlers, and the Blackfeet, referred to the mountains as the Crazy Woman Mountains. The name has been shortened over time."

"That's sad," Briana murmured. Her heart hurt for the woman who'd witnessed the death of her husband and children. Two days ago, she might not have been able to relate with the woman's anguish. Having witnessed her roommate's death, she could understand.

"I think you have a friend in Lucy," Rafe said.

Briana glanced down at the dog, stirring at her feet. Lucy looked up at her with her big brown-black eyes. "She's beautiful."

"Did you have pets growing up?"

"We always had a couple of dogs in the house. They would alternate whose bed they would sleep in. On some nights, they'd sleep with Ryan, on others, with me. My parents were glad they didn't sleep with them."

"What kind of dogs were they?"

"We had a pair of miniature Shetland sheepdogs. Shelties." Briana smiled. "Sam and Trixie. They were with us for most of our young lives. They didn't pass until I left for college." She sighed. "I missed them terribly."

"College kept you busy?"

She nodded. "It was good to be running all the time. When I wasn't in class or studying, I worked at an ice cream shop part-time for extra spending money."

"What's your favorite ice cream?" he asked. "Or did you leave the ice cream business hating ice cream?"

She laughed. "I didn't eat ice cream for a solid year after I graduated. But I eventually came back to my favorite, Rocky Road. What's yours?"

"I'm boring. I love vanilla ice cream. But I like a thick hot fudge sauce poured over it."

"Mmm. You're making my mouth water." She looked out at the miles and miles of empty plains. "Do you know if Eagle Rock has an ice cream shop there?"

He shook his head. "I've never been to Eagle Rock. I just left the military and was on my way there when I got the call."

She gave him a grateful smile. "I'm lucky you were as close as you were. I doubt anyone would've gotten to me from Montana any sooner." She shivered. "What I don't understand is why they didn't attack me along the way? I was alone the entire trip from Joliet to Springfield. They had ample opportunity to run me off the road."

"I've been thinking about that," Rafe said. "Like we thought, it had to be your phone they followed. It might've taken them time to figure out where you were. They caught up while we were sleeping."

Briana trembled in the seat beside him. "I'm just glad the bullet missed."

"You and me both." Rafe smiled. "I have Lucy to thank for that. If I hadn't bent to pet her, I could've taken that bullet square in the chest."

"Do you think they'll hack into your phone's GPS now that they know I'm with you?" Briana asked.

"Hank sent me my cellphone before I left Texas. He said it has special security apps and encryption loaded into it to keep that from happening. We should be all right. And I haven't seen anyone following us since we ditched your phone in the back of that truck headed east from Springfield."

"I'll have to call the phone company and have my service cut off," Briana said.

"Another day. The less communication you have with your old life, the less of a chance *El Chefe* will have of finding you now."

Soon, they entered the foothills of the Crazy Mountains, zig-zagging along winding roads. They came to a town, the name posted on a quaint wooden sign, indicating they'd found Eagle Rock. Rafe didn't stop in the town.

"Shouldn't we stop for supplies?" Briana asked as they passed a small grocery store.

Rafe shook his head. "Hank said they had the cabin fully stocked and ready for us. Again, the less contact we have with others, the less chance of *El Chefe*'s men finding us."

Briana nodded and brushed her hand over Lucy's smooth head. "I'm glad we stopped back in South Dakota for supplies for Lucy. I think we need to keep her on a lead until she gets used to us. If we let her run free, I'm afraid she'll try to find her way back to her owner's grave."

"Good idea. There have been dogs that have done that, finding their way across several states to get back to the home they were familiar with."

"Should we text Hank and let him know we're here?" Briana asked.

"He has access to my cellphone's location. He'll know. He said he'd head to the cabin when he saw we were near. Most likely, he'll be there before us."

Using the directions Hank had sent, they passed through town and out the other end, heading deeper into the mountains. Eventually, they turned off the paved road onto a gravel track, climbing up the side of a hill. The road wound through trees and around hills. When it forked south, Rafe turned north.

As they neared the top of a rise, the trees thinned. They emerged into a small clearing where a rustic log cabin perched in the middle. Beside it stood a shiny black pickup with a tall, dark-haired man and a petite, beautiful blond woman Briana found vaguely familiar.

She carried a toddler on her hip, and her belly was swollen with a baby yet to come.

Rafe parked beside the pickup, climbed out and came around to help Briana and Lucy to the ground.

Lucy leaped out and ran to the end of her lead, eager to explore her new surroundings.

Briana was glad she'd snapped the leash onto her collar. She hated to think of the dog getting lost in the woods. She'd read about the bears that made their homes in the mountains and the wolves they'd reintroduced to the area. Lucy wouldn't stand a chance alone in the hills.

Rafe rested his hand at the small of her back as he led her over to where Hank stood with the woman and child.

Hank greeted Briana first. "You must be Briana Hayes. It's a pleasure to meet you. Your brother was very worried about your safety."

"Thank you for sending Rafe to help. I don't know what I would've done without him."

Hank shook Rafe's hand. "Welcome to the Brotherhood Protectors. Glad to have you aboard."

Rafe nodded. "I appreciate the opportunity."

Hank turned to the blonde. "This is my wife, Sadie."

Briana frowned. "Sadie…I feel like I should know you."

Hank chuckled. "You might know her for the all the movies she's made. Most people know her as Sadie McClain."

Briana blinked. "You're Sadie McClain, the movie star?"

She laughed. "I know. Out here, I don't look like I do on the big screen. I'm just Sadie, Hank's wife and Emma's mom." She looked down at the child in her arms. "This is Emma, our daughter."

Emma leaned toward Briana, her arms outstretched.

"Do you mind if I hold her?" Briana asked.

"Please," Sadie said. "She seems to want to go to you."

Briana handed the leash to Rafe and took Emma in her arms.

"You must have a way with children. She usually takes a minute or two to warm up to new people," Hank said.

"I'm good with the little ones," Briana said, smiling down at Emma in her arms. "It helps in my job. Doesn't it, Emma?"

"Your brother said you work with the Child Welfare Department in Chicago," Hank said.

Briana nodded.

"Is that how you got into trouble?" Hank asked.

"Not exactly," Briana said.

Sadie held out her arms. "Here, let me take Emma while you three talk."

Briana handed the child back to her famous mother, took a deep breath and launched into what had happened back in Chicago that had led her to her fleeing the city and traveling all the way out to Montana.

"Until he finds Alejandra, he won't leave Briana alone," Rafe concluded. "She's the key to where he can find his child."

"In the meantime, I'll fly some of my men to Illinois

to bring Alejandra and her little girl here, where we can provide her the best of protection." Hank glanced at Sadie and Emma where they walked around the yard in front of the cabin. "I can imagine how terrified the woman is that she'll lose her child."

"There could be a problem with sending someone to Alejandra," Rafe said. "They know Briana's with me. They could link me to your company and follow anyone you send back to Illinois to Alejandra. They've already proven they can follow a cellphone." He frowned down at his. "Are you sure these phones are hack-proof?"

"Your phone isn't registered in your name. But it wouldn't hurt to ditch it now that you've come this far. I have a satellite phone in my truck. You can use it until we can get a burner phone for you to use. They're really hard to trace, and you can change out phones quickly and easily. For the time being, you can hole up in the cabin. We'll bring out anything you might need. If there are specific items of groceries you'd prefer, make a list and we'll get them for you, so you don't have to make the trip into town."

Briana gripped Hank's hand with both of hers. "You don't know how much I appreciate all you've done for me."

"Are you going to go inside and see if there's anything you might need in the way of food or household goods? I shopped based on my tastes." Sadie smiled as she rejoined them. "You might not like what I like. I'm okay with that, but we'll need to get what you like on our next trip out."

"I'm sure it will all be fine," Briana smiled at the

beautiful actress who looked as at home on the big screen as she did in the Crazy Mountains.

Sadie led the way into the cabin. "This is one of our hunting cabins. There's only one bed, but I had Hank bring a sofa in, in case you need another place to sleep."

She moved to the side with Emma and let Briana walk past her into the small space.

"I'm sorry, but it's rustic. And by rustic, I mean electricity. It has a generator to run the lights and the pump to get water. You'll be able to shower, but the stall is very small. Still, you won't have to use the old outhouse." Sadie grinned. "I don't mind roughing it, but I draw the line at outhouses."

Briana laughed. "It will be perfect."

"My computer guy, Swede, will dive into the dark web and see what he can find out about *El Chefe Diablo*'s activities," Hank said from behind her. "It might give us a heads-up on what he plans next."

Feeling a bit overwhelmed by all Hank and his wife had done, Briana swallowed hard on the lump in her throat. "Thank you."

Sadie turned and hugged her. "I know how it feels to be scared. You don't know who to trust, where to turn and how to get out of a situation you didn't instigate. Hang in there. And if you need anyone to talk to, call me on the satellite phone."

"Speaking of which," Hank turned and left the cabin.

Rafe stepped across the threshold. "We should be safe here. It's far enough off the beaten path to discourage intruders from stumbling in."

Hank returned, holding a phone, which he handed

to Rafe. "Based on what you told me about the weapons you own, I brought additional ammo and a small .40 caliber handgun for Briana."

Rafe smiled at Briana. "Good. We'll get right on those lessons."

Hank's jaw hardened. "Hopefully, she won't have to use it."

"Better to know how and not need it than need it and not know how to use it," Rafe said.

"Exactly." Sadie nodded. "I have my own little pistol. I take it out every week and shoot to keep up my skills."

Briana nodded. "That's what I'll have to do. First, I need to learn how to handle it."

"Look out, world." Rafe chuckled.

"Why are you laughing?" Briana demanded. "You're the one who'll be teaching me."

His face sobered so quickly, it was Briana's turn to laugh.

Her lips twisted. "See, it's not so funny when you're forced to teach the city girl how to shoot."

"That's not why I quit laughing. It is serious, and we need to start those lessons today."

"I'll get that gun and ammo," Hank said and ducked out of the cabin, again.

"I'd prefer to wait until Sadie and Emma are out of here," Briana said. "I don't want to scare them with my ineptitude."

"Oh, sweetie," Sadie grinned, "everyone has to start somewhere. But yes, the loud noises will scare Emma. We need to be going anyway. She'll be ready for a nap right after lunch. And I could use one, too." Sadie patted her perfectly rounded belly. "I find myself easily tired, these days."

A twinge of envy had Briana questioning her life choices. Soon, she'd be twenty-eight. She wasn't dating, didn't have a husband prospect, and she wasn't getting any younger.

Wasn't the big three-zero about the time her biological clock should start ticking? She'd known so many of her women friends who'd waited until they were in their thirties to have children, only to discover they'd waited too long. Some, even after long months of fertility treatments had yet to get pregnant. "When is your baby due?"

Sadie smiled. "Two months. But you'd think it was any day as big as I'm getting."

"You're all baby," Briana said.

Suddenly, Sadie's eyes widened. "Oh, well, there he goes, kicking me. I think he'll be a football player, as active as he is. Or maybe she'll go for hockey, as violently as she plays in my belly."

Hank stepped back through the door and handed a small case, and what appeared to be a shoulder holster, to Rafe. Then he dug in his front shirt pocket and his back jeans pockets for boxes of ammunition. "I'll bring more tomorrow. You'll burn through a lot, practicing. The good news is that there aren't any neighbors to disturb way out here."

"Sweetie, we need to get going," Sadie said, as Emma tugged on her hand. "Your daughter is restless."

Rafe set the gun, holster and bullets on the hand-hewn table and reached down to take Emma's hands. "Wanna come up with Uncle Rafe?"

Emma raised her arms without hesitation.

Rafe swung her up into the crook of his arm and walked with her out into the yard. "You need to come visit Uncle Rafe often."

"After the threat is past," Briana reminded him.

"After the mean ol' bad guys are gone," he said, blowing a raspberry on the toddler's belly.

Emma giggled and grabbed Rafe's ears.

"Hey, those are mine, and they don't come off easily." Rafe nuzzled the child's neck and blew a loud sound against her throat.

The toddler laughed and squirmed.

Briana watched, mesmerized by how easily the big Delta Force soldier interacted with the toddler.

"You're a natural, Rafe," Sadie said, echoing Briana's thoughts. "You don't have children, do you?"

"No. Never considered it. But I love playing with other people's kids. And they seem to like me." He grinned at the little girl in his arms. "You're a cutie," he said, "aren't you?"

"Come here, Emma." Hank reached for his daughter. "We need to get going before those giggles turn into angry squalling. She's a good baby, but she needs her recharge naps to keep those pretty lips smiling."

Hank settled Emma into the car seat in the middle of the back seat of his truck.

"If you come up with a list of items you'd like to have," Sadie said, "call us on the satellite phone. We'll pick them up in town and run them out to you."

"Thank you," Briana said. "I hate to ask for anything else. You've done so much already."

"Nonsense. We don't get that many visitors this far north. It's our pleasure to welcome the newcomers." Sadie gave Briana a hug. "I'm sorry about what happened to your friend. Just know, we're here if you need anything." Hank helped her up into the passenger seat and fastened her seatbelt around her, kissing her gently as he did.

Briana nodded, afraid to say anything lest it come out on a sob. The reminder of Sheila's death hit her, again.

Hank drove out of the yard and down the gravel path, leading away from the cabin, Rafe and Briana.

As the engine noise faded, silence wrapped around the little cabin in the mountains.

Lucy nudged Briana's hand, sliding under it. She leaned her fluffy black and white body against Briana's leg and whined softly.

"I know. It's really quiet out here."

Rafe snorted. "Wait until dark. Then every little sound will be like rockets going off. And you won't know what any of them are."

"You're not painting a calming picture for this city girl," Briana muttered.

He chuckled.

Briana wrapped the lead around her wrist and squared her shoulders. "Come on, Lucy. Let's explore our little patch of heaven."

Rafe joined her. "While we're at it, we can look for a place to set up our firing range."

"Good," she said. "The sooner I learn to fire a gun, the sooner I'll feel better about being out in the woods, far away from everything and everyone I ever knew."

Rafe slipped an arm around her waist and pulled her close. "Not everyone you ever knew. You know me, now."

She leaned into his warmth and strength. "That's right. You're my friend." Her friend she was having more than friendly thoughts about. There could be a lot worse things than being alone on a mountain with a sexy former Delta Force soldier.

CHAPTER 6

Rafe walked around the perimeter of the hilltop, checking out all the potential blind spots an enemy could leverage. While he explored, he found a sparsely treed hill not far from the cabin that would make a perfect backdrop for target practice.

He hurried back to the cabin, collected the weapons and left Lucy with bowls of water and dog food. With Briana, he returned to the hillside. They took advantage of the late afternoon sunshine to familiarize her with the .40 caliber HK pistol Hank had left for Briana.

Rafe set up several soft drink cans on a fallen log. Then he marched five long strides away from the target and motioned for Briana to join him. He handed her a pair of sponge ear plugs and showed her how to roll them between her thumb and fingers and stick them in her ears, where they expanded to fill the space.

She stood beside him, her hands clutched together in front of her. "I really don't know much of anything about shooting a gun," Briana said, staring at the .40 caliber pistol Rafe removed from the case.

"You'll learn," he said and went into describing each part of the weapon, how it worked and what could make it jam. He showed her how to hold it in her hands, balancing it on her opposite palm while it remained unloaded.

She listened carefully, asking questions and doing everything he said.

"You have to treat the weapon as if it were loaded at all times. Never point it at something, unless you intend to shoot it. If you're not shooting, point the barrel at the ground.

Then he had her face the cans and hold the gun out in front of her, her finger along the side of the trigger guard. "Now, switch the safety off, and place your finger on the trigger."

She thumbed the safety. "Like this?"

He nodded. "Yes. Finger on the trigger?"

"It is," she responded.

"Line up the sights like I showed you and pull the trigger by squeezing it gently until it clicks."

Her eyes narrowed as she looked down the top of the barrel and slowly squeezed the trigger. When it clicked, she flinched then relaxed.

Rafe grinned. "It's not so bad, is it? This weapon doesn't have much of a kick. You'll barely feel it jerk in your hand." He held out a full magazine. "Once we add the bullets, this weapon becomes lethal."

She nodded, drew in a deep breath and took the magazine from his hand.

"Slide it into the handle, while pointing the barrel at the ground. Not at your feet, but the ground in front of you. I don't know how many slap-happy recruits have blown off their toes because they weren't careful."

Her head shot up, her eyes rounding. "Really?"

He grinned. "No, but it pays to be super careful."

She nodded and slipped the magazine into the handle of the pistol.

Rafe stood at her left. "Now, do the same thing you just did with the empty gun. Aim down the sights at the target, and squeeze the trigger gently."

He stepped back and nodded. "You can do this."

Briana held the gun just as he'd shown her, switched off the safety and squeezed the trigger. The loud bang made her jump slightly.

The bullet hit the log below the can, sending splinters of rotted wood in all directions.

"That's good," he said.

"But I missed the can," she argued.

"You did, but only by hitting low. Aim a little high of the target this time."

She did and nicked the can, making it spin and fall from the log. Briana laughed and glanced his way, her smile bright in the afternoon shadows.

They fired over a hundred rounds, adjusting her stance and the gun's sights, until Briana was comfortable with how the gun felt in her hands and she could consistently hit the target.

By the time they finished, the shadows had lengthened, and the sun had ducked behind the highest peak of the Crazy Mountains. Without the sun to warm the air, it got cold quickly.

Rafe helped Briana fit the shoulder holster over her arms and buckled it around her torso, his knuckles brushing against her breasts.

His groin tightened. "Sorry."

"Don't be," she said with a smile.

When she looked up at him, her gaze melted into his, making him even more aware of how close they were standing and how much he wanted to kiss her. But it was getting late.

"We need to get back to the cabin." Rafe took a step backward, shifting his gaze upward to the darkening sky.

Briana's chin dropped, and she fiddled with the straps around her arms before sliding the now empty pistol into the holster. "Lucy will be beside herself, thinking we left her."

"I was thinking more along the lines that this is bear country. Now that we're not shooting and making a lot of noise, they might come out of the woods to check things out."

"Bears?" Briana glanced around.

He nodded. "Let's get back so we can walk Lucy before it gets too dark to see."

Briana carried her gun case in her right hand.

Rafe carried his gun case in his left hand. He reached for her empty hand and curled his fingers around hers. "You did good today."

"I had the best instructor." She looked down at his

hand holding hers. "Do you always hold hands with your students?"

He started to let go, but she tightened her grip. "No," he said. "But then I've never had as pretty a student as I did today."

She leaned against his arm. "Thank you for being patient with me. This is all new, but I'm sure I'll get the hang of it."

"You will. It just takes practice."

As they approached the cabin, Lucy started barking.

Rafe entered first, grabbing her by the collar and holding on long enough to snap the lead onto the metal loop. The border collie darted through the door and out into the yard, coming to an abrupt halt at the end of the long lead. Then she raced back to Briana and wagged her entire body at her feet.

Briana laughed and ruffled the collie's coat. "You have to wait for us, girl."

The three of them wandered around the perimeter of the yard until Lucy had done all of her business for the rest of the day.

When they returned to the cabin, Briana closed the door and let Lucy off her lead.

Rafe ducked back outside to start the generator and was back a couple minutes later.

Together, they went through the pantry staples Sadie had stocked the cabin with and settled on making chili.

"You can hit the shower while I cook." Rafe suggested.

"Are you sure?" she asked.

"Chili is about the only meal I can cook, besides

steak on the grill. All the ingredients are here. I think I can handle the meal for tonight."

She smiled. "Deal. I'll come up with something for tomorrow night."

"Hopefully, we won't be here too many nights."

"I'm okay with it. I don't have any place else to go." Briana lifted her chin. "Besides, this is my chance to see some of Montana. Albeit a small corner of the Crazy Mountains. But what I've seen so far is stunningly beautiful."

Rafe nodded. "Agreed. One of these days, I want to try my hand at fly fishing in some of the mountain streams in the area."

"It could be one big vacation." Briana shook her head. "If we didn't have a drug lord breathing down our necks."

"There is that little kink in our Montana getaway." He tipped his head toward the only other door besides the exit. "Go. The water should be hot by now."

He pulled cans from the shelves, plunked a pot on the gas stove and made chili, trying really hard not to think of Briana only a few feet away, naked in the shower. He could easily step into the bathroom and join her…if she wanted him to.

Rafe sighed. She was a client. They'd only known each other a little over twenty-four hours. He needed to keep his pants zipped and his hands to himself.

Protecting the beautiful Briana could be the toughest mission he'd ever been assigned.

. . .

Briana stripped out of the clothes she'd worn for over forty-eight hours that now smelled like gunpowder and dog. The water pressure was questionable, but at least there was a shower in the cabin and she didn't have to find a creek in which to bathe. After shampooing her hair with the sweet-smelling shampoo Sadie had provided, she applied conditioner, and then scrubbed her body with the scented bodywash. Five minutes after entering the shower, she was clean, rinsed and feeling better than she had when she'd stepped in.

Several towels were folded neatly on a wooden shelf. Briana grabbed one and dried off. The chilly night air made her shiver in the small bathroom.

On another shelf, Briana was glad to find a stack of gently used clothes. They included a soft T-shirt and a pair of stretchy leggings she could wear the following day. She dug deeper, hoping to find a sexy nightgown. Had she really thought *sexy*? All she needed was a night gown or pajamas she could sleep in to save the clothes for the next day.

Sadly, there weren't any night clothes among the items, but there was a midnight-blue silk robe... She pulled on the robe that covered her down to the middle of her thighs. The silk was cool against her skin and made her shiver. Whether from cold or excitement, she didn't want to contemplate. After running a brush she found on the counter through her tangles, she left her hair hanging down around her shoulders to dry naturally. Other than the dark circles beneath her eyes, she didn't look too awful after having fled across the country. She looked at the stack of clothes and almost grabbed the T-shirt and leggings to cover her nakedness beneath the robe. Sadie had provided a brand-new package of sexy white lace panties, so at least Briana had those to wear beneath the robe. Firmly tying the sash around her waist, Briana left the bathroom and stood on the threshold, inhaling the rich, tantalizing scent of chili cooking on the stove.

Rafe sat on the couch, rubbing Lucy's neck. He looked up when Briana stepped through the door. He had opened his mouth to say something, but nothing came out.

Briana's cheeks heated at the hunger in Rafe's eyes. "Is dinner ready?" she asked, knowing the hunger had nothing to do with the fact they'd skipped several meals in their twenty-plus hours on the road from Illinois to Eagle Rock. Apparently, the robe was sexier than any leggings she could have worn.

Rafe nodded, cleared his throat and leaped to his feet. "Yes. Yes, it is. You can get started while I jump in the shower." He scooped chili into a bowl, added a spoon and set it on the table. "I'll only be a few minutes."

"That will give the chili time to cool a little. I'll wait for you," she said.

Rafe grabbed his duffle bag and ducked into the tiny bathroom.

Briana refilled Lucy's bowl of dog food and scratched her ears. "He's pretty cute, isn't he?"

Lucy looked up at her and whined softly.

"Yeah, he has that effect on me, too."

Briana spread out the blanket they'd purchased for Lucy across the wood floor.

Lucy circled several times, pawed at the fabric to arrange it just the way she liked it, and then dropped down and was asleep in seconds.

Less than five minutes later, Rafe stepped out of the bathroom, wearing jeans, a T-shirt draped around the back of his neck and nothing else.

Briana swallowed hard, her tongue suddenly dry. The man was built like a brick house. Muscles stretched across his broad chest then tapered down his torso to a narrow waist and hips. And then all that muscle flared out again over massive thighs. He padded barefooted across the floor to the pot on the stove and stirred it several times before he laid the spoon on the stove and shrugged into the T-shirt.

If she'd thought donning the shirt would make him any less sexy, she'd have been wrong.

The T-shirt stretched across his muscles, emphasizing rather than hiding them.

Swallowing hard again, Briana slipped onto the bench at the table and lifted her spoon, having a really hard time tearing her gaze away from Rafe.

"How's the chili?" Rafe asked, turning around with a bowl full for himself.

"What?" Briana glanced down at the bowl in front of her, heat rising up her neck to fill her cheeks. "Uh…I don't know. I was…waiting for you," she lied. She'd been admiring the way his shirt fit his shoulders and wishing she could lay her head on his chest and listen to the beat of his strong heart. Maybe then, she'd forget the reason why they were in Montana to begin with.

"Don't wait on me. Dig in." Rafe sat on the bench

across from her and dipped his spoon into the steaming chili.

Briana focused on the food in front of her, though her mind didn't lose sight of the man in her peripheral vision. She'd slept with him the night before, and he hadn't done anything more than hold her. What made her think he might want to do more than that?

Well, he had kissed her. Had it only been his way of comforting her?

Her gaze went to the only bed in the cabin and the couch. "I can sleep on the couch," she offered, taking a bite of the lukewarm chili.

His head came up. "That's not necessary. You can have the bed. I'll take the couch."

"It makes more sense for me to sleep on the couch. It's not long enough for you."

"I've slept in worse places," he said and scooped another spoonful of chili into his mouth.

"Or we could share the bed." Once again, her cheeks heated, and she looked down at the chili on her spoon. "I mean it's not like we haven't already slept together."

"True. But that was because you were scared and in shock."

"What if I'm the same tonight?" she asked. "But if it makes you uncomfortable…"

His lips twisted. "As a matter of fact, it did. After all, I'm a man. You're a beautiful woman."

"Never mind. I don't want you to do anything that doesn't feel right to you." She ate another bite of chili though she had to swallow hard to make it go down.

He lowered his spoon and captured her gaze with

his. "Sweetheart, it felt too right to me. I'm just not sure it's the right thing for you."

She tilted her head. "Why?"

"I wanted a whole lot more than to simply hold you all night. Not that I didn't enjoy that."

"Oh," she said.

"Wait until we call it a night. You can make the decision then. I don't mind the thought of sleeping in a real bed versus a lumpy couch."

Briana finished the food in her bowl and helped clean the small kitchenette, standing beside Rafe as he dipped dishes into soapy water then rinsed them thoroughly, before handing them to her to dry.

They bumped into each other several times, sending shocks of electricity throughout Briana's body. The longer they worked side by side, the more aware Briana became of the soldier.

Still distracted, she turned to hang the dishtowel on a hook on the wall and spun, running into the solid wall of Rafe's chest.

His hands came up to rest on the swell of her hips, long enough to steady her.

"Sorry."

"I'm not," he whispered, his tone even, deep and sexy as hell. He cupped her face in his palm and bent, lowering his head and face to within a fraction of an inch from hers. "I don't know what it is about you that makes me want to kiss you."

"Is that a bad thing?" she asked.

"Yes. It makes me vulnerable."

Her brow furrowed. "But you're so strong and

courageous."

"Strength isn't just about the muscles. Find a man's Achilles heel, and you can take him down with a pinch." His lips hovered over her mouth, his warm breath tempting her. "Tell me no, and I'll back off."

"I can't," she whispered, her body burning in anticipation. "I want you to kiss me, too."

"It could lead to so much more. I'm not sure I can stop once I start down that path."

"Do you need me to lead the way?" Her gaze shifted from his mouth to his eyes. His dark brown irises smoldered to black.

"I'm willing to follow," he breathed against her lips.

The first night they were together, all he'd done was hold her as they'd rested in the same bed. Yes, Briana wanted him to hold her. And she wanted so much more. Sliding her hands up his chest, she laced them behind his neck and raised up on her toes, closing the distance between them.

When her lips touched his, his arms slipped around her back and crushed her to him, his mouth claiming hers in a kiss that shook her to her very core.

Briana opened to him, meeting his tongue with hers in a sensuous caress that started a fire low in her belly and burned outward. She pressed her body to his, the silk of her robe sliding across her skin, reminding her that she was almost naked beneath. All she had to do was release the belt and let it fall to the floor.

Rafe lifted his head and stared down into her eyes. "I didn't take this job to seduce my client."

"Would it make you feel better if I seduce you?" she

asked, a smile pulling at the corners of her lips. She stepped back, released the belt on the robe and let it slide off her shoulders. The silk floated down her body to pool at her ankles. All she had on were the lacy panties and a tentative smile.

Please, like what you see.

For a long moment, he stared into her eyes. Then his gaze swept down her body. Rafe drew in a deep breath, bent, scooped her up into his arms and carried her to the only bed in the one-room cabin.

When he reached it, he set her on her feet, cupped the back of her neck with one hand, and kissed her slowly, as if savoring the taste of her.

Briana slipped her hands between them, bunched her fingers into his shirt and tugged it from the waistband of his jeans.

Rafe stepped back, yanked his T-shirt from around his neck and tossed it over the end of the bed.

Meanwhile, Briana loosened the buckle on his belt and pulled it free of the loops on his jeans. She pushed the button loose and slid his zipper down. Then she reached inside and cupped him over his boxer briefs, feeling the swell of his cock, hard and thick against her fingers, nothing but the cotton of his briefs between them.

Blood rushed through her body, her pulse pounding through her veins.

Rafe shoved his jeans down his legs, kicking free of the denim.

Finally naked, he stood before her in all his masculine glory. "Are you sure about this?"

She nodded, her breath too tight in her lungs to push air past her vocal cords.

Rafe bent to retrieve his wallet from his jeans and plucked a condom from inside.

Briana took the packet from him, tore it open and rolled the rubber down his engorged shaft, pausing to palm his balls before withdrawing her hand.

With a sexy growl, Rafe hooked his thumbs into the elastic band of the lace panties and dragged them down over her legs. He dropped to one knee and followed the path of the panties, pressing his lips to the inside of her thighs, licking the curve of her knee and tugging the lace free of her ankles.

Completely deficient of air, her breath hitched in her lungs. Briana couldn't move, couldn't resist.

As he rose, he dragged his fingers up her legs to cup her sex, a finger stroking her damp entrance.

Briana sucked in a breath and released it on a moan.

Rafe slipped his hands over the swells of her ass and lifted; she wrapped her legs around his waist.

With her hands resting on his broad shoulders, Briana lowered herself onto his thick shaft, her slick channel accepting him.

He filled her, sliding deep inside until he was fully sheathed.

For a long moment, he didn't move, giving her body time to adjust to his girth before he gripped her hips and lifted her, sliding out of her to the very tip of his cock.

Sensations rushed over her like fireworks bursting throughout her body.

When he pulled free of her, she cried out.

"Shhh," he murmured as he laid her on the bed and crawled up between her legs, leaning on his arms, a hand positioned on either side of her head. "I want to explore all of you."

And he proceeded to do just that, starting with her mouth. He kissed her, summoning her tongue to dance with his. When they needed to breathe again, he swept his lips across her chin and down the length of her neck to tongue the pulse beating rapidly at the base. From there, he trailed kisses and nips across her collarbone, over the swell of her breast to the hardened nipples puckered and ready for whatever he had in mind.

He took one between his lips and scraped his teeth across it.

Briana arched her back against the mattress, pressing her breast deeper.

He sucked inward, taking as much as he could inside his warm, moist mouth, flicking the tip with his tongue until Briana moaned and writhed beneath him.

Moving to the other breast, he massaged it with his fingers, then sucked at the nipple pulling hard, igniting Briana's insides with a desire so strong she couldn't wait for him to go lower.

And he did.

Abandoning her breasts, he tongued and nibbled his way across her ribs, dipping briefly into her bellybutton and, finally, arriving at the puff of hair covering her sex.

Parting her legs wider, Briana raised her hips, wanting him inside her, the sooner the better. "Please," she moaned.

"Please, what?" he said, his breath stirring her curls, making her ache with longing.

"I want more. I want you inside me," she said, her fingers curling into the comforter.

Rafe chuckled, parted her folds and dipped a finger into her wet channel, swirling around, making her crazy.

He slid the damp finger up between her folds and stroked the tender nubbin of flesh.

Briana gasped, her body tensing; her breath lodged in her throat.

He flicked that flesh and rubbed it again.

"Oh, sweet Jesus," she called out.

"Like that?" he asked, blowing a warm stream of air over her damp clit.

"Oh, yes!" She lay back against the pillow, her head rocking side to side. "Don't stop."

"I won't. Not until you're completely satisfied."

"*Yesss.*"

He slipped his finger back inside her and lowered his head to take that nub of flesh between his lips and suck gently. When he released her, he flicked her there, tonguing and tapping, swirling and sucking, until she exploded into a thousand sparkling lights. Her body shook with the force of her release, pulsing and thrumming as she rode the wave to the very end.

Still, it wasn't enough. She wouldn't be completely satisfied until she had him buried deeply inside her.

Lacing her fingers in his hair, she tugged gently, urging him upward.

He licked her one last time then climbed up her

body and settled between her legs, the tip of his cock nudging her entrance.

Briana reached low, captured the swells of his taut ass and brought him home. He filled her, sliding deep inside, his cock pressing against the walls of her channel, fitting her so perfectly, she felt as if the two of them made one.

When he moved, he set off an entirely different charge of electricity zipping through her body.

He pumped in and out of her. She dug her feet into the mattress and met him thrust for thrust. The bedsprings squeaked and the headboard banged against the wall with the force of their efforts.

On the way up to her second orgasm for the night, Briana felt Rafe tense, his body grow tight and his breath catch. He thrust one last time, sending her catapulting over the edge.

He held steady, his cock buried so deep inside her, she couldn't tell where he ended, and she began. His shaft pulsed within her as he came. For a long moment he leaned over her, his head thrown back, his jaw tight. Then he dropped down on her, stealing the breath from her lungs with the weight of his body.

Briana didn't care if she ever breathed again. She loved how he felt, crushing her beneath him.

Then he gathered her in his arms and rolled the two of them onto their sides, retaining their intimate connection. He pulled one of her legs up over his thigh and rested his hand on her naked hip.

Briana rested her head on Rafe's arm and circled one of his hard brown nipples with the tip of her finger, loving that they were still together in the most intimate of ways.

It felt so natural and right, she didn't feel at all embarrassed. "I know I'm just a client to you, so I don't expect anything from tonight." She glanced up at him. "No strings."

His arms tightened around her, and a frown settled between his eyebrows. "Damn, woman. How can you talk like that when we're lying here like this?" He pulled her closer. "And you're not just a client. You think I would do this with every client?"

She shrugged. "I don't want you to think I'll be needy. You have your life here in Montana. I have a life back in Chicago." She sighed. "I had a life back in Chicago. I like to think I was making a difference."

"Sweetheart, you're making a difference in my life, right now."

She looked up into his eyes. "How so?"

He brushed a strand of her hair back behind her ear. "I left the army because I felt like something was missing in my life. I didn't know what it was…until I met a woman over the phone, and we talked for hours getting to know each other."

"We did talk for a long time," she said, her fingers sliding over his shoulder, loving how smooth his skin was and how hard the muscles were beneath it.

His gaze narrowed, capturing hers. "The point is, you showed me what I was missing."

"And what was that?" she asked, her breath catching and holding in her chest.

"Connection. And it's more than having a date, it's

more than sex. All we did was talk. And I felt more connected to life, and what I want out of it, than I'd felt in a very long time… Hell, ever."

She laughed softly and stared at his chest. "I'd say we're even more connected, now. But I don't want you to think I'm a clingy woman. Being confined together can make people think there's more to their relationship than really exists."

He tipped her chin up, forcing her to look him square in the eyes. "Is that how you feel?"

She lifted a shoulder. "I don't know how I feel," she said, though she really did. However, she wasn't prepared to admit it.

"Tell you what. Let's leave tomorrow to tomorrow and concentrate on today," he said. "Do you want to be with me today?"

She nodded. "Yes. Do you want to be with me?"

He smiled down at her, and his cock hardened inside her. "Yes. And I think you know it."

Her heart fluttered at the sexy way his lips curled. She slid her leg down his thigh and then back up to curl around his hip. "Are you tired?"

He shook his head. "Not in the least. Are you?"

She shook her head and pushed him onto his back, rolling with him so that she was straddling his hips. She bent to claim his lips with a soul-searing kiss. When she came up, she gave him what she hoped was a sexy smile and practically purred, "My turn to drive."

CHAPTER 7

Rafe woke to the sound of Lucy whining. When he sat up, the room was so dark, he couldn't see the dog much less the hand in front of his face. Before they'd gone to sleep, he'd turned off the battery-powered lantern, plunging them into the inky blackness of a night in the deep woods, far away from nightlights plugged into electrical sockets or streetlights shining through windows.

In the Crazy Mountains of Montana, they had neither streetlights nor electricity, unless he fired up the generator again.

"Why's Lucy whining?" Briana rolled over and pressed her warm breasts against his back.

He wanted nothing more than to pull her naked body into his arms and make love to her again.

Lucy barked, cutting that fantasy short.

"I'll take her out for a walk," he said.

"You can turn on the lantern. It won't bother me," she said and yawned. "Want me to go with you?"

"No. I'll be right back. I'm sure she just wants to relieve herself. I shouldn't be long. You can stay here and keep the bed warm."

He turned on the lantern, pulled on his jeans, boots and a jacket and snapped the lead on Lucy's collar.

By then, Lucy was pacing in front of the door, whining and sniffing.

"She must need to go really badly." Briana sat up in the bed, pulling the sheet over her naked breasts.

His cock twitched and grew hard in an instant. "I'll be right back," he said, opened the door and stepped out into the night.

The moon and starlight provided enough light he didn't need the lantern; he could see almost as well as he could during the day.

Lucy took off, straining at the leash, growling low in her chest.

"What's wrong, girl?" Rafe asked. He hadn't taken three steps from the cabin when he remembered this was bear and wolf country. About the time he decided to turn around and get his gun, Lucy went berserk, barking like a mad dog. It was all Rafe could do to hold her back. He tried dragging her in, but she twisted and jerked at the leash, making it impossible for Rafe to pick her up and carry her back inside.

Rafe had just grabbed Lucy by the scruff of her neck when a bear burst out of the shadowy tree line, rose up on his hind legs and lumbered toward them, roaring. Moonlight glittered off his long, wickedly sharp teeth.

Barking fiercely, Lucy broke free of Rafe's hold and lunged toward bear.

The lead pulled tight, catching her up short. She flipped over, turned, and then tried again to get to the bear.

Without a gun in his hand, Rafe couldn't help her. And he couldn't drop the lead and run back into the cabin. He reeled the dog in, pulling on the long lead, one foot at a time, the dog's lunging motions making it almost impossible.

The bear followed as if being lured by the promise of a snack, roaring and swiping at the air with its massive paw.

The bear was almost on Lucy. Rafe could smell the animal and feel the heat of his massive body. He didn't fear for himself, but he worried that he wouldn't get Lucy away from the beast before he swiped her with his heavy paws and razor-sharp claws.

Just when the bear pulled his paw back to deliver a killing blow, a low bang sounded behind Rafe.

He ducked and spun toward the cabin.

Briana stood in the doorway, her silk robe hanging open over her naked body, holding the pistol she'd practiced shooting the day before.

"Get out of here," she yelled.

The bear roared, the sound ripping through the night air.

Lucy strained at the leash, barking so much her voice went hoarse.

Briana fired again, aiming over all of their heads.

Rafe ducked low, dragging Lucy toward him.

The bear dropped to all four feet, turned and ran into the woods, grumbling as he went.

Lucy tried to follow, but now she was close enough, Rafe grabbed her around her middle and carried to the cabin.

Briana backed into the cabin, pointing the gun at the ground. "Holy shit, Rafe. Holy shit."

Rafe carried Lucy through the door and kicked it shut behind him before he dropped her on her feet.

Briana's face was chalk white, and her eyes rounded. She trembled from head to toe. "Did you see that bear?"

He chuckled, took the gun from her shaking hands, dropped the magazine out of the handle, cleared the chamber and laid it on the table. Then he pulled her into his arms and held her tight. "Thank you for having the foresight to bring a gun with you."

"He was so close."

"Yes, he was." So close, Rafe had felt his breath when he'd roared. "That was some quick thinking on your part."

"I got up as soon as you left, thinking you might need a gun. Everyone says this is bear country." She looked up into his eyes. "Holy hell. It is."

"He's gone. I think he was more scared of you than you were of him." He smoothed the hair back from her forehead. "You were amazing. Fierce."

"Terrified," she whispered. "It almost got you and Lucy."

"But it didn't." He tipped her chin up. "Because of you."

"I almost forgot to flip the safety off."

"But you did." He kissed the tip of her nose.

"I did it," her lips curved into a tremulous smile, "didn't I?"

"Yes, you did." He pulled her close, slipping his hands inside the silk of her robe and rubbed his hands over her smooth skin. "Thank you for saving Lucy and me." He held her close, his cock hardening as her naked breasts pressed against his chest. He shrugged out of his jacket and draped it over the bedpost. Then he scooped her up into his arms, carried her to the bed and made sweet love to her.

They slept until the sun shone through the only window and Lucy insisted on going outside to relieve herself.

Rafe was more prepared this time, taking his gun in the shoulder holster. He was still kicking himself for being so clueless the night before. Making love to Briana seemed to have sucked his brain free of all braincells. He'd have to be more aware and stay on his toes. The bear could have been *El Chefe*'s hired thugs, and he'd have had less of a chance of surviving them. They'd have shot him on sight. From now on, he'd have to take all the precautions. For that matter, he might want to set out some kind of early warning system to alert them to incoming intruders.

With nothing but time on their hands, they could come up with something.

He left Briana in bed while he walked Lucy around the cabin looking for places he could rig a trip line of something like cans filled with rocks that would rattle when someone ran over the line. Hell, he could ask Hank if he had some kind of early warning or security system that ran on batteries. He could use it for people as well as for angry grizzly bears. Then he wouldn't be surprised in the middle of the night when he'd rather be in bed making love to Briana.

When he came back into the cabin, Briana had omelets made of fresh farm eggs, canned ham and minced onion. As they ate, they talked about the bear, Lucy and what they might do for the rest of the day. They settled on clearing away brush from the nearby tree line to allow them to see more clearly into the shadows and to disallow the enemy, or bears, to move in so closely, undetected.

Rafe contacted Hank via the satellite phone, requesting something in the way of a surveillance system that ran on batteries and would provide some kind of warning should man or beast approach the cabin

At the end of the day, Hank arrived with a tall, broad-shouldered man with a shock of light blond hair.

"Donovan, this is Axel Swenson, Navy SEAL, and the brains behind the Brotherhood Protectors," Hank said.

"Hank's the brain. I just work the electronics and computers." The blond-haired man held out his hand. "Call me Swede."

Rafe shook the man's hand. "Nice to meet you, Swede."

Rafe turned to Briana. "This is Briana Hayes. My... client." He got stuck on the word. Already, Briana was so much more than a client. He was afraid he was falling for her. Never in all his thirty-four years had he felt the way he did about another woman. Hell, he didn't trust most women. His mother had barely given a damn about him. None of the women he'd gone out with had held his attention for more than a night in bed, and he doubted they would've shot at a bear to save his life. Yeah, Briana was different. Still, he wasn't sure how things would play out between them when the threat went away. He had a job in Montana. She would move back to Chicago and do good things for the children there.

"We brought you the surveillance equipment you requested. The cameras run on batteries and will also work on infrared at night. We can set up a way to check them using a battery-powered unit you can recharge when you have the generator running."

Rafe helped unload the boxes from the truck and laid them out on the tailgate. Soon, they had cameras positioned all around the perimeter of the cabin, and the base unit installed with a monitor on the table inside.

When they were all done setting up, they tested with Hank and Swede walking out by the units. Each time, a signal sounded, alerting Briana and Rafe to intruders.

Hank and Swede returned to the cabin and dug out another device for them to use to monitor their location —a drone they could operate to give them a birds-eye view of the road and land leading up to the cabin. Swede showed Rafe and Briana how to operate it and had them practice a couple of times before he was satisfied they could handle it.

Before Hank climbed into his truck to leave, he fished in his pocket and pulled out a silver necklace with a gemstone pendent. "Briana, I'd like you to wear this necklace at all times, even when you're in the shower or swimming. It's got a GPS tracking device embedded beneath the gemstone. If you're kidnapped, or even just lost in the woods, we'll be able to locate you by computer or one of the handheld tracking devices we have back at the ranch. Also, I wanted you to know my guys made it to Illinois. They'll move Alejandra from the shelter to a safe house here in Montana sometime in the next forty-eight hours."

Briana frowned. "The more people who know where she is, the greater chance someone will slip up and reveal her whereabouts."

Hank shook his head. "My guys are all special forces. They know how to keep their mouths shut and how to slip in and out of places without being detected. You can trust them completely."

Briana chewed on her bottom lip. "I promised Alejandra she'd be safe."

"And she will be," Hank said. "And we'll keep you safe, as well."

"I'm not as worried about me as much as I am about Alejandra and her baby," Briana said. "Will you let me know when you get her moved into the safe house?"

"I will," Hank said. "One last thing." He reached into the back seat of the truck and removed a cooler, handing it to Rafe. "Sadie sent out some ranch-raised beef steaks for you two to enjoy, plus a bottle of her favorite wine. She cooked the potatoes, and the steaks are medium rare. All you need to do is warm them up. She included a green salad, dressing and two pieces of apple pie. I told her she'd better have some left for me when I get home, or I'll stay and eat with the two of you." He winked. "Enjoy and try not to get eaten by the bear."

Hank and Swede left, driving away as the sun slipped below the mountaintops, casting them into shadow.

Rafe carried the cooler to the cabin and waited while Briana and Lucy entered before he followed. "I don't know about you, but roughing it in the Crazy Mountains ain't all that bad."

Briana grinned. "It could be a heck of a lot worse. We have running water, great food and good company. What more could we ask for?"

Rafe's grin faded. "For *El Chefe* to back off and leave you alone. I'd feel better if we had an end in sight. We don't know if he'll give up trying to find you, or by some miracle, locate you here in the Crazy Mountains. I'd almost rather confront him than be forever in limbo."

She shrugged. "I look at this as time I get to spend with you. And now that we have the surveillance system, we can relax a little."

Rafe nodded. He'd let her think they'd be just fine with an early warning system. Truth was, until *El Chefe* backed off, they had to be hyper-aware at all times. Surveillance system or not, if the drug lord sent enough men in to extract Briana, they could be overrun before Hank and his team had time to provide backup.

Rafe hoped it didn't come to that. In the meantime, they had a wonderful meal and another night together.

Life could be a whole lot worse. He could be stuck with a client he couldn't stand instead of Briana, a woman he was quickly learning to like a little too much.

But then, what was too much? She was an amazing woman. The kind of woman he could see himself staying with for a very long time.

CHAPTER 8

After the meal Hank and Sadie had provided, Rafe and Briana walked Lucy outside once more before calling it a night.

They made love until midnight and fell asleep in each other's arms. The bear didn't return that night, and nothing set off the alarms, allowing them a full night's sleep.

Briana woke the next day fully refreshed and ready to do something with the day. She suggested they take the drone higher up the mountain and get a feel for the terrain around the cabin. Rafe agreed, and they packed a picnic lunch and the drone, snapped a leash on Lucy and spent the day tromping through the hills, getting to know each other better and laughing a lot.

She learned she was pretty good at operating the drone. Her hands were more adept at subtle changes in direction than his, and she maneuvered the drone all around the hilltop where the cabin perched.

Lucy chased rabbits and drank from mountain streams full of clear, cold water from snow melt.

The day was idyllic, the sun shone down on them, and they didn't see a single bear or bad guy. Just her, Rafe and Lucy in the beautiful Montana mountains. She could almost believe it was a vacation. And she loved everything about Rafe. He was smart, understood how to get around in rough terrain and took good care to make sure she didn't walk off a cliff or fall into a ravine.

By the end of the day, she was gloriously tired and happy. Which felt strange, considering she was on the run from a drug lord, the head of a cartel in El Salvador, who had contacts and thugs he could tap into in the States. Who knew how far his reach extended? She should be more afraid, but it was hard to be when she had Rafe with her and she was surrounded by the beauty of the Montana mountains.

They spent another night in each other's arms, making love until after midnight. Early the next morning, they were awakened by the buzzing of the satellite phone.

Rafe rolled out of the bed and padded barefooted across to the table to answer. "Donovan here."

He listened for a few minutes, and then nodded. "I'll tell her... We will. Let us know if you have any trouble. Yes, sir. Out here."

"Did they get Alejandra moved?" Briana leaned up on an elbow, letting the sheet slide down to expose her breasts. She hoped it would be enough to make Rafe come back to bed and make love to her again. They'd have to add condoms to the list of supplies they needed Hank and Sadie to pick up in town.

That would be awkward.

"Hank said they have Alejandra in a safe house here in Montana with a couple of his guys providing round-the-clock protection. They flew her out on a private plane in the middle of the night and landed in the dark. She and the baby are safe. He wants us to be extra vigilant."

A knot formed in Briana's gut. "Why do we need to be *extra* vigilant? The way I see it, you don't need to protect me now. I don't know where Alejandra is hiding. I couldn't tell *El Chefe* even if I wanted."

Rafe laid down in the bed beside her and gathered her in his arms. "You know that, and I know that, but *El Chefe Diablo* doesn't. As far as he knows, you're the only one who knows where Alejandra is hiding."

"Then we can just tell him I don't know anymore. That she's gone from the location where I left her."

"He may or may not believe you. And if he does believe you, he might want revenge against you for interfering in the first place. And if we contact him, he might figure out where you are. We can't risk that."

Briana sighed. "How long can I hide from this man? It doesn't make any sense. Maybe we need to come out in the open and flush out his minions."

Rafe pressed his lips to hers. "No."

"I can't live like this forever. I have a job. A life."

"And he could snuff it out in a heartbeat."

She captured his face between her palms. "Seriously,

as much as I love being with you, I can't live like this forever. You can't protect me forever."

"Are you tired of me already?" Rafe leaned over her and kissed her forehead, her cheeks and her nose.

Her pulse quickened, and an ache built deep down in her core. "Far from it. But we have to be real."

Rafe kissed a path down her neck, across her collarbone and lower to claim one tightly budded nipple.

"Are you listening to me?" she asked, her voice more of a moan.

"I'm listening," he said and sucked the nipple into his mouth.

God, the things he was doing to her made her come apart at the seams. She tried to focus. "Life has to go on."

"Can it wait until after we make love?" he asked, as he switched to the other breast.

"Rafe," she started to argue, but the air left her lungs as his hand slipped over her belly to cup her sex.

"Yes, Briana?" he said and blew a warm stream of air over her damp nipple. "I'm here." Rafe kissed her nipple and moved lower to her rib. "And here." He kissed another rib. "And here."

"Oh, who am I kidding?" She gave up and made love to him in broad daylight with Lucy lying on the floor in front of the door. If *El Chefe Diablo* was coming for her, she'd at least have enjoyed the time she spent with Rafe. When it was all over, she'd go back to Chicago, and he'd go on to his next assignment with the Brotherhood Protectors.

After they made love, they lay for a long time in each

other's arms, while birds sang outside, and sunshine streamed through the single window.

"I'll miss this, when it's all over," she whispered.

"Why should you miss this?" he asked.

Before she could answer, an alarm went off on the surveillance system.

Rafe sprang from the bed, grabbed his handgun and ran to the video monitor. He studied the six display windows on the screen. One had a red outline. In the display image stood a four-legged animal.

Lucy paced at the door but didn't whine or bark.

After several minutes staring at the monitor, Rafe was joined by Briana, pulling her robe around her. "Anything?"

"An elk and her baby." He pointed to the red-rimmed image.

Briana laughed. "Better them than the bear." She handed him his jeans. "Come on, let's go for a walk. Lucy needs some exercise."

They spent the day wandering over the hills, returning to the cabin before the sun sank below the ridgeline. They fed Lucy, ate dinner and settled in to read books Sadie and Hank had left on a shelf beside the canned goods.

When it was time for bed, they made love until late in the night. Sometime later, Lucy whined at the door to be let out. Rafe dressed in jeans, boots and his jacket, tucked his handgun into his pocket and checked the monitor for any blinking lights. The infrared display showed nothing amiss. He snapped the lead on Lucy's collar and let himself out through the door. "Lock it behind me," he said.

Briana locked the door behind him and shivered in the cool mountain air. She pulled on a pair of leggings and a T-shirt, and then slipped her feet into her shoes and wandered over to the surveillance monitor. An alert went off, and one of the screens blinked red.

Her pulse leaped as she studied the monitor. In the blinking square, she could see the infrared image of Rafe and Lucy walking near the edge of the clearing. She smiled as they stopped to let the dog sniff at every little thing on the ground.

Lucy had seemed to settle in with them, glad for the attention and love she'd missed with the passing of her previous owner.

As Briana watched, Lucy braced herself, lowered her head and bared her teeth.

At the same time, another alarm went off on the surveillance system. Briana expected it to be from the camera closest to the one near Rafe and Lucy as they crossed into its sector.

However, the screen that lit up wasn't from the cameras closest to Rafe and Lucy. It was from a camera on the back side of the cabin.

Briana leaned closer to the monitor, studying the image. At first, she didn't see anything, but then a white silhouette pushed up from the ground and moved toward the cabin. Another white silhouette rose up and followed the first. They were hunkered over, and when they straightened, Briana could tell they were people, and they were carrying guns. A third alarm went off and another screen blinked with a red outline. More men emerged from the trees, running toward the cabin.

Her heart leaped into her throat. She had to warn Rafe before they reached him and Lucy.

Briana reached for her pistol, slammed the magazine into the handle and ran for the door.

CHAPTER 9

As soon as Lucy took up a defensive stance and growled, Rafe stiffened, yanked his gun out of his jacket and started back toward the cabin.

Before he reached it, headlights blinked on, and vehicles raced up the drive and through the trees, heading directly for him and Lucy.

He ran, but he wasn't going to make it to the cabin. Not before the vehicles reached him first. He prayed Briana would stay in the cabin with the door locked and call Hank on the satellite phone. Hank wouldn't get there in time to help, but he might catch up to them before they disappeared with Briana.

When he realized he wouldn't reach the cabin in time, he released Lucy's lead and told the dog, "Go, Lucy!"

The dog ran into the woods.

Rafe turned, braced his handgun in his palms and fired at the headlights and the tires, hoping to slow the lead vehicle.

A dark Jeep with its top off barreled toward him.

Rafe fired in the direction of the driver, but the vehicle didn't slow. At the last minute, Rafe threw himself to the side, hit the ground, rolled and came up on his feet. Another Jeep raced up to him. A man leaned out the side of the vehicle and hit Rafe in the side of the head with a baseball bat.

Pain knifed through his head, and Rafe fell to his knees, the gun slipping from his hand. Another man leaped out of the vehicle and ran toward him with a club like what the policemen carry. When he cocked his arm to hit Rafe with it, a flash of black and white leaped out of the tree line.

Lucy grabbed the man's arm before he could swing it at Rafe and bit down hard.

The man screamed and flung his arm backward, knocking Lucy away.

Rafe felt the ground, searching desperately for the pistol. When his fingers curled around it, he staggered to his feet and aimed at the man trying to hit the dog with the club.

As Rafe leveled his weapon and took aim, the man swung hard and hit Lucy in the head.

The border collie yelped and crumpled to the ground, lying still.

Rafe pulled the trigger too late to save the dog. The man with the club tipped sideways and collapsed, unmoving in the dust.

His head spinning and a gray cloud closing in on all sides, Rafe turned back to the cabin. The lead Jeep had come to a halt in front of the door, and four men jumped to the ground.

"Briana, don't come out!" he yelled.

Two men raced up beside Rafe and grabbed his arms. Through the gray cloud, he fought them, swinging and missing. When one of them coldcocked him in the jaw, he hit the ground, his vision blacking out for a moment. Long enough for the men to grab his gun, yank his arms behind his back and slap a zip-tie around his wrists.

They jerked Rafe to his feet, dragged him to the lead Jeep, and stood him in front of the headlights.

"Briana Hayes, if you want this man to live, come with us," a man in a black leather jacket and a ski mask called out.

"Don't," Rafe shouted.

The man beside him slammed a meaty fist into his gut.

Rafe doubled over, fighting back the black abyss threatening to consume him.

The man in the black leather jacket waved a pistol toward Rafe. "Bring him closer."

The two men on either side of him dragged him forward.

The man in the leather pointed his gun at Rafe's head. "You have until the count of three to come out or the man dies."

The door remained closed.

Briana, don't. Too dizzy to form words, Rafe hung between the two men, praying Briana didn't cave in to their demand.

"One... You really want to watch his head splattered

all over the ground? Two…I ain't shittin' you. It's your decision. You want him to die?"

"Wait!" Briana's voice called out through the wood-paneled door. "How do I know you'll let him live?"

"You don't. We'll get you one way or another. But you have my word we won't kill him if you come with us without a fight."

Briana snorted. "The word of a thug?"

"It's the best you'll get. You don't have much choice either way."

"Let him go, and I'll come out," Briana said.

"No," Rafe said.

Again, he was punched in the gut, knocking the wind out of him.

"Don't hurt him. I'm coming out," Briana cried.

Rafe tried to tell her no, but he couldn't get air past his vocal cords.

The men holding his arms were the only reason he hadn't fallen on his face. He hated that he couldn't fight back, that they were outnumbered, and that Briana was giving up her freedom to save his sorry ass. He should have been more prepared. He should have been ready.

But they'd never expected *El Chefe* would send an army of men to secure one woman when he'd only sent one before.

The cabin door opened, and Briana stepped out, her hands raised in the air. "Don't shoot him. I'll go with you. Just let him live."

The man in the black leather jacket tilted his head toward the Jeep. "Get in the back."

Briana walked toward the Jeep, her brow furrowed,

her gaze on Rafe. "Don't hurt him," she said as she climbed into the backseat.

Two men got in with her, one on either side.

The man in the leather jacket slid into the passenger seat, and his driver got behind the steering wheel.

"What do you want us to do with him?" one of the men holding him up asked.

"Leave him," their leader said. "Maybe the bears will eat him and put him out of his misery."

The men on either side of him shoved him to the ground and left him lying there as they grabbed their guy on the ground, leaped into their Jeep and followed the lead vehicle out of the yard.

Rafe lay with his face in the dirt, his vision fading in and out. He knew he had to get help fast. The longer they had Briana, the farther away they'd get. But every time he tried to move, his head spun, and he blacked out for a few seconds.

"Can't give up," he muttered. "Bree needs me."

He tried again to roll onto his back. He blacked out only to feel something warm and wet scraping across his skin. When he opened his eyes, Lucy lay beside him, licking his face.

"Hey, I thought you were dead."

She continued licking, whining softly.

This time when Rafe rolled onto his back, he didn't black out. He was able to sit up without falling again. Then he folded his legs beneath him and staggered to his feet, swaying. He thought he'd fall to the ground, but he managed to remain upright long enough to get to the cabin and through the door Briana had left open.

Once inside, he found a knife in the kitchen utensils and fumbled to get it into his hands behind his back. After several failed attempts, he finally sawed through the plastic and freed his wrists. He lunged for the satellite phone and dialed Hank.

"Briana?" Hank answered.

"No. Donovan."

"Fuck," Hank cursed. "They got her, didn't they?"

Rafe had a lot more curses he wanted to say, but they would serve no purpose. "Yes."

"You okay?" Hank asked.

"I will be," Rafe said. "I hope they don't hurt Briana. I should've been more prepared. They brought more than a dozen men to secure her."

"I've gathered as many of my guys as I could. We're on our way."

The roar of rotor blades echoed off the hillside.

"I have a feeling it's too late. Sounds like they're taking her out by chopper."

"Was she still wearing the necklace I gave her?" Hank asked.

Rafe squeezed his eyes shut against the throbbing in his head. "I think so."

"I'll get Swede monitoring her progress on the computer right away. I have the handheld device. We'll be able to see where she's going and hopefully intercept them."

"God, I hope so. I can't believe they sent so many men to get her. The other two times were one- or two-man jobs," Rafe said.

"*El Chefe* must want Alejandra really bad to send a

dozen mercenaries in to retrieve someone who might know where her and the baby are hidden. Seems like overkill."

Rafe cringed. "Let's hope they don't kill her once they discover she has no idea where Alejandra is hidden."

"Are you in any shape to meet me at the highway?" Hank asked. "Looks like the chopper is headed in the direction of Bozeman."

Rafe fought back waves of nausea and pressed a hand against the growing lump on the side of his head. He didn't have time to pass out. Briana needed him. "I'll be at the highway when you get there."

He shed his jacket, pulled on a T-shirt, slipped his shoulder holster over his arms and buckled it across his chest. Grabbing his AR15, he stowed it on the back seat of his truck and called to Lucy.

The border collie dragged herself up into the truck and settled in the passenger seat. She hadn't run off when he'd released her leash. She seemed to have bonded with him and Briana in the few short days they'd been together. He was glad the blow she'd sustained hadn't killed her. Briana would've been heartbroken.

Briana...

Sweet Jesus, he'd failed to protect her. Even with the surveillance monitors, he'd let them get past him to her. And she'd willingly stepped out of the cabin to save his sorry ass. She was amazing and courageous. By God, he'd bring her back safely, and then go after the man who'd taken her.

Rafe raced down the mountain road, fishtailing around curves, skidding on gravel. The men in Jeeps were long gone, as was the helicopter in which they'd airlifted Briana.

By the time he reached the highway leading into Eagle Rock in one direction and Bozeman in the other, Hank's truck was slowing to a stop. Two more trucks pulled in behind him, and several men climbed out, carrying rifles or handguns.

Hank left his truck and joined Rafe next to his. "The chopper landed at a private airstrip on a ranch this side of Bozeman. I notified the sheriff, but by the time they got out to the ranch, a small jet had taken off. The helicopter was gone, and the jet was well on its way to wherever they're flying her. I'm in contact with the ATC. They're researching the flight now. So far, they don't have a tail number to allow us to identify the owner. The ranch owner where the landing strip was located is an absentee owner. He flies in once a year during hunting season. He didn't know someone was going to land on his property, and he didn't authorize it."

Rafe's fists clenched. "So, at this point, we have no idea where they're taking her."

"Unfortunately, no."

Rafe's jaw hardened. "I want to talk to Alejandra. It's got to be more than a jilted man wanting his woman and child back. Why is he so desperate to get to her that he'd hire a dozen thugs, mercenaries, a helicopter, and a jet plane to find her? And then to transport another woman back instead… It doesn't make sense."

"If someone stole Sadie away, I'd do everything in my power to get her back. But it bears questioning Alejandra to know what *El Chefe* might do next. I'll have my guys bring her to the ranch. Maybe she can shed some light on why the man is so anxious to get her back that he'd kidnap another woman. In the meantime, you might as well come back to the ranch with me. We can monitor Briana's progress on my computer. If they're heading for an airport, we can call the sheriff or police in that area and have them waiting when they land."

"And if they're headed out of the country?" Rafe asked, cold dread settling like a lead weight in the pit of his belly.

"I can call in all my men and organize a rescue operation. I know someone who owns and operates a large cargo plane who could transport us. I also have contacts in Washington with decision-making power over the Special Operations Command. If push comes to shove, we'll launch an extraction operation to get her out."

He'd heard Hank had connections in high places, but to be able to tap into Spec Ops authority was huge. "You can do that?"

"There are a lot of people who owe me a favor. I can cash in my chips. However, we'll need to have all our ducks in a row and all the intel we can dredge up to plead our case."

"Sounds like it'll take a lot of time."

"Most likely, it won't happen overnight," Hank said, shrugging. "But I think we could mobilize in under forty-eight hours." He frowned at Rafe's truck. "What kills me is how he found you in the first place." His eyes narrowed. "I'm betting he had a tracker placed on your truck."

Rafe stared at the vehicle in the glare from Hank's headlights. "It's possible. They could have tagged it when they found Briana's cellphone. She'd left it in her purse, locked up in the truck when we stopped for the night in Springfield, Illinois."

"And they waited to attack until you two came out of the hotel." Hank nodded. "It makes sense. Let's leave your truck here. He can find my place easily enough, but why make it easy?" Hank jerked his head toward his men and his truck. "Let's get this ball rolling."

Hank led the way. Rafe climbed into the passenger seat of Hank's truck.

Within the next fifteen minutes, they were rolling through the gates of White Oak Ranch.

Sadie came out on the porch, dressed in jeans and a sweatshirt, her brow furrowed. "I'm so sorry to hear about Briana." She held the door as the men marched into the house and downstairs to the Brotherhood Protectors' HQ-bunker beneath Hank and Sadie's ranch house.

Hank made quick introductions to the men standing around. "You've met Swede." He motioned to a barrel-chested man with brown hair and brown eyes. "Tate Parker, former Delta Force."

Rafe's eyes narrowed. "Don't I know you?"

The man's lips curled upward at the corners. "We met briefly on a mission in Afghanistan a couple years ago. You might remember me as Bear. That's what people call me."

Rafe nodded. "That's right, Bear Parker. You ran into that building to pull a few kids out after the Taliban lobbed a grenade at it."

Bear nodded, his lips thinning. "Got all but one out alive."

Hank jerked his thumb toward a man with dark hair and darker eyes. "This is Taz Davila, former Army Ranger."

Rafe shook hands with the man.

The next man had black hair and blue eyes. "This is Boomer, or Brandon Rayne, former Navy SEAL," Hank said.

Next was a man with dark hair graying significantly at the temples. "Chuck Johnson is the old man of the team. Prior Navy SEAL."

Taz leaned toward Rafe. "Don't underestimate him. Chuck's in top physical condition and can outrun, outshoot and out-bullshit any of us, any day of the week." He grinned and held up his hands in surrender when Chuck glared at him.

After shaking hands with all the men. Rafe turned to Swede. "Where is she now?"

"They're flying over Colorado right now," Swede reported.

"There has to be a way to intercept that plane."

"It would take too much red tape to scramble fighter planes to intercept a private jet for a civilian," Hank said. "All we can hope is that they land somewhere in the States, and we can get local law enforcement to seize them."

Rafe paced the room. "We can't just stand around

waiting for them to land."

"We're not." Hank glanced up from a simple cellphone. "My guys are on their way now with Alejandra. We can spend the time we're waiting to see where Briana lands by questioning Alejandra."

"By bringing Alejandra here, you're exposing her."

Hank held up the cellphone. "We're using burner phones to communicate, and we're using a van painted like a mail delivery vehicle to get her in and out. I have six guys in the van with her and several positioned at the gate for when they arrive. They're on their way now. Should be here in the next ten minutes."

"Anyone want coffee or something stronger to drink?" Sadie descended the stairs carrying a tray with a carafe of coffee and mugs.

Hank hurried to her, relieved her of her burden and set the tray on the table. "I told you that you don't have to wait on us. Besides, you're not supposed to carry anything heavy," he chastised her. Then he pulled her into his arms and kissed her soundly. "Go back to bed. Emma will be up at dawn, and you'll be exhausted."

"I gave Daphne a heads-up," Boomer said. "She and Maya can come over and help watch Emma while Sadie catches up on her sleep."

"Thank you, Boomer," Sadie said. "I'd love to see Daphne, and Emma enjoys playing with Maya."

Boomer smiled and ducked his head to send a text to Daphne.

Rafe liked how everyone knew each other. Being the new guy, he felt as though he was still on the outside looking into a tight-knit organization. He knew he'd get over that soon enough, and he sure as hell didn't have time to worry about anything other than getting Briana back safely.

A few minutes later, Swede announced Briana's tracer showed her currently over Texas.

Hank's burner phone pinged. He glanced at a text message coming through. "They're here." He shot a look at Swede. "Let them in the gate."

Swede hit a button on his computer keyboard. "Done."

"Thanks." To Rafe, he said, "I'll be right back." Hank left the bunker, running up the steps two at a time and disappearing through the door at the top.

Sadie followed at a more sedate pace, her hand resting on her swollen belly.

When Hank returned, he escorted a dark-haired woman carrying an infant in her arms. She lifted her chin as she walked into the room full of men. Her gaze swept them, coming to rest on Lucy. "I understand the woman who rescued me off the streets of Chicago has been taken by *El Chefe Diablo*'s men."

Rafe crossed to stand in front of the woman. "She helped you. Now, it's time for you to help her. What is it *El Chefe* wants? Is he upset that you ran with his child?"

Alejandra held her baby close to her chest. "*El Chefe* is not in the least interested in this child," she said. "Except that he would use my baby as insurance."

Rafe's brow twisted. "Insurance?"

"He threatened to kill Bella if I did not cooperate with him."

"Holy hell…what kind of cooperation did he want?"

Alejandra looked toward a blank wall. "I kept the books for his organization. He wants me back to continue to do so. And if I don't come back, he will try to kill me." Her lips curled into a cruel smile. "But I have some insurance of my own."

Hank frowned. "How so?"

"I have an actual book identifying every one of his business partners and what kind of money, services or products have passed between them. There are names in there that could cause major upset in many countries, including the United States. I have hidden that book with an attorney, who has special instructions to mail it to the DEA if I don't call every three days to tell him not to."

Rafe's heart sank to the pit of his belly. Briana was caught up in something even more dangerous than a drug lord wanting his girl and baby back.

"If word gets out that this book exists, there will be a huge uproar in Mexico City, Bogotá, Paris, London and on Capitol Hill in Washington, DC. Major political players could lose their positions, even go to jail. *El Chefe* will do anything to keep that from happening. If that book goes public, he himself will be murdered."

"So, it was never about the child," Rafe stated. "It's all about *El Chefe*'s connections and the trouble you could stir up if that information is revealed."

She ran a hand through her hair, the shadows beneath her eyes a deep purple. "When I first started doing books for the cartel, I was fresh out of college. I'd just returned from university in the United States to my home in El Salvador. I didn't realize I was going to work for a cartel. I thought it was a regular accounting job. The money was good. Better than anywhere else around. I couldn't resist. By the time I figured out what was happening, it was too late. Once you go to work for the cartel, there's only one way out—in a body bag." She smoothed a hand over the baby's shock of dark curls. "Then I had Bella. I realized I couldn't raise her in that environment. I knew *El Chefe* would use her to keep me working for him. He'd threaten to kill her, and carry out that threat, if I tried to leave."

"That's awful." Sadie had joined them in the basement, carrying a sleepy Emma on her hip. "I don't blame you for wanting to escape."

Alejandra gave Sadie a brief nod. "I started documenting all of the clients, partners and connections to the cartel. I noted how much money was involved, what products and services. Once I had all that information, I compiled it into a notebook and mailed it to a lawyer in the States, asking him to hold it without opening it. If I did not call him every three days, he was instructed to mail it to the DEA. I'm due to call today."

"How did you escape?" Rafe asked.

She glanced down at her baby, her face softening. "*El Chefe* didn't know that I wanted to leave. I kept my plans to myself. I had fake passports made. I told him that a good friend of mine from college was dying of cancer, and that she'd asked to see me and Bella before she passed. I told him she lived in Chicago. He allowed me to fly to the States to see her. I kept my cellphone and called when I landed to reassure him I was indeed visiting a friend and would be back soon.

"As soon as I left the plane, I tried to disappear into the city, but he'd arranged to have men follow me. At first, I think to keep me safe. When I noticed I was being followed, I ducked into a shopping center and then into a women's changing room. From there, I made my way through a rear exit. I'd lost them, but I knew they would report back to *El Chefe*. Before they could notify him, I called him to say I had enjoyed a little shopping and was stopping to get something to eat before I joined my friend. I had hoped when his men called, he'd be placated by the fact I'd initiated a call and checked in. I'd hoped it would buy me time to find a safe place to hide. Then it started to rain. That's when I spotted *El Chefe*'s men and ducked into an alley. They passed the alley and kept moving. That's when Briana found us."

Rafe studied her expression, trying to determine whether she was telling the truth. "Briana said she found your phone in her purse after she'd dropped you at the shelter."

Alejandra's cheeks reddened. "When I realized *El Chefe* would eventually figure out that I had not gone to a friend's death bed, I knew he could trace my cellphone. So I put it into Briana's purse, figuring she would take it away with her. It's my fault he went after her. If she hadn't helped me, she wouldn't be on her way to El Salvador."

"Why would he take Briana when he wanted you?"

Alejandra shrugged. "Apparently, he figured out that Briana helped me. And he knows me. I won't let someone else die because of my defection. He'll offer to make a trade. And when he does, I'll go to El Salvador, so that Briana can come home."

The baby stirred in her mother's arms and whimpered.

Alejandra looked up. "I'll make that trade, but I have one request."

"And what would that be?" Hank asked.

"Please, someone take my baby. Give her a home and the love she needs to flourish. Bella deserves a better life than the one she had with me."

Swede called out. "They stopped in Monterrey, Mexico."

Alejandra nodded. "They'll fuel up there. There's a ranch outside of Monterrey with an airstrip and jet fuel for men who don't want to land their planes at public airports to refuel. *El Chefe*'s shipments stop there when they fly from El Salvador to the US and back. It won't be long before they land, full stop, in El Salvador."

"At this point, everything we know is conjecture," Hank said. "We don't really know what he plans to do with Briana."

Tears glittered in her eyes, but she blinked them away. Her chin lifted. "I guarantee he will try to make a trade. He wants me. He thinks that all this information is in my head," she said, tapping her temple, "and that if I get loose, I can tell whoever wants to know about all of his dealings. Leaking that information could bring a stop to his operations, or make his clients lose their trust in him and want him dead." She held out her hand. "If you have a burner phone, one that can't be traced, I'll prove to you that this is his plan."

Hank fished in his front pocket for and pulled out a cellphone. He handed it to her. "This is the burner phone I used to communicate with the men who've been guarding you. The number is taped to the back."

Alejandra dialed the international number direct to *El Chefe* and waited. She switched the phone's audio to speaker so that all could hear. Voicemail picked up on the other end. The message was in Spanish. She left a message, also in Spanish. Then, in English, she added, "Call this number." She left the number for the burner phone.

Moments later, the phone buzzed. Alejandra answered using the speaker option.

A man speaking angry Spanish yelled into the speaker.

She spoke to him in a calm, resigned tone.

Rafe only picked up a few of the words she spoke in Spanish, but at one point, he heard her mention "*Señorita* Briana Hayes." He wished he'd paid more attention in high school Spanish class. At the end of the conversation, he picked up the words, *"Estaré ahí pronto."* I will be there soon.

Alejandra ended the call and looked across at Hank.

Hank turned to his man, Taz Davila.

Taz nodded. "It's like she said. He wants to make a trade. He has Briana, and he's not going to give her up until Alejandra shows up in El Salvador."

Rafe turned to Hank. "So, what are we going to do? I know Briana wouldn't want us to turn over Alejandra to the cartel."

Alejandra shook her head. "It's the only way. He will

not let her go, until he has me. If I'm not there in a certain amount of time, he'll start hurting her. Eventually, he'll kill her."

"She's not in El Salvador yet," Hank said. "Let me talk to some of my contacts and see what we can come up with."

Rafe's eyes narrowed. "Sounds like an extraction mission to me."

Alejandra frowned. "What do you mean by contacts?"

"I have some friends in high places who might be able to help us," Hank said.

She shook her head. "Some of the clients and partners on my list are high up on the political chain in the US. If you stir that hornet's nest, I won't be able to get to El Salvador to make the trade. They won't let me live that long."

Hank nodded. "Understood. I'll present it as purely an extraction case of a US citizen. I won't mention that it's a trade."

"*El Chefe* gave me twenty-four hours to get back with him on arrangements for my return to El Salvador. He will expect me there shortly afterward."

"Good," Hank said. "That gives me time to work my connections."

Over the next twenty-four hours, Hank performed miracles. He organized a plane to transport his team of Brotherhood Protectors. He contacted his source in the Special Operations Command and arranged for an extraction mission using Rafe's former Delta Force team out of Fort Hood, Texas. He also contacted the

DEA, who had undercover boots on the ground in El Salvador. They would perform reconnaissance of the cartel's stronghold.

Two DEA agents were mobilized quickly and were at the airport when the plane carrying Briana landed. They witnessed a dozen of the cartel's men escorting Briana off the plane then departing in a convoy of vehicles that headed toward *El Chefe's* compound.

Rafe was amazed that by the time the Brotherhood Protectors boarded the plane Hank secured to fly them to El Salvador, that they were fully equipped with weapons, ammunition and protective gear. The items had been stored in crates marked as movie cameras, props and electronics, supposedly destined for a remote location within the country of El Salvador to prepare to film an action-adventure film, starring Sadie McClain.

They remained in close communication with the Delta Force team that had been mobilized and was scheduled to arrive by commercial flight around the same time. They would meet on the ground in the target country and form a formidable team that would be ready, and in place, when Alejandra appeared to make the trade for Briana's freedom at *El Chefe*'s compound.

Rafe hoped all went according to plan, and that they were able to extract both Briana and Alejandra from the cartel leader's clutches without losing either woman or any of the team of Delta Force soldiers.

He understood plans were only good for starting a mission. They rarely executed exactly as intended.

CHAPTER 10

The men who'd loaded Briana into the Jeep and transported her down the hill to a clearing where a helicopter waited didn't say a word to her. She asked them where they were taking her, but they remained stoically silent, refusing to give her an answer. They secured her wrists with zip-ties, thankfully in front of her, and then strapped her into the helicopter, an armed guard on either side of her.

Thirty minutes later, the helicopter set down on a landing strip on a large ranch where a jet airplane waited. Briana's heart sank into the pit of her belly. She was in for a much longer ride than she'd imagined.

A couple of men speaking Spanish marched her up the steps and onto the jet. At that point, she figured she was on her way to meet the man Alejandra had tried to escape. She was on her way to El Salvador to answer to *El Chefe Diablo*, the Devil Boss. The only thing that kept her from breaking down into tears was the knowledge that they'd spared Rafe's life. Even if she never saw the

United States again, she would know that Rafe was alive and he'd be doing everything in his power to find her and bring her home.

The men who accompanied her on the plane carried military-grade rifles. If she wasn't mistaken, they were AK-47s. Russian-made rifles she'd seen pictures of in news clips from all over the world. They did give her water to drink and allowed her to use the lavatory aboard the plane. It wasn't like she could escape through a window. Not at 35,000 feet in the air. She must have fallen asleep somewhere over Oklahoma or Texas. When they landed to refuel, it was daylight and the signs at the landing strip were in Spanish. She wasn't sure where they were, but she suspected Mexico. The men with the guns didn't allow her to leave the plane, and they were on their way again as soon as the fuel trucks had finished filling the plane's tanks.

By the time they landed at their destination, Briana was bone tired. She'd slept a little, sitting up, but she was worried about Rafe and heartsick for Lucy. The last she'd seen the dog, she'd been lying on the ground after being hit with a club. The pain in Briana's wrists, where the hard plastic of the zip-ties had rubbed the skin raw, seemed inconsequential in comparison to Rafe's and Lucy's suffering. So far, the men who'd kidnapped her hadn't done more than shove her a couple of times. She was sure the Devil Boss had a harsher punishment in store for her once she arrived at his compound.

Dread built with every passing mile they drove away from the airport and into the jungles of El Salvador. If she could, she'd escape, but making her way back to civilization might prove to be difficult and dangerous. She wasn't sure what kinds of animals she might encounter, but they would be preferable to the men of the cartel who had, as Rafe had warned, killed entire families, including women and children, because their boss didn't like the sound of their dogs barking.

Briana had read that cartels were notorious for making examples out of people who crossed them. Sometimes they hung them in their villages or mowed them down at family gatherings. The fact that Briana had assisted Alejandra in her escape and evasion of *El Chefe*'s men made her a prime target for retribution.

By the time they reached the cartel compound, Briana's belly rumbled. She hadn't eaten since the night before, and the heat and humidity of the jungle left her feeling dehydrated. What she wouldn't give for a tall jug of ice water.

The compound consisted of high stucco walls with a heavy wooden gate. Two guards stood on either side, also equipped with AK-47s. When their cavalcade arrived, the guards met the first vehicle, their weapons drawn, ready to fire into the vehicle. Whatever the driver of that vehicle said was enough to convince the guards to stand down and allow the vehicles to enter the compound.

Once inside, Briana studied the layout. If she planned an escape, she'd need to know how many buildings stood between her and the walls and how many guards she'd have to get past to get through the gate or go over the top of the wall. Two guards at the gate, men on the wall behind the gate. A man on the top of the first building closest to the gate with a rifle aimed at the vehicles entering. Her heart sank deeper. She wasn't a trained combatant. She didn't have the skills to fight her way free. But she had a brain and courage. She would figure out how to free herself.

Briana couldn't wait for someone to rescue her. That might never happen. She wasn't an important political figure or a celebrity. The US government didn't send the army to rescue a single female kidnapped from the mountains of Montana. Especially one they'd never heard of. If she wanted to live, she had to get herself out of the compound and to the nearest US consulate or embassy.

First, she had to get the zip-tie off her wrists.

The caravan of black SUVs came to a halt in front of a palatial stucco house with white columns and curved arches.

Briana half expected the Devil Boss himself to step out of the building to greet his prisoner.

He didn't.

She was dragged out of the SUV and marched into the building, through a wide foyer and down a hallway to a tall wooden door. The guard in front of her knocked and said something in Spanish.

A voice inside barked a response.

The guard opened the door. Her escorts shoved her through and stood beside her in front of a large desk made of ornately carved mahogany. A man with thick black hair and a dark mustache sat behind the desk, his arms crossed over his chest. For a long moment, he stared at Briana, his eyes narrowing.

Finally, he stood and walked over to her. "You are responsible for depriving me of my property."

Briana's brow twisted. "And what property is that?"

"Alejandra Villareal," he said, his lip curling back in a sneer.

Briana lifted her chin. Though she was shaking inside, she refused to let the man see an ounce of fear. "I'm not familiar with how things work in El Salvador, but in the US, slavery has been abolished. People aren't considered property."

He backhanded her, the heavy ring on his finger cutting into Briana's cheek.

Pain shot through her face. She lifted her bound hands to press against the gash his ring had opened on her face. Tears welled automatically in her eyes. Briana blinked, refusing to let even one fall.

The cartel leader glared at her. "You should not have interfered in a matter that did not concern you."

"Helping people in need is always my concern. I would do it all again. Alejandra is not your property."

"You are wrong. Alejandra belongs here," he said, his tone forceful. "Tell me...where is she?"

Briana lifted her chin. "I don't know."

He nodded. "I thought not. We found the women's shelter where you took her outside of Chicago. They said they did not know of a woman and a child meeting Alejandra's description. We searched the building and did not find her."

Thank God. Briana fought the urge to smile. She hoped no one had been injured during the search.

"Alejandra was there. We know from tracking her

cellphone. We didn't get there in time. Your friends took her before we arrived. It's funny how people will talk when you threaten their children. The shelter organizer refused to answer our questions, but one of the guests was eager to give us answers when we took her three-year-old daughter."

Briana gasped. "You bastard." Anger burned deep in Briana's gut. If she'd had her .40 caliber pistol on her, she'd have shot this man who would use a child as a pawn in his vicious game.

"When we had all the information they had to give, I had my men burn the shelter to the ground."

Briana sucked in a sharp breath. She felt as if she'd been sucker-punched in the belly. "You are not a man. You're not even an animal. Animals have more compassion than you."

His lips curled in a sneer. "I did not build an empire by being kind to strangers." His brow lowered. "Alejandra *will* return to El Salvador, or she will be responsible for your torture and eventual death."

Briana's gut clenched. Death didn't worry her, as long as it was swift. The idea of being tortured sent shivers of fear throughout her body. She refused to let it consume her. Her mother had always told her and her brother to never borrow trouble. Never fear something that had yet to happen. And in this case, she had to do something to keep it from happening. Briana had to find her way out of this situation before the Devil started down the path of torture.

He said something in Spanish to one of the guards.

The guard left the room and returned with a tray of food and drink and set it on a small table near a chair.

The Devil Boss nodded to the tray. "For now, you are my guest. But that will change if Alejandra does not come to her senses and return."

Briana's belly rumbled loudly. She wanted to tell the man where he could shove his food and drink. She wanted to rebel against anything he wanted her to do. But reason forced her to consider her need for sustenance to help her in her escape. She might have to traipse through the jungle for days without food or water. Better that she consume what she could when offered. She didn't know when her next meal might come.

The Devil Boss spoke again in Spanish. One of the guards pulled a wicked-looking knife out of a scabbard strapped to his leg and came at Briana.

She backed away, running into the guard behind her.

The guard laughed, grabbed her bound wrists and sliced through the zip-tie, scraping her skin with the sharp edge of the blade.

Briana winced. As soon as the plastic tie popped free, she pressed her wrists to her sides to stop the bleeding.

El Chefe frowned. "He cut you?"

Briana's chin rose. "It's nothing," she lied, holding her wrist tightly against her jeans.

The Devil Boss grabbed her wrist and yanked it toward him, getting blood on his hands. "*El idiota!*" he shouted and let out string of curses in Spanish. He took the rifle out of the offending guard's hands and spoke angrily in Spanish.

The guard raised his hands and answered, as if pleading.

"Really. It didn't hurt," Briana said.

El Chefe pressed the rifle into the man's chest and stared at him through slitted eyes. For a long moment, he held that stance. Then, he said, "Bang."

The guard's eyes widened, and his body tensed. When the gun didn't go off, he let go of the breath he'd been holding in a relieved whoosh.

The Devil Boss spoke softly, *"Pagas por tus errores."* Then he shot the man pointblank.

Briana screamed and staggered backward as the guard's eyes rounded and his mouth opened as if to say something. Then he collapsed to the floor and lay still.

The Devil Boss turned to Briana, pointing the rifle at her chest. "I will translate for you," he said. "You pay for your errors."

Briana sucked in a breath, her heart pounding hard against her chest. She fully expected the cartel leader to shoot her next. She almost welcomed it to end the tumult of fear roiling inside.

Instead, he tossed the rifle to another guard and waved a hand toward the body on the floor. *"Limpia este desastre,"* he said and walked away from Briana.

A couple of his men grabbed the arms and legs of the dead guard and carried him out of the room.

As the cartel leader reached his desk, he turned and jerked his head toward Briana. *"Llévala lejos."*

The remaining guard clasped her arm and dragged her toward the door.

"You might as well let me go," Briana said, her voice shaking. "I don't know where Alejandra is."

"Your friends know where to find her. If they want you to come home alive, they will bring Alejandra to me." The phone on his desk rang, and a smile curled his lip. "I suspect this will be Alejandra now. She called earlier. She knows what is at stake. Now, it's only a matter of time as to when she will return to her country. When she does, we might decide to let you go." He shrugged. "Or maybe, we will keep you and sell you to the highest bidder or use you as an example to others who might interfere in our operations." He waved his hand.

The guard dragged her toward the door.

The cartel leader let the phone ring a few more times, tapping his fingers on the desktop, as if letting Alejandra stew.

As her captor escorted her out of *El Chefe*'s study, Briana heard the man talking. She couldn't make out the words and wouldn't have been able to translate, anyway.

If it was Alejandra, it meant Hank had been successful in moving her to Montana. It also meant that all Briana had done to protect the woman and her baby was for naught. Thankfully, Hank's men had moved her before the Devil Boss's men had arrived at the shelter.

She hoped Alejandra would refuse to make the trade. The woman's baby needed her more than Briana needed to live.

At the same time, Briana worried about the forms of torture the cartel leader would inflict on her to force Alejandra to comply. Could she withstand the pain?

The guard took her to a room at the end of a long hallway, unlocked the door and shoved her inside. As soon as he released his hold on her arm, Briana spun and darted around the guard. She almost made it past him when he grabbed her hair and yanked her backward.

Briana fell, landing hard on her ass.

Instead of letting her rise to her feet, the guard dragged her by the hair into the room, stepped back, pointing his rifle at her chest and backed through the doorway.

Scrambling to her feet, Briana ran for the door. It shut before she reached it. The metal click of a key being turned in the lock let her know she was well and truly stuck in the dark prison. With no windows and no lamps or light fixtures, she had to wait for her eyes to adjust to the darkness. The only thing saving her from pitch blackness was the sliver of light coming from beneath the wooden door.

Briana closed her eyes and willed her vision to adjust quickly. The sooner she could see, the sooner she could inspect her prison for possible ways to escape.

When she opened her eyes again, she looked around at the dim interior of a small, square room. In one corner was a toilet and a sink. In the other was a cot, bare of pillows or blankets. Not that she needed blankets in the heat of the El Salvadoran jungle. She tested the sink. The water appeared to be clear and fresh. She washed her face and hands, careful not to ingest any for fear of parasites. Eventually, she'd have to have water, but for now, she preferred to do without.

Footsteps sounded on the Saltillo tile outside the door of her prison, and the metal lock clicked.

The guard who'd brought her there pointed his rifle at her and said something in Spanish she assumed translated to "Stay where you are, or I'll shoot your ass." Another guard brought the tray of food she'd left in the study into the room and set it on the bed. Then he backed out, the door closed, and the lock sealed her inside.

The tray contained a small round pancake-looking things that appeared to be thick flour tortillas.

Briana lifted one, sniffed and tested a bite, only to find the interior filled with refried beans. It tasted all right and wasn't too spicy. She ate all of one and started into another. On the tray was also a plastic bottle of water. Trusting it only slightly more than the water out of the tap, she sipped it, trying to quench her thirst. The humidity and the close confines of the room already had her sweating. She'd need the water to keep from dehydrating. After she'd finished two of the small, stuffed pancakes, she fit one into her pocket to hold in case she managed an escape.

Another careful study of the room helped her to identify items she might use for weapons. If she could knock out a guard, she might sneak past him to get out of the main house. The challenge would then be getting out of the compound. The wall was too high for her to scale without help. If she could find a ladder or something to help her get over the top, she'd need to climb over away from the main gate and hope there weren't guards posted all around the perimeter. She just needed a chance, and she'd make the best of it. The jungle looked pretty tame compared to the kind of justice *El Chefe Diablo* dished out. Briana needed to figure a way out. The sooner the better. Then Alejandra wouldn't have to risk her newfound freedom to get Briana out of a tight situation.

There had to be a way.

Briana went to work pulling and tugging at the legs of the bed. The metal was firm and needed a screwdriver and a wrench to dismantle the frame. The plumbing was bare bones. She might have used the lid to the toilet, if it had one. The tank was one that was mounted high on the wall with a string to pull for flushing. She might be able to use the string to stretch across the door to trip or confuse the guards. Filing that thought away, she skimmed her hands along the walls, searching for any holes or soft spots she could dig out to carve an exit through the wall. The wall was smooth. Tapping her knuckles against it, she realized it was probably made of concrete blocks. Without a chisel and several weeks of painstaking work, she wouldn't make much of a dent in the structure.

If she wanted out of that room, she had to leave through the door. Unless the guard got careless, she doubted an opportunity would present itself. What guard wanted to face *El Chefe Diablo* after losing a prisoner? Especially after one of the guards was murdered for scraping Briana's wrists with his knife.

An hour passed. Two guards showed up to escort her back down the long hallway to the cartel leader's study.

"Give them proof of life. Talk to the camera." He nodded toward a man who held a smart phone.

This was her chance to get her message across, not fight the monster who held her hostage. Briana stared at the smartphone camera, her head held high. "Alejandra, if you get this message, don't come to El Salvador. Seek asylum from the US government, stay in the States and raise your baby."

El Chefe cursed and started toward her.

Briana continued, talking faster, "You were right to leave this monster. Stay away. Don't worry about me. I don't have a child. You do."

The Devil Boss grabbed her hair and yanked back her head. He stuck a wicked, long knife up to her throat and spoke to the phone. "If you want her to live another day, you'll be on a plane in the next twelve hours. After that, I will start taking her apart, one piece at a time, starting with her pretty ear." He touched the tip of the knife to Briana's ear and pricked it, drawing blood.

Briana bit down hard on her lip to keep from crying out.

"Twelve hours." *El Chefe* lowered the knife, released his grip on her hair and backhanded her hard enough that she flew across the room and landed on her hands and knees.

He made a cutting motion across his throat. The man holding the smart phone stopped the video and handed the phone to his boss. He pressed a few buttons, keyed a message and pressed send.

"Now, we will see if your life is worth anything," *El Chefe* said, motioning to the guard. *"Llévala lejos."*

The guard jerked her to her feet, walked her out of the room and back down the long hallway to her prison.

Still dizzy from being hit in the face, Briana could barely keep up with the man. He half-walked, half-dragged her until they reached the room. Then he shoved her inside and slammed the door shut.

Briana stumbled and fell to the floor, the same cheek he'd cut the first time bleeding again. She lay there for a few minutes, praying Alejandra did as she'd said and stayed in the US. If she came home, she would have no freedom and live in constant fear for her life and for that of her little girl.

Briana understood what it meant for her if Alejandra didn't come, and she prayed that if she couldn't find a way out, that she'd die sooner rather than later.

CHAPTER 11

Thirty-six hours after Briana's abduction, the plane greased the landing and came to a halt in San Salvador, the capital of El Salvador. They couldn't get there fast enough for Rafe. After seeing Briana bleeding at the hand of *El Chefe,* Rafe was ready for a fight. Being cooped up on a plane for hours, did little to reduce his anger.

He was glad to be on the ground again. They hadn't saved Briana yet, but at least he was in the same country as the pretty social worker and had more of a chance of saving her than when they were back in Montana.

Hank had tapped on one of his movie star wife's friends who owned a large plane they used to transport movie-making equipment and personnel to foreign locations. They'd loaded the cargo hold with everything they'd need to mount an operation to extract Briana from the clutches of one of the most notorious cartel leaders in Central America.

The plane parked in the general aviation side of the

airport and was met by the customs officials of the country. Hank had arranged for them to see a crate full of movie equipment. After they'd checked the crate, they allowed the team to load the crates into waiting trucks inside a hangar.

A bus arrived from the commercial side of the international airport, and the Delta Force team from Fort Hood joined them.

Rafe had never been happier to see his old team as he was that day.

"Dude, I send you to protect my sister, and this is how you treat her?" Ryan "Dash" Hayes pulled Rafe into a bear hug. When he leaned back, he frowned, staring at the blood on his hand. "Get in a fight with one of those Montana grizzlies?"

"A grizzly would have been easier to deal with." Hope built in Rafe's chest. With his team there, they had half a chance against an army of cartel thugs. "I wasn't sure they'd send you guys. I thought you were on a mission."

"We were on the way back when I got the call from Bree," Dash said. "I didn't realize just how bad it was."

"Neither did we. Obviously. *El Chefe* sent in a dozen of his mercenaries to get her out, along with a chopper and plane."

"We heard. You're lucky to be alive from what Hank told us." Hayes tipped his head to the others standing behind him. "The guys are all glad to see you. We're hoping we can talk you into re-enlisting. It's not the same without our token Irishman." He stepped aside.

"Yeah, man. I don't have anyone to nag me to clean

my weapon or change my socks on mission," Doug "Dog" Masters said. He hugged Rafe then punched him in the arm. "You need to come back."

"No shit." Craig Bullington, otherwise known as Bull, pulled Rafe into a bone-crunching hug. The big mountain of a man could bench press four hundred pounds without breaking a sweat. "We miss having you around."

"Speak for yourself." Mike "Blade" Calhoun clasped forearms with Rafe. "Now, I have half a chance with the ladies without Donovan around to steal them. Unless he's found one of his own. Then he can come back."

Dash frowned. "You ain't been hitting on my sister, have you?"

"Dash, I hope your sister is better looking than you," Sean "Mac" McDaniel said, pushing him aside to get close to Rafe to hug him. "*Is* she better looking than Dash?"

"Much better," Rafe said. "And she's amazing, kind and selfless. Unlike her brother."

Dash's eyes narrowed. "You didn't answer my question. You been hitting on Bree?"

"If he has, he's smart enough not to tell you," John "Tank" Sanders, the old man of the team, said. He shook Rafe's hand. "Good to see you."

"Great to see you, Tank. You ever buy that piece of property out by Copperas Cove?" Rafe asked.

Tank nodded. "Closed on it the day before we shipped out on our last mission. Haven't had a chance to get out there and see what needs to be done. Hope to build a house out there, someday."

"Are you the next man to bail on the team?" Rafe asked. "You should be getting close to your twenty-year mark."

"I have three more years to go," Tank said.

"Tank, you should see about getting a desk job," Rucker Sloan said, reaching in to shake Rafe's hand. "You're getting too old for Delta Force. Or maybe, we all need to be like Donovan and bail before we're too old."

"Shut the fuck up," Tank said. "I'm not old. I can still outrun, outshoot and outfight any one of you dumbasses."

Mac clapped a hand on Tank's shoulder. "A little sensitive, are we?"

"It's good to see you all," Rafe said. "I didn't realize just how much I missed you bunch of jerks."

"Yeah, you'll be back," Bull predicted.

Rafe shook his head. "Nah. Montana is pretty amazing."

"Montana? Or my sister?" Dash's eyes narrowed.

Rafe's jaw hardened. "We're getting your sister back. I shouldn't have let them get to her."

Hank joined them. "You were far outnumbered. I should have provided more support."

"We had no idea he would send so many or launch such an elaborate attack to capture Briana. He wanted Alejandra. Still does."

"It's how he operates." Alejandra approached the group of Delta Force men. "If he can't get what he wants directly, he makes certain he can negotiate for what he wants. He just has to get the right carrot to dangle." Alejandra touched Rafe's arm. "You couldn't have known. I shouldn't have taken up Briana on her offer to find me and my Bella refuge. She would never have been a target if I'd just moved on my own."

"We can stand around swapping regrets all day, but we're better off getting to the compound," Hank said. "The undercover DEA agents have agreed to meet with us in a conference room inside this hanger to pass on what information they were able to gather. Let's get this operation underway."

The team moved into the conference room, where they met with the two agents who'd been as close as they could get to *El Chefe*'s compound in the jungle. They'd counted as many as thirty of the cartel leader's men coming and going from that location. Since they'd taken Briana into the compound, she hadn't come back out, that much they knew.

They'd been covering *El Chefe*'s movements for some time now, gathering information about his contacts, clients and partners.

Hank had briefed his team of Brotherhood Protectors on the way to El Salvador. They weren't to mention anything about the book Alejandra had with all that information. He didn't want anyone in El Salvador to know of its existence for fear Alejandra wouldn't make it to the compound to trade for Briana.

The Deltas and the DEA didn't need to know about the book. That was information best kept for another day.

"We have to assume *El Chefe* has people watching us already," Hank said. "Hopefully, he hasn't seen just how many people we brought with us. He'll expect my team to bring Alejandra to the compound. Before that, we need the Deltas in place for backup and to provide cover for when Alejandra makes the trade. We can't let them keep Briana."

"How do we know she's still alive?" Rafe asked, though he hated the thought that she might be otherwise.

At that moment, Hank's burner phone buzzed. He pulled the phone from his pocket. "*El Chefe* just texted a video." He brought the video up on the phone, and they waited while it buffered.

Rafe leaned in and gasped when Briana's image came onto the screen.

"Alejandra, if you get this message, don't come to El Salvador," Briana said. "Seek asylum from the US government, stay in the States and raise your baby."

Briana continued, talking faster, "You were right to leave this monster. Stay away. Don't worry about me. I don't have a child. You do."

El Chefe grabbed her hair and yanked her head back. He stuck knife to her throat and looked straight at them. "If you want her to live another day, you'll be on a plane in the next twelve hours. After that, I will start taking her apart, one piece at a time, starting with her pretty ear." He touched the tip of the knife to Briana's ear and pricked it, drawing blood.

Rafe's fists clenched, rage rising in his chest.

"Twelve hours," the cartel leader repeated. The time stamp on the message was from six hours earlier.

That gave them six hours to contact *El Chefe* to

arrange the trade. Six hours to get the Deltas in place to support them.

The DEA guys had a hand-drawn diagram of the exterior of the compound and the likely locations of guards posted outside. They'd pulled a satellite image that gave a birds-eye view of the buildings within the compound. The main building appeared to be a large white house, and there were barracks-like buildings at the rear of the walled compound. Several smaller buildings were on either side, possibly for storage. Jungle surrounded the compound on all sides with a gravel road leading in. The trade would have to be made somewhere along the gravel road.

"We don't send Alejandra in until they send Briana out," Rafe said.

"The trade has to be made outside the compound," Hank agreed. "To have any chance of bringing both women back, we need them to be where we can see them. If they get Alejandra inside the compound, it'll complicate her extraction."

"Don't worry about me," Alejandra said. "We need to get Briana out alive. If I go in, take Briana and get the hell out of El Salvador. *El Chefe* cannot be trusted."

"The compound is two hours out of the city," one of the DEA agents said. "You need time to get there and get in place. We've arranged for a couple of produce trucks to get your advance team to within a couple of miles of the compound. They'll go in on foot from there."

The Delta Force team gathered their weapons, protective gear and communications equipment then loaded their duffle bags into the back of the truck. They wore civilian clothing, having agreed that arriving in uniform would alert the cartel to their presence sooner than they wanted.

One of the agents made a call, and minutes later, trucks pulled into the hangar loaded with boxes of produce arranged so that the soldiers could climb into the back, hunker down amid the boxes and not be seen from the road.

"Great. Let's get this party started," Hank said. "I have a wife and little girl waiting for me back home."

"And I have a baby girl I hope to see again," Alejandra said.

"If all goes according to plan, you should see your daughter soon," Hank said.

If.

Rafe prayed the operation that night went according to the plan. At the very least, he hoped they got Briana and Alejandra out alive. Trading one woman for another didn't sit well with him. He preferred to go in with just the team and duke it out. Having the ladies in the line of fire made it trickier and more dangerous.

After his week in the mountains with Briana, Rafe didn't want their time together to end so soon. He liked her a lot and could be well on his way to loving her. Rafe wanted more time with Briana to get to know her even more. At the end of the day, he hoped they'd have that chance.

BRIANA SPENT the day working on the legs on the bed, trying to break a leg free. The metal didn't bend, and the screws were in tight, holding the legs to the frame. She needed a screwdriver and a wrench to free the bolts holding it together. Since she had neither of those two items, she moved on to the other items in the room. The bed had no sheets or blankets she could use to throw over the guard. The toilet had no lid she could use to hit the guard with, but the food tray was made of metal. If she could get the guard far enough inside the room, she could hit him with the tray and make her escape.

Getting the guard to open the door would be the first challenge.

Briana stood to the side of the door holding the empty tray. She moaned loudly. "I'm sick. Please, get me a doctor. I'm so sick." She moaned again.

When the door didn't open, she pounded the wooden panel with her fist. "Please, I'm sick and need help. *Por favor.*" She stopped and dropped to the ground with as loud a thump as she could manage and not hurt herself. As soon as she hit the floor, she quietly crawled to the side of the door, lifted the tray and stood, ready for when the guard might finally open the door to check on her.

She waited silently.

And waited.

Just when she thought the guard might not even be on the other side of the door, the lock clicked.

Briana's pulse quickened as she raised the tray over one shoulder, her arms cocked and ready.

A guard pushed open the door with the barrel of his AK-47 and looked inside.

Because it was so dark in the room, he had to push the door wider to let in some light.

Holding her breath, Briana waited for the man to cross the threshold.

When he didn't see her in the triangle of light shining across the floor, he stepped into the room.

Briana swung the tray as hard as she could, slamming it into the man's face.

The man released his hold on the AK-47. It clattered to the hard tiles.

Briana would've dived for the weapon, but the big guard dropped to his knees, landing on the gun. Instead, she hit him on the back of the head and leaped over his shoulder, landing in the hallway. She ran as fast as she could, aiming for the only door she knew led out of the building.

When a man stepped into view in the grand foyer ahead, Briana ducked into an open door that led into a sitting room with dark wood tables and brightly colored sofas. French doors on the other side of the room lured her to the outside light. She ran across the room and had just reached for the door handles when a shout rang out in the hallway.

Grabbing the handles, she yanked open the French doors and ran out into a garden. Unfortunately, the garden was a courtyard, surrounded by four walls. Each had French doors leading onto the garden, but which one would bring her closest to exiting the house? She ran to the door directly across from the one she'd just passed through. More shouts echoed throughout the huge house.

If she hoped to escape, she had to do it soon. The door on the opposite side led into a bedroom with a solid wood, four-poster bed with a white eyelet lace comforter that seemed incongruous for a drug lord known for killing.

Footsteps clattered on the paving stones in the garden behind her. Briana dropped to her belly and rolled beneath the bed, wishing she'd had time to close the garden door. Alas, someone was running toward her, giving her no time to hide anywhere but beneath the bed.

She moved to the center, praying whoever it was would run straight through the room to the other side, searching for her. That might give her time to find another way out.

Booted feet entered the room and ran for the door as Briana had hoped. The door opened, but the boots didn't pass through it.

Briana couldn't see what he was doing but guessed he was peering out into the hallway. He called out in Spanish to someone passing by. That person responded, and the man stepped out into the corridor.

Briana held her breath, waiting for the man to leave the room. With the house in an uproar to find her, she knew she wouldn't make it out of the compound without being captured. The thought depressed her, but she wouldn't give up. This was her first attempt. She would try again.

Easing out from under the bed, she crawled out the open French door into the garden and sat on a bench beneath a tree and pulled in a deep breath. She stared at a bird bath, waiting for the guards to find her and return her to her prison.

Footsteps on the paving stones made her stiffen. She wouldn't fight this time. Not with all the cartel's minions searching for her. But she was prepared to duck if one of them decided to take a swing at her.

"You've upset my staff," a voice said behind her.

Briana didn't turn toward *El Chefe*. "You have a lovely garden," she said.

"I like to come out here to read when I want peace and quiet," he said, walking around to stand in front of her. "You know, you can't escape."

"So you say."

"Even if you'd gotten out of the house, you wouldn't have made it past the wall."

"You could be right," she said. "Then again, no one likes to be held prisoner. Some are just more determined than others to be free."

He stared at her, eyes narrowing. "Are you talking about yourself or Alejandra."

Briana pushed to her feet. "You are not a king or a god. You cannot control the lives of others with your money."

He dipped his head. "No, but I can control them with my army and the mercenaries my money can buy."

"And does it make you happy?" Briana stood in front of the Devil Boss, her shoulders back, her face set in grim lines. "Are you happy controlling other people? Don't you wonder if it's all worth it?"

He spread his arms wide. "I have all this."

"Things," she pointed out. "You have things. What

about love and kindness? The people in your life should be what make you happy, not the things. Things don't have feelings."

He snorted. "Things don't stab you in the back or steal from you."

"Is that what happened to you? Did someone you cared about turn on you? Was it Alejandra?"

"No!" he shouted. "It was not Alejandra. She is but an employee, who knows too much about my business to let go. You know nothing about me. And you never will." He looked past her shoulder and said something in Spanish.

Two guards appeared. One had blood drying beneath his nose and a bruise on his cheek. They gripped her arms and half-carried her back to her cell. The food tray had been removed. There was nothing else in the room she could use as a weapon. Her heart sank into her shoes.

Briana could have wallowed in her despair and let loose the tears waiting to fall, but the thought of maybe seeing Rafe again kept her going. They'd had so little time together. She liked him. A lot. She could even see herself falling in love with the man—if given the chance.

The next time the door opened, she'd have to be ready to throat punch the guard and make sure he didn't yell for help as soon as she ran.

If she got another chance, she'd take it.

CHAPTER 12

With Brotherhood Protectors Hank, Swede, Boomer, Taz, Chuck and Bear by his side, and his old Delta Force team supposedly in place around the compound, Rafe dared to hope all could go well once they arrived with Alejandra to make the trade. They didn't try to sneak in like the Delta Force team. Their job was to be there for the trade. The Deltas were there to cover their sixes and make sure *El Chefe* didn't try to take them all out and keep both females.

Hank's men gave the Delta Force team plenty of time to get to their positions and for the sun to sink into the horizon. Two hours out from the designated time, Hank handed Alejandra the burner phone to make her call to the Devil Boss.

She set the audio on speaker and spoke in Spanish, repeating her words in English. "I'll be there in two hours. We will make the trade outside your compound. We will see that *Señorita* Hayes is well and uninjured before I step out of the vehicle. Understood?"

"*Si.* We will have bullets reserved for Miss Hayes if anything goes wrong during the transfer. Understood?"

Rafe's lip curled back in a snarl. He personally wanted to kill *El Chefe* with his bare hands. To watch him choke to death slowly. How a man could torture and kill innocent people on a whim was beyond Rafe's comprehension. Men like the cartel leader needed to be eliminated from society completely.

After Alejandra made the call, they loaded the team into three SUVs then lined up for the drive out to the compound. Taz, Chuck and Boomer took the lead. Hank, Alejandra and Rafe rode in the middle vehicle. Swede and Bear brought up the rear. The Brotherhood Protectors were fully equipped for combat, wearing bullet proof vests, helmets with radios, rifles, handguns, grenades and night vision goggles.

The Delta Team would be in place with a sniper on either side of the entrance, ready to pick off anyone who might try to take out Hank and his team.

They drove in silence to within a mile of the coordinates the DEA agents had given them and slowed to a stop, where they performed a communications check with the Delta Force team. Once everyone was accounted for, the procession continued on to the turnoff. The sun was well on its way toward the horizon, casting the surrounding jungle into deep shadows.

The closer they got to the compound, the faster Rafe's heart beat. He wanted to see Briana, to know for sure she was alive and well. And he wanted to kill *El Chefe* for taking and hurting her. The woman only wanted to do right by people, to ease their suffering.

She'd helped Alejandra because she couldn't stand to see a woman and her child exposed to the elements and afraid to seek assistance lest she draw attention to herself and be discovered by the man she'd escaped.

Briana had a big heart and courage like no other woman he knew. Yes, he could be falling in love with her and, for the first time in his life, he was okay with that. He wasn't tempted to return to the Delta Force teams. He realized he wanted a life outside constant deployments to war-torn nations where he could be shot at, blown up or tortured if caught. No, he wanted more in life. He wanted someone like Briana to come home to at night, to explore the mountains with and maybe raise children of their own. Not *like* Briana. He wanted Briana.

As they came to a halt fifty yards from the compound's gate, the lead vehicle stopped, and the men climbed out, standing with their doors open, providing a little protection from potential gunfire.

The gate opened, and several of *El Chefe's* men emerged.

Rafe held his breath, waiting for the most important person to come out of the compound. When she did, he let go of the breath and tightened his hand on his rifle.

Briana stood between two large men, each holding one of her arms. Behind her stood a man with black hair and a black mustache, wearing a white guayabera shirt and dark trousers. He stood with his arms crossed over his chest, his eyes narrowed, surrounded by his men who would take bullets to protect him should anyone decide to start shooting.

Alejandra squared her shoulders, her face pale beneath her naturally dark complexion. "It's time." She leaned close to Hank. "Thank you for helping me. If this plan does not work out, promise to take care of my child. She needs a good home and the love of a family."

"We're going to get you out of this," Hank said.

Alejandra stared hard into his eyes. "Promise."

Hank nodded.

Alejandra turned to Rafe. "I will do my best to make sure your woman gets out alive. Be ready to grab her and get her out of El Salvador. *El Chefe* does not forgive or forget when someone crosses him. If he lives through this, he will seek his revenge."

"Our goal today is to get you and Briana out of here alive," he said.

She cupped his cheek and gave him a gentle smile. "You love her, don't you?"

He nodded without realizing it.

"In some ways, you are like him." She jerked her head toward the compound. "You care enough to go after her."

Rafe frowned. He never wanted to be compared to the cartel leader.

Alejandra raised a hand. "The difference is, you would let her go, if that was what she wanted."

He wouldn't like it, but he couldn't keep someone who wasn't his.

Hank got out of the driver's seat and opened the back door. Rafe got out of the back seat and held out his hand to Alejandra.

She took it and let him help her out. Once her feet

were on the ground, she leaned up on her toes and kissed his cheek. "Thank you for coming with me." Then as she stepped away, she plucked one of his grenades off his vest and smiled. "Be ready."

"What the—" Rafe took a step after the woman.

Hank caught his arm. "Let her. She has a plan. We need to be ready."

He glared at Hank. "You knew?"

He tightened his jaw and nodded.

"What if it goes off when she's near Briana?"

"She knows how to use it."

Rafe shook his head. "It's too dangerous."

Alejandra called out in Spanish, and then in English. "Let her go. We meet halfway. Alone."

The Devil Boss said something to his two men.

They released their hold on Briana and stepped back, forming a wall between *El Chefe* and the Americans.

Hank and Rafe passed the other Brotherhood Protectors standing behind the doors of the front vehicle and stood ready to help in whatever way they could.

Alejandra and Briana walked toward each other.

Rafe prayed the cartel men didn't see the grenade or they might shoot her before she got close enough to make the grenade count. If she'd already pulled the pin and they shot her, the grenade could kill both women.

Rafe's muscles bunched. He'd be ready to run in and grab Briana as soon as she got close enough.

God, he didn't like this. His breath caught and held

in his lungs as the scene played out in front of him in excruciatingly slow motion.

He'd been involved in a lot of high-risk, high body-count battles, but this one had him the most on edge because he had very little control over what might happen. All he could do was be ready to respond and hope the Deltas were in good positions to pick off the cartel members before they could pick off Briana and Alejandra.

Briana had spent the afternoon pacing in her prison. Time dragged so slowly she thought she might go crazy. She even did pushups and sit-ups to keep fit while confined. If she stayed much longer, she considered making marks on the wall to count the days.

She'd finally laid on the cot and closed her eyes, hoping to fall asleep so that time would seem to pass quicker. Sleep wouldn't come. Not long after she laid down, the key clicked in the lock, and two guards appeared, glaring at her as if daring her to try something.

They took her by her arms and propelled her down the long hallway to the front entrance and out into the yard of the compound.

Briana looked around, wondering if she could break free of the big men and make a run for it. Or was this what the Devil Boss had been after all along…the trade?

Hell. Briana hoped it wasn't a trade. Alejandra needed to be with her baby, not this lunatic. He would make their lives miserable and possibly end them without a second thought. Because she'd made a run for it, he might even torture her before he killed her.

Torture.

Was the Devil Boss about to perform his first act of torture on her? Would he record it and send it to Hank and Rafe to make them convince Alejandra to make the trade?

All these thoughts raced through Briana's head in seconds. Then they were at the gate, and the cartel leader was there as well.

As soon as the gate opened and the path cleared of cartel men, Briana could see three SUVs standing at the end of the drive. The lead one stood open and men were outside the vehicles, using the doors as shields.

Briana's heart skipped several beats. She couldn't help but think that shit was about to get real in El Salvador.

Then Hank Patterson got out of the second vehicle and opened the back door.

Rafe emerged.

Briana gasped, and her heart fluttered. He was there. He'd come for her. Her eyes welled with tears she quickly blinked back. The two guards at her side walked her forward a couple of steps and stopped, still holding tightly to her arms.

After Rafe got out of the SUV, he turned and extended his hand.

Alejandra emerged, leaned up and kissed Rafe's cheek.

A short stab of something hit Briana square in the gut. Jealousy? No, the kiss had been quick, as if in thanks. Envy. Probably. She wished she could kiss Rafe's cheek and lips and hold him close.

Then Alejandra called out in Spanish and then English. "Let her go. We meet halfway. Alone."

Her heart pounding, Briana nearly collapsed, when upon a command from their leader, the cartel guards released her arms. She was free but had to walk the gauntlet of the road leading into the compound.

Alejandra stepped away from Hank and Rafe, walked around the open doors of the lead vehicle and kept coming.

"Go," *El Chefe* barked.

Briana lurched forward, rubbing her arms where the men had held her so tightly there would be bruises. The fifty or so yards to the SUVs seemed like a lot more.

As Alejandra neared, it dawned on Briana that she didn't have her baby with her. Where was Bella? The men behind her didn't seem to have her. Was she in one of the vehicles? Her heart stopped for several beats. Had she left Bella in the States?

Her heart squeezed hard in her chest. This woman was sacrificing herself to save Briana. Leaving her baby in the hands of others…

Oh, her heart hurt.

As she approached Alejandra, she shook her head. "You shouldn't have come. Where's Bella?"

"I had to. She's with Sadie. Be ready to run."

Briana frowned. "What?"

Alejandra glanced down at her hand, holding something green with a handle clutched against it. "Just run,"

Alejandra said as she continued to walk toward the compound.

As the item registered in Briana's mind, she picked up her pace, walking faster. Holy shit. Alejandra had a grenade.

Dear Lord, please don't let her martyr herself for me.

Briana glanced over her shoulder as Alejandra approached the phalanx of men surrounding *El Chefe*. In an underhanded toss, she rolled the grenade between the legs of the men guarding the cartel leader. They scrambled, dancing away from the object.

Alejandra spun and ran toward Briana. "Run!" she yelled.

Briana stumbled over her own feet then righted herself and ran as fast as she could.

Alejandra caught up with her, took her arm and pulled her along with her.

An explosion rocked the ground beneath their feet, the force at their backs pushing them forward so fast, they fell to their knees.

Gunfire exploded all around.

"Stay down," Hank called out.

"Cover me!" Rafe cried and ran toward them, hunkered down.

Briana crawled on all fours toward him.

Alejandra did the same, moving as fast as she could.

When Rafe reached them, he pointed to the ground in front of Alejandra. "Stay flat on your belly. I'll be right back."

Alejandra dropped to her belly.

Rafe bent, helped Briana to her feet and, shielding

her body, ran her toward the vehicles. As soon as he had her safely behind the bulk of an SUV, he left her and went back for Alejandra.

Briana watched from the relative safety of the SUV as Rafe started to run toward the other woman.

Hank caught him before he got too far. "Cover me."

The founder of the Brotherhood Protectors ran across the open ground, dropping down beside Alejandra.

Briana held her breath, praying Hank and Alejandra made it back to safety, alive.

Hank wrapped his arm around Alejandra, effectively shielding her body with his as he ran with her to the waiting SUVs. He helped her into the back seat of the middle vehicle and slid in beside her. One of his men took the driver's seat.

Rafe returned to Briana and ran with her to the last vehicle, the one closest to the main road. As they reached it, Briana heard the thunder of rotor blades beating the air. She looked up to see a helicopter rising above the canopy of trees.

She turned to Rafe. "Did *El Chefe* get away?"

Rafe's jaw was so tight it twitched as he helped her into the backseat. "I don't know for sure, but he jumped behind the gate and slammed it shut before the grenade exploded."

Briana cursed as she slid across the seat. "That man doesn't deserve to live. He's a monster."

Rafe slipped in beside her and pulled her into his arms.

Swede and Bear climbed into the front seats and

closed their doors. Bear spun the vehicle around and raced for the main road heading back to San Salvador, followed by the SUV carrying Hank and Alejandra and the last vehicle with two more of Hank's men.

Rafe spoke into the mic on his helmet's radio. "I have Briana in the lead vehicle." He listened. "That's what I thought. This isn't over as long as *El Chefe* is still alive." He looked across at Briana. "He got away."

"Son of a bitch," Briana said.

He took her hand and held it in his. "The good news is that all of the Delta Force team members got away without injury."

Briana raised his hand to her lips and pressed a kiss to the backs of his knuckles. "Thank you for finding me."

"I wouldn't have stopped looking until I did." He brought her hand to his lips and kissed the tips of her fingers.

"Did you know Alejandra was going to throw a grenade?"

"Not until she stole one from me at the last minute."

Briana cocked an eyebrow. "When she kissed you?"

He grinned. "You saw that?"

Her brows formed a V over her nose. "I did."

"Were you jealous?"

She sighed, her brow smoothing. "Truthfully, I was, a little." Briana leaned her head against his shoulder. "I thought we had a connection up there in the Crazy Mountains, unless it was all one-sided…?" She glanced up at him from beneath her eyelashes.

"If by one-sided, you mean, all on my side, that could

be. Because, you see, I have no idea where I stand with you, Briana Hayes. When you left, I felt we had just gotten started. I was falling for you. Now, we've all been traumatized, and we're likely to think we're in love when we're just getting to know each other."

"Why not accept the fact we're in love?" Briana asked. "Life's short, and none of us get out of it alive. Unfortunately, some sooner than others."

He nodded. "You have a point." He leaned close and kissed her lips. "Lucy and I missed you."

"Oh my God, Lucy! She made it?" Briana smiled, her heart swelling. "I thought that bastard killed her when he hit her with the club."

"She made it. I'm sure she's got a headache."

Briana reached up to unbuckle his helmet and pull it off. Then she touched the bruise and knot at his temple. "You should have seen a doctor."

"I'm okay."

She leaned up and pressed a gentle kiss to his injury.

"You're the one I'm worried about." He brushed the backs of his knuckles below the gash on her cheek. "Who did this?"

Her eyes narrowed. "The Devil Boss. I'm glad we got Alejandra out of there. She doesn't deserve to live in that kind of fear. The man is horrible." She shivered, remembering how he'd toyed with the guard who'd cut her before killing him.

She lay her cheek on Rafe's shoulder. "I'm worried."

"You're out of there."

"I know. But *El Chefe* is still alive. He won't let this slide. He'll be back for more. I'll be surprised if we make it out of El Salvador without further backlash from him."

"The Deltas will be right behind us. They'll make sure we aren't tailed by the cartel men. The DEA agents are guarding the plane at the airport. If all goes well, we'll be on our way back to Montana within the next couple of hours."

"If all goes well." She sighed. "I'm not holding my breath. I don't feel like this is over. *El Chefe* doesn't give up that easily."

"We'll be ready." Rafe smoothed a hand down her arm. "We'll get you home."

"Home." She sighed. "Where is home? I can't go back to my apartment."

"Then make Montana your home. There are plenty of children who need someone like you to look out for their best interests."

She smiled up at him. "You make it sound so easy. My life was in Chicago."

"And is it still?" He kissed her forehead. "What's keeping you there?"

"What do I have in Montana?" she asked.

"Me and Lucy," he answered.

She cocked an eyebrow. "For how long?"

"As long as we both shall live?"

"Ah, put the poor guy out of his misery," the driver said.

Rafe laughed. "Briana, you might not have had the pleasure of meeting Bear and Swede. They work with Hank as some of his Brotherhood Protectors. Swede's prior Navy, and a SEAL. Bear was Delta Force, like me. And they're interrupting a private conversation."

"Problem is, you two lovebirds are making things too difficult," Bear said from the driver's seat.

"Bear's right," Swede said. "Admit you care for each other and get on with life."

Briana laughed. "We've only known each other for a week."

"A week…a month…" Bear shrugged. "You know what you know. I knew within the first couple of days I loved Mia."

"Same with me and Allie," Swede said. "In our line of work, we have to rely on our instincts…you know…gut feel. What is your gut telling you?" Swede turned and pinned Briana with his gaze.

Heat rose up her neck. "I've never been happier than the week we spent in the cabin in the mountains. But that doesn't mean Rafe feels the same."

Rafe pulled her into his arms, the hard bulletproof vest digging into her. "Oh, sweetheart, I do."

"There you go. End of discussion," Bear said.

"Not really," Swede argued. "It's only the beginning."

"The beginning," Briana sighed. "I like the sound of that."

CHAPTER 13

Rafe held Briana in his arms the entire trip back to Montana. He felt that if he let go, she'd slip through his fingers and be gone again. He wasn't ready to let her go and hoped she'd stay with him in Montana.

The big question was *as what?*

Was a week together enough to know if you were right for each other? Did he want a commitment from her? Did he want to marry her? Maybe the question he should've been asking himself all along was whether he was willing to lose her.

After her abduction, he knew the answer to that question.

No.

When they arrived at the airport in Bozeman, Hank called Sadie, waking her up, to let him know he was on the ground and would be home in less than an hour. The other guys all called their ladies and let them know they'd be home soon as well. The atmosphere was jovial, if not completely happy. They'd extracted both women and none of their people had been killed or injured badly.

The big downer was that *El Chefe* had gotten away.

Alejandra and Briana rode in the SUV with Hank and Rafe. Swede, Taz, Bear, Boomer and Chuck rode in the other. Rather than go to Hank's ranch, where they'd all parked their own vehicles before they'd loaded up weapons, communications and personnel for the trip to El Salvador, Chuck would drop them off at their homes so they could get some sleep.

In the early hours of the morning, Hank drove up to the ranch house. The lights were all out.

"That's unusual," Hank said as he shifted the SUV into park. "Sadie always leaves a light on the porch and one in the living room when I'm away."

"Maybe she forgot," Rafe suggested.

"Maybe," Hank said, a frown settling between his eyebrows. "Leave the gear in the vehicle. We can unload it all tomorrow. Everyone will want to get sleep. And speaking of home…Donovan and Briana, you two can stay here for the night. It might be safer than the cabin. Alejandra, you'll stay with us until we can figure out something. Right now, we all need sleep." He pushed open his door and stepped down.

Rafe got out and held the door for the two women. He'd stripped out of his bulletproof vest but wore a shoulder holster with his Glock. With *El Chefe* loose, he could have his mercenaries make another attempt on Alejandra or Briana. He'd had enough time to make some calls while they were in the air.

Hank led the way up the stairs to the porch, shaking

his head. "It's not like Sadie to leave the lights off. At the very least, I would've thought Maddog would've left one on. He was in charge of ranch security while we've been gone." When he reached for the door handle, it turned without resistance. Hank held up a hand with his fist clenched, the sign for his team to stop. He pulled his weapon from the holster beneath his jacket, stood to the side of the door and nudged it open.

"Both of you get behind the SUV," Rafe said to Briana and Alejandra. He pulled his weapon from his holster and climbed the porch steps, moving to the opposite side of the front door.

Hank nudged the door wider and dove in, rolling to one side and to his feet in a hunched position behind a table in the foyer.

Rafe dove in as well and remained in a prone position on the floor.

A light blinked on, illuminating the living room.

Hank cursed.

Sadie sat in a straight-back wooden chair, her arms secured behind her, duct tape across her mouth.

In a playpen beside her lay her little girl, Emma, sound asleep.

Sitting in a wing-back chair beside them was *El Chefe*, holding Alejandra's baby, Bella, in his arms, a gun pointed at her little head.

Two of his men stood behind him, AK-47s in their hands, pointed at Hank and Rafe.

"It took you long enough to get here after you destroyed my home," the cartel leader said. "I don't forgive transgressions easily." He shrugged. "Actually, I don't forgive transgressions at all." The man glanced down at the baby in his arms. "I get what I want. Every. Time." He glanced toward the door. "Is that not correct, Alejandra?"

Alejandra entered through the front door, her eyes rounded and shaking her head. "I'll go with you. Just don't hurt her. She's innocent. She's your daughter."

"I thought as much. Another reason for her to return to El Salvador with her mother." He brushed the baby's hair back with the barrel of the gun he held. "It would a shame for her to die for no reason but that you didn't care enough about her to stay where you belong."

Alejandra looked from *El Chefe* to Sadie, Hank and Rafe. "Leave these people alone, and Bella and I will go with you. Now. This minute. No argument."

"You'll go with me no matter what I do with the rest of your friends."

"Please, they only wanted to help me," Alejandra begged.

"As I told your beautiful friend, Briana, I didn't get where I am by being kind to strangers. I take my business seriously. When people interfere in my business, they pay." He pushed to his feet.

The baby whimpered.

"Let me hold her." Alejandra walked forward, her arms out. "She's probably hungry and hears my voice."

As if to prove her mother right, Bella's whimpers turned into soft cries. She stretched and raised her arms, as if seeking Alejandra.

The cartel leader quickly became impatient with the

baby and struggled to hold onto her and his gun at the same time. He almost dropped her.

Alejandra rushed forward to catch Bella.

El Chefe let her have the child and grabbed her instead, shoving his gun up against her temple. "Now, we are going to walk out of here, and none of you will stop us. If you do, I will kill the woman and the baby." He held out his hands. "The keys to your vehicle."

Hank dug in his pocket and pulled out the key fob, tossing it at the cartel leader. The fob landed at his feet.

"Get it," he told Alejandra.

Balancing Bella in her arms, Alejandra bent to retrieve the key fob.

El Chefe held the gun to the back of her head the entire time until she handed it to him. He pocketed the key fob and hooked his arm around Alejandra's neck, again pointing the gun at her temple.

With the keys to the SUV, the man was about to walk out of the ranch house with exactly what he'd come for. Alejandra and her baby.

Rafe's heart skittered to a stop and then raced. He prayed Briana had headed for the woods to hide until the cartel leader and his men were gone. The farther away she was, the better. Especially if *El Chefe* was taking the SUV she was supposed to be hiding behind.

El Chefe backed toward the door, holding Alejandra in a chokehold. His men followed, also backing toward the door, their AK-47s pointed at Rafe and Hank.

"If they move, shoot the woman," *El Chefe* said. Then he backed through the door and out onto the porch.

A loud crack rang out in the darkness.

The cartel gunmen turned toward the sound.

At that moment, Rafe sprang at the man nearest him, grabbed his rifle and shoved it up in the air.

Hank went for the one on his side and did the same.

Rafe's guy pulled the trigger, shooting a hole in the ceiling. They struggled for control of the weapon. Fueled by searing anger and pure determination, Rafe slammed the weapon into the man's face. It hit the guy's nose with a sickening crunch. Blood gushed from his nose, and his eyes teared. His grip weakened on the gun.

Rafe seized control and slammed the butt up hard, catching the man in the chin. He fell backward, hitting his head against wall. He slid down, knocked out cold. Rafe flipped him over, yanked the cord from the nearby curtains and tied the man's wrists together behind his back and leaped to his feet.

Hank had the other man on the ground, the AK-47 pressed against his throat.

The man's face was turning purple as he choked off his air supply.

Rafe ran for the door. He had to stop *El Chefe* before he got away with Alejandra and her baby. And he had to find Briana.

With his gun in his hand, Rafe stepped through the door. What he saw made his heart leap into his throat.

Alejandra stood on the ground below the porch, holding her baby close to her chest. "Please, don't hurt her."

The Devil Boss stood nearby with his hand twisted in Briana's hair, a knife pressed to her throat, blood trickling from a gash on the side of his head. "Bitch," he said through clenched teeth, swaying slightly. "I should have killed you in El Salvador. *Eres un problema.*"

Alejandra spoke in rapid Spanish, her voice passionate, desperate. Then in English, she said, "Kill her, and I will expose all of your clients, in every country."

"If you do not come with me, I will kill her." He lifted his chin and winced. "Who will win this argument?"

Briana captured Rafe's gaze and mouthed the words, *Shoot him.* Then she slammed her head backward, hitting *El Chefe* in the nose. The arm holding the knife shook.

Before he could tighten his hold, Briana cocked her arm and jammed her elbow into his side then ducked.

Rafe aimed and shot the cartel leader in the chest.

El Chefe's eyes rounded. The knife fell from his hand, and he clutched his chest. *"Debería haberte matado."* He fell to the ground and lay still.

Alejandra walked over to the man and pushed his face with her foot. "But you didn't kill her." She spit on him and turned away, holding Bella close. "And I am thankful for the woman who was kind to this stranger." She hugged Briana and let the tears fall.

Hank ran out on the porch, breathing hard, a bruise turning purple on his cheek. "Is he dead?"

Rafe descended the steps, holding his gun out in front of him. He nudged the cartel leader with his foot then bent to feel for a pulse at the base of his throat.

"He's dead," Rafe said and stood. He went to Briana and pulled her into his arms.

Hank ran back into the house. Moments later, he

emerged with his wife and daughter. "Sadie said Maddog went out to the barn to check on the horses because they were making a lot of noise. He didn't come back." He handed Emma to Sadie. "I'm going to check on him."

"I'll go with you." He handed his gun to Briana. "You know how to use it."

She nodded. "Be careful."

Rafe followed Hank out to the barn behind the house. As they approached, they could hear the muffled sound of someone yelling and pounding on the wall inside. The barn door had been wedged shut with a two-by-four board jammed into the dirt.

Rafe kicked it out of the way and flung open the door. The yelling grew louder.

"He's in the tack room." Hank flipped a switch on the wall. Nothing happened. "They cut the power to the barn." He turned and grabbed a flashlight from a hook on the wall and pressed the button, sending a beam of light through the building.

The horses in the stalls stirred, whinnying at the disturbance.

Hank hurried to a door on the right side of the barn. Another board had been jammed into the ground, bracing the door to keep it from opening. He kicked it aside, and the door burst open.

A big man with black hair and dark eyes charged through, blood on his hands and shirt. He grabbed Hank by the front of his shirt. "Sadie?"

"Is fine. As is Emma."

"They hit me from behind. I fought them, but they

won and threw me into the tack room. When I came to, I couldn't get out."

"At least they didn't just shoot you."

"They didn't bring silencers. Maybe they didn't want to wake Sadie," Rafe said.

"You're alive. My family is safe. That's what's important," Hank said. "Their leader is dead, and the two goons he brought with him are tied up in the living room."

Maddog shook his head and winced, rubbing the back of his head. "I shouldn't have let Kujo take Lucy to his place for the night. She would've warned me."

Rafe nodded. "I was about to ask. I'm glad to know she's okay."

"Come on, let's get back to the house. It's been a long night, and you might need medical attention," Hank said.

"I'm fine. Just pissed that they got the jump on me."

Rafe led the way back to the house, eager to get to Briana. He didn't like her being out of his sight. Not with all that had happened.

She was inside the house with Sadie and Alejandra, standing guard over the two cartel men.

"I called the sheriff and Homeland Security," Briana said. "They're on their way, along with an ambulance to collect this scum." She nodded toward the two men she had her weapon pointed at. "You want your gun back?" she asked Rafe.

He grinned. "Not unless you're tired of holding it. You're amazing."

She shook her head. "I'm not amazing. I'm shaking."

Rafe crossed the floor and took the gun from her trembling hands. "I've got it. You might want to sit before you fall."

"I'd rather stand here with you," she said and wrapped her arms around his waist.

He pulled her close with his free hand and kissed the top of her head. "I've been thinking about it. I really want you to stay in Montana."

She laughed. "Why? It doesn't appear to be any safer than Chicago."

"Maybe not, but I want you to stay with me. Like Bear and Swede said…go with your gut. Mine is telling me you're the one." He frowned down at her. "Unless your gut isn't saying the same thing."

Her arms tightened around him. "My gut is saying the same."

"If you really want to go back to Chicago, I'm sure I can find something to do there," he offered. "But Lucy wouldn't be nearly as happy as she is here in Montana."

Briana smiled up at him. "We do need to consider what would make Lucy happiest. She's ours now."

"And we can't break up a family, can we?" Rafe said, bending to claim her lips.

"Why don't I take that gun for now," Hank drawled.

"I believe I see headlights coming this way," Sadie said. "And the sun's starting to rise. Emma will be awake in an hour or two. I'm going to take her to her room and tuck her in." She turned to Alejandra. "I'll show you to the room Bella's been sleeping in. It has a bed you can sleep in. You can nurse her there. Poor Bella hasn't been too happy with the formula."

Alejandra turned to Hank.

He nodded. "Go with Sadie, for now. I'm sure the police and Homeland Security will want to speak with you before you call it a night...or day, in this case."

"I'll be out as soon as I've fed Bella." Alejandra and Bella followed Sadie and Emma out of the living room.

Two sheriff's vehicles arrived with an ambulance following close behind.

Homeland security arrived an hour later.

The sun had fully risen by the time authorities left with the two cartel men and the body of *El Chefe Diablo.*

Emma woke. Sadie and Hank moved to the living room where Emma could play while Hank napped on the couch.

Sadie showed Briana to a room down the hall from Alejandra. She frowned. "Do you two need separate rooms, or just one?"

"One," Rafe and Briana said at the same time

Sadie laughed. "I kinda thought so, based on all the canoodling you've been doing since you got back. Besides, the Crazy Mountains have a way of bringing people together. You must be exhausted. I'll bring you some night clothes, and this suite has its own bathroom, so you don't have to leave it."

"Thank you, Sadie," Briana said. "Seems like I'm always borrowing clothes from you. I'll be glad when I can retrieve my own things."

Sadie's face brightened. "So, you'll be staying in Montana?"

Briana looked up into Rafe's eyes. "Looks that way."

His heart bursting, Rafe grabbed Briana up in his

arms, kissed her soundly then pushed through the door into their suite. They didn't come out for a full day, thanks to Sadie leaving trays of food and piles of clothes outside the door.

Rafe would've stayed locked in the room forever. He knew without a doubt Briana was the one for him. When they finally had to come out and be social, he'd do something to make it more permanent. But for now, he was happy to make love and sleep with the woman he loved. Tomorrow would get there all too soon.

EPILOGUE

"Briana, will you grab that other tray of steaks and bring it out to the porch?" Sadie called out as she left the kitchen with a bowl full of corn on the cob drenched in butter and wrapped in foil, ready to go on the grill.

"Got it," Briana said. "Are the baked potatoes nearly done?"

"Hank swears they'll be ready in five more minutes," Alejandra said. "And a good thing. Five trucks just pulled up."

"I hope we have enough food." Sadie turned to back out of the front door onto the porch. "I didn't really think the Deltas would actually come all the way from Fort Hood, Texas, for our 4th of July celebration."

"Are you kidding?" Rafe held the door for her. "They would've come even without the invitation. I've been telling them about the fly fishing and rafting and wildlife they're missing out on. They all decided to pack up and come for a long weekend. Briana and I have got them all lined up for some Crazy Mountain fun."

"Where are you going to put them?" Sadie asked as she handed the bowl of corn cobs to Hank at the giant grill.

"We arranged for them to stay at the bed and breakfast in Eagle Rock," Briana said. "They'll like that, since they can walk over to the Blue Moon Tavern for dinner and drinks after a full day of hiking, fishing or rafting."

"Oh, good," Hank said. "Here they are now. Looks like my team is bringing up the rear."

"I think you could use a parking lot guide." Briana laughed. "Look at the caravan of vehicles heading this way."

The Delta Force team parked, grabbed beers and found chairs on the lawn.

"You weren't kidding about this place being amazing," Rucker Sloan lifted a beer to Rafe. "Glad you talked us all into coming up. Nearly gave the CO a coronary when we all asked off at the same time. If anything happens and we need to deploy, we'll do it from here."

"Man, I'm looking forward to the fly fishing," Bull said. "But right now, I'm looking forward to that steak Hank's got grilling."

Blade leaned back in his chair and stared out at the setting sun. "What's the nightlife like around here? Any lonely females in the neighborhood?"

"Can't you go an entire weekend without sniffing out a girl?" Mac clapped a hand on Blade's shoulder. "Problem is, you haven't found the right one. Not like our team jumper, Donovan." He tipped his head toward

Rafe. "You look too stinkin' happy, man. You'll have us all convinced we need to get hitched by the time we leave Montana."

"What are you talking about?" Dawg frowned. "Did you get hitched, Donovan? When were you going to tell us?"

"Keep your britches on," Tank said as he climbed the porch steps and shook Rafe's hand. "They aren't hitched, yet." He smiled at Briana. "Make him do it right. Down on his knee and everything."

Briana grinned and looked at Rafe. "You might need some tips from Tank." She narrowed her eyes at the man. "You know so much, why haven't you gotten down on one knee yet?"

He shook his head. "Too stuck in my ways. No woman would have me."

"You're wrong," Briana said. "I'm sure the right one is out there, waiting for you to find her."

Joseph Kuntz arrived with his woman Molly Greenbrier and their dog, Six. "Did you start the party without us?"

"Hey, Kujo," Hank called out. "We were waiting for you." He slapped a beer in Kujo's hand and turned to Molly. "Beer, wine or a margarita?"

"I'll have a beer," she said.

Kujo twisted the top off the beer and handed it to Molly.

Six found Lucy lounging in the shade on the porch and laid down beside her.

Boomer and Daphne arrived with Maya. They

spread a blanket on the ground beside the one where Emma was playing with a plastic horse.

"Won't be long before Maya is chasing Emma around the barnyard," Sadie said.

"I can't wait to teach them how to ride horses," Daphne said.

"How are your riding lessons coming along?" Hank asked.

Daphne grinned. "Good. Boomer's going to get me a horse as soon as we build a barn on our place."

Hank grinned. "Then you'll need to get a pony for Maya."

"We will, when she gets a little bigger," Boomer said.

Taz Davila and his woman, Hannah Kendricks, the physical therapist at the local veterans rehabilitation ranch, arrived at the same time as John Wayne Morris—the Duke—and Angel Carson, his stuntwoman fiancée. They claimed the horseshoes and started a game far enough away from the little ones to keep them safe.

Swede and Allie had come earlier to help with setting up tables and making side dishes for the growing crowd of people.

Bear and Mia Chastain arrived with Chuck, Kate and Kate's niece Lyla.

Maddog and his woman Jolie pulled in shortly after.

Bringing up the rear were Viper and his woman, Dallas.

"Is that all of us?" Hank asked.

"Flannigan is out on assignment," Sadie reminded him.

"That's right." Hank dropped a foil-covered corn cob on the grill.

Sadie smiled and rubbed her growing baby bump. "Hank's really built quite the empire of protectors. I might decide to give up acting to help him keep organized. That and be a fulltime mom."

Hank handed the grill duties over to Swede and came up onto the porch to hug his wife. "You can do whatever your heart desires." He kissed her soundly and bent to kiss her belly. "Us guys will keep you busy here on the ranch."

"We don't know if the baby is a boy or a girl. We said we'd wait and be surprised." Sadie frowned. "You didn't peek at the ultrasound, did you?"

Hank grinned and waggled his eyebrows. "If I did, I'm not telling."

"Hank!" Sadie swatted at his arm.

Rafe slipped up behind Briana and covered her belly with his hands. "I can't wait for you to be as big as Sadie."

Briana leaned back in his arms and smiled. She'd meant to wait and tell him later that night when they were in bed at the hunting cabin, but now was as good a time as any. "Careful what you wish for, babe." She turned in his arms. "In eight and a half months. I'll be just as big."

Rafe's brow dipped in a frown. "Wait...what?" His frown deepened. "Are you saying what I think you're saying?"

She nodded, her smile spreading across her face. "I'm pregnant."

"What?" Sadie's head came up. "Briana? You're pregnant?"

Briana's grin broadened. "I am."

Dash Hayes glared at Rafe. "What the hell, Donovan?"

"Well, damn," Rafe muttered. "I was going to save this for a private moment, but since you're making announcements, I'd better make one of my own and also make an honest woman out of you." Rafe dropped to one knee. "Am I doing it right, Tank?"

Tank rolled his eyes. "If you have to ask, you aren't."

Briana's heart fluttered and swelled to twice its size, filling her chest with all the happiness she felt.

"Briana Hayes…" Rafe paused. "Hell, I had it all memorized, and now I can't remember a word."

"From the heart," Tank prompted. "Speak from the heart."

"Oh, right." Rafe cleared his throat and started over. He took her hand in his.

Briana's entire body trembled. She thought she might pass out or throw up, she was so nervous.

"From the heart," Rafe said. "From the moment I heard your voice talking to me from Chicago to Springfield, I felt like I'd come home. You have the most beautiful voice. Sometimes, I close my eyes and just listen to you talk. But I digress. The point is, I want your voice to be the one I wake to every morning. You're beautiful, courageous and fun to be with. Will you be my wife and make me the happiest man on earth?"

Briana cupped his cheeks in her palms. "Rafe Donovan…I thought you'd never ask." She laughed. "Yes! I've loved you since we met over the phone, and I'll love you when we're old and gray. And I can't think of anyone I'd rather have as the father of my child."

"Our child," he corrected. "And, oh yeah." He rose to his feet, dug in his pocket and pulled out a ring with a fat diamond solitaire surrounded by a halo of smaller diamonds. "Guess I should have started with this." He slipped the ring on her finger. "I love you, Briana. Now, tell your brother not to kill me. Unless he wants to raise his nephew."

"Niece," Briana corrected.

Rafe frowned down at her. "Did you peek at the ultrasound?"

"If I did," she grinned. "I'm not telling."

"Well, we'll just have to wait and see who's right."

"Donovan, you've got a lot to learn," Hank said. "The woman is always right."

Rafe nodded. "And she's right. The right one for me."

"And it's too early to tell the sex anyway," Hank added.

Sadie clapped her hands. "Well, yay! We're going to have a wedding. And we'd better make it before the baby's born. Double congrats!"

Rafe pulled Briana into his arms. "Do you have any idea how happy you make me?"

Briana brushed her lips across his. "If it's anywhere near as happy as you make me, I might have a clue."

THANK you for reading DELTA FORCE RESCUE in the Brotherhood Protectors series. Don't miss the first book in the DELTA FORCE STRONG series BREAKING SILENCE and see the Delta Force team on their next mission!

Interested in more military romance stories? Subscribe to my newsletter and receive the Military Heroes Box Set
Subscribe Here

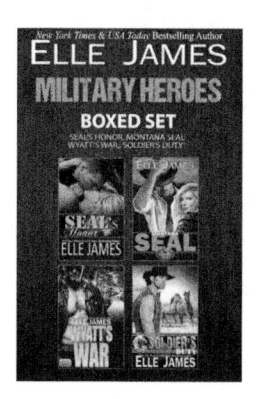

Keep reading for the first chapter of Wyatt's War, Book #1 in the Hearts & Heroes Series.

ABOUT THE AUTHOR

ELLE JAMES also writing as MYLA JACKSON is a *New York Times* and *USA Today* Bestselling author of books including cowboys, intrigues and paranormal adventures that keep her readers on the edges of their seats. When she's not at her computer, she's traveling, snow skiing, boating, or riding her ATV, dreaming up new stories. Learn more about Elle James at www.ellejames.com

Website | Facebook | Twitter | GoodReads | Newsletter | BookBub | Amazon

Or visit her alter ego Myla Jackson at mylajackson.com
Website | Facebook | Twitter | Newsletter

Follow Me!
www.ellejames.com
ellejamesauthor@gmail.com

ALSO BY ELLE JAMES

Shadow Assassin

Delta Force Strong

Ivy's Delta (Delta Force 3 Crossover)

Breaking Silence (#1)

Breaking Rules (#2)

Breaking Away (#3)

Breaking Free (#4)

Breaking Hearts (#5)

Breaking Ties (#6)

Breaking Point (#7)

Breaking Dawn (#8)

Breaking Promises (#9)

Brotherhood Protectors Yellowstone

Saving Kyla (#1)

Saving Chelsea (#2)

Saving Amanda (#3)

Saving Liliana (#4)

Saving Breely (#5)

Saving Savvie (#6)

Brotherhood Protectors Colorado

SEAL Salvation (#1)
Rocky Mountain Rescue (#2)
Ranger Redemption (#3)
Tactical Takeover (#4)
Colorado Conspiracy (#5)
Rocky Mountain Madness (#6)
Free Fall (#7)
Colorado Cold Case (#8)
Fool's Folly (#9)

Brotherhood Protectors
Montana SEAL (#1)
Bride Protector SEAL (#2)
Montana D-Force (#3)
Cowboy D-Force (#4)
Montana Ranger (#5)
Montana Dog Soldier (#6)
Montana SEAL Daddy (#7)
Montana Ranger's Wedding Vow (#8)
Montana SEAL Undercover Daddy (#9)
Cape Cod SEAL Rescue (#10)
Montana SEAL Friendly Fire (#11)
Montana SEAL's Mail-Order Bride (#12)
SEAL Justice (#13)
Ranger Creed (#14)
Delta Force Rescue (#15)
Dog Days of Christmas (#16)

Montana Rescue (#17)

Montana Ranger Returns (#18)

Hot SEAL Salty Dog (SEALs in Paradise)

Hot SEAL, Hawaiian Nights (SEALs in Paradise)

Hot SEAL Bachelor Party (SEALs in Paradise)

Hot SEAL, Independence Day (SEALs in Paradise)

Brotherhood Protectors Vol 1

Iron Horse Legacy

Soldier's Duty (#1)

Ranger's Baby (#2)

Marine's Promise (#3)

SEAL's Vow (#4)

Warrior's Resolve (#5)

Drake (#6)

Grimm (#7)

Murdock (#8)

Utah (#9)

Judge (#10)

The Outriders

Homicide at Whiskey Gulch (#1)

Hideout at Whiskey Gulch (#2)

Held Hostage at Whiskey Gulch (#3)

Setup at Whiskey Gulch (#4)

Missing Witness at Whiskey Gulch (#5)

Cowboy Justice at Whiskey Gulch (#6)

Hellfire Series

Hellfire, Texas (#1)

Justice Burning (#2)

Smoldering Desire (#3)

Hellfire in High Heels (#4)

Playing With Fire (#5)

Up in Flames (#6)

Total Meltdown (#7)

Declan's Defenders

Marine Force Recon (#1)

Show of Force (#2)

Full Force (#3)

Driving Force (#4)

Tactical Force (#5)

Disruptive Force (#6)

Mission: Six

One Intrepid SEAL

Two Dauntless Hearts

Three Courageous Words

Four Relentless Days

Five Ways to Surrender

Six Minutes to Midnight

Hearts & Heroes Series

Wyatt's War (#1)

Mack's Witness (#2)

Ronin's Return (#3)

Sam's Surrender (#4)

Take No Prisoners Series

SEAL's Honor (#1)

SEAL'S Desire (#2)

SEAL's Embrace (#3)

SEAL's Obsession (#4)

SEAL's Proposal (#5)

SEAL's Seduction (#6)

SEAL'S Defiance (#7)

SEAL's Deception (#8)

SEAL's Deliverance (#9)

SEAL's Ultimate Challenge (#10)

Texas Billionaire Club

Tarzan & Janine (#1)

Something To Talk About (#2)

Who's Your Daddy (#3)

Love & War (#4)

Billionaire Online Dating Service

The Billionaire Husband Test (#1)

The Billionaire Cinderella Test (#2)

The Billionaire Bride Test (#3)

The Billionaire Daddy Test (#4)

The Billionaire Matchmaker Test (#5)

The Billionaire Glitch Date (#6)

The Billionaire Perfect Date (#7) coming soon

The Billionaire Replacement Date (#8) coming soon

The Billionaire Wedding Date (#9) coming soon

Ballistic Cowboy

Hot Combat (#1)

Hot Target (#2)

Hot Zone (#3)

Hot Velocity (#4)

Cajun Magic Mystery Series

Voodoo on the Bayou (#1)

Voodoo for Two (#2)

Deja Voodoo (#3)

Cajun Magic Mysteries Books 1-3

SEAL Of My Own

Navy SEAL Survival

Navy SEAL Captive

Navy SEAL To Die For

Navy SEAL Six Pack

Devil's Shroud Series

Deadly Reckoning (#1)

Deadly Engagement (#2)

Deadly Liaisons (#3)

Deadly Allure (#4)

Deadly Obsession (#5)

Deadly Fall (#6)

Covert Cowboys Inc Series

Triggered (#1)

Taking Aim (#2)

Bodyguard Under Fire (#3)

Cowboy Resurrected (#4)

Navy SEAL Justice (#5)

Navy SEAL Newlywed (#6)

High Country Hideout (#7)

Clandestine Christmas (#8)

Thunder Horse Series

Hostage to Thunder Horse (#1)

Thunder Horse Heritage (#2)

Thunder Horse Redemption (#3)

Christmas at Thunder Horse Ranch (#4)

Demon Series

Hot Demon Nights (#1)

Demon's Embrace (#2)

Tempting the Demon (#3)

Lords of the Underworld

Witch's Initiation (#1)

Witch's Seduction (#2)

The Witch's Desire (#3)

Possessing the Witch (#4)

Stealth Operations Specialists (SOS)

Nick of Time

Alaskan Fantasy

Boys Behaving Badly Anthologies

Rogues (#1)

Blue Collar (#2)

Pirates (#3)

Stranded (#4)

First Responder (#5)

Blown Away

Warrior's Conquest

Enslaved by the Viking Short Story

Conquests

Smokin' Hot Firemen

Protecting the Colton Bride

Protecting the Colton Bride & Colton's Cowboy Code

Heir to Murder

Secret Service Rescue

High Octane Heroes

Haunted

Engaged with the Boss

Cowboy Brigade

Time Raiders: The Whisper

Bundle of Trouble

Killer Body

Operation XOXO

An Unexpected Clue

Baby Bling

Under Suspicion, With Child

Texas-Size Secrets

Cowboy Sanctuary

Lakota Baby

Dakota Meltdown

Beneath the Texas Moon